Death Claims its Prize
(A Mike Cannon jumps racing mystery)

Eric Horridge

Death Claims its Prize

Copyright © 2024 by Eric Horridge
All rights reserved.

Front Cover Design: Beth Kate Ierino

Book design by Eric Horridge

No part of this book may be reproduced in any form or by any electronic or mechanical means including information storage and retrieval systems, without permission in writing from the author. The only exception is by a reviewer, who may quote short excerpts in a review.

This book is a work of fiction. Names, characters, places, and incidents either are products of the author's imagination or are used fictitiously. Any resemblance to actual persons, living or dead, events, or locales is entirely coincidental.

Eric Horridge

DEDICATION

This book is dedicated to all the horse racing trainers throughout the world.

"From sire to sire
It's born in the blood
The fire of a mare
And the strength of a stud
It's breeding and it's training
And it's something unknown
That drives you
And carries you home"

Dan Fogelberg
Run for the Roses

Death Claims its Prize

Death Claims its Prize

Prologue

Warrington, Cheshire:
Saturday 20 March 1993, 12:25 pm

The crowd of shoppers on Bridge Street stumbled their way past each other. The cold grey day had caused many to wrap themselves in heavy coats, carry plastic Macs and hide umbrellas inside bags just in case rain decided to unleash more misery upon them.
The man sat in the driver's seat of the van, a pair of binoculars resting on his lap, his passenger fidgeted nervously, looking continuously at his watch.
"We should get going," the passenger said, his voice now an octave higher than a few seconds before. He was becoming more agitated and continued to fidget in his seat.
"Another minute," the driver said, raising the binoculars to his face and directing them towards where he expected to see the result of their actions. "The timers are never a hundred percent accurate."
Two hundred yards away from where the men sat, multiple lives were in the balance. Fate would determine who was in the area of the McDonalds restaurant and Boots' chemist and who had entered or left the Argos store another hundred yards away.
Both bombs had been placed inside litter bins and those who had used them during the morning had no idea of their deadly contents.
The passenger looked at his watch again, the situation was becoming desperate. "Are you sure they sent the message, Conor? I haven't seen hide nor hair of a cop since we've been sitting here."
The driver continued to stare through his binoculars, conscious that despite the side windows having been deliberately tainted, a curious passerby could potentially notice what he was up to.
"Yes, it was," he answered. "The coded message was sent to the police in Liverpool, along with one of the charities, at least half an hour ago."
"How do you know?"
"Because I do, Cillian, I just do!" the driver replied angrily, slamming the binoculars down onto the middle seat, scattering empty take-away boxes and soft drink cans onto the floor.
The silence between the two men in the next fifteen seconds became palpable, the tension almost unbearable.

Death Claims its Prize

"C'mon, c'mon," Cillian Lynch said, under his breath, his left leg bouncing up and down, his nervousness beginning to affect his colleague. "Where the feck are the police?" he asked, out loud. "Why haven't they cleared the area?"

"I don't know," Conor Boyle replied, suddenly jumping in fright, after hearing and feeling the effects of a bang on the back door of the van and along the sides. It was followed by jeers and hoots as three teenagers dressed in dark hoodies and dirty jeans ran past the front of the van. The boys then turned, jostling other pedestrians in their way, before throwing an egg each at the van's windscreen.

"What the feck!" Lynch shouted, as the teenagers jogged away from them, turning around as one, and showing the two men inside a V for victory sign while mouthing numerous expletives that those inside could barely hear. The grins on the boys faces said everything about their attitude to the egging.

"Bastards!" Boyle shouted. He started the engine and turned on the windscreen wipers which did little to clean the mess, merely smearing yellow yoke and pieces of shell across the glass.

"We'd better get going, Conor," Lynch said, his voice modulating with fear. "We're going to get caught if we stay here much longer." Both men noticed that some of the pedestrians had shouted at the three hooligans that were continuing to make a nuisance of themselves. The youngsters walked towards the McDonalds restaurant where they were obviously heading, laughing and joking at their own antics. A couple of middle-aged women pointed towards the van as they stood on the pavement discussing what they had just witnessed. Others continued with their business, heads down, ignoring the commotion that some had reacted to, content to remain prosaic, refusing to get involved, focused on their own issues and concerns.

"You're right," Boyle said, finally relenting to his passengers plea. Putting the van into gear he slowly drove twenty yards and turned into Friars Gat. The wiper blades along with the water sprayed from the van's reservoir tried their best to clear the mess that continued to smear egg and shell across the glass. As that van merged into the traffic coming from the right, the vehicle was hit with the shock wave from the bomb left in the dustbin in front of the chemist, followed immediately by the roar of the explosion. The bomb had ripped into the buildings, smashing the various frontages and sending shards of glass, chairs, tables, people (both inside and out) and other shrapnel flying in all directions. Prostrate bodies lay on the ground, over tables and under chairs. For a few seconds there was absolute silence before groans, screams and cries filled the air. It was clear to those who had escaped the disaster that some of their fellow shoppers were badly injured, some possibly dead, others would lose limbs. Other pedestrians decided to run to safety but the second bomb, left outside Argos, showed no mercy when it exploded sixty seconds later.

The white van with the eggshells stuck to the edge of the windows sped off in the direction of Irlam, Eccles and Manchester. The men inside had planned to dump the van and torch it in Stockport and then catch a train to Stoke-on-Trent. There, they would stay for a couple of days then split up before taking another train to Holyhead. The men expected the ferries to be watched but were confident that by travelling alone they would not be singled out for questioning. Even if they were, each had a readymade alibi and a reason for being in England. Getting back home was something that both men were looking forward to. They had been away for nearly a month, living on their wits, careful not to draw attention to themselves. The mission they had been given had gone exactly to plan. As they merged onto the M62, a soft rain began to fall. Within minutes there was no trace of the eggs that had splattered onto the windscreen.

The ten-mile drive out to Consall Woods, east of Stoke-on-Trent, took twenty minutes. They posed as 'twitchers' when they arrived at the visitors centre, each carrying binoculars and a copy of 'Bird book of Britain' in their individual backpacks. This pleased the attendant of the bird sanctuary. A third man, Ronan Buckley, who had arrived with Cillian Lynch had done all the talking. He had some knowledge of the subject and used it to give credibility to their visit. They had gone to the site in separate cars, two in each. Boyle had been joined by Darragh Kelly who had been in country for two days. His cover was that he was Boyles' cousin, which was indeed true, and should he ever be questioned by the authorities, his answer was that he was over in England to help Boyle move back to Ireland. That was a lie. There was another reason.

The two cars had been supplied by others in the cause and had been left where they would not arouse any suspicion. The keys had been dropped off in envelopes, placed in individual post boxes attached to entry hall walls at the base of flats that had been rented specifically. Once they were well inside the woods, the silence was only broken by the birdsong of Wrens and Blackbirds, and in the distance, near the river Churnet, Willow and Marsh tits. Buckley suggested that they move off the path and deeper into the trees.

"I need to show you something," he said, "it relates to your next mission."

Lynch glanced at Boyle, then at Kelly. "What mission?" he asked, "I thought that it was agreed we wouldn't be doing anything else until the summer. I thought…"

"You thought what?" Buckley asked, indicating that they should lower their voices. He continued to lead them away from the path and further into the dense woods.

"I thought that Conor and me were to go back home, down the farm in my case, so that we can get back to normal for a while."

"You can," Buckley replied, "both of you," he continued, pointing at Boyle then back to Lynch. "However before we can do that, I need to show you where I've hidden the cache."

"Cache?" Lynch queried again.

"Yes, come on, I'll show you."

Buckley turned away and ventured deeper into the woods, dodging between Birch and Ash trees that towered above him and stepping over Wild Garlic and Wood Anemone that covered the ground. The others seemed to hesitate for a few seconds before deciding to follow.

They passed a few open spaces before Buckley stopped in a small clearing. It was a spherical opening with a five-yard radius, which seemed to mirror the type of spot where covens of witches may have met in years gone by.

"Just here," he said, pointing at the ground. "Just here," he repeated, unnecessarily.

"What's here?" Lynch asked, looking down at the bare earth in the centre of the clearing. He removed his backpack and dropped it onto the musty forest floor. All he could see was damp soil and soft mud from recent rains. As he raised his face to question Buckley, he had a brief glance of a silver object which slashed towards him. The

serrated blade of the hunting knife which Boyle had surreptitiously removed from underneath his jacket sliced through Lynch's back, with a force that plunged the blade down to the hilt. The blow was hard enough to sever the spinal cord, pierce the ribs continuing through the heart. Blood gushed from his mouth like a torrent and his eyes immediately lost their focus. The last thing Lynch saw was Buckley's face. He was dead before he landed hard on the ground, the knife still protruding from his lifeless body.
"Now we just need to dig," Buckley said, without any sign of emotion or compassion to what had just happened. He pulled out a collapsible spade from his backpack and threw it over the body towards Boyle, who let it land on the ground.
"Both of you get going. Leave this to me," Boyle said, pointing towards Lynch's body, which lay spreadeagled like a ragdoll where it had fallen in the dirt.
"Are you sure?" Kelly asked. "I'm happy to help you, cousin."
"No, it's fine…. I'll do it."
"Okay, have it your way," Buckley replied, holding out his hand. Boyle looked into the man's face. He smiled cynically, grunted, then bent to pick up the spade from the ground.
"Perhaps we'll meet again?" Buckley said.
"Maybe."
"Well, until the cause is won, we'll just have to keep on fighting then."
"Aye, we will that."
Buckley stared back at Lynch's killer. His own job now done, there was nothing else to say. What had just taken place was all in the name of the cause. Weak links were not acceptable as they endangered everyone. They could not take any chances. He picked up his backpack, and stepped towards Boyle, silently brushing passed him before disappearing into the trees.
Kelly followed a few seconds later. "I'll see you when you get home," he said, slowly drifting away to join Buckley back at the car park.
Boyle waited for a few minutes, standing quietly, staring at the body on the ground, listening for any other signs of life in the immediate vicinity. All he could hear were the birds that flew from tree to tree, their songs echoing throughout the canopy. Satisfied that there was no one around, he began the task of burying the body of Cillian Lynch.

CHAPTER 1

"He's done really well," Cannon said, "I couldn't be happier with him, Rich, all thanks to Jim."
Jim Cochrane smiled at the sound of his name, happy that his customer was enthused with his work. They were standing under a gable looking out towards a row trees in the distance, the boundary of the Ballyneed Stud farm and the expansive farmlands beyond. They were only a five-minute drive to the Curragh racecourse, which unfortunately for Cannon was not a track that White Noise, the horse he had come to collect, would ever race on. The Curragh was for flat races only, so Punchestown, a jumps and flat racing track, some twenty kilometres east, was where the horse would race next.
"That's good to hear," Rich Telside replied, his voice breaking up slightly on Cannons' mobile. It was a long way from Oxfordshire to County Kildare, Cannon mused, as Telside his longtime assistant added, "So when do you intend to bring him back then, Mike?"
"As soon as possible, Rich," Cannon replied, noticing that Cochrane was nodding in agreement. He had done his job getting the horse through an injury, now it was up to Cannon as trainer to get the horse fit enough to race.
The horse had been earmarked to run in the Champion Hurdle at Cheltenham the previous season but during the build up to the festival had suffered an injury and the plan had been scuppered. Fortunately it meant that the horse would be a year older when the opportunity presented itself again, and despite the injury had the potential to be fresher and tougher after such a long layoff. There was still the task of getting the horse to the event and that would require careful planning. Decisions would need to be taken about which races to compete in leading up to the Festival the following March, but Cannon's thinking in relation to the horse had changed over the past six months. He knew the horse had ability, which was evident from the success he had enjoyed before the injury, but what Cannon needed to do was work out how to get the best out of him now that the injury had healed. Questions such as how to improve the speed that the horse could maintain and over what distance? The Champion Hurdle was run over slightly more than two miles, (just less than three thousand three hundred metres), and the winning

time in recent years varied from around three minutes fifty seconds to four minutes five seconds. This time achieved while also jumping eight hurdles during the race. Hurdles or flights, as some called them, were significantly easier to navigate than Steeplechase fences, so speed was essential if a horse had any chance of winning the event. During the previous season Cannon had set his sights on just participating in the race, but not on winning it. With the support of the horse's owner Joel Seeton, a self-made millionaire from York who had made his money in packaging, it had been agreed that the previous season was to have been a trial run before a proper tilt was to be made. Unfortunately due to the horse incurring the injury things had gone awry. But now, thanks to Cochrane who had worked his magic, Cannon was much more upbeat about the horse's chances this season. At the very least being much more competitive.

"I'm arranging for the horse to be transported home in the next few days," Cannon continued into his phone, hoping that Telside could still hear him. "And we'll bring him over for a run in a month or so, probably in mid-October when the ground isn't likely to be too wet. As we discussed before, starting his campaign over here where he's been recuperating and where he obviously thrives will hopefully bring him on."

"Agreed," Telside answered, before adding, "Oh, by the way Mike, I've had an enquiry as to whether we are interested in taking on one of Chester Sutcliffes' horses."

"Chester Sutcliffe, the ex-politician?"

"Yes, that's him."

Cannon asked Telside to wait for a second before he responded to the question. He apologized to Cochrane, who had been waiting patiently, that his conversation was taking longer than expected and suggested that they catch up again in Cochrane's office once he had finished his call. Cochrane agreed to do so and walked away from where they had been watching White Noise trotting around, his tail swishing and his mane blowing in the early autumn sunshine. Here was a thoroughbred who had a new zest for life as indicated by the occasional leap made and the kicking out of the back legs as he jogged around the fringes of the white fenced paddock.

"I didn't know he had any jumpers, Rich. I thought he only had flat horses," Cannon said, referring to Chester Sutcliffe, a former Cabinet Minister, now TV personality.

"Well it seems he does. His manager has asked if we had any places available and whether we were interested?"

"His manager?" Cannon queried.

"Yes, his manager," Telside repeated, before adding, "A guy called Tony Burke. It's a new world for me, Mike, but don't all personalities on TV have managers nowadays? Just like footballers and musicians, rock bands and whatever?"

Cannon smiled to himself at Telside's comment. The man was well passed retirement age and many would consider him a relic. Someone who the present had left behind and consigned to history. But to Cannon the man was a friend, a confidant and a tireless worker in the yard who would likely drop dead on the job rather than slowly drift away into slippers and a pipe. He was also very good at seeing through people, at finding a way past the front, or the screen, behind which they often hid. In short, he was invaluable to Cannon, having kept the stable going whenever Cannon had been dragged away from training his horses, due to him getting involved in other matters because of his policing background. As an ex-DCI, his experience and his own curiosity had been tested throughout his time as a racehorse trainer. It wasn't something he was proud of or even wanted to be involved with, it just seemed to happen, to follow him. The racing industry was like any other where money was involved. Someone was always trying to take advantage. Jockeys, owners, bookmakers, punters, trainers like himself, even officials had the potential to try and beat the system. Cannon had hoped initially, perhaps naïvely, that when he had retired from the police for the quiet of the countryside, he had left all the shit of the past behind him. That the ghosts of the cases he had investigated over the years had been buried forever. Unfortunately that wasn't the case and on occasion they would resurface to haunt his memory. It was only due to Telside that Cannon had been able to survive. Incidents within the yard, on racecourses and abroad had tested him. His relationship with his wife and his now married daughter had been in danger at times, both emotionally and physically. Without Telside, his friend, his mentor in the racing game, Cannon's career would have ended well before it had even begun. As it was, his yard, his racing stable, had grown from virtually nothing to its current number of thirty-two horses. Of which, there were twenty-four horses in training, and accommodated in the stables, at any one time.

"Did he mention which horse he wanted us to take on?" Cannon asked, curious as to why Chester Sutcliffe would have chosen him to train a horse the man owned.

"No, but I can call him back and find out," Telside offered.

"That would be useful, I think. I don't want to agree to anything without knowing what we are in for. As I said before, I didn't even know that Sutcliffe was involved in our game."

"Well obviously he must be," Telside said, "though, like you, I'm surprised he's come to us given his personality and his ego. I would have thought that he would have approached a more high-profile yard than ours, don't you think?"

"I do, Rich," Cannon answered, a thought running through his head, a thought that first tickled his brain then fell flat as if to counter his own cynicism. He told himself that he should be grateful of the approach, as it would likely boost his personal profile if he accepted the offer. While Cannon was not a user, he knew from his wife, Michelle, that Chester Sutcliffe was extremely active on social media. He was always posting and forwarding articles of interest about himself, as well as commenting on world affairs and sport. He was known as someone who constantly changed his profile picture on Facebook in order to keep relevant and 'current'. Cannon did not use any platform; Facebook, Twitter (or X), Snapchat or Tik-Tok. He left that to Michelle and his daughter Cassie, now living in the small town of Bolsover, thirteen miles east of Chesterfield, where her husband Edward worked as a Haemotologist at Chesterfield Royal Hospital. Cassie was a junior partner at a law firm in Mansfield.

"Okay Mike, I'll get back to you after I've got a bit more information," Telside confirmed. "I'll give Burke a call later."

"Fine with me."

"Are you still coming home the day after tomorrow?"

"Yes, unless my flight gets cancelled," Cannon said sarcastically. His original flight over to Ireland had been delayed twice, due to what was termed by the airline as 'bad weather'. He and his fellow passengers believed that it was more to do with bad planning than any meteorological issue given the crew on board his flight over from Birmingham had been complaining of staff shortages and a dispute over the hours they were expected to work every day.

"By the way, I'm still planning to go to Sam Quinns' place later today to have a look at a couple of those horses he is selling," Cannon continued. "And with any luck I'll also get up to Aidan Murphy's farm in Dunboyne tomorrow as he has that 'chaser that we talked about that may be worth taking a risk on."

"The one you mentioned some time back?" Telside asked, "I can't remember what it's called now."

"Rory's Song."

"Aye, Rory's Song, that's the one."

"Yes, if he's sound and has a good attitude.."

"And the price is right," jumped in Telside.

"…then I might take a chance, perhaps look to syndicate him, now that we know all about the tax implications," Cannon concluded.

Telside laughed. It was only eighteen months or so prior that Cannon had received a tax windfall due to his financial advisors resolving a query with HMRC about syndicating horses. The refund that had come his way had helped pay for some of the cost of Cassie's wedding.

"I'll leave that to you, Mike," Telside said. "In the meantime I need to get going. As you know there's a fair bit of painting and fixing up in the stables that I need to supervise, not to mention keeping the normal routine going."

"Thanks Rich, what would I do without you?" Cannon asked rhetorically. It was a question that neither of them wanted to consider, nor indeed wanted to answer. Both men knew that time would eventually catch up with them, but now wasn't the moment or place to give it any further thought. They had discussed the issue of Telside 'slowing down' several times in recent months, and despite his age and having had a triple bypass after a heart attack only two years prior, he had stated quite categorically that he would remain working with Cannon until he was "carried away in a box."

Finishing the call, Cannon made his way to Cochrane's office which was about two hundred yards away. The small structure where the rehabilitation expert ran his business was a typical white painted brick building with a grey slate roof. It was situated near to a group of ash and oak trees that lined the extremity of the property on three sides and which cast a shadow across the small window through which Cochrane saw him approaching. As Cannon reached the threshold of the building, the front door opened and Cochranes' Office Manager, a middle-aged woman by the name of Candice McGurk welcomed him in, holding the door ajar. She was a short woman, originally from

Northern Ireland but who had married years earlier to a local man. She was a little over five feet tall, slightly overweight with the potential to be called dumpy. She had an open face surrounded by shoulder length grey hair, tied back into a girlish ponytail. Cannon wasn't sure whether the hair was coloured on purpose to hide premature greys or if it was all natural. Trying to be non-judgmental he deliberately ignored it, despite the style seeming to suggest something he had little knowledge of. He knew that Cochrane relied on her and that was all that mattered. Her face consisted of extremely white skin, slightly ruddy in places along the nose and chin, with green eyes that seemed to hold your gaze at all times, and a mouth full of NHS teeth. Cannon thanked her, guessing that she must have seen him making his way to the building.

"I was just going to check on whether the transport company you are using to take White Noise home had made all the necessary arrangements," she said. "They are not the usual company we use, and I want to make sure they know that I've arranged for the export health certificate to be issued. Hopefully they've done the rest."

"I think they are pretty much a full-service entity," Cannon replied, hoping that his faith was not misguided. He had decided to use 'CB & Sons Transport' as they were a small business and happy to take on smaller jobs which many of the larger Horse Transport businesses would not, especially transporting a single animal back to England. When White Noise had been brought over several months prior, he was one of a group of twenty animals shipped across the Irish sea as part of a consolidated lot. Some of the animals he had travelled with included ex-racehorses, some going to stud, others into retirement and others to be used in pony clubs. That process had been handled by a larger company which had collected horses, including White Noise, in Oxfordshire, Lambourn in Berkshire and in other counties before shipping them across the sea. Moving horses around the country was expensive at the best of times. Moving horses across international boundaries was even more so. Many stables shipped several horses together in order to lower the cost per individual by consolidating shipments. In the case of White Noise, he would again be returned to England by sea, which was much cheaper than flying, though obviously took much longer. Many owners with large bank balances used air transport to move their animals to various racetracks throughout the UK, into Europe or even across the pond to the US. Some even went further, especially in flat racing, transporting their horses to Japan and Australia. While Joel Seeton was a wealthy man, he was also very cautious with his money and because there was still plenty of time for White Noise to prove himself before the season began and also show that he was over his injury, Cannon had suggested that taking his time to get the horse back to Oxfordshire and into his yard was not unreasonable. There was no need to rush. Seeton had agreed to this, leaving Cannon with the responsibility to make any decisions necessary to expedite the process.

"Okay, well can I confirm a few other details with you after you've finished with Jim?" McGurk asked, politely.

"Of course. I don't think I'll be very long."

"Great," she replied, "I'll speak to you then." She turned and made her way to her own office, which was a small room, 3m x 3m, in one corner of the building. With her left door open, she went to sit back down at her desk. Cannon noticed the window through which she must have seen him approaching. On the same side of the building but standing opposite to McGurk's office, separated by what seemed to be a small team of administrators who were working feverishly at their workstations, was Cochrane's own office. It was larger than his Office Managers' and was filled with a desk, two chairs and a multitude of books and magazines that filled every shelf including some that stood in untidy piles on the floor. Cannon had had a number of meetings with Cochrane over the past couple of days and was used to the jumble and mess that pervaded his senses every time he sat down in the solitary visitors chair. There were books on Horse Rehabilitation, Confirmation and the Horse Skeleton, Equine Medicine and many others. Piles of the magazine 'RacingAhead' and other publications stood under the windowsill, leaning precariously against the wall. Cochrane had been a veterinarian for many years before he started his own business and Cannon guessed that some of the books were from that time in Cochranes' life.

"I've just had a chat with Candice about the company I'm using to get White Noise home for me," he began. "It seems she wants a bit more information before she contacts them this afternoon about collecting the horse."

"Oh yes, CB & Sons."

"You know them?" Cannon asked.

"I know of them, but I haven't used them myself. I see they are up near Oldtown, the other side of Dublin."

"Well, they were the closest business that was willing to do single shipments, so that worked for me," Cannon added, "and depending on what I see tomorrow I may be going back with another one soon."

"Are you still looking to buy?"

"Perhaps."

"Well if you need me to look at anything, just let me know."

Cannon admired the way the offer from Cochrane had been made. The 'upsell' didn't bother him at all, and indeed it made perfect sense. From what he had observed of White Noise's recovery, he had no doubts that the man sitting opposite him knew his stuff. If Cannon ever had any reason to doubt a horse's soundness and have someone cast an eye over it, then that man was Jim Cochrane.

"If I find it necessary, I will Jim. I certainly will," Cannon confirmed.

"Good," Cochrane replied. A smile of appreciation spread across his face. He was a tall man in his early fifties. A full head of reddish-brown hair, curly and without shape. His face was slim like the rest of his body. He had long languid limbs that seemed to flow like waves as he walked or moved his arms. His face was pale despite working outdoors at times, though Cannon guessed the sun seldom saw the man. He was normally either under a roof inside a stable, or alternately under grey and rainy skies that frequented the country on a regular basis. Cochrane's skin was smooth, but his chin was covered with a healthy and well-trimmed beard. He wore a blue and white checked shirt under a khaki green sleeveless jacket, denim jeans and brown elasticated boots. It was the same style of clothing that Cannon had seen the man wearing every single time they had met.

"Anyway back to White Noise and the next steps," Cochrane continued. The tone of his voice had changed to emphasize his thoughts on the seriousness of the injury the horse had originally suffered from, and whether it would reoccur in the future. "The tendon problem and associated impact on the shoulder has responded extremely well to the treatment. As you saw earlier the three-month rest and the stem cell transplant we did has worked much better than we expected."

"Agreed."

"So you'll also know that with any injury, and one which will be put to the test multiple times over the remaining life of the horse, there are no guarantees that there will be no reoccurrence."

"I understand," Cannon replied. He was completely aware of what could happen at any time, and conscious of the fact that the injury that White Noise had suffered could have meant the end to his career as a racehorse. Fortunately, due to the commitment and money of Joel Seeton and the belief within Cannon himself as to the horse's future potential, they had both decided that it was worth trying to get the gelding back to full fitness. From what he had seen this morning and in earlier visits, they had made the right decision. Proof of the pudding however would be in the eating and they would start with 'breakfast' as soon as the horse arrived back in Oxford. "I expect to build up his fitness before putting him over the sticks, and then I'll bring him back here for an easy run before we start getting serious," he added.

Cochrane smiled. "I don't think there are too many easy runs at Punchestown," he said, "Billy likes to win every race he puts his horses in."

Cochrane was referring to Billy Milligan, one of the top Irish trainers. Renowned for placing more than one horse in many of the races that he contested, Milligan was usually battling for the title of Champion trainer of the country and had nearly two hundred horses in his stable at any one time. In addition to his success in Ireland, he was also very competitive in England, particularly in the bigger meetings at Aintree and Cheltenham, not to mention some of the smaller festivals. It was likely that should White Noise make it to the Champion Hurdle then Milligan, amongst other larger stables, would have runners in the race.

"I'm sure you're right," Cannon replied, acknowledging Cochranes' comment. "I'll just have to place my horse in the right race," he added, with a smile.

"Well on that note, I wish you good luck, Mike. It's been a pleasure looking after him and I'll be following his career very closely, especially if his first run back at the track is over here."

The two men stood, Cannon thanked Cochrane again and offered to take him and Candice out for dinner as an additional thank you for everything they had done. Cochrane accepted albeit reluctantly, noting that his bill for services rendered was enough appreciation. Cannon laughed as they shook hands, suggesting that they meet at

Harrigan's on Lower Main Street in Newbridge later that evening. "Say at seven-thirty?" Cannon said, "I'll arrange a table."

"A bit upmarket for me," Cochrane chortled, as he showed Cannon out of his office and took him across to where Candice McGurk was still sitting at her own desk, "but I'll be there. How about you, Candice?" he asked. She turned around to face them, her back having been to the door as they entered the room.

"How about me, what?" she asked, as Cochrane patted Cannon on the back and left him alone to explain what had been agreed. He filled her in.

"Unfortunately I won't be able to make it," she said. "My daughter has just come back from Spain after a short holiday there. She goes off to university in Leeds next week, so we need to sit down and sort out a few things before she does."

"I understand," Cannon said, sympathetically. He knew all about daughters going away to university. He went through the experience when Cassie did the same. Thankfully that was a few years back but at the time it was quite nerve racking. Emotions ran high with the thought of his only daughter going away to live and study on campus, particularly with all the distractions that came with it. Fortunately things worked out well. "Anyway, there is always next time," he added.

"When I'll be happy to accept," she said, a smile creasing her face. "Now about that detail I need for CB & Sons Transport," she added, changing the subject.

It took twenty minutes for Cannon to provide all the information she required, which predominantly related to indemnity waivers and insurances once White Noise had been passed from Cochrane and on to the transport company. After verifying all the necessary detail and signing the applicable forms, McGurk confirmed that she would contact the transport company immediately and thanked him by providing a printed copy of Cochrane's bill.

"I'll send you a soft copy by email as well," she added, as he made to leave the office.

"That would be appreciated," he replied, noting that the figures on the paperwork in his hand wouldn't get any less even if the invoice had been sent to him electronically in the first place. He had expected a figure but blanched slightly at the size of it once it was in black and white and on paper. Fortunately it wasn't his money and Seeton *had* given him the go-ahead to proceed, but if things quickly went south with the horse he was sure that the businessman wouldn't be too happy with him.

"Oh and thanks again for the invitation to dinner," she added, "I hope you and Jim have a good night."

"I'm sure we will," Cannon said, looking at his watch, aware that his next appointment with Sam Quinn was in less than two hours and he still needed to find his way there. Fortunately, 'Siri' was able to get directions for him using Apple maps on his iPhone and as he climbed into his rental car he requested her to obtain the necessary route. While he waited for the app to get the fastest available, he took a quick look over to where White Noise continued to walk around his enclosure, his head held high and his tail swishing around. Cannon could tell the horse was happy. Soon the work to get him race fit again would begin.

"It's a horse called Santa's Quest," Telside repeated, his voice dropping the odd syllable occasionally. Cannon was driving his rented car to the small village of Foulksmills in County Wexford. Mobile coverage was a little dodgy in places but he got the gist of what Telside had said. He hadn't anticipated that the journey from Cochrane's facilities would take him nearly ninety minutes. The plus side however was that he could talk with Telside for as long as needed as he drove along the M9 and then the N80 which traversed the Irish Countryside.

"And you said you'd had a look at the horse's form and the breeding?" Cannon asked, still having no idea why Chester Sutcliffe would want to give him a horse to train.

"Yes I did, and I must admit he's not a bad prospect."

"Oh yes?" queried Cannon.

"Well he won his first race, a bumper at Sandown, just less than three years back by six lengths. Since then he's run seven times, all over the big fences. He's been lightly raced during the past two seasons but had four wins, two seconds and a third."

"Pretty impressive," Cannon agreed.

"What's even more interesting is that he's never been beaten by more than two lengths in any race."

"And who's been training him up to now?"

"Warren Hawker, down Taunton way."

"Oh, the late Warren Hawker?"

"Yes. Remember he died in a car crash a month or so ago in the 'States. California or Nevada I think it was. It was in Racing Post the day after it happened."

"That's right," Cannon replied, recalling the article that Telside was referring to. "It was a single car incident wasn't it? Late at night or something?"

"Seems he fell asleep at the wheel driving back from Las Vegas to LA. The police report said he been drinking and ran off the road into a ditch or something."

"A gully," Cannon replied, smiling to himself. "They call it a gully over there, Rich."

"Well, whatever they call it, he drove into it and ended up dead. Poor man. To die alone like that…terrible."

Cannon agreed. While he hadn't known Hawker very well, they had crossed paths on occasion and he seemed a very nice man, and quite successful too as evident by the results of the horse now potentially being offered to him by its celebrity owner.

"So when do we have to make a decision?" Cannon asked, knowing that he had limited resources at his yard. There were only so many stalls within his stable blocks and White Noise would soon be arriving back to take up his place, plus his visits over the next twenty hours could quite easily result in a few more horses joining him.

"The manager, Burke, said that he needed an answer by close of play today, but I told him that you were away and that I would have to speak to you before we could commit to anything."

"Which means?"

"We have until midday tomorrow."

Cannon put a hand to his mouth as he considered what Telside had indicated, leaving his other hand on the steering wheel. Suddenly a large truck carrying a cargo of live sheep hurtled past him, causing his own car to shake from side to side from the slipstream. He was aware that by being unfamiliar with the road had meant that he was driving a little slower than others would expect but was surprised at the speed of the truck that raced past him. Keeping half an eye on his GPS and the other on the road ahead he watched as the truck tailgated another driver before forcing it to move aside, allowing the truck to steam on.

"Bloody idiot," he muttered under his breath, before giving Telside some feedback. "Rich, I think it would be better if I give this a little more thought. I'm not too far away from Sam Quinn's place and I've still got to see Rory's Song at Dunboyne tomorrow, so I need a bit of time to work through our options. This horse of Sutcliffe's sounds interesting but coming out of the blue it has thrown me a bit."
Telside laughed. It wasn't too long ago, especially during Covid, that many stables, like that of Cannon, were unsure whether they would be able to survive or not. The pandemic had added to the financial problems that some in the industry were already feeling. Covid felt to many as if there was another nail being knocked into their coffin. Smaller trainers had required as much support as they could get, and owners were fickle at the best of times. Depending on their own circumstances some owners had been required to offload their horses completely. Some had culled the number they owned and others retired their horses or had left the game entirely. The result was that as some small yards folded, many of the bigger yards got more horses to train. This often led to scenarios where some races were dominated by the same trainer, like Billy Mulligan in Ireland or Paul Slochin in England. This left punters bewildered and an inferior quality of racing on the track. Accordingly it was imperative for the good of the game that stables similar to Cannons' thrived as much as they could. Turning a good horse away was perhaps not the best idea, but Cannon needed to be sure that by considering Sutcliffe's offer, he wasn't jeopardizing the possible success of any another horse already in his stable. He had other owners who had supported him through the hard times to consider first, despite the prestige he would gain by being seen in the presence of a TV personality. Telside knew exactly what Cannon was thinking and suggested a solution.
"Look Mike, I'll call Burke back once we are finished here and tell him that he'll have an answer before the deadline. That will keep our options open."
"Thanks Rich," Cannon replied, pushing his indicator to the left as the sign to Foulksmills came up to meet him. "I'll call you later if I get the chance. If not, I'll call you first thing in the morning before I leave for Aidan Murphy's farm."
"No problem, Mike. I have enough to do here anyway," Telside said, adding, "just take care of yourself and drive carefully."
Reaching a T-junction at the bottom of a long dip into the village,

Cannon took a quick look at the SatNav/GPS and flicked the indicator to show that he was intending to turn left again. Simultaneously he acknowledged Telside's comment with a "goodbye" and let his friend close the call. Looking to his right he noticed that the road curved out of sight and the arc of the road created a blind spot that made it difficult for him to see if any traffic was coming his way. He glanced left again and noticed the road was clear, then he looked back to the right. As he was about to edge his car forward a large red tractor with wheels that seemed to dwarf Cannons' own car came barrelling along from the right like a demented apparition, flashing past and missing the front of his vehicle by millimetres. The roar of the diesel engine was deafening, causing him to flinch in fear of his life.

"Jesus Christ!" he shouted at the windscreen, "what the….?"

It took him a few seconds to regain his composure, his heart beating loudly in his chest as he contemplated what had just happened. He checked the rear-view mirror suddenly realizing that his indicator was still on and wondering if there was another car stuck behind him? Fortunately there wasn't. The road was empty, but in the immediate silence, not five seconds after the incident, Telside's words came back to taunt him. "*Drive Carefully.*"

Cannon did not believe in premonitions or coincidence, but he did trust his intuition and his own driving skills. He decided that he would need to be extra vigilant from now on as he continued on his way. It was clear from what he had experienced over the past hour or so that he needed to be wary of the driving habits of local farm workers. One near miss was enough for the day.

Taking another look to his right he edged the car forward again, slowly turning left into the road and tried to see if the tractor that had gone in the same direction was still visible. He would have liked to have given the driver something to think about, but by the time the terrain allowed him an opportunity to see the road ahead more clearly, there was no sign of the tractor anywhere. With several farms and farm roads between the T-Junction and the turn off to Sam Quinns' place, it could have pulled in anywhere. Putting the incident behind him, Cannon continued driving following his GPS through a number of twists and turns of unnamed roads until he found the farm that he was looking for. He turned off the road and stopped in front of a closed gate. Climbing out of his car, he stretched, feeling a slight crack in his spine. Rubbing the back of his neck, he raised his shoulders while twisting his head from side to side to ease the tension that had intensified during the drive. The sun shone on his face though a cool breeze which wafted over the fields that stretched as far as the eye could see, caused him to shiver slightly. Late autumn could deliver some nice days, he thought, and today was one of them but he sensed that it wouldn't be long before the Emerald Isle was in for more rain. Opening the gate inwardly, he noticed the two separate locks connected to a large chain that had been wrapped around the metal frames of the gate in order to keep it closed. Pushing the gates to either side of the rutted driveway that disappeared from view due to the contour of the land, he let the chain drop onto the dry grass. Jumping back into his car, he drove three hundred metres over the bumpy ground before pulling up near to Sam Quinns' house. Turning off the engine, Cannon scanned the immediate area. The driveway had surrendered to a gravelled square which stood to the right of the house. It was big enough to park several cars or to conduct a three-point turn with a four-horse van. Cannon assumed that Quinn would need to do this many times given his business was the buying and selling of racehorses. The house itself was a typical two-storey home. Painted with traditional whitewash, which had now yellowed slightly, it had six windows facing towards the front, three upstairs and three on the ground floor. With a black slate roof and an annex to the left-hand side, the building was a carbon copy of most of the farmhouses that littered the area. To the left of the annex the driveway continued, and Cannon could just make out some additional buildings. They were low and he guessed that they were stables. He assumed that there were other buildings that he could not see, those that would contain feed, farm implements, workshop equipment and other typical items that a farmer would need to do his job. At some point, if time permitted, he hoped that Quinn would offer him some traditional hospitality and show him around the place. Climbing out of the car, he suddenly realized that no one had ventured out of the house to greet his arrival, and he had not seen any movement anywhere. He found the silence a little unsettling given the fact that he had confirmed his expected arrival time with Quinn just that morning. Listening to hear for any sound of activity anywhere, he stood against his car for a few seconds conscious only of the faintest of bird song. He took a quick look around to check if there was anyone working in the surrounding fields but could only see a few green and red tractors dotted across the valley beyond the boundary of Quinns' land. Farmers were ploughing their fields after recent harvests of barley, beans and oats. In the far distance there were small dots of black and white littering some green fields. Dairy and sheep farms complimenting the rich tapestry of Wexford's rural landscape.

Cannon knocked on the red painted front door, hearing an echo from within that reverberated throughout an obviously vacant building. He moved to a window on his right, peering through the glass to see if he could see anyone inside. With a hand against one side of his face to shield his eyes he stared into a well-kept lounge. It was empty of people. He knocked several time on the glass pane but was greeted with a silent response.

Turning away he looked at his watch. It was almost three. Before he had left Newbridge he had texted Quinn again to let him know that he would have to leave by four as he needed to get back to Newbridge for the dinner he had arranged with Jim Cochrane. Cannon had not received a reply but it hadn't concerned him too much, as from recent experience he knew that Quinn wasn't adept at responding very quickly, if at all. Cannon had sent text messages and left voicemails previously without acknowledgement.

Deciding to take a walk around to the back of the house, Cannon shouted a casual "Hello" a number of times but was again greeted by silence and the mocking of various birds. Taking the long way around, he strode past the front door heading to the left of the house and the annex. As he did so, he made a conscious decision to check on whether the front door was locked or not. Twisting the handle he confirmed that it was. Disappointed, he realized that without any other vehicles around, it was likely that Quinn had gone somewhere and perhaps that was the reason he had not responded to Cannons' text message? Unsure if his conclusion was correct he decided to check one final time whether Quinn was at the back of the property working in another building or possibly in one of the stables. Having walked around the annex he found himself in the back garden. It was there that he found the body of Sam Quinn. He was slumped onto the ground just outside the backdoor, his hands had been tied behind his back and he had been shot twice. Once in the back of the head, the other right through the heart.

CHAPTER 2

By the time Detective Inspector David Walsh of the Wexford Division (Eastern Region) Garda had arrived on site, Cannon had made three long phone calls. He had been asked to wait in his car while a Sergeant and two other Garda members secured the area around Sam Quinns' body and members of a Forensic team began getting themselves ready to search the area once they had been given permission to do so.
Walsh was a large man, nearly six feet four (one metre, ninety-three), a hundred and five kilograms of muscle and balding. What was left of his red hair was fighting a losing battle as it struggled with his cauliflower ears for the worst feature of the forty-two-year-old former rugby player. Once a captain of Leinster's seconds team, he had a reputation in the force as being as pugnacious in his job as he was on the rugby field. Known to take no nonsense, he was an intimidating character. Dressed in dark blue chino trousers, a white unbuttoned shirt which strained at the neck and a black peacoat, if he had been wearing a fisherman's beanie he would have looked more like a sailor than a cop. He had clambered out of the unmarked silver Hyundai Tucson driven by himself and before making any attempt to look over the scene had made a bee-line to where Cannon was waiting. Tapping on the driver's side window with a large knuckle, he flicked his head indicating that he wanted to join him inside the car. Leaning across to the passenger side, Cannon pushed open the door as Walsh stepped around the back of the vehicle and then climbed in. It was obvious that Walsh had been provided some detail about the situation already and that he was aware that Cannon was the person who had called the police to notify them of the murder.
"I suppose this came as a shock to you, Mr...err....?"
"Cannon."
"Cannon. Yes...Cannon," Walsh repeated, looking through the windscreen at the flapping blue and white, *Police - Do not cross*, tape that fluttered erratically in the now late afternoon breeze. It was six thirty, the sunset still two hours away.
"Yes, it certainly did Inspector," Cannon said, answering the

Detective's question.

"Not something one comes across every day," Walsh said, bluntly, in response.

"No, not every day…fortunately."

Walsh noted the subtlety in Cannon's voice. He turned to look at the man alongside him, staring for a few seconds, then asked, "You were a cop?"

"Was. Once."

"How long?"

"Long enough to know what happened here," Cannon said, pointing in the direction of the house. Walsh considered the reply for a second then held out his hand.

"David Walsh, a pleasure to meet you," he said, making up his mind that Cannon was a witness and not a suspect. Cannon was surprised at the immediacy of the approach but gratefully shook the man's hand which seemed to swallow that of his own.

"Let's take a walk," Walsh said. "You can fill in the details for me."

The two men climbed out of the car into the stillness of early evening. It was as if the day had refused to give in to night. The sun was low on the horizon but its rays were still evident, making long shadows across the ground. A calm seemed to drift across the fields until arriving at a multitude of individuals going about their business with unspoken efficiency. Men and women were arranging equipment just outside of the blue and white tape that set the immediate boundaries of the crime scene that Cannon had stumbled into.

Stopping a step away from the flimsy fluttering barrier where they had strolled silently together, Walsh said, "Did you know the victim?"

"No, not really," Cannon replied.

"Meaning?"

"I've never met him."

While he waited for a response, Cannon sensed that Walsh was a man of few words. His size and demeanour were enough to get people to answer questions and share what they knew or had seen.

"So you…?"

"Came to look at some horses he had advertised for sale," Cannon offered.

"Where?"

"On-line."

Walsh looked around, then pointed where Cannon had guessed previously the stables would be. "Did you get to see any?"

"No. When I got here I tried the door but got no answer, so I took a walk around the back and…."

"Found the body," Walsh said, interjecting, and finishing Cannons' sentence. Cannon was aware that it was a habit. He had developed the same mannerism when he became a Detective. It was also often used as a tactic. One could easily trick people into saying something they didn't mean to. The brain often going into automatic reaction mode. Markers in language could cause one to answer without thinking, the tongue responding like a guitarist who has played the same song multiple times. Muscle memory doesn't require thought and the tongue is an important muscle.

"Yes," Cannon replied, watching as Walsh took out a vaping device from his coat pocket, and within seconds began puffing away on something with a menthol smell. While he waited for Walsh to continue, a slight young woman in a white paper forensics suit, the hood not yet covering her short blond hair, wandered over from a group of four people that had been unpacking boxes and lighting equipment and placing it beside the van that they had come in. At the time of their arrival, Cannon was on the phone to Michelle and subsequently to Jim Cochrane, explaining to her what had happened and apologizing to him for cancelling the dinner that he had offered only hours before.

Ignoring Cannon, she greeted Walsh, saying something in Gaelic.

"English please, Caoilinn," Walsh answered, her name pronounced Kee-leen. "Our witness here, Mr. Cannon, doesn't speak our language."

After looking the witness up and down, she said, "Are you ready to have a look at the body, Daithi? We've been busy unpacking while you've been in transit and we have a lot of work to do. Also I don't want to move anything until you've given us the go ahead to get a mortuary van out here, but in the meantime I'll get things started."

Cannon noticed the use of the Walsh's name in Gaelic, said almost as a retort to his request to speak in English. It sounded like Dah-hee to his ear but he wasn't totally sure. David would have to do.

"Carry on. I'll be there in fifteen minutes," Walsh replied. "I want to have a chat with Mr. Cannon here and have a quick look around first."

Shrugging her shoulders, she turned without further comment and called to the rest of her team. She had reverted back to using Gaelic so Cannon had no idea what she was saying.

"Let's look at the stables," Walsh said, eventually, pointing in their general direction.

Cannon was surprised that Walsh didn't want to see the body first, but he guessed that the Detective had his reasons, though he couldn't figure out what they were. In lock-step the two men began the two-hundred-metre walk to the stables which were now clearly seen at the back of the property, on the left-hand side of the house. Passing the immediate area of the crime to their right, Cannon noted the size of the area that the police had cordoned off with tape. The flapping plastic stretched all the way around the perimeter of the house and included most of the back garden as well. He watched briefly as two individuals, he wasn't sure if they were men or women as they were completely covered from head to toe in white, took photographs of the body using little numbered plastic boards and small rulers to reference size, distances and other possible clues. A third person was writing something down on a clipboard while Kee-leen called out various observations. The body had been covered with a grey blanket.

Once completely out of sight of the others, Walsh finally spoke again. Cannon knew that the silence that had separated them over the last thirty seconds as they walked towards the stables had been allowed to intensify in order to unsettle him. Not an unusual tactic, but one compounded by the continuous vaping by Walsh, the output of which drifted occasionally across Cannon's face, irritating him.

"So what do you think?" Walsh asked.

Cannon turned to his left, looking at Walsh's profile, surprised at the Irishman's question. "Why do you ask?" he replied.

"Because something's not right."

"And you're telling me this….?"

"Let's put it this way, Mr. Cannon. I think there is a lot more behind this killing than meets the eye."

"And you think I'm involved?"

"At the moment no, but I'm keeping my options open. In the meantime let me ask you something."

"Go on," Cannon encouraged.

"How long were you in the force?"

"Why?"

"Just answer the question," Walsh replied, his tone neither sharp nor aggressive.

"Long enough. I spent more years there than I care to remember."

"Because of scenes like this?" the Irishman asked, pointing over his shoulder.

"Yes. I was a DCI. Eventually I'd just had enough."

"I thought so," Walsh smiled, before taking another pull on his vaping machine then placing it into his trouser pocket. "Which is why I asked for your view."

They had reached the small stable block. There were four individual stalls built into the white painted building. Hay nets were attached to the inner walls of each, and pea straw was strewn across the cement floors, littered with manure that to Cannon's eye was obviously fresh.

"No horses," he said, quizzically, "that's strange."

Walsh watched as Cannon looked around at the ground. The path they had walked on from the house to the stables was made of crushed rock, littered occasionally with a few weeds and with grass verges on either side.

"I can see a few hoof marks and the odd footprint, but there's no sign of a trailer anywhere. Perhaps we missed it at the front of the house?" Cannon said.

"Which means?"

"That someone has walked the horses that were in here to some form of transport. Maybe there are some tyre impressions near the house and along the pathway to the gate?"

"Which you and I and the rest of the team will have ridden all over when we came in." Walsh said, matter of factly.

Cannon acknowledged the point but suggested that if it was he in charge he would be asking Forensics to look at everything they could, even where evidence may have been compromised.

"I agree. I'll see what I can do," Walsh replied. "Though as I'm sure you will understand, we have limited resources here, just as I know you have in England. I'll ask Caoilinn to get her team to look into it, though I doubt it won't be until tomorrow. They have enough to do as it is, which I'm sure will last well into the evening. Plus, it will be dark in a few hours. Let's just hope that it doesn't rain."

Cannon looked up, the sun was heading towards the western horizon. There was no redness in the clouds. The shepherds would not be delighted by what he observed. After suggesting the two men go back to where the cars were parked, Cannon asked, "Do you still want my opinion, given you've already indicated that there is something unusual about this killing?"

"Yes, I do."

Taking his time as they walked back to the edge of the crime scene, Cannon eventually remarked, "My immediate reaction was that this was an execution style killing, but if that's the case then why take the horses?"

"To make it look like something else?" Walsh answered, playing devil's advocate.

"What kind of something else?" Cannon queried.

"A robbery gone wrong? The culprits caught red-handed then somehow managing to overpower Quinn."

"And kill him?"

"Yes."

"But why would anyone do that, particularly execution style?" Cannon asked. "It seems a bit extreme for a bunch of horse thieves, doesn't it"

"Do you know what type of horses they were?" Walsh asked, deflecting Cannon's question.

They had reached the still rustling blue and white tape, stopping to watch. A couple of Forensic team members looked up from their work, small faces peering out from the hood of the white suits they wore. Cannon noticed that all four of the team had grass stains on them, at the knees and along the elbows. He said, "I'm not aware of all his horses but he had two that we had corresponded about. Both were 'chasers. Neither of them were particularly valuable as they were geldings. I'm not sure what else he had."

"Which means there was another motive?" Walsh asked.

"Possibly. Has anything been stolen from the house itself?"

"I don't know yet, I'll have the team go over the place. In the meantime while I have a look around, I'd like you to give a statement to my Sergeant. After that you can go, Mr. Cannon."

"Mike."

"Mike," Walsh repeated, holding out his hand to shake for a second time.

"Do you know if he had any family?" Cannon asked, noting that Walsh had not mentioned anything, and he was curious to know why not. Those closest to the victim were often the first considered as possible suspects. "With Quinn being a local in such a small community I'm sure someone would know if there were any issues between them. Break-ups, fall-outs that type of thing?" he continued. Walsh smiled, he wasn't sure if he should take the inference within Cannons' comment of locals being nosey about each other's business as a dig or as a compliment. He decided to ignore it, answering the question the only way he knew. The irony of his detailed response was not lost of him however. "I understand from the Sergeant that Mr. Quinn has a surviving daughter, Julie, a twin. The other daughter, Rachel, apparently drowned while they were both on holiday in Europe. Julie apparently emigrated to New Zealand over fifteen years ago now. Seems she married over there, then subsequently got divorced after it was found out that she couldn't have children. The latest information we have is that she still lives in Dunedin on the South Island."

"A bloody long way away," Cannon said, conscious of his twenty-four trip to Melbourne some years before. New Zealand was another four-hour flight beyond that.

"Agreed. I'm not looking forward to the phone call either."

"You're going to make it?"

"Yes."

"Poor woman," Cannon said, sympathetically.

"Indeed."

After a few seconds Walsh made a comment about needing to get on and Cannon nodded, knowing that what lay ahead for the Detective was a mountain of paperwork and hours of conversations and analysis. Phone records would be trawled through, enquiries of neighbours and friends would be made, ballistic checks would be undertaken, forensics would be collated and reported on, links would be made….

The real question to be answered however was whether there would be an arrest and a conviction for the crime?. Time would tell. Cannon was sympathetic of Walsh's plight but it was no longer his concern.

As the two men parted, Walsh ducked under the blue police tape, talking briefly with the Garda Sergeant in Gaelic that he had referred to earlier. The policeman made his way towards Cannon.

"Are you happy for me to take your statement in my car rather than down at the local station, Sir?" Sergeant Seamus Brady asked.

"Of course," Cannon replied, "I've got to drive back to Newbridge afterwards, so I appreciate the offer of doing it here."

"That's no problem, Sir. I understand you are a former member? Inspector Walsh has advised me of your service."

Cannon offered a subdued smile in response, "Yes, I've seen my fair share," he added.

With a brief gesture towards the police car, Brady encouraged Cannon into the front passenger seat while he climbed into the driver's side.

The whole process took just short of an hour. Cannon providing what he could. He kept to the facts about what he had observed, what he had touched and some background as to why he was visiting Quinn. After reviewing the statement and satisfied that it was correct, he signed the document and passed it back to Brady who advised him that he would likely be contacted again as the investigation continued.

"I think I'm aware of the process," Cannon responded, trying not to sound condescending, "and I'm more than happy to help as required, Sergeant….anytime."

"Thank you, Mr. Cannon," Brady replied. "As I'm sure you are aware not everyone is as cooperative with the police, especially when it revolves around a murder."

"Don't I know it," Cannon agreed, recalling how many times he had been put in a position of witnesses refusing to cooperate or changing their statements as a murder investigation unfolded. Often as the truth came out, he uncovered the dark underbelly of the human condition. Jealousy, hate, spite, abuse, torture, mind games, depravity amongst other human frailties. He tried to ignore what had affected him, but at times like this, the memories came flooding back. It was as if the spirits of those who had been killed had immersed themselves in his psyche and were constantly trying to reveal themselves, looking to claim their rightful place in his thoughts.

Cannon climbed out of the police car. As he did so, he noted how the dark of night was slowly creeping over the hills in the distance. The last light of day was fading quickly. As he walked to his own car, he saw eerie shadows thrown across the side of the house from the stark bright floodlights that the Forensics team had set up as they continued with their investigation.

"Good luck," he said to himself, as he slid back into his rental cars driver's seat and started the engine. As he waited for his phone to connect via Bluetooth to the media system, so that he could get the satnav up and running to guide him back to his hotel, a sharp tap on his window made him jump.

The large frame of Walsh covered the glass obscuring anything else behind him. Cannon pressed the button on the armrest to lower the window.

"Before you go Mike, just have a look at this."

Holding a small piece of paper in the palm of a gloved hand Walsh pointed towards a single sentence typed in the middle of the scrunched sheet, it was less than half the size of a mobile phone.

"Snitches get stitches," Cannon read out, aloud. "Where did you find it?"

"It was stuffed down Quinns' throat. One of Caoilinn's team found it. I'll get it bagged, but I'm interested in what you think."

"I'm not sure I'm the right person to comment to be honest. I don't know much about the man as I told you earlier."

"Ummm?" Walsh replied, his attempt to hide the doubt hidden in his question was not lost on Cannon.

"Are you suggesting that Quinn was involved in something other than horses and that I know about it?"

"I'm not sure what I'm saying to be honest," Walsh said, innocently.

"But you think this note suggests a motive for the killing?"

"It could do," Walsh replied, "but as I said before, something seems odd about this case."

"Well I wish I could help you, Inspector Walsh."

"Call me Dave."

"Okay…Dave," Cannon replied, pleased that the two men had now finally settled on first name terms.

"Good….anyway Mike, maybe you can help me with this."

"I would prefer not too, to be honest. I've got enough on my plate as it is," Cannon exclaimed, as he looked at the clock on the car's dashboard.

"I'm with you," Walsh replied. "But I sense that there is more to this than first meets the eye and if required I may need to call on you again. Obviously that depends on where this all leads," he continued, pointing back over his shoulder to where the Forensics team continued with their work.

"I understand Inspector..err Dave, though I doubt I'll be of use because as you'll see from my statement I'm effectively just an innocent bystander."

"But one caught in the middle of something," Walsh answered.

"Maybe, though I have no idea what."

"And that's why I may need your assistance. Until we know where this all leads I can't rule anything…or anyone…in or out."

Cannon let the last sentence slide by. A strange silence stood between the two men for a few seconds. Then, with a brief smile Cannon put the car into gear, Walsh moved away from the window keeping the piece of paper cupped inside his hands. "Take care," Cannon said as he nudged the car forward before turning it 180 degrees and heading back down the driveway and then on towards the main road. As he drove the short distance to the farm gates he suddenly realized that he would be riding over tyre tracks that may contain clues to what had happened back at the house. He rationalized that the local police had not seemed too concerned so perhaps they knew something he didn't. As he turned onto the unnamed road he checked the time that his satnav was suggesting he would get back to the hotel. Given he had another long drive the next day, he would probably go straight to bed after calling Michelle. He considered stopping to buy a burger at some point on his long drive but decided to give it a miss, hoping to get something at the hotel. Concentrating on the winding road ahead he began the long journey, disappointed that he had to cancel his dinner with Jim Cochrane.

The grey Kia Sportage had pulled into the layby on the unnamed dirt road that stood on a hill above Quinn's farm. A pair of infra-red night vision goggles held to the man's eyes watched as the visitor drove away leaving the police *in situ* to continue with their work.

Having used a telephoto lens to get a photograph of the registration plate of the departing car, the man continued with his observation of those working at the scene. As he watched a song began to play on his mobile phone, Thin Lizzy, Whiskey in the Jar.

Answering the phone with a "Yes, Liam?" he waited for the caller to speak.

"Is it done, Finn?" the caller questioned.

"Yes."

"Did you find what you were looking for?"

"No…. I was interrupted before I could look around."
"By who?" the caller asked.
"I don't know Liam, but I had to get out of there bloody quickly."
"And you're sure that no one saw you?"
"Yes, I'm sure. I left by the back door and hid in the bushes to one side of the house until I could sneak away. I did get the registration number though of the visitor who must have called the police after he found Quinns' body. Unfortunately it's a hire car. Hertz."
"Where is he now?"
"He's just left."
"And the Garda?"
"Still busy….at the house."
"Okay, maybe we can try again once the Garda have left the place, though I suspect that could be in a few days. In the meantime send me the details of the hire car, I'll try and find out who the visitor was."
"Will do, Liam. I'll send you the photograph from my phone."
"Good. After that, I suggest you get yourself home. No point in waiting around. A satisfactory day I'd say."
"Yes…but we still need to get that document."
"Agreed, Finn. With luck the Garda won't find it either," Liam replied, cutting the call between the two men without any form of farewell.
Taking a look through the binoculars, the infra-red lenses allowed Finn Campbell to observe what the police were doing. Ten minutes passed before he had seen enough. Starting the car, Campbell ensured that all the running lights and headlights remained off. He needed his eyes to accustom themselves to the darkness before moving, having originally planned to drive away from his position with only his running lights on. However he soon realized that such a move would be risky due to the pitted terrain. Concerned that even the low beams of his car would be noticed by the police because of his elevated position and being less than a quarter of a mile from the farmhouse, he decided to take a chance using the small amount of moonlight that existed to guide him down the uneven road.

It was probably an unnecessary step to take, but it worked, finally finding himself at the beginnings of a tarred road. With so little traffic about, he was reluctant to come across a Gardai car and be caught driving without any lights, so he turned them on, finally relaxing. The sweat running down his back was cold to the skin. Any entanglement with the police within a reasonable distance of Quinns' house could potentially wreck what they were trying to do. He drove away as quickly as he dared but was concerned about the need to return.

CHAPTER 3

Cannon awoke from a disturbed sleep to the sound of rain on the window. It didn't concern him at first but as he showered he realized that it may have impacted the ongoing investigation out at Quinns' farm. Having arrived back at his hotel he had been able to get a sandwich delivered to his room along with some tea, after which he had called Michelle to fill her in on what he and Walsh had discussed. Their conversation was relatively short, Michelle expressing her concerns while he tried to play them down, outlining the fact that he was just a witness, with no future involvement. However while drying himself, he reflected again on Quinns' murder and Walsh's comments about the apparent attempt to make the killing seem like something it wasn't.

Putting his own observations to one side, after he had dressed he made his way downstairs to grab some breakfast, planning to call Telside once he was in his car.

As he began his trip to Dunboyne, the rain began to fall more heavily so he decided to take the shortest route as suggested by his SatNav/GPS. It would take forty minutes, just touching the outskirts of Dublin, which would be more than enough time to advise Telside of his decision regarding Chester Sutcliffe's horse and for them to make the necessary plans.

"I've decided that its worth a try," he said, "particularly as it's an opportunity to train a horse for a celebrity. It can only do wonders for our profile, don't you think?"

"Or maybe damage it," Telside countered.

"That's possible I suppose," Cannon replied, suddenly aware of a large silver tanker starting to tailgate him. He had been on the M7 for around twenty-five minutes and was close to the off ramp to Naas, recalling that he had never been to the racecourse there, either as a spectator or as trainer. Maybe one day? he thought, as the truck behind carrying thousands of litres of milk, turned into the fast lane to his right and sped past him causing a stream of water to sluice across his windscreen. Cannon cursed, turning his windscreen wipers on to high speed in order to improve his visibility of the road ahead. He noticed the tanker continue to pull away from him as it barrelled along the highway, almost oblivious of the treacherous conditions.

"Thank God for that," Cannon muttered to himself, confusing Telside in the process, but feeling relieved that he was no longer sitting with fifty tons of metal and milk, moving at eighty miles an hour, on his rear bumper.

"So should I give Burke a call then, Mike? I can take him through all the things to be arranged and talk about the necessary paperwork we need," Telside asked.

"Yes, go ahead. Also, find out when they would like the horse moved. I'm assuming they'll be wanting us to take him as soon as possible?"

"I would think so," Telside answered. "When Burke called me with the offer, he said that Warren's place has been pretty badly impacted since his passing, which was why they wanted a quick answer. Sutcliffe is apparently very concerned about the horse not getting any work done, particularly with the new season fast approaching. Being only lightly raced, he wants to get it back into work as soon as possible so that it can maintain its form and get back on the track."

"That makes sense," Cannon said, suddenly noting that his GPS was showing a delay of almost twenty minutes on his route, due to an accident further up the road near the City West Business Campus. He decided to take an alternative route as suggested by the machine. It required him to turn off the motorway near Steelstown and onto the R405, which he anticipated being a quieter road with fewer trucks.

"So what's your concern about Sutcliffe," he asked, conscious of Telside's earlier comment about taking on the TV presenter as a client.

A short silence passed between them, filled only by the whoosh of tyres on the wet road, and the swishing of the wipers across the windscreen, creating a musical soundscape that seemed almost hypnotic with its metronomic tempo. Cannon concentrated on his driving as he waited for his friends response.

"I'm not sure, Mike, to be honest."

"In what way?"

"Well it's just a feeling. The man seems pretty demanding on the TV, almost too determined to get his own way and I think he may want more from his investment than anyone can guarantee, least of all, us."

Cannon smiled to himself as Telside was quite right. The ex-MP and Cabinet Minister was demanding, but as a politician fighting for his

Death Claims its Prize

constituents one would have expected him to be nothing less. It had been his job. The son of a former Defence Minister, who had become a Cabinet member in his own right, he had moved into TV after leaving politics and was now hosting an evening talk show. The man hadn't changed his spots since his move into TV, just the seat that he occupied. It was almost a case of horses for courses. He could now ask questions of those who sat opposite him, whereas in the past he would have had to answer them himself. Cannon was aware from the media, both electronic and print, that Sutcliffe, an extremely good-looking man, tall, thin, tanned with a wife of thirty-two, fifteen years his junior, and with a single daughter, had been talked of as a possible Prime Minister in Westminster circles before he gave it all away. The reason given for his decision to leave politics was muddled and unclear for the most part. Burnout, death threats, family reasons and opportunity were all offered, but many of his colleagues didn't believe any of them. However, as there was no whiff of a scandal, no fingers pointed at any largesse or the use of a privileged position, something didn't make sense but no one had been able to get to the bottom of it. Whatever else it was behind his departure would remain Sutcliffes' secret.

"Listen Rich," Cannon said, "we've had lots of demanding owners over the years, so what's another one, even if he is a personality? If he interferes too much then we'll just pull the plug. The horse may be a good one but Sutcliffe can't expect miracles. After all, we have a number of good horses whose owners pay just as much as he would and who also expect results. We'll just do our best and that's all we can do."

"So we're going ahead?" Telside asked, a little disappointed. His attempt at getting Cannon to reconsider or at least take on board what he was thinking having disappeared through the ether and the wires and poles that made up the mobile phone network.

"Yes we are, though I still need to decide if we will take on Rory's Song as well. I'll give it some serious thought when I see him at Murphy's place. I should be there in about fifteen minutes or so."

"Okay, well just remember White Noise was picked up yesterday from Jim Cochranes' place and is being readied to be transported home tomorrow. If you want to buy Murphy's horse then you'll need to decide quickly especially if you want the two of them to travel together."

Cannon only heard half of what Telside was saying, letting out an awkward sigh. The incident at Sam Quinns' place had suddenly resurfaced. While driving he had tried to suppress it, ignore it, despite the sight of Quinn's body having toyed with his thoughts all evening and throughout the night. He had occasionally woken during the early hours with disconnected strings of vision and words having been spoken, that made no sense. Since waking and repeatedly reliving Quinn's murder in his mind, he knew that he had forgotten about the day to day, suddenly realizing that the intent of his trip was to bring White Noise home and if possible buy more horses. It was not to get involved in murder and he had to remind himself of that. Rory's Song, who he would see soon, was a possibility, but the horses of Quinn, who were now God knew where, were no longer an option. He castigated himself for not concentrating on the objective of his visit.

"Sorry, Rich," he said, apologizing, "my mind was somewhere else, but I got the message. Anyway, I'll be in touch later as I'm almost at Murphys place. I'll let you know what happens after I've had a look at the horse and anything else he's offering."

Pressing the button on his mobile to end the call, Cannon failed to notice the small white car that had been following him since he had left his hotel. Lost in the rain and spray that swept across the roads, the non-descript Kia had maintained a steady pace, consistently remaining a hundred yards behind.

After his call with Finn Campbell, Liam Kennedy had used his contacts at the rental car company's insurer to find out who the driver was and where the man was staying. It was easy when you had a network. Credit card information had been quickly correlated between the bank, the hotel and the car hire company and he had what he needed. Deciding to investigate what the man was doing in Ireland and what association he had with Sam Quinn, a quick look on-line confirmed his suspicions. Mike Cannon was an ex-DCI, a retired cop, someone who Quinn would likely have sought out as a safe pair of hands. With Cannon also a racehorse trainer, the pretext of meeting with Quinn to look at buying a racehorse from him would be a perfect ruse, Kennedy thought. He knew a little bit about thoroughbreds from his time working on various farms, and from what he had observed at Quinns' place on an earlier nighttime visit there, were certainly not quality animals as far as he was concerned. Accordingly he suspected Cannons' visit to see Quinn was for some other reason. He had a view about what that was, and that had made him more suspicious. Accordingly just after midnight he had made a call and let his employer know what he thought was going on, reluctantly filling him in on how things had gone so badly wrong.

What should have been a simple matter had become extremely messy, particularly because the search had been interrupted by Cannon's arrival on the very day they had anticipated being able to go through the house from top to bottom. The operation had gone tits-up on two fronts and it was just as well that the other members of the team had been able to remove Quinns' horses just before Cannon arrived, taking them away to be destroyed, their carcasses burnt in a field just north of Bridgetown some ten miles away. It was a cautionary move they had taken intending to throw the police, but it was one made on the spur of the moment.

When Kennedy had sent Campbell and the others to search Quinns' house they had expected the place to be empty and Quinn to be in town for a few hours as was his habit every Tuesday morning. What they had been unaware of was the visit from Cannon, which meant that Quinn had unexpectedly remained at home. Everything went wrong when Campbell had been surprised as he searched through the property. Quinn had come down from the stables and had confronted him, finding him inside one of the upstairs rooms. The resultant killing was a matter of "him or me" Campbell had said, when he called Kennedy immediately afterwards to advise him of what had happened. The panic that ensued from the shooting had necessitated Kennedy to change plans, deciding to have the horses removed by Healy and Flannery who had been keeping watch for Quinn's return, lying in wait at the front gate of the farm. They had been able to do so just twenty minutes before Cannon arrived, but Campbell was still inside as Cannon pulled up. Fortunately he had evaded being seen leaving the building by seconds, using the trees and bushes to the right of the house as cover, before ultimately making his way back to his car.

From the information that Campbell had later provided from his vantage point, Kennedy knew that Cannon had never entered the house. He expected that the Garda were likely to have done so at some point, but if they had, it was probable that they were unaware of what Campbell had been looking for. So, unless the police were lucky, the secret was still likely to be hidden inside.

Cannon drove through Aidan Murphy's farm gate which had been left open for him. The rain had slowed to occasional showers, though the dirty grey sky above suggested that any significant change in the weather was unlikely in the short term. As his car shuddered along the short gravel driveway, the white Kia that had followed him for the past forty minutes drove on. Arriving at a roundabout some eight hundred metres further along the road it conducted a one hundred and eighty degree turn and headed back from where it had come from.

CHAPTER 4

Chester Sutcliffe was in a contemplative mood. He had been kept waiting by his Producer who was still messing about trying to get hold of his guest for the evening. While the show was only on air in nine hours the guest's agent had still not confirmed that his client would be available to attend. Without the guest on the show that they had been heavily promoting over the past month, there was a likelihood that the whole thing would be a damp squib. "A bloody disaster," Sutcliffe had said when he had been told of the problem. While they had other items 'in the can' should they need, the interest gained through the teasers the TV station had put out had been unprecedented. The guest was one both loved and loathed in equal measure. Edgy, divisive and with a history of bad behaviour, it was a coup for the media team who had been able to entice him to appear. The public's expectation had been heightened, incrementally over the preceding weeks, anticipating that Sutcliffe would be able to use his considerable interviewing skill to peel back the layers that the guest often hid behind and uncover something that would cause a sensation. Social media was abuzz with the hype and the channel Executives were almost apoplectic with excitement. The interview could only increase viewership and with it, revenue.

Sutcliffe, along with two other men and a woman sat quietly in their chairs. They waited for the conversation between the Executive Producer of his show, Charlie Scott, and Walt Finkelstein, the agent of US actor, Timothy Westwood, to end. An argument had been raging for several minutes, the agent seeking assurances that certain topics about Westwood would not be raised during the interview with Sutcliffe.

"We don't want anything said about any alleged drug use, or violence towards women," Finklestein repeated. "Any such allegations made will result in immediate legal action. Do you understand me, Charles?"

"Of course," Scott replied, offering a sly wink in Sutcliffe's direction. "It goes without saying that Chester will focus on Tim's acting career, but we do need to think about the elephant in the room."

There was a brief silence on the far end of the phone. The star shaped instrument that lay in the middle of the long table of the windowless production office, became the focus of attention. The open phone-line crackled as static played with Finkelstein's laboured breathing. The earlier robust conversation had drained him slightly of energy. At eleven in the morning, and when he had least expected it, he had been required to defend his client extremely rigorously when he would have much preferred to be drinking coffee at a small café somewhere, with his partner Seth.

"I've told you before, no questions about Tim's personal politics!" Finkelstein said, his voice containing an element of steel as it rasped the internal speaker of the phone. "This interview will be about the film and nothing else. No scandal mongering, no reference to his recent divorce settlement, nothing to do with who he supported in the last US election, nothing…. just the movie. Do I make myself clear!?"

"But we've been promoting…"

"I know what you've been doing Charles, I'm not an idiot. But if you want any more publicity for Sutcliffe and his show then you'll need to get it somewhere else."

The subtle reference to the TV host was not lost on Scott. The change in tone obvious, and he knew that Finkelstein was getting to the end of his tether. He looked over at Sutcliffe, then at the others in the room. The threat he was faced with made his choice a simple one. Making a wrapping up signal with his hand to the others in the room, he stuck his tongue firmly in his cheek, offered a meek apology to the agent and procured the attendance of Timothy Westwood at the evening's show.

"Fuck me," he said in exasperation, once the line was confirmed dead by Jill Sinclair, Scott's production secretary.

Sinclair was a mousy looking girl, almost non-descript. In her early thirties with light brown hair and a face so pale due to working deep inside studio buildings and barely seeing the sun. She had a vampirish quality about her. She was of medium height, dressed in pale blue jeans, a rolltop cream jersey and black leather jacket. She was efficient and had heard enough profanity in similar meetings that any outburst washed over her like waves on a beach.

"You would think that Westwood would welcome the publicity," Scott continued, "particularly given his last few films were complete flops."

"Not to mention that disastrous episode at the Old Vic last year," Carol Boyd, the program's publicist added. It was she who had been feverishly using every option open to her to promote the interview. Her comment related to an attempt by Westwood to direct a modernized version of Macbeth which went horribly wrong, not least because of the actor's attempt to use the streets of New York as the background for the play. 'Hoodlums' replaced witches, jealousy was fuelled by gang drug deals, guns replaced swords, and betrayal was accompanied by the sound of hip-hop. The idea wasn't particularly new but the execution was shocking, and the show had closed within a week. Advance ticket sales had been poor, and after the critics had savaged the show, the promoters and producers had been left with no choice but to cut their losses. Westwood had left the UK with his tail between his legs, the fallout to be cleaned up by others. With his reputation badly burnt he had used the last fifteen months to stay out of the limelight until recently. It had emerged that he had been secretly filming his latest offering, a political thriller set in East Germany during the cold war and was the reason Finkelstein had suggested to Westwood that Sutcliffe's show was the right vehicle to promote the film. This was because the hosts late father had been politically active during that time.

James Sutcliffe had been a spy for MI6 working as a diplomat behind the iron curtain, looking for traitors against the crown. It was around the time of the Profumo affair and he was secretly swapped at the Brandenburg gate in 1963 just a few weeks after the US President, JF Kennedy, had visited the Berlin Wall. Sutcliffe had been arrested in Prague a year earlier. The exchange, for a number of Russian spies who had operated out of the Soviet embassy in London, was only revealed some forty-five years later. The explosive details made public in a book ghost-written for the senior Sutcliffe, and only released a few months before his death from Parkinson's disease. The book had captured the public's imagination and the content had created a stir in Westminster. The prevailing conversation excited the wider press, encouraging them to relook at that period of political scandal and ask whether there was still the same undercurrent of mistrust throughout the government of those in the civil service today? Chester Sutcliffe had been a recently appointed MP when the book was released. He was only thirty-one at the time and was inundated with a barrage of questions about what he knew of his

father's role.
Was James Sutcliffe a double agent?
Were there any secrets not revealed in the memoir?
Why did it take more than four decades to tell the stories that were included the book?
Who was being protected by the passage of time?
The hounding by the press, and the subsequent fallout resulted in the younger Sutcliffe needing to keep his head down for several years. Working for his constituency he slowly emerged as a future party leader as those above him crumbled and self-imploded through hubris, arrogance and internal bickering. Eventually after his side of politics won power he was given a Ministerial position. However when the opportunity arose sometime later to take on the highest role within the party, Sutcliffe suddenly resigned his seat and headed for the bright lights of the media. His move was a shock to his colleagues, but he had his reasons and he was determined to keep them to himself.

The room fell silent, all eyes turned to Sutcliffe waiting for him to respond to what had just taken place. With his hands together, held just below his chin, he looked to the others as if he was praying. He remained looking down at the table, then as if addressing no one in particular began to speak, his voice soft but clear, his tone authoritative. "It's a pity that we've spent so much time and money promoting tonight's show, given what we've just heard. However let's not forget that once Westwood is in the chair, he is fair game."

He looked up from the table, lowered his hands and stared into each face. All of them appeared to be hanging on his every word.

"And it's a live show," Scott added, jumping in. "He's got nowhere to go if he doesn't like the discussion."

"Other than to walk out," Sinclair said.

"And how will that look?" Scott queried.

"He'll certainly get some publicity," chimed in Stephen Crumm, the TV network's lawyer, who had remained mute until now. He had been listening carefully to what had been discussed and argued over, making copious notes as the debate had continued. "However," he continued, "if Mr. Finkelstein had been less hasty and more thorough regarding his client's interest, he would have reviewed the contract we have with Mr. Westwood. In so doing he would have noticed that the terms and conditions related to his appearance on the show

indicate that nothing is 'off the table'. There are no caveats, nor any exclusions stated, except for...."
"His fee?" Sutcliffe interjected, a subtle smile on his face.
"Yes, Chester, that's right. If he bails out during the show, doesn't arrive in time or refuses to attend, in whatever form, then all publicity costs incurred are recoverable from him, his appearance fee will be waived and the Station will be able to sue for any other costs or damages."
"Not the sort of publicity he needs."
"No, Chester," Crumm continued, "but I'm guessing that Finkelstein was looking for the best fit for his client's comeback film, given the subject, rather than just any old talk show."
"And is now trying to limit the damage?"
"The potential for it, yes."
Sutcliffe smiled again, his open lips and whitened teeth creating a line across his tanned face. He glanced at Scott. The two of them had worked together very successfully for a long time, having known each other for many years. From the very beginning of their friendship, they had immediately fallen into a symbiotic relationship. As post-grad students and well before Sutcliffe went into politics, Scott and he had travelled throughout Europe as well as through North and South America together. They worked on farms, in cafés and restaurants, doing anything to fund the next leg of their journey. They became so close that Scott, now his Producer, knew exactly what Sutcliffe was thinking. It was a friendship that ultimately became an issue between Sutcliffe and his wife. Secrets from their past that he refused to share, were eventually too much for her and the marriage failed. Nodding imperceptibly at the star presenter, he let him respond to Crumm's commentary.
"Don't worry Stephen, I've been around long enough to know what we are faced with. A hack of an actor whose holding on by his fingernails and who needs a break."
"And is looking for us to provide it to him," Scott added.
"Precisely," Sutcliffe went on, his mind turning with questions he would raise later on. He was determined to delve into Westwood's personal demons. It would make great television and would be a boost to the show which was rapidly becoming the 'must watch' program of the week.
"As long as you are careful not to cross the line, Chester," Crumm

insisted, "then I agree, you should be able to probe as deep as you want to. In my opinion Finkelstein and Westwood need us, more than we need them."

Without replying, Sutcliffe turned to Boyd who was smiling at the prospect of using the interview to further enhance the standing of the show. The publicist was figuratively licking her lips at how to publicise future episodes, her mind reeling at the potential. She could see the viewership figures increasing exponentially after the show aired later that evening. In her mind she had visions of the famous interview with Prince Andrew and the Epstein affair or Martin Bashir's interview with Princess Diana in 1995. While that might be deemed overkill by some, Boyd was of the view that the travails of Westwood, a famous actor, who was once accused of being a communist, being exposed so brutally by Sutcliffe would be a fascinating juxtaposition given Sutcliffe's own family background. She could almost taste the delicious irony.

"I think we are going to have an interesting show," Sutcliffe said, his eyes sparkling at the prospect.

"Without a doubt, Cliff, without a doubt."

Scott glimpsed at Boyd, then looked back across the table towards Sutcliffe. He noticed the way that the two of them had exchanged glances but decided to ignore it. He called the production session to an end then instructed his assistant to write up the running order of the show.

"Don't forget to draft some questions for Cliff as starters, and make sure we have the necessary grabs to play during the interview."

"No problem," Sinclair answered, as she made for the door, held open for her by Crumm.

"And I'll catch up with you later," Scott continued. "In my office for a run through at four."

With a wave she was gone, followed by the lawyer and the publicist. Sutcliffe had remained seated, he appeared be looking at his mobile which had been kept on silent during the meeting.

"Is everything okay?" his Producer asked.

"Oh, yes, everything's fine," Sutcliffe answered pointing at the screen of his phone. "I had a text from Tony, he asked me to give him a call after we finished."

"Nothing serious I hope?"

"I don't think so. He would have called and left a voice mail if it was.

And, if he really needed to talk with me urgently, he would have had one of the production assistants come and interrupt us."
"Okay, then if it's not urgent, I'd like to talk to you about something."
"What about?"
"Westwood....close the door," Scott replied.

CHAPTER 5

Rory's Song had all the physical attributes of a good 'chaser. He had well developed hindquarters, a huge chest and strong legs. "Unfortunately he's not very quick," Aidan Murphy said, as one of his staff, a young girl of no more than eighteen, with a slim figure wearing tight black jeans, riding boots and an unzipped blue parka coat, led the horse around in a circle. The hooves of the animal clipped and clopped on the still wet cement of Murphy's yard. The occasional splash of dirty brown water flew up from the boots of the girl and landed in the various puddles that lay on the uneven surface. Fortunately, the threat of more rain had diminished slightly as a gusty cool breeze sent the clouds scattering in different directions, allowing a saddened sun to burst through on occasion, revealing an even sadder grey/blue sky. The groom continued with her perpetual walk, allowing Cannon to make an assessment of the horse as it moved away from where he and Murphy stood. They shared a canvas awning attached to the side of a white painted stable block. Dotted with mud and streaked with black lines where rain had run down its sides the building was large enough to house twenty-four individual boxes. Murphy had mentioned to Cannon earlier that he only had twelve horses in work and was trying to reduce his workload to eight.
"I'm a bit too old now for any more than that," Murphy had said. A short man and a former jockey who had ballooned in weight since he had stopped riding some twenty-five years earlier. Now he was almost round, with a head bereft of hair except for a few white tufts on either side which seemed to force their way from under his checkered cap and swamp both ears. "And since my wife passed away a couple of years ago," he continued, "it's been a very lonely existence," he added, with a forlorn smile. "Nowadays once everyone goes home it's a real bugger if something happens. While I used to be able to manage things, I don't have the strength or the energy to handle it anymore."
When he had been greeted on his arrival, Cannon had noticed the arthritic hands and the unsteady gait of the Irishman. The sight of this old trainer standing under the awning and waiting for his arrival

in the cold and damp of mid-Autumn made Cannon realize how fortunate he was to have his Michelle and his team back home to support him. Cannon was sympathetic and understood where Murphy was coming from, instantly turning his mind to Telside back in Woodstock. He and Cannon had discussed retirement several times, but Telside had convinced him that the subject was taboo and that it was never to be raised again, indicating that he would rather die on the job before he would ever set foot in a care home or aged facility.

Dressed in a green raincoat that had seen better days and which seemed to hang like a smock over his grey jersey, grimy blue jeans and well-worn wellington boots, Murphy told Cannon why he wanted to sell the horse.

"Apart from the obvious physical issues," he began, removing his hands from the pockets of the coat and letting Cannon see the gnarly fingers that were twisting like the claws of a bird of prey, "it's really all about the money." The cold gave the digits a blue appearance and Cannon wondered why Murphy wasn't wearing gloves. He decided not to say anything, allowing the Irishman to carry on with his explanation. "I'm sure you're aware that you need critical mass…"

"And a bit of lady luck?" Cannon suggested, indicating that he knew where Murphy was going with his explanation.

Every trainer needed a good horse or two in his stable to ensure that those owners who removed their animals to seek pastures new, looking for success elsewhere, did so under their own recognizances. A poor horse wouldn't make a trainer successful, a good horse did that. Accordingly a successful stable usually had owners wanting their horses to be part of such a set up. Less successful trainers had to fight to get good horses into their facilities. Unfortunately the difference between a good and a bad establishment was often a single animal, not the approach or philosophy of the man whose name was in the race book or race card as the trainer. Cannon, like all those in his position, knew that he was one horse away from the limelight and just a few more away from failure.

"Exactly, and unfortunately 'she' has deserted this Irishman," Murphy continued, a brief smile creasing his face at his attempted joke.

"So why are you selling this particular horse?" Cannon asked, as the groom walked Rory's Song past the two men again, continuing to parade him in the same concentric circle. The girl's long dark brown hair blew in the breeze, occasionally merging with the horse's mane, their brown-coloured strands embracing each other in a muted dance against the poor light of the day.

For a few seconds it appeared as if Murphy was going to change his mind and tell him that the horse was no longer on the market. Cannon waited.

"Because he deserves an opportunity to show what he can do," Muphy answered eventually, turning side on to look at Cannon's profile.

"But didn't you say he was slow?" he asked.

"No, I said he wasn't very quick."

Cannon smiled to himself, making a mental note that he should be more careful with the words he was hearing. In his former life words were extremely important. They often held the key to solving a mystery, the unravelling of a story, an excuse or a lie. Being so attuned to what was said to him had allowed him to be successful as a Detective and he chastised himself for making such a simple error in relation to Murphy's comment. He sensed that he may have lost his chance, should he decide to buy the horse, to lower the price. He needed to remember his negotiation skills and reconsider his tactics. It may be that he had lost his edge, he thought. He decided to try another tack knowing that Murphy needed the money, the man perhaps inadvertently having told him so. The only question was whether Rory's Song was worth what Murphy wanted for him.

"So what are we talking about here?" Cannon asked.

"What are you offering, Mr. Cannon?" Murphy replied, his accent more pronounced as he emphasized his potential buyers surname. It was the old game of answering a question with another question. While it was something Cannon was used to, the setting wasn't right for it and time was against him. He had a plane to catch early the following day and if he did decide to buy the horse he still needed to contact CB & Sons to collect the animal so that it could be transported along with White Noise to his yard in Stonesfield. Making such arrangements, then getting back to have the rescheduled dinner with Jim Cochrane in Newbridge would mean that he would have little time for anything else. It could be done if he made a quick decision, the bank having already approved a facility for him to pay in Euros, however he wanted to be sure it was the right thing to do first, especially given the pending arrival of Chester Sutcliffes' horse. Cannon had already researched the form and the results of the races that Rory's Song had competed in and had reviewed the Vet's report that he had commissioned before he left Stonesfield for Ireland. The report had been sent to him a few days earlier and he believed that given the horse's breeding and strong confirmation, it did have some potential once fit and having been properly schooled. Watching the animal continue being walked around, he was trying to keep his powder dry and his money in his pocket for as long as possible. He wanted Murphy to make the next move.

"I reckon Thirty Thousand," Murphy said finally, pointing in the direction of the girl. Cannon decided to stay silent for a while, to stretch out the process a little, despite his own time limitations. After all, time was indeed money and if he could use it to his advantage in the negotiations, he would. Pretending to consider Murphy's proposal, which he had no intent of accepting, he waited thirty seconds before responding. "Euros?" he asked.

"Pounds," came the instant reply.

Learning from his earlier mistake, Cannon answered, "Then I think I'd better get on my way, Aidan. It's clear that we won't be doing any business today at that price." He held out his hand to indicate that he was thankful for Murphy's time, but the Irishman didn't take it.

"Twenty-five then, Mr. Cannon, and pounds at that," Murphy said. Again Cannon pretended to be considering the offer. He pointed towards the sky and complained about the weather. It was a distraction, the idea being that the longer he held out, the more likely that Murphy would need to decide to sell or walk away and fight another day. The silence between the men was only broken by the snorting and neighing of the horse and the repeated sound of clip-clopping on the wet cement. Cannon eventually broke the impasse. "Twenty Thousand, no more," he offered.

"Euros?" Murphy questioned, cynically.

"Pounds," Cannon answered, accepting the irony of his own currency reversal. "And that's my one and only offer."

This time it was Murphy who had to consider what was on the table. While he did so, Cannon asked him if he knew of Sam Quinn.

"I've come across him at a couple point-to-point meetings over the years, but I don't know him particularly well. I know he bought a few horses that he raced there at times, and occasionally he'd get one that would run at Cork or Fairyhouse, but he was more a trader than an owner." The description by Murphy of Quinn's business seemed to tie in with what Cannon had seen at the farm in Foulksmills.

"Why do you ask?" Murphy enquired. "Are you looking to buy from him as well? I don't think he has anything like this one on his books."

"I was considering it," Cannon answered nonchalantly, still wondering whether his offer for Rory's Song would be taken. "But I assume you haven't heard?"

"About what?"

"That he was murdered."

"When?"

"Yesterday."

"Jesus!" Murphy exclaimed, the obvious shock at the news written on his face. "How? Why? Who the..?"

"He was shot…in the head. Execution style."

"Bloody hell! How do you know this? It wasn't on the news last night or even this morning."

Cannon understood the reason why the killing had not been publicised as yet. Until the next of kin had been informed in New Zealand, the police would not mention the names of a victim unless it was essential. It appeared that they had decided not to say anything to the general public as yet. Cannon assumed that Walsh still believed that it was a targeted killing rather than something opportunistic and that the general public were not at risk from whoever had pulled the trigger.

"I found the body," he said, quietly.

"Holy Mary, Mother of God!" Murphy said, making the sign of the cross on his chest. "What is world coming too?" A rhetorical question and one that neither men wanted to answer.

Cannon nodded, there was nothing to be said.

"So what do you think?" he asked, after a short pause, turning the conversation back to his offer. He noted that the news of Quinn's murder had inadvertently created some confusion in Murphy's mind and that he was clearly shaken. In a few seconds his demeanour had changed and Cannon sensed the level of unease. Something was obviously troubling him.

"Oh, err….yes, done!" he said, holding out a hand.

The deal concluded, Cannon pondered for a second on how quickly Murphy had accepted the offer once he became aware of Quinn's death. It was obvious that the news had come as a shock but what relevance, if any, did the murder have to Murphy, such that he reacted the way that he did? There were numerous questions that swarmed through Cannon's mind like bees inside a hive. He was tempted to raise them but decided to keep his peace for now. What had happened to Quinn was a question for the police to solve and not for him to get involved any more than he already was. The need to constantly remind himself of that fact continued to play havoc with his natural instincts. His time in the force had left an indelible mark on his psyche, but he had voluntarily walked away from it, years ago….which had allowed him to keep his sanity. Finding Quinn's body however had brought back the ghosts of the past, suddenly reliving what he wanted to forget. While he fought against the memories, trying to bury them again, he struggled to let them go. He knew that death was never far away and would come to claim what it believed was owed. His experience while on the roads yesterday a simple example and was enough to confirm that view. Putting the thoughts of the near miss with the tractor to the back of his mind he let Murphy know that he would arrange for the horse to be collected by his preferred transport company that afternoon. All they needed to do was complete the necessary paperwork and he would arrange for payment to be made immediately.

With a smile and a shrug of agreement, Murphy pointed towards a small building about twenty yards away on the other side of the yard. It was daubed in chalk white, the base and walls streaked with mud and dirty veined lines where rain had overflowed from the gutters and ran down the outside, flaking the paint that had cracked in the occasional sunlight. The tiny windows of the structure seemed to be struggling to let the cold light of the gloomy day in while the closed black barn style door tried to keep the heat inside from getting out. "My office," he said, then calling to the young groom requested her, "put the horse away."

The two men jogged across the open space and entered the office. Cannon noted the similarity with that of Jim Cochrane. There were papers and documents everywhere. On the floor, on the windowsills, on chairs and on top of a battered four drawer filing cabinet. The drawers themselves seemed unable to close. The coloured tabs of various files and folders peered above the ridges of each drawer suggesting how full they were. It looked like a tsunami of A4 sheets trying to escape.

"Forgive the mess, Mr. Cannon," Murphy pleaded, "but my assistant who normally helps me with all the necessary documentation has recently had a child, and the poor little thing has been unwell, so I've been on my own for the past few weeks."

With a smile, Cannon indicated that he understood the issue, though doubted that the problem had only begun in the past month. It took them more time than he expected before the transaction was completed, and he found himself on his way back to Newbridge. Along the way he made a call to CB & Sons, giving them all the necessary details of Aidan Murphy, including address and contact details before requesting the company arrange to transport Rory's Song along with White Noise to Stonesfield. Once satisfied that his requirements were fully understood and a promise had been given that both horses would arrive at his yard within less than three days, he made another call to Jim Cochrane apologizing that once again he may be late for dinner.

"I'll be there just after seven," he said, looking through the windscreen at the darkening sky ahead. While the showers had stopped for now it was obvious that rain was not far away again. Even though the sun was still somewhere above the horizon and not yet ready to set, it was impossible to know of its presence. Heavy cloud was rolling in. After he finished his call with Cochrane, he was about to dial Telside's number to give him an update on Rory's Song when a police car overtook him, roaring past him on his right-hand side. Without any flashing red or blue lights nor any siren, Cannon had not noticed the speeding vehicle galloping past the stream of traffic behind. Many of the cars in the fast lane had moved over to let the police car pass and it caused him to jump in his seat as it shot by. In the gloom of early evening and with the spray from the other cars on the road ahead splattering surface water across his windscreen, he hadn't noticed the Garda car rapidly approaching from the rear. Caught by surprise, he swerved slightly into the right-hand lane, earning the ire of a driver that had decided to follow the police car and take advantage of the empty stretch of road created by the rushing Garda's Hyundai. A loud blast on a horn and an angry fist greeted Cannon as an indistinguishable pick-up truck screamed alongside him. Over correcting and swerving back towards his own lane, he almost hit a car that had sidled up alongside in the left-hand lane. He cursed the driver of the pick-up as it accelerated away, oblivious of Cannons' futile message of disdain for the way he was driving. With his heart pumping rapidly, uncontrollably, Cannon realized that he not been concentrating fully on the road, and his mind had been elsewhere. He had been too busy talking and thinking about the events of the previous twenty-four hours that he had not focused on his driving. He noticed that his hands were shaking. "Shit!" he said, out loud. "Get a grip, for fuck's sake....concentrate!" Touching the brake pedal slightly, causing a number of cars behind to slow down in concert with him, he flicked on the indicator and moved left into the slow lane.

Once his heartbeat had returned to near normal, he called Telside letting him know that he had bought Rory's Song and the price that he had paid for the horse. Telside agreed with him that they may have acquired a bargain. "And he'll be travelling with White Noise. They're expected to arrive sometime the day after tomorrow subject to the weather and any issues with the crossing," Cannon confirmed. "That's good news, Mike. I'll make sure we have a stall ready for both of them."

After thanking his assistant for making the necessary arrangements at the yard, Cannon turned his attention to the other matter on his mind, Chester Sutcliffe's horse. "So what did Tony Burke have to say about our decision?" he asked.

"He said that Sutcliffe would be very happy to hear it and that they would get in touch with you in a couple of days. He explained that they wanted to give you enough time to get home before they came up from London to meet with you."

"Burke *and* Sutcliffe?"

"Yes."

"Okay, well I guess it's not unexpected, given who we are dealing with," Cannon replied, suddenly hoping that he wasn't going to regret his decision. The idea of having a good horse in his yard but needing to work with a very difficult owner, one that was used to getting his own way, was not something that pleased him particularly. There was something about entitled people with large egos that always rubbed him up the wrong way. He tried hard not to let Telside hear his concern through the tone of his voice, but he was unsuccessful. Telside tried to play down any negatives by suggesting that should Cannon feel uncomfortable at any stage, then he could always ask Sutcliffe to move the horse on. It happened all the time. Owners and trainers didn't always see eye-to-eye. It was par for the course across the industry, the only difference this time as far as Telside was concerned was the high profile of the owner and the high expectations that came with it. Acknowledging the principle, Cannon knew that Telside was right. They had been through similar situations before, just not with such a public figure. The two men then ended their conversation, Cannon letting his friend know that he needed to concentrate on the road ahead given the weather, and the approaching darkness. Looking at his GPS/SatNav he still had some way to go before he met with Jim Cochrane.

With his heartbeat now back to normal and Telside's simple philosophy echoing in his ears, Cannon accepted that the risk he was taking training for Chester Sutcliffe was countered by the opportunity to increase the stables' profile with other owners. In some way he could see the irony. Would the training of a horse for someone with such a high profile affect his own ego? Would being successful or otherwise with the horse start to change him? Was it possible that another person's ambition would alter his own expectations of himself? To date he had been happy with his personal progress, both as a trainer, a father and a husband….to Sally… and now Michelle. He had started small and progressively, along with Telside, had increased the stable size. While he had been close to the top of the hill, almost winning the Grand National for a wealthy owner, he had never trained for someone with such a national persona, an easily recognizable figure. His decision to do so was making him uncomfortable for some reason, something he had never experienced before. He wasn't sure why but realised that he had to go with it. The die had been cast.

CHAPTER 6

Tony Burke had been waiting for Sutcliffe's meeting to finish. He hoped that the text he had sent over an hour earlier was enough to get his client, the ex-politician, now TV presenter, to return his call asap. Burke was impatient, waiting for the phone to ring, but continued working through the correspondence on his desk. His office looked out over a slightly untidy garden, notwithstanding the manicured lawn that he could see through the three-quarter length window. After the rush of colour from the perennials which were now fading, daisies and hollyhocks would soon provide some sparkle to the garden beds that ran along the fences of the half-acre grounds at the back of the Esher property. A rare but occasional burst of sunlight streamed into the room, before quickly disappearing again.

Standing, Burke raised himself to his full height, stretching his arms and rubbing the back of his neck as he walked towards the window. On the way over he picked up the cup of coffee that he had started but had not yet finished. It had been placed next to his mobile phone on the right side of his desk and was now tepid, but he swallowed it anyway. As he looked up at the thick grey clouds above, they appeared to resemble an angry sea which had suddenly learned to ignore gravity and take flight above the earth rather than rest upon it. At five feet six or one hundred and sixty-seven centimetres tall, Burke could have been a jockey had it not been for his weight. His seventy-nine-kilogram body made him appear more like a bulldog than the lithe greyhound which most jockeys were. However it was his tenacious nature away from the saddle that had made him successful, the trappings of which were all around him, the early days of growing up in Derby long forgotten. At forty-nine, twice married and twice divorced, a father of one from his first marriage, he ran his own management company. The business looked after the affairs of a number of celebrities, along with several former sports stars who worked the speaking circuit. Dressed casually in a sky-blue polo shirt, beige chino trousers, black loafers on his feet and no socks, he was warmed by the expensive Scandinavian wall panel-heaters that he had had installed throughout the five bedroomed house shortly after acquiring it six years earlier. Despite his rotund body he was often described as handsome. With a full head of jet-black hair, dyed when necessary, and cut like Hugh Jackman, he had striking blue eyes that seemed to see right through anyone who had the temerity to stare back at him. His nose and mouth centred perfectly in his diamond shaped face gave him a slightly boyish look. A full set of teeth, regularly whitened, completed the picture that he had fashioned. He believed that he had to look the part, in order to play the part. It was a philosophy that had made him successful in his business dealings, leveraging the social media trend of celebrities wanting to be seen and the public wanting to watch or experience how the 'other half' really lived. His contacts were extensive, and his networking had brought him clients like Chester Sutcliffe. The relationship had worked for both of them since Burke had signed the contract to represent the former politician. He had a vested interest in what Sutcliffe could bring him as an agent and Sutcliffe likewise relied on Burke to maximize his earning potential through sponsorships and any other lucrative deals. It was Burke who had put forward his client's name to the TV studio Executives that had hired Sutcliffe some two years earlier. The rest, as they say, was history. Sutcliffe's show was the number one talk show in the country, rivalling and usurping many of the long-established programs. Controversial, edgy yet entertaining, it always seemed to have the right guest on who was willing to spend an hour talking about themselves. With Sutcliffe's skill at finding holes in the front that many tried to hide behind and knowing where to push or probe his guest for answers, the program with the tag line, 'Going beyond the spin and getting under the skin', had gained a huge following and with it Burkes' own profile. He had been praised as the man who had found the perfect niche for his now extremely high-profile client. Until that stage, Sutcliffe had been somewhat on the outer. Having walked away from his political party and his constituents without any apparent reason, he had been floundering until Burke had put the idea to him. After getting Sutcliffe's endorsement of the idea he had then sold it to the TV station who had jumped at the chance to take on the charismatic former MP. With a glamorous young wife in tow, and the potential to do a 'fly on the wall' reality exposé of their life together after the first season of the show, (which would also reveal why he had turned his back on his political career), the decision to sign him up was a no-brainer. Unfortunately for the original Producer of the show, Sutcliffe subsequently reneged on both matters. This caused several of the Executives and the Producer a tremendous amount of consternation and anger with threats being thrown around like confetti. Under his contract Sutcliffe could have been sued and even lost his position, but due to the ratings achieved and the show's success having substantially increased advertising revenues across all forms of media, the decision was made to kick the can down the road for a period. The parties ultimately agreed by way of a compromise to make a documentary about Sutcliffe, his lifestyle, and his love of expensive wine, cars, and exotic destinations to be filmed in subsequent years. The rights would belong to the TV station, but the program would only be aired after Sutcliffe had left the show or within three years from its making, whichever was the earlier. The original Producer of the show had resigned in disgust at the backflip. Charlie Scott had subsequently replaced him, taking on additional Executive duties from those he already had.

Burke turned away from the window, noticing as he did so a few spots of rain dabbing themselves on the double glazing. He took the few steps towards his chair when his mobile began to ring; the first few bars of *Eye of the Tiger* by Survivor. Reaching for the device he noticed the name on the screen, it was Sutcliffe.

"Hello Chester, thanks for calling back. Are you well?"

"I'm having a few issues, but they are not unexpected," Sutcliffe replied, not bothering to ask what Burke wanted to speak with him about.

"Let me guess….with the lawyers?"

"To some degree yes, but actually it's more of a problem with an agent…," Sutcliffe answered, letting the title slide.

"Timothy Westwood's?" Burke asked, tentatively, knowingly. He was aware that the actor had been invited ten days ago to appear on this week's program and the promo cycle had emphasized Westwood's attendance continuously. But, what Burke didn't want to see was his star client ending up in some legal wrangle for defamation or slander with a movie star or his agent, particularly an American one. It would be costly on so many levels and with Sutcliffe's propensity to push the limits at times, that possibility was never too far away.

"Yes, Walt Finkelstein," Sutcliffe answered. "He's such a prick. On the one hand he wants us to give Westwood a platform to plug his new film, yet on the other he doesn't want me to ask any difficult questions."

"What is he happy with then?"
"Just those that relate to the movie."
Burke took a deep breath. He knew that Sutcliffe was not the type of man to sit back and just do what a representative of his guest asked of him. It was Sutcliffe's show and it was meant to be balanced, in-depth, challenging and ultimately serious. It wasn't for the faint-hearted guest, but it was for those that had something to say and weren't afraid to say it. Controversial subjects of any type, be they from a book, a film, a philosophical idea or anyone's own personal viewpoint were what made the program successful.
Taking a pragmatic position, Burke let Sutcliffe know that the decision of how far to push things with Westwood was for him to decide. "Just be careful though, these film stars can get a bit edgy if you get under their skin, particularly those that are in a career crisis. Their egos can get in the way and make them extremely sensitive."
Sutcliffe laughed. "If Westwood is so sensitive then he shouldn't be appearing at all. He needs the exposure and that's why he agreed to be on the show."
"Okay, but I'll be watching," Burke replied, trying to hide the fact that he wouldn't be. He had other things to do. He hoped his lie wasn't obvious to Sutcliffe as he changed the subject. "I've got some good news," he said, "I've found a replacement trainer for the horse."
"Who?"
"A guy called Mike Cannon. He's in Oxfordshire. His stables are in a place called Stonesfield near to Woodstock."
"Is he any good?" Sutcliffe asked, cautiously.
"I did some research. He's done well over the last few years. His stable is quite small but he's had a bit of success, in fact he nearly won the Grand National a few years ago."
"Nearly?"
"It's a long story. There are a number of articles about it on the web. I can send you a link if you want?"
"No, I'll take your word for it. As long as he can do the job with the horse then that's fine with me. I'm happy to give him a go as long he as he understands where I'm coming from…."
"That he prioritizes the horse?" Burke interrupted.
"Yes. You know I prefer smaller yards over big ones. Those TV trainers as I call them are all about themselves rather than the horses.

If it wasn't for the owners, they would be nothing."

Burke listened to his client, inwardly noting the irony of Sutcliffe's words. It was obvious that egos and visibility in the media, social, print, radio or TV were the breeding ground of narcissism and hegemony and the trend was becoming increasingly rampant. However it was this craze, this fad, that helped Burke get to where he wanted to be. As an agent of personalities, the biggest of which was on the phone, he knew which side of the bread was buttered and he devoured it.

"Which was why I chose Cannon for you," he continued.

"Sounds good," Sutcliffe replied. "So when does the horse get up there?"

"I've suggested that Cannon and his team make contact with Warren's Head Lad directly and between them make the necessary arrangements. Once they've done that, they will let me know and I'll send you the details. I've already indicated to Cannons' offsider that once the horse arrives up there then you and I can go up together and we can have a look around. If you'd like to that is?"

"I would."

"Great."

"Is there anything else?" Sutcliffe asked, his tone hinting that he needed to move on and that he was finished with their conversation.

"No, I think that's the lot."

"Good." A monosyllabic reply, confirming that the subject was closed.

"Have a great show tonight...," Burke began, before realizing that the call had been disconnected prior to him having uttered the first word. Putting the now silent phone down onto his desk, he sat back in his chair, a sound of exasperation escaping from his lips. He stared at the wall opposite, a painting by Tracy Emin that he had bought for eighty-thousand pounds mirrored his mood which had changed from pleased to indignant in a matter of seconds. He was annoyed at the offhandedness that Sutcliffe had shown him. While his client's behaviour was nothing new, and there were others who did the same, Burke found himself reacting in a way that he hadn't done before. "Perhaps I'm getting old?" he said to himself, knowing that what he had experienced was nothing more than self-pity and was a fruitless response to Sutcliffe's behaviour. His clients weren't always his friends, and most of them were mere commodities. Like any object they were sold to the highest bidder, the party that was prepared to pay the most for them. Sutcliffe was no different despite his previous high-profile position in government. Unfortunately, he sometimes forgot how significant Burke had been in helping resurrect his career. His agent had negotiated a lucrative deal for him to become a TV host, which brought him back from near obscurity to national prominence. Sutcliffe would argue that it was his own talent and experience that secured him the position, but without Burke none of it would have happened.

Removing his gaze from the black and blue artwork he turned his attention back to the paperwork on his desk. He then revived his computer screen that had gone to sleep while he had been giving Sutcliffe all of his attention. Stroking a number of keys, the screen came back to life. Staring at the spreadsheet now facing him, he moved his mouse until he found what he was looking for. Picking up the phone again, he dialled the necessary number.

CHAPTER 7

Cannon sat with Jim Cochrane, both men had a drink in front of them. Each table in the middle-snug part of the pub was occupied and the noisy chatter throughout drowned out the softly sung song from a local singer/songwriter who was trying to get himself heard.
"A lot busier than I had expected it would be," Cannon said, raising his voice so that Cochrane could hear what he was saying. He sipped his tea, the drink of choice to accompany his meal.
His guest answered with a nod of the head. "It's a very popular venue and it doesn't have any TV's as you can see. Not like some of the other pubs have today," Cochrane shouted in reply, hoping to be heard.
Cannon looked around. The décor of dark wood, soft lighting and polished tables gave it an ambience of class and style. The venue was much more than a pub, it was also a cocktail bar with a very good restaurant. The clientele were a mix of ages. Some were young upwardly mobile men and women of differing professions who laughed and joked together while they sat at the high bar. Others ranged from middle-aged couples who were enjoying a meal through to those who had retired and were out for an evening, socializing with like-minded friends. All of which kept the waiters and bartenders extremely busy.
Putting down his cup next to his empty plate, Cannon asked Cochrane whether he was in attendance when White Noise was collected by the transport company.
"Yes, I was."
"And how was the horse? Did he behave?"
"He was a gentleman. He took everything in his stride."
"That's good to hear. I was a bit concerned that he may get a little excited given how fresh he appeared yesterday."
"I don't think you need to worry. The boys who collected him did an excellent job handling him."
Cannon smiled, he was relieved that one of his best horses was now on its way home.
"Just as an aside," Cochrane said, "where did you find them, CB & Sons?"

"By doing a bit of research, detective work shall we say," Cannon added with a grin. "Why do you ask?"

"Well, as I told you yesterday, I had never heard of them but they definitely know what they are doing. The horse box they used was state of the art with heating no less. They also had all the gear, float boots, tail wrap, new ties, head collars and it even had CCTV inside the box. I was very impressed."

"Glad to hear it," Cannon responded, trying to stifle a yawn. It had been a long day and he needed to get some sleep before his flight the next morning. "I'm hoping that the horse I bought from Aidan Murphy travels just as easily. I would hate for it to arrive stressed at my yard."

"They are travelling together?"

"Yes, I wasn't sure if I would buy the horse initially but he looked well so I decided to take a chance on him. I gave CB & Sons a call while on my way back here and they were happy to collect him for me. By taking both together it will save me a bit of money."

"Sounds like you're going to be a busy man," Cochrane said, as he slugged the last of his Guinness, the pint glass remaining speckled with a beige foam as the dark liquid disappeared.

"Yes, I will be but that's not unusual. The only issue I have is for me to get three horses into the yard at the same time."

"Three?"

Cannon stifled another yawn, he was starting to feel weary. He didn't want to appear keen to leave as Cochrane was at dinner at Cannons' invitation but at some point he would need to bring the evening to an end. Inwardly he was hopeful that his guest was able to read the signs. "I've picked up a horse owned by Chester Sutcliffe, and I need to get him into the stable in the next few days," he continued. "Apparently the horse has been standing in its box for a week or so while they looked for someone to take it on."

"Whose Chester Sutcliffe and why was the horse not exercising? Was it injured?"

Cannon sighed, sensing that he would need to explain what he meant. He guessed that Cochrane had no interest in UK politics nor was he a fan of late-night television, particularly talk shows, which was why he had not recognized the name. Looking at his watch Cannon noticed that it was just after nine-thirty.

"Sutcliffe has a program on TV that starts in half an hour....at Ten. He's a talk show host, a former politician who likes to rub people up the wrong way, but he's very popular."

"Never heard of him. I guess he must be English?" Cochrane enquired, with a smirk.

"Yes, he is."

"Umm," Cochrane replied, his eyes raised heavenwards. It was a response that indicated an element of disdain, and he followed it with a 'I thought so' shrug of the shoulders.

Cannon decided that it was almost time to call it a day thanking his guest for joining him for dinner and for everything the man had done for White Noise. He then, out of courtesy, asked whether Cochrane wanted another drink.

"No, I've had my fill, Mike, thank you. It's only a short drive home but one can't be too careful. The Garda are around every corner don't you know."

Cannon smiled at the exaggeration. It was what he liked about the Irish. They were prone to embellishment but always with a twinkle in their eyes. Cochrane was no different to those of his countrymen on the tables around them, the young and the not so young who seemed to be enjoying telling tall tales to their fellow drinkers. The evening had been relaxing and the atmosphere had been jovial, friendly, warm, but with Cochrane mentioning the police Cannon suddenly felt a chill run through him. The killing of Sam Quinn raced into his mind like a galloping colt under a vigorous ride. He hadn't mentioned anything about it and was pleased that he had escaped the urge to do so. He assumed however that Cochrane was aware of what had happened, just as Aidan Murphy had been. The bush telegraph that most horsemen in the country would be naturally attuned to had surely made its way to the Curragh? Deciding to leave the subject alone, Cannon picked up the bill that had been conveniently placed on the table by their waiter.

"Thanks again for joining me, Jim, and I'm sorry about yesterday," he apologized. "I'm glad though that we were able to catch up tonight, it's been great."

"Oh, that's no problem, Mike. It's always a pleasure to have a happy client, especially one whose buying the drinks."

Death Claims its Prize

Both men laughed. Overall it had been a relatively cheap meal. Two pints of Guinness and a steak for Cochrane, Salmon, a cider and a tea for Cannon.

"I think I got off quite lightly overall," Cannon indicated, as he settled the bill at the counter. Cochrane stood a few feet away, coat at the ready, the weather outside meant that they would feel the change in temperature the moment they left the warmth of the building. Cannon had already put his jacket on, anticipating the cold.

With a final handshake the two men went their separate ways, Cannon promising to keep Cochrane abreast of White Noise's progress back to fitness and when he would be back to race at Punchestown. As he walked the few blocks to his hotel he yawned several times, his body letting him know that he needed to get some sleep. Once back in his room and given how tired he felt, he decided not to call Michelle rather deciding to text her to say that with his early start he would call her in the morning. Shortly thereafter he had set the alarm on his mobile phone and had climbed into bed, asleep the moment his head hit the pillow. Two hours later the dreams began.

If Cannon had turned on the TV before he drifted off to sleep and had tuned into the applicable channel then he would have seen Chester Sutcliffe at his best, breaking all the promises that he and Tony Burke had made to Walter Finkelstein.

Timothy Westwood was fair game the moment he walked onto the set. Two chairs placed in an adversarial position sat on the stage in front of a live studio audience of two hundred people. Monitors displaying the two combatants were dotted around the room showing Sutcliffe and Westwood facing each other from various camera angles. Westwood was dressed casually in a dark blue sports jacket, crisp white shirt and grey chinos and looked remarkably relaxed. His hair was fashionably ruffled and the TV make-up made him appear more tanned than he usually was. Not all Americans were as bronzed as they seemed to be on film, especially New Yorkers in their mid-forties. Charlie Scott as Producer of the show leveraged the vision to get the best of the exchanges that he could. With twenty minutes of the hour long interview now gone, Scott spoke rapidly into Sutcliffe's ear via a small earpiece secreted into the hosts ear canal, hidden beneath his mid length hair style.

"Ask him about his stance on abortion, his view on the upcoming US election, the allegations of intimidation and inappropriate behaviour while performing at the Old Vic…make him uncomfortable," Scott said excitedly, noticing a slight tick on Sutcliffe's face as the rapid-fire topics burst through the small microphone. Imperceptibly to anyone other than those who were aware of the exchange, Sutcliffe made a small nodding motion that Scott and the others in the control room took to mean that he had understood what had been said. However he ignored the subject matter, deciding to take a different line of questioning instead. Those involved with the show waited with bated breath for the fireworks to start, while in the wings of the set Walter Finkelstein loitered just out of sight, glued to every question posed and every response given. He had been happy until now. The questions and discussion had been primarily about Westwood's role in his new film, *Torn Apart*, his fellow actors, the director and the storyline itself.

As Westwood rambled on about the movie and the industry in general, Sutcliffe saw the gap and took it.

"I'm sorry to cut across you, Tim, but with all due respect can I ask about you and Layla Anderson, your co-star in this film? Is it true that you had a relationship with her during the making of it?"

Westwood was a little taken aback by the sudden change in Sutcliffe's posture. To date everything had been amicable, almost collegiate, a boys will be boys kind of feeling. While Westwood tried to gather his thoughts, Sutcliffe attacked again using the lowest common denominator…the dirt his team had dug up during their research on the man.

"Ms. Anderson is still married to Peter McLaughlin, the textile entrepreneur is she not?" he asked, "Is he aware of the fling you had with his wife while on set?"

Caught out by the sudden change of tack, Westwood was unsure how to answer. He had been told by Finkelstein that there would be no questions about his personal life. As he hesitated, Sutcliffe added further fuel to the fire. "I also understand that before starting the making of this film you were also seeing Jade Peyton, the well-known runway model. Is she aware of your affair with Ms. Anderson?"

The actor squirmed in his chair, trying to find Finkelstein who was still standing in the wings but edging ever closer to the stage itself. "I…," Westwood mumbled, finding himself facing number two camera, its red light burning brightly like an evil eye that stared into his very soul. The light indicated that the camera was live. Scott in the control room asked the cameraman via their two-way comms system to zoom onto the actor's face. As he did so, Sutcliffe posed another question. Finkelstein moved back behind the set, unable to do anything without causing a scene. His anger was palpable at the car crash of an interview and he intended to make his way to the Producer's suite as soon as he could. He needed to shut down the conversation before any more damage could be done to his client's reputation.

"And is it true that you and Layla Anderson were seen taking drugs on set, Mr. Westwood? I heard that cocaine and other items were found in your trailer while making the film?" Sutcliffe continued.

"What? Where did….?" Westwood stammered, his face like thunder.

"And we also understand that Ms. Peyton, your current girlfriend as noted on a number of social media platforms, has announced recently that you and her are expecting a child together. What does Ms. Anderson, think about that, or was the fling just something to pass the time while filming?" Sutcliffe asked conspiratorially.

Westwood realized that he was in a difficult position but rather than walk off the set as Finkelstein would have preferred, he tried to fight fire with fire and act his way out of trouble. "I'm not sure where you are getting your information from, but it is totally incorrect," he said, trying to refute Sutcliffe's allegations.

"So it's also false that you and Chelsea Cunningham, your co-star in Macbeth, were never lovers?"

"What the f…?!" Westwood shouted, the expletive stuck in his throat as he realized that he was on live television. His hands gripped the arms of his chair, his body language suggesting that he was about to walk off the set.

Sutcliffe decided to push the knife in deeper. "I also understand that you are a supporter of California's Governor who wants to challenge the recent changes to the abortion laws in the US, and is insistent upon LGBTQI+ actors, blind and deaf actors and obese people amongst others, playing those specific roles in films or on TV."

"Yes, I am," Westwood croaked, pleased that the conversation had quickly turned to something that he was happy to talk about.

"So on the matter of abortion does that mean if Ms. Payton is indeed pregnant, given your relationship with Layla Anderson, then you would suggest she aborts the child?"

With nowhere to go, Westwood became so enraged, getting to his feet and violently kicking his chair away, ripping off the microphone attached to his lapel and throwing it across the floor. The audience erupted as he stormed off the set angrily shouting about being set up and brushing aside Finkelstein who had stayed out of sight of the audience, standing a few yards back from the edge of the stage. His own attempt to shut down the questioning had come to nothing as he had been unable to get into the control room. Security and access control defying him.

Sutcliffe meanwhile began to summarize his reasons behind his questions. It was a method he regularly used to justify to his TV (and studio) audience his line of enquiry, showing footage of various incidents that he had touched on during the conversation. Some of the film had been leaked to his research team by insiders, some had been inadvertently put on social media feeds by Westwood's friends, and other information had been gleaned from third parties who were only too happy to spill the beans about what they saw/knew about Westwood's behaviour on various movie sets. The actor was misogynistic, callous, bullying and self-centred, made worse by his failing popularity and marketability.

"And that ladies and gentlemen," he added, staring into camera number one with a serious look on his face, "is why I want you to see and hear what actually happens inside Hollywood. We've known for years about the casting couch, the men preying on those actresses who are trying to make their way in the business. Alternately there are women who use men to get parts and roles that other actresses deserve but lose. You see, actors and actresses make lots of money as they apparently work to entertain us, but under the skin, the veneer, there is a lot that is hidden and it's my job to question what we think we know and find the truth behind the spin. My conversation with Mr. Westwood was just such an attempt." After a few seconds pause and a brief smile, he stared directly into the camera again with its lens focused directly onto his face. With a strong clear voice he ended the show with a simple, "Goodnight all."

As the credits began to roll across the multiple screens the audience rose as one, a thunderous ovation rippled throughout the studio. Sutcliffe stood and theatrically bowed to the adoring fans. The reaction from the interview had been exactly what he and Scott had hoped for. As the clapping and cheering started to dissipate, Jill Sinclair walked onto the set, taking Sutcliffe by the arm and whispering into his ear. The message was brief, Westwood and Finkelstein had already left the building. There would be no post interview chat or drinks in the studio lounge, the actor's agent having promised retribution. Sutcliffe shrugged his shoulders. It wasn't the first time such comments were made, and he doubted it would be the last. He was successful because of the angst and controversy he created. It was what the public wanted and he believed that those who complained after appearing on the show were secretly content with the amount of publicity created for them, as it did for Sutcliffe himself. As the old adage suggested, any publicity was better than no publicity.

"Let's get a drink," he said, in reply to Sinclair, "I could do with one and I expect Charlie will too. I'm keen to hear what Finkelstein actually said to him, if anything. Also we may need Steve Crumm to get involved and smooth things over if there were any threats made against me."

Pointing the way, he let Sinclair walk ahead of him. They made to leave the set, the cameramen were busy closing down their machines, and the audience had almost all been ushered out of the auditorium. Sutcliffe looked out at the rows of empty seats and the backs of the few remaining audience members who were making their way through the exit. As he watched, a head turned to look back at the stage. The face was shrouded in shadow for a second, then the light from the exit door creased a diagonal line across the features. Sutcliffe stopped, recognizing the individual. Instantly his mouth became dry. He tried to call out but the individual had been ushered through the door. His blood suddenly ran cold. Was it really who he thought it was? If so, how was it possible? His mind began to race, the issue of Finkelstein and Westwood instantly disappearing from his thoughts. There was something more disturbing to occupy his mind now. Something far bigger!

Death Claims its Prize

The increasing breeze caused the plastic tape that cordoned off the crime scene to flutter madly. That, and the rustling of leaves in the trees were the only sound that pierced the early hours. Rapidly moving clouds cloaked the halfmoon, allowing occasional tiny glimmers of light to seep through like a dripping tap before it was quickly turned off again. Finn Campbell crouched down in the field that bordered the driveway leading to Sam Quinn's house. He was fifty yards away from the building. Dressed in black jeans, a black windbreaker and with a balaclava over his head it was impossible for the Constable seated in the relative warmth of his car to notice him, even if he passed within a few feet. The fact that the Garda were still on site had initially concerned Campbell, but once he had completed a 360-degree reconnaissance of the immediate area he was satisfied that there was only one person to worry about. Using his infra-reds he had noticed that the young policeman had pushed back his seat and appeared to be sleeping. Checking his watch he saw that it was just after two fifteen. He had been watching the car for the past ten minutes and it was time to move. With Liam Kennedy's tongue lashing still ringing in his ears from their meeting earlier that afternoon, Campbell crept deeper into the field making his way around the right-hand side of the house. Using trees as additional cover he eventually found himself able to reach the edge of the garden at the back of the house, a small hedge the perfect spot to keep him hidden while he surveyed the area again. Once he had spent another five minutes waiting, listening for any movement, he carefully removed the backpack that he had been shouldering and before replacing the small night-sight binoculars that had been slung around his neck, he removed a pair of rubber soled plimsolls which he exchanged for the boots that he had been wearing. The plimsolls had been chosen for their lack of markings on the bottom of the soles. Their lightweight ensuring that there would be limited impressions made should Campbell happen to stand in a flowerbed or in any mud or dirt. Leaving the bag in the bushes, he bent down low before skimming across the ten yards of open lawn and pressing himself against the white painted wall of the house. Breathing slowly, his training ensuring that he kept his heart rate measured and even, he took the nylon cord that had been wrapped around his left shoulder like a bandolier and made a rudimentary lasso. He had done the very same thing less than forty hours earlier when he had originally infiltrated Quinns' house. Having decided not to break-in using the more discernible and easily noticeable way of a window or door, he had taken a rope and using the chimney as a fulcrum, had climbed up onto the roof. After removing a few of the slate tiles he had been able to slip into the loft space and make his way into the house, carefully searching each room, trying to find what he was looking for. Unfortunately, Quinn had unexpectedly returned from the stables at the back of the property, discovering him in one of the rooms, leaving him with no choice but to act. With the help of Healy and Flannery, he had been able to continue his search while the others removed the horses from the stables and had taken them away. The arrival of Cannon however had meant that he had to stop his search and leave the house the same way that he had entered it. He had expected that going back into the house again was likely to be more of a challenge given the strength of the wind and the almost complete darkness that surrounded it. With his eyes having slowly adjusted to the dark, he found however that he was able to repeat the process without too much difficulty. He had no idea what the young policeman was expected to do either, whether he intended to circle the house regularly or was required to stay put and make sure no opportunist came looking to steal from the place was the unknown. Whatever the requirement, Campbell was conscious of the need to get in and out as quickly as he could. Once inside he took a few deep breaths, and with a sense of déjà vu, methodically began to make his way again from room to room. Using a small torch with a beam that focused a warm light with a focal length of only fifteen centimetres, his gloved hands found nothing of interest as he began his search in one of the bedrooms. He knew what he was looking for but it could be anywhere and he needed to revisit the rooms, the shelves, the numerous possible hiding places that he had searched previously. He soon realized that the exercise was going to take him much longer than expected. The silent and darkened rooms with curtains that remained open, the need to be careful where he pointed the beam of his micro-sized torch and the ever-present threat of the garda turning up unexpectedly, made the task all the more difficult. With the occasional creaks and ticks sounding throughout the building as the gusting breeze outside encouraged leaves and branches to scrape against the walls or tap against a window, Campbell held his breath as he listened for any other movement, his ears straining underneath the balaclava. After searching for an hour plus he had made little progress other than being able to eliminate three of the seven rooms. On his previous search during the daylight he had been able to rifle through the building quite easily as the house was kept extremely neat. It had made things much easier than he had anticipated and initially he had expected to find what he was looking for within minutes. He had eventually found the small safe hidden inside the wardrobe of an unused bedroom but had been instantly aware that the room was different from others. Multiple folders and papers had been scattered on the bed which was devoid of sheets or coverings. Similarly there were numerous cardboard boxes stacked five or six high in one corner of the room. Some leant at an angle effectively designed to act as an invisible picture that only the creator was aware of. The boxes were positioned such that they prevented the wardrobe doors from being opened. If any of them were moved then the picture would be disturbed and it would be obvious that someone had gotten into the wardrobe and likely found the safe. Campbell's training had taught him to be aware of such ruses. Having photographed the set up by using his mobile phone, he had been able to access the inside of the wardrobe, returning the scene to its original layout once he had examined the safe. He had quickly established that the safe was another ruse. The door was partially closed but also unlocked, and again had been set up to trick anyone who hadn't been as careful as he was. The repository itself was empty. If what he was looking for was still in the house, it obviously wasn't inside the safe. He had barely replaced everything as he had found it when he heard Quinn coming back into the house. With access to the loft and the roof compromised by Quinn having made his way almost immediately upstairs, Campbell had challenged him to reveal what he had been looking for, the butt of the Glock 17 viciously used as an incentive but to no avail. Taking Quinn outside and pointing the gun at the man's head, Campbell had expected that the threat of death would have encouraged Quinn to tell him what he wanted to know. He had been wrong. Eventually the decision had been made for him. Quinn had stonewalled, wasting time trying to negotiate a way out for himself finally giving up a single piece of information that turned out to be a lie. It was not enough and the result was a single gunshot to the head, followed by a second to the chest.

Campbell looked at his watch again, the light from the torch dancing on the face. He had been searching for eighty minutes now and it was obvious that to continue for much longer would increase the possibility of being discovered. Not by the sleeping policeman but by leaving unnecessary traces of his probing and foraging. If he left anything misplaced, an overturned ornament, a piece of clothing that dropped unseen from a hanger or anything that did not seem right to a trained eye, he could be in trouble. He knew that Kennedy wouldn't be happy but he knew that he needed to be sensible. There would be other opportunities. Another few days, a week or a month wouldn't make any difference as far as he was concerned as long as he was paid and he doubted the Garda would have any knowledge of what he was searching for anyway. Despite this, for him, for the others, finding the item was a priority, their sole objective. It was just a matter of time.

CHAPTER 8

Cannon was pleased to see the gates of his yard. The flight back from Dublin had been delayed for longer than those catching the plane had been made aware. Just as he was getting ready to shower, a message came through on his mobile phone that the flight had been delayed by ninety minutes. The revised departure time had been scheduled for seven thirty in the morning, it eventually lifted off from the runway at ten fifteen. During the expected one hour twenty-minute trip, they had incurred bad weather, a deep low which had creased the south of Ireland was now circling across the southern parts of England and the Midlands. The plane had diverted to Manchester and the three-hour National Express bus ride to the Birmingham airport, where he had left his car, meant that it was just before five in afternoon when he was finally able to park in front of his own office. The journey had taken him nearly twelve hours.

During the trip to Birmingham he tried to ignore the rain that slashed down continuously from the dark laden sky causing heavy spray to shoot upwards from behind the multitude of large trucks, vans and the never-ending string of cars that ignored the met office warnings about wet roads. At one point the bus had been required to stop suddenly as the traffic ahead slammed on brakes to avoid crashing and it reminded him of the madness he had seen on the roads over the past couple of days.

"Thank God, I'm not driving this thing," he had said under his breath, as he chatted with Telside on his mobile. They had been discussing the need to get the stables ready for the imminent arrival of White Noise and Rory's Song. In addition they still needed to formalize the transporting of Sutcliffe's horse to the yard and Cannon had suggested that one of them needed to contact Warren Hawker's stables in Taunton, the next day. The expected visit by the TV presenter was also a subject that required resolution but Cannon decided to have a further conversation on the matter once he had an idea when the horse was expected to arrive.

Walking into the house, he placed his suitcase just inside the front door and Michelle greeted him with a passionate kiss and an extended hug.

"I guess that means you're glad I'm home?" he said, with a smile.
"Is it that obvious?" she replied, coquettishly, a naughty sparkle in her eyes.
"Sort of. Anyway, how are you?
"I'm fine. I've just got home myself, about ten minutes ago. It's been a very long day."
Cannon smiled again as he looked at his wife. He had missed her. She was dressed in black slacks, a cream ribbed jumper and a sky-blue shirt with a small butterfly motif on the left collar. Her hair, in shoulder length waves, was ruffled as if she had run her hand through it a number of times. He guessed that as a senior member of staff at her school for girls, she probably had reason to do so.
"I got your text by the way, about the delay," she continued.
"I assumed you'd be at the school, so I didn't want to bother you if you were in class. That's why I did the same when I was on my way from Manchester."
"You're right, I was at the school very early this morning. There was no point in me waiting around while on my own in this big house anyway, so I went in. Also the summer school classes I've been teaching finish tomorrow so there are tests to mark before then."
Nodding in reply, he said, "No wonder it's been a long day."
"Yes, it never ends. We're already having meetings with the new staff members that have come on board so that we can get organized for the new school year."
"Which starts in…..?"
"In just over a week."
"Bloody hell," he replied. "Between the two of us I doubt we'll be seeing much of each other in the next little while then. I've got three horses coming into the stable the day after tomorrow and…."
Before he could continue, she put a finger to his lips. Silently she shushed him, before kissing him again. Her mouth lingered on his and he pulled her closer, both of them feeling the warmth of each other's body. For a few seconds it was as if they were the only people on earth, lost in an embrace that could only lead to one place. Pulling away he said teasingly, "Does this mean I can't see Rich before he goes home? There's still a couple of hours of sunlight left, unless the rain that's coming our way, hits."
Taking him by the hand towards their bedroom, she answered, "You can see him in forty minutes…if you can last that long?"

He doubted he could but offered to try.

Ninety minutes later he was almost dressed again. Michelle lay naked in the bed, the sheets crumpled around her. Subconsciously she pulled them up to cover her exposed breasts. Her hair was spiky and ruffled, a sign of their lovemaking. Cannon had always been a gentle lover, a quality that she admired and appreciated in him, but today they had both been hungry for each other. It was as if him having been away for a few days had lit a spark between them and they had responded like newlyweds. Afterwards as they lay beside each other, Michelle had whispered to him that she hoped that no one had heard their collective cries as they had reached climax.

"You forgot to close the curtains," she said with a smile, her eyes looking towards the uncovered window that looked out onto a small garden. The sun was now low in the sky under a increasing layer of cloud. Occasionally a shadow stretched out across the grass as a patch of sun briefly came and went. The rain that had been creeping its way across the country was less than an hour away.

"Too late now," he said playfully, pulling the two ends of the fabric together, temporarily pitching the room into darkness. She switched on a small bedside table lamp. Kissing her, he let her know that he wouldn't be long with Telside and that she should be 'prepared' for when he got back. "Promises, promises," she replied, climbing out of the bed and starting to dress herself.

With a vision of Michelle's body still firmly in his mind, Cannon left the house. He looked up at the darkening sky as he crossed the short distance to the stable block and Rich Telside's office.

The post show meeting had been positive at times and fiery at others. Scheduled for Ten am that morning, it had only begun at one-thirty in the afternoon and was still underway three hours later. The delay caused by the outpouring of anger

Christopher Blakman, the TV Station's CEO had felt the full force of Walt Finkelstein's wrath. "He's threatening to sue," he had said to the Production team, Presenter and Program's Lawyer. He then went on to advise them that the preliminary numbers for the show indicated that a lot more eyeballs were watching it than ever before, and that it was clear the public seem to be embracing what they had to offer in ever increasing numbers.

"So what's the problem?" Charlie Scott had queried. "If the public vote is on our side, that's all that counts isn't it?"

"And Finkelstein can threaten all he likes," Crumm added, emboldened with his legal advice after rewatching the previous night's program earlier that morning. "There was nothing said by Chester here that was untrue or contentious in nature. Finklestein and Westwood can try to claim that there was, but our research folk had done their due diligence and investigated what was said, beforehand. We have the necessary proof to affirm what was alleged should this ever get to court."

"Maybe," Blakman answered, not totally convinced, but was happy to take Crumm's guidance. "However when you challenge Hollywood like we did last night, it can often bite you in the arse."

"What, by shunning the program?" Scott challenged.

"Yes, exactly that."

"Well as far as I'm concerned, let them do that," Scott continued. "As the Producer of the show I believe that we've got something to sell to the public and the numbers watching obviously substantiate that. I'd also suggest that anyone whose uncomfortable with appearing on the show doesn't. We've got a guest list as long as your arm already penciled in until the end of the season, so…"

"And no one has indicated yet that they want to drop out either," Carol Boyd interrupted. What had happened overnight across social media and the wider press had been sensational. As Publicist she had spent a significant part of the morning trawling through a multitude of comments about the show. The stations website had also been inundated with commentary. Most of what had been written had been positive, supportive of Sutcliffe's style, but there were also a number of negative posts, as expected. The most sinister were death threats made by anonymous trolls. As was usual she had passed them on to the police, but she knew that they would be ignored. After every show there were always threats made and every time she did the same thing, and in response so did the police. She had been advised many times and had relayed the feedback to everyone on the production team, that the police were too busy, too constrained, to follow up anything written in reaction to a program. The response from the police had been the same every single time, such that Boyd could effectively write it for them.

'Until there is an actual crime having been committed, the Metropolitan police are unable to respond to or investigate any commentary related to your show. While we take any threats of violence seriously, we note that responses to each episode of your show is encouraged by you and we believe that the vast majority of negative commentary is intentionally provocative rather than intended to be acted upon. The Metropolitan police will however investigate any criminal activity should it occur.'

After a short pause, Blakman sucked his teeth before rising from his chair. "I'll give Finkelstein a call tomorrow," he said. "I'll also talk with the board. I'm sure this won't go anywhere but if you could draft me a note Stephen, confirming our position," he pointed at the lawyer, "I'll get that off and hopefully that will resolve the matter once and for all."

He looked towards Sutcliffe who had stayed quiet for the past fifteen minutes, his mind seemingly elsewhere. Deciding to ignore the Presenter's silence, Blakman patted Scott on the shoulder, thanked the others for their input and strode out of the room.

"Fuck me!" Scott said, once Blakman had closed the door behind him. "What an ungrateful bastard."

Suddenly the room was alive with chatter, separate conversations began about Blakman as CEO, the nature of his comments and how his negativity was in contrast to the public response to the program. After allowing a couple of minutes of gossip, Scott advised everyone that the meeting was over but not before he indicated to Sutcliffe that he wanted to talk with him privately. Leaving the two of them behind, the rest of the group departed to their desks and offices. Once they were alone, Scott closed the door again.

"What's wrong?" he asked, "you've hardly said a word for the past hour or so."

"You were right," Sutcliffe replied, without emotion.

"About?"

"The girl. I saw her."

"When? Where?" Scott queried, his voice rising slightly.

"Last night, after the show. She was in the audience."

"Are you sure?"

"Yes, she specifically stayed behind until most of the audience had left the studio. She stared right at me. She wanted me to see her."

Scott rubbed a hand through his hair. "Shit!" he exclaimed, "I didn't think she would ever turn up here."

"Well she did."

"And she didn't say anything to you?"

"No, she just made eye contact."

Scott began pacing around the room, continuously rubbing his chin as if by doing so a solution to their problem would pop out of his mouth. He muttered to himself, his words spoken so softly that Sutcliffe couldn't hear anything he was saying other than the occasional expletive.

"Leave it to me," he said eventually. "I'll see what I can do. Perhaps I can call in a few favours."

"Like what?" Sutcliffe asked, concerned with what his Producer was thinking.

"Never you mind," Scott replied, "never you mind."

"I'm glad you had a good trip, Mike, but I'm pleased you're home now," Rich Telside said, shaking his friend's hand.

"Me too," Cannon answered, smiling briefly as he thought of how he had spent his time over the last hour or so.

"I was about to come over," Telside added, "but I guessed you wanted to catch up with Michelle first, so I thought I'd leave you be."

Acknowledging the sentiment gratefully, Cannon sat down opposite his assistant. Telside looked fit for a man in his early seventies. Ever since his heart bypass he had trimmed down a little, though there hadn't been much to lose in the first place and despite his health scare he had continued to maintain a regime of rising early every morning to help with the training and schooling of the horses in the yard. It was his life, a point he had made to Cannon many times, who had once upset Telside by suggesting that the man should consider retirement. The idea was only ever floated that one time, Cannon quickly realizing his mistake by doing so. Despite his age, Telside put in a full day's work and was also the last of Cannon's team to go home each night. Without him Cannon would never have been able to do what he did. The development of his reputation as a trainer was built on their partnership and the mentoring that Telside had provided him throughout their journey together. Their relationship began nearly twenty years ago and they had been through a lot in that time. They had been able to build up the business, achieving some success but not without a number of disappointments either. These included a jockey's death while schooling one of Cannon's horses; the loss of a talented apprentice/conditional rider who got in with the wrong crowd, eventually leaving the stable by mutual consent; and the death of an owner while preventing his own horse from winning the Grand National. There were others too but Cannon was ever hopeful that the forthcoming season would be better than the last one. Whenever he reflected on that point, he realized that the same thought was likely being considered by all the trainers across the country. However, with White Noise's return, his new acquisition Rory's Song and the arrival of Sutcliffe's horse being added to his existing fold, his optimism grew.

Eventually, he answered Telside's comment with a straight face, saying, "You're right Rich, I think she was definitely pleased to see me."

Telside looked at his watch, there was only forty-five minutes of light left in the day and the darkening sky would soon likely put an end to it. Rain could be heard softly pattering on the roof of the stable block. It had just started but both of them knew that it was forecast to get much heavier in the coming hours.

"If you want to get going Rich, we can catch up again in the morning," Cannon advised, noting Telside check his watch for a second time. "I'm happy to do evening stables myself as I assume all the horses have been fed and watered already?"

"Of course, Mike," Telside replied.

"Any issues?"

"Well that's why I wanted you to see. We've got a couple of things that need attention."

"Such as?"

"Thunder Three and Silicon Chips both sustained injuries this morning. The Vet had a look and suggested specific treatments for both of them. I agreed with him so I've moved them out already. I told the owners first and they understood."

"So what happened?" Cannon asked, concerned at what he was hearing. His earlier optimism suddenly dissipating with the news.

"I'll get to that in a second because there is something else."

"Go on."

"Winter Garden is off her feed, and there are signs that a couple of the others are heading the same way."

"Jesus."

"It seems we may have received some contaminated food, fortunately it might be just a couple of bags. The other horses that may be sick all ate from the same batch though. The vet is not sure if it's a result of something like a mycotoxin or an additive in the feed, but he has taken some swabs for testing."

"When did this start?" Cannon asked, concerned for his animals welfare.

"First signs started late morning. Luckily the vet was on his way to look at the injuries I just mentioned, so I told him about the issue at the same time. I didn't want to concern you while you were in transit as there was nothing you could do anyway."

Knowing Telside had as much knowledge about the issue of food contamination as he did, Cannon agreed with him. Before he could ask another question however, Telside said, "I've isolated Winter Garden and the other two horses who ate the same feed by moving them to the far end of the barn and left the two boxes vacated by Thunder Three and Silicon Chips empty as a sort of barrier between the rest. If it turns out to be a virus and not a feed issue that's making them sick then at least there is some protection for the others."

"If it's a virus then we will have to move those three out," Cannon said, figuratively crossing his fingers, "but tell me about the other two. How did they get injured and what's the prognosis?"

Taking a deep breath which concerned Cannon even more, Telside said, "Thunder Three was kicked. He has sustained lacerations to his off-fore and has some considerable bruising to his shoulder and neck, but we think he'll make a full recovery. He's been taken to the Valley Equine Hospital in Lambourn. The vet thinks that if there is no internal damage the horse should be back with us in about a month."

"And Silicon Chip?" Cannon queried, fearing the worst.

"Believe it or not…a bowed tendon."

"Shit!"

"I'm sorry Mike."

"So that's him out for the season, and it's not even started yet."

"Which is why I arranged for him to be boxed at Alan Chaplin's place straight away. He's going to need a lot of TLC and be confined to his box for at least six months. "

"If not more," Cannon replied sadly.

"Once you've had a look, we can decide where to take him for treatment. I just thought that as we needed the space, sending him to Chaplin for a couple of days at his agistment farm would be useful. We were able to bandage the horse up and put his leg in a temporary splint. The vet was able to give him some pain killers and he seemed comfortable when he left us."

With the day having started off badly it had now gotten much worse. Cannon hoped that Telside didn't have any more bad news.

"Is that it?" he asked.

"Yes."

"Thank God. Okay, let's take a quick walk and look at that feed and those three horses, then you can be on your way, Rich. I'm sure you want to get home before the weather closes in for the night."

As the two men began to make their way through the tack room and into the barn, the sound of heavy rain on the roof began to drown out their voices.

CHAPTER 9

It had been a challenge after his short time away. Getting up at five in the morning seemed particularly difficult for some reason. If it hadn't been for the rehearsal the previous day, having to get to the airport for his subsequently delayed flight, the warmth of Michelle's body almost emboldened him to ignore the constant beeping of his mobile. They had gone to bed earlier than usual but only turned off their lamps much later. Behind the now closed curtains they had made love for a second time.
"I can get used to this," he had said, before closing his eyes and holding her tightly to him. In response she had playfully dug him in the ribs with her elbow. It was the last thing he remembered before falling into a deep but troubled sleep, the sight of the body of Sam Quinn invading his dreams.

Sitting together in Cannon's 4 x 4, the windscreen wipers flicked backwards and forwards across the glass, the car's heater kept the late Autumn chill from seeping into their bones. The rain that had increased in intensity overnight was still falling intermittently. During the past two hours they had been watching their horses school, canter and gallop, some jumping the fences spread out across the heath while others were asked to maintain their cruising speed over extended distances. The first lot had already gone back to the stables for washing down and returning to their individual stalls. During the rest of the day the stable hands would ensure that the individual stalls were properly 'mucked out', fresh straw, food and water provided before the yard quietened down until evening stables. When he could Cannon liked to do the late-night check himself which included looking into each stall and ensuring every horse was settled. New horses coming into the yard meant that he needed to take his time to understand their specific moods, foibles and quirks. Keeping a horse happy was what made one trainer better than another and the challenge always excited him. Attention to detail was Cannon's approach. His time in the police had instilled such a mantra and it was a philosophy that he had subscribed to throughout his training career.

"I'll be glad when White Noise and Rory get here tomorrow," he said, looking across at Telside who continued to watch the final pair of the second lot clear the closest fence to their vehicle. It was their last bit of schooling for the morning.

"Me too," Telside replied, referring to White Noise. Turning his head to look at Cannon, he said earnestly, "I've missed the old fellow, and can't wait to see him again."

"Well you don't have to worry anymore, Rich. He was looking good out at Cochrane's place and I think he'll be in for a great campaign."

"I certainly hope so."

"So does Joel," Cannon said. "The man has been very patient and very supportive of us since the horse got injured, but like any owner I suspect he'll be wanting to see a bit more success this coming season."

"Which is fair enough Mike, given the talent the horse possesses. It's why Seeton pays his bills and why it's our job to have the horse fit again and get him to Cheltenham."

With that thought in mind, the two men climbed out of the warmth of their vehicle just as the rain began to ease. Cannon called the riders together and as they gathered in a line, steam rising from the flanks of their charges, Telside conducted a physical inspection of each of the horses checking for any obvious injuries. As he did so, Cannon queried the individual riders, making appropriate notes in a small notepad based on their responses. He would take the feedback they gave and collate it onto his computer once back in his office.

While questioning his new apprentice, a seventeen-year-old boy called Tom Crichton, about his mount Simply Guessed, he listened carefully to what the boy had to say. It had been a gamble to take on another apprentice (conditional rider) after what had happened with the boy's predecessor, a young girl called Angela Fryer. She had moved on from the stable a few months earlier after getting involved with a drug dealer, a situation that didn't end well.

Despite what had happened to Fryer, Cannon was determined to keep the memory and the name of one of his former track riders alive. Ray Brollo had been killed while schooling one of Cannon's horses a few years prior. Crichton, as Fryer had been before him, was the beneficiary of the Trust that had been established in the young man's name and even as an apprentice he was expected to live up to the high standards that Cannon set for every member of his team.

"So how does he feel compared to Chocolatier who you schooled in the first lot?" Cannon asked, wanting to see if the youngster was beginning to get a better understanding of the differences between a 'chaser like Simply Guessed and the novice hurdler that he had ridden an hour or so earlier.

"Well boss," Crichton began, his voice strong and assured. "The Choc' has a lot to learn still. He was a bit keen to attack the flights and he seemed to want to smash them down rather than just clear them, so he's not as efficient as he could be just yet." Cannon was impressed. The clarity of the response was a trait that had helped the young man become the successful applicant, the interview process to replace Fryer having been conducted by both Cannon and Telside early in the off-season.

"And old QM here then?" Cannon asked repeating his question, while patting the horse's neck and looking up at the young man in the saddle. QM was the nickname given to Simply Guessed. Most stable hands and track riders had other names for the horses they rode or cared for and it could be confusing at times. The nicknames usually came about to describe the characteristics of the specific animal. Simply Guessed became QM, short for 'Question Mark', because you never know what you were going to get from him. As a nine-year-old gelding, the horse could be gentle some days, cantankerous occasionally or just plain obstinate at other times. If he was the latter on a race day he would just refuse to race, effectively baulking at the very first obstacle. If the horse was in the mood to race, he would simply fly the larger fences. Cannon had requested that Telside put Crichton on the animal so that the young man could get a feel for a horse that could be difficult to ride on occasion. He did this so that the blond-haired, fresh-faced teenager learnt how to handle such horses before he was allowed to ride in a race under National Hunt rules. Cannon did not want to put his apprentice in any danger and needed to be satisfied that the boy had built up the necessary experience and courage to meet the challenge of jumps racing. The death of Ray Brollo was never far from Cannon's mind no matter how much time passed and he was determined that it never be repeated.

"He was as good as gold boss," Crichton answered, in response to the question Cannon had posed. "In fact he taught me a little trick about how to shift my weight and when to move myself closer to his neck as we jump. He seemed to adjust himself to cover for my mistakes which was great. I'll work on what I was doing wrong though."

Cannon nodded in response. He knew that experienced horses often made allowances for poor horsemanship when and if they could. A bad ride in a race could occasionally cause a horse to fall, unseat the jockey during the event or even lose the race, which was why Cannon was particular about who he put in the saddle. Owners usually accepted his choice but sometimes they weren't always as keen when it came to apprentices. Fortunately Angela had been an excellent rider, despite her personal problems. Cannon was hoping that Tom Crichton would be just as good. From the response given, it was clear that Telside and he had made a good decision.

"Okay," Cannon said, taking a few steps back in order to see the rest of the lot that were still standing quietly, waiting for him to question the other riders about the work done by each. He made one final comment to Crichton, something he would repeatedly say to any apprentice jockey. "I'm pleased that you are learning, but remember you'll need to be quick in doing so. Whenever you get onto a horse's back you'll have seconds to get a feel for it. Every day is different, no matter how many times you will have ridden that horse. Like humans they can have good days and bad days, and it's why I gave you QM to ride today, because of his moods. Once you are on the track, you are on your own and it's up to you to get the best from your mount. Owners rely on you, as do I, as do we all, and we expect nothing but your best."

"Understood, boss," the young man replied, with humility.

"So, here endeth the lesson," Cannon said smiling, moving on to talk with the next rider who had been waiting patiently, his horse pawing the wet ground with his near side hoof as if to ask Cannon to "get on with it." After receiving the feedback from the jockey, he repeated the same process with the remaining riders, carefully noting whether the specific animals demeanour was in line with what had been relayed to him verbally.

Once he had completed the exercise he asked one of his most experienced riders, Simon Brooks, effectively Telside's Head Lad, to return the lot back to the stables and once there carry on with the daily routine. Turning to Rich he suggested that it would be good if they could spend a few minutes discussing what they had noticed during the two sessions and what their collective thoughts about each horse were.

Back inside the SUV the two men decided on a course of action for each mare and gelding. Cannon had always been a traditionalist believing that the jumps season started during late September and ran until the end of April the following year. Basically a winter sport. He believed that softer ground was better for the horses legs and rarely ran his horses on frost affected ground. During his training career he had stuck to a timetable of getting horses ready for their seasonal debut from October onwards. This was around the time of the annual Chepstow meeting, held in mid-October. Some of his owners over the years had pointed out that the sport had become much more commercial and had requested to have their horses run at meetings held at any time during the year, even during the summer. Cannon had refused to do this and if an owner was unhappy with his decision, then he or she was welcome to take their horse(s) elsewhere. Some owners did so, while others stayed with him thereby accepting his position on the matter. To some degree it was a merry-go-round of opinion but both he and Telside took it in their stride. Money wasn't everything and Cannon was more interested in getting the best out of the horses rather than racing them just for the hell of it. Risking the life of a horse with a broken leg or damage from a fall was not worth it as far as he was concerned.

"I noticed Carillion seemed a little out of sorts," he pronounced to Telside, referring to a 10-year-old bay gelding who was one of several new acquisitions to the stable over the past couple of months. He had been moved to Cannon at the end of June from another stable. The owner having fallen out with the previous trainer over the horse's lack of success.

"Aye, I think he may need a bit of a rest. His action seems fine but he may need a break. I don't think he's a world beater by a long shot. He does have talent but it seems his attitude is the problem, he doesn't have his mind on the job at times."

"That ties in with Andre, his jockey, had to say," Cannon replied, looking at his notes. "So let's give the horse an extended rest and we can use the stall for one of our newcomers."

The two men then discussed what else they had observed from the two lots; which horses needed vet care, which needed water walking to relieve muscle soreness and which seemed to be getting close to being race ready. They then made plans for upcoming meetings, addressing when and where each horse would start their season, while noting that they needed each horse to improve their race fitness over time. Their agreed philosophy was that for each campaign they wanted to see progress every time a horse raced. If they over trained the animal, like a boxer could do when preparing for a fight, then the season could be over before it even started. Cannon's view was that National Hunt horses generally needed a break between each run as racing in heavy ground and over long distances, whether that was over hurdles or the bigger fences took a lot out of them.

"When White Noise is about eighty to ninety percent fit I want to take him back to Ireland for his first race," Cannon pointed out. "I told Jim Cochrane that I would, so that he could see the result of his handiwork, and I want to give the horse a run on the grass at Punchestown as I think the course will suit him."

"Okay," Telside replied, happy with the suggestion. "So given what we've just discussed, if we add Rory's Song into the mix along with Sutcliffes' Santa's Quest then apart from anything else we are going to get pretty busy over the next few days and weeks."

"Nothing like being busy. Rich," Cannon answered, placing a hand on his friend's shoulder, watching the windscreen being peppered with raindrops that had begun to progressively increase in size.

"Just in time," Telside said, pointing at the glass.

"Yes, well let's get back home," Cannon replied, turning the ignition switch. As the engine burst into life, he said, "Once Sutcliffes' horse gets here and he's had twenty-four hours with us, I'll give his agent a call to arrange a visit."

"I'm sure he'll be keen to see the place," Telside replied, "but I still have my doubts about him. I think he may be a challenge for you Mike."

Cannon laughed. He had worked with and fought against all types of individuals in the past. The good, the bad and the downright evil. An ex-politician who was now on TV was nothing to be afraid of as far as he was concerned. "We'll see," he replied. "My immediate concern is the arrival tomorrow of White Noise and Rory's Song. I'm trusting CB & Sons to look after them properly and get them here without any problems. However with the weather as it was yesterday and the delays to flights from Dublin, I've been worrying about the ferry crossing and whether there could be any issues."

"Have they been in touch with you?"

"No."

"Well, no news is good news, so hopefully everything is fine."

"I hope so, Rich. I'll be happier though, when they get here."

Telside nodded his head in agreement. As Cannon drove them the short distance back to the stables, the rain was much heavier, impacted by a strong wind that had sprung up from the South West.

"It's getting a bit messy," Telside said, "might get a little colder too."

"I agree. We may have seen the last of the nice weather, but hey that's why we do this, Rich. This is our time, our season, so let's hope we have a good one. If we can get White Noise to Cheltenham and maybe Sutcliffe's horse or QM there as well, then it will be."

"Or Aintree," Telside added, "along with one of two other meetings, like the Tingle Creek at Sandown."

"Let's not too far ahead of ourselves, Rich," Cannon said with a smile, as he drove into his yard and parked the vehicle in front of his office. Switching off the car he faced his friend again, saying, "After last season's issues with Angela, I hope that this coming one will be straightforward and that the only thing that we will have to worry about, is the horses."

"I hope so too, Mike," Telside replied.

Climbing out of the car into the now heavy rain, Cannon shivered as the cold water invaded his eyes and ran down the back of his neck. For some reason he suddenly thought back to finding Sam Quinns' body. Thank God it wasn't his problem anymore. He had had enough of seeing death come searching to satisfy its hunger, for death looking to claim its prize.

CHAPTER 10

He had spent the entire day working at his computer. The task of collating the information from the morning's exercises along with the feedback from Rich after the horses had cooled down and were back in their stalls, had caused him a significant amount of work. This included phone calls to owners to advise them of his thinking as to where to place their animals in upcoming races and at which meetings. Other calls to discuss treatment plans, rest plans and other advice given by the veterinary staff all added to the workload. As he had been about to log-off, he received a call on his mobile from the local representative of CB & Sons that everything was on track for the delivery next day of the "Irish Shipment."

Cannon had smiled at the description the rep' had used and had thanked him for the update. Shortly thereafter Telside had popped into his office to tell him that he had been in touch with Warren Hawker's Head lad, Bryce Kidd, and that Sutcliffe's horse would be on a float from Taunton the next day.

"He should arrive the day after tomorrow, as they are bringing him overnight. That will give me enough time to decided which rider and groom I want to work with the horse," Telside advised.

"Well if the horse is as promising as he seems, I think we'll need someone with experience. It's way too soon for Tom to get on him. Let's use Lester, he's one our best. I'm sure Simon would be okay with that, especially if we let him look after White Noise again," Cannon replied.

Lester Crouch had been with the yard for several years. He was a gangly lad, from a small village called Long Hanborough only ten minutes by car from Woodstock. Now in his late twenties, he had originally set his sights on being a jockey, but his weight had prevented him from achieving that dream, however he was a very good horseman and an excellent worker around the place. A good friend of Simon Brooks, Cannon doubted there would be any issues with his choice.

Telside agreed. "Done," he said.

Walking into the kitchen, his senses were met with the sounds and smells of cooking. The last of the day's light, grey and dull, filtered through the window that looked out onto the back garden. Three LED recessed globes overhead, removed the shadows and dark corners from the room, burning luminously. Cannon watched Michelle for a second as she worked on the countertop cutting up some vegetables.

"Sorry I took so long," he said, "I didn't even hear you come in earlier. It's been a long day. How did it go at school?" He asked rapidly, before putting his arms around her waist and snuggling his face into the base of her neck.

She squirmed slightly, twisting away from him, knife in hand. "Hey, hey," she replied with a smile, the knife pointing directly at Cannon's chest. "Later, later" she said, teasing him with her suggestive tone. "But to answer your question, it was a bloody nightmare again."

"Why?"

"Just the usual. Last minute changes to timetables; whose teaching what year levels and why; arguments about set book delays, just the normal chaos before next week."

"Glad it's not me," he replied. A comment he had made many, many, times before.

He was just about to ask her about what she was making for dinner when his mobile phone began to ring. Taking it from his pocket, he noticed that it was Cassie and pointed at the screen so that Michelle could see who it was. She whispered that he should give his daughter her regards and turned back to the counter.

"Hi there, stranger," he said, pleased to hear from her. It had been at least three months since they had spoken, though he knew that Michelle and Cassie had regular catch-ups on the phone.

"Hi dad. Yes, I'm sorry about that," she replied, sounding particularly excited.

"What's up?"

"I have some news."

"Oh yes?" he replied, curiously. "A promotion perhaps? Or did Ted get another posting somewhere exotic?"

"No, much better....I'm pregnant."

Cannon let out a shout that caught Michelle off-guard. She turned to look at him just as he said, "That's amazing! That's brilliant! How far?"

His words spilled out like water from a burst pipe. He wanted to know everything, then he noticed that Michelle was smiling. Putting a hand over the mouthpiece he enquired of her, "Did you know?"

With a slight nod of the head she answered him.

He let Cassie respond to all his questions. She was well, had few symptoms of morning sickness, her employer was supportive and more importantly Edward was doting on her continuously.

"That's great," he said once she was finished. "We'll need to come up there as soon as we can."

"That would be great, dad, but no rush. We've got plenty to do but also plenty of time, I'm only eight weeks gone but we'll soon have enough to keep us busy. Setting up a room, buying a cot, looking at prams and lots and lots of baby clothes."

"A boy or girl?" he asked.

"I don't want to know. So we'll be buying white outfits just to get us going. Edward said that once the baby is born we'll know what to buy."

"Sensible I suppose."

"Yes, anyway I've got to go. I just thought I'd let you know. I've got a meeting with a client at seven."

"Wow, doesn't the law stop for babies?"

"No. I've just finished one meeting and I thought I'd call you in-between that and the next one."

"Thanks Cassie, I appreciate you letting me know."

"Well *grandad* I wanted to let you know earlier, but I thought it best that I get through the shock first."

"Michelle knew though?" he queried.

"Yes, us girls have to stick together."

Ending the call with a series of "love you's" Cannon put down his phone on the countertop and contemplated what he had just heard.

Michelle continued with the cooking and waited for him to speak. Eventually he said, "This calls for a bit of a celebration."

"Anything in particular you had in mind?"

"What's for dinner?" he asked, conscious that she had put all the vegetables she had been cutting into a roasting dish that was now in the oven.

"Roast lamb, roast potatoes, carrots and cabbage with some gravy and mint sauce."

"So I suggest a red wine, and we need something special," he continued.

"Sounds good to me," she said.

"I still have a couple of bottles from our trip to Australia. What's it called…Heathcote Shiraz I think. I'll open one of them."

With her agreement he went off to his rarely used wine rack to find what he was looking for. Not drinking much anymore, they drank a single glass each as they ate dinner. A toast to the as yet unknown baby, the mother and grandfather was the highlight of the evening.

CHAPTER 11

Tony Burke and Stephen Crumm had been able to close down the threat made by Westwood's management team, pointing out the T's and C's of the actor's contract he had signed with the studio were clear and that there was nowhere legally for them to go. Whatever the fallout from the interview with Sutcliffe it was now Finkelstein's problem and he and his client would need to handle it accordingly.

Burke called Sutcliffe to advise him of the outcome of the discussions. Standing in his conservatory he looked up at the grey sky. Dried streaks of dust like empty river beds left by the overnight rain clung to the glass windows. The coffee in his cup steamed as he slowly sipped the dark liquid. Outside the wind had eased allowing the heavy clouds to hover in one place, the threat to smother everything below with their weight, obvious.

"I knew that he didn't have a leg to stand on," Sutcliffe said. "I should have gone harder."

"Maybe, but I think you dodged a bullet in some ways. There is a line that can't be crossed, which I know you know where that is, and remember you do need to keep the audience on side at all times."

"True."

"I'd be a little more circumspect with a guest that is universally liked. Tearing into someone who is popular nowadays would not go down as well as it did when you were in parliament."

Sutcliffe laughed, remembering how he could say whatever wanted to under parliamentary privilege, and there were no repercussions. He was however distinctly aware of the difference between then and now but occasionally he found himself reverting to his previous behaviour, nearly being caught out several times in recent months. Being encouraged by Charlie Scott didn't help either. As the Producer of the program he continued to have Sutcliffe push the boundaries, something that Burke quietly seethed about.

"Anyway, changing the subject for a second. I wanted to let you know that your horse, Santa's Quest, is being transferred to Woodstock today. Cannons' stable have been in contact with Warren's team and the horse is expected to arrive up there tomorrow."

Death Claims its Prize

"That's good. When can I see my boy again?"
"I believe they want to get him settled with his surroundings for at least a day or two and to get him into their routine before we show up. You know I don't know too much about this stuff but once they are happy they'll let us know when we can visit."
"I hope it's not too long."
"Well as I told you previously, from what I've found out about him the guy has a good name, and he looks after his horses only racing them when they are ready. He runs a good ship and with the relatively small number of horses he has compared to other trainers, he seems to get the best out of them."
"I'll take your word for it. That's why your my agent. I trust your judgement."
"Thank you," Burke replied. "By the way your other horses with Fred Aspinall and Stu Grenfell are staying where they are, and Stu has agreed to take on Whiplash Kid and Honeyeater from Hawkers' yard."
"Not Cannon?"
"No, he didn't have much space left when I first called his assistant. In fact I was lucky to get a spot at all. Cannon has been away looking to buy another horse for himself and also bring back to the stable one of his owner's horses that had been injured but has since recovered. As I mentioned, he only has a small yard."
"Couldn't Fred or Stu have taken on Santa's Quest?"
Burke sighed, "Not really, they also had limited space."
"But you said that Stu…," Sutcliffe interrupted.
"Yes, had taken two of your three, but remember they are big yards. I thought you wanted someone to focus on Santa's Quest and not have him compete for attention with a multitude of other horses?"
"I did."
"So that's what I arranged," Burke replied, starting to get annoyed. He was starting to see how some of Sutcliffe's guests may feel when question followed question.
For a few seconds there was silence between the two men. Burke sipped his coffee while waiting for his client to respond. Eventually he did. "I understand, Tony," Sutcliffe replied. "So you'll let me know when we can go and see him?"
"Yes."
"This weekend perhaps? It's the best time for me, because of having

no shows."

"That's up to Cannon, as I've just pointed out. I suspect it depends on what happens tomorrow and Friday. I'll let you know."

"Okay, good," Sutcliffe answered, ending the call without any apology for his challenge to Burke's decision of where to resettle his horse and why. Pissed off at his client's response, he sculled the rest of his coffee and as he walked back to his kitchen found himself speaking to himself, calling Sutcliffe, "a prick!"

The arrival from Ireland of Rory's Song and White Noise was greeted with much fanfare, particularly with regards to the latter.

When he had last been seen in the yard, he had been much lighter, sickly and having lost weight due to not eating for several days. His injury had taken its toll, but as he walked down the ramp from the dual horsebox with the freshly painted signage of CB & Sons Transport along its side, he looked in magnificent order.

"Cochrane did an amazing job," Telside said, as Simon Brooks led the horse around in front of Cannon and Telside who had been waiting patiently for the horse's arrival.

"As I told you the other day, the man is a miracle worker," Cannon said. Calling to Brooks, he asked, "What do you think, Simon?"

"He looks fantastic, boss. I can't wait to get on him and see what he feels like."

"Well get him into his stall, give him some feed and some water. I think we've gotten rid of all the contaminated stuff, thank God." He turned to Telside who nodded in agreement.

"Simon and the boys did a good job in clearing everything out, so yes, we hopefully won't have that problem again. Winter Garden seems to be progressing well as do the other two so while we are not out of the woods yet, we're not far from it."

"Okay," Cannon answered, feeling relieved. He called to the driver of the horse float who had gone back up the ramp to bring down Rory's Song. While they were waiting, he watched Brooks lead White Noise away, then he turned to Telside as Rory's Song was led down. "Tell me what you think?" he said, watching the older man's face, noticing how Telside's eyes scanned the new arrival.

"Thirty Thousand?" he asked, sceptically.

"Twenty. Pounds."
Telside watched as the horse was led around. He noticed the strength in the hind quarters and the way the animal carried himself. His walking action was good.
"I can see why you wanted to give him a try, but didn't you tell me that he was a bit slow?"
"For hurdles probably, but I think he'll do alright over fences. He's got a big reach and if his minds on the job and he has a heart for it, then maybe we can win a few races with him?"
"He hasn't had the best career so far though has he?" Telside questioned, before calling over a young rider named Chad Bryant, who was standing in a small group of grooms watching the unloading and asked him to take the horse to his allocated box in the horse barn. The driver gave the lead rope to the youngster then began to return the ramp to the vertical position at the back of the horse box, locking it shut with four large bolts. There were two on either side, one at the top, the roof of the box, and the other level with the internal floor.
"We still have to decide whose going to look after him," Telside added, noncommittally, pointing at the rear of Rory's Song as Bryant led him away.
"Agreed," Cannon replied. "I think I have just the person."
"Want to share it?"
"Tom Crichton. I think it will work for both of them as the horse has potential and if we can improve his fitness, slowly working him up to his best, then that may also improve Tom's confidence too. If that works it may give him a chance to race the horse before the end of the season?"
"That's a long ways off, but I'm happy to give it a try," Telside said, just as the driver came over to say that he was about to leave and make his back to Holyhead to catch his boat.
"Are you sure you don't want a drink, a coffee, tea, a sandwich before you go?" Cannon asked, apologizing for not offering any refreshments earlier. "Mr. err…..?"
"Kelly, Fionn Kelly. Me daddy's one of the owners of the business, even though it's called CB & Sons Transport. It's a long story," he added, with a smile. "And while I appreciate the offer, I do need to get going."
Kelly appeared to be in his late twenties. He had dyed hair, part

blond and part black, the sides being the former and the scalp the latter. He was dressed in jeans, a green jumper over a checked shirt and wore heavy boots. At just over five foot ten (one metre seventy-eight) tall, he had ruddy skin, pale and easily touched by the sun. He had green eyes and a pugilistic nose as if he had been a boxer in his earlier days. He spoke with a strong accent which made his mouth turn down slightly on the right-hand side.

"Ok, Fionn, I understand, but I want to thank you for delivering the horses safely. I really do appreciate it," Cannon replied. "I'll probably be using your company again when I take White Noise, that's the Grey you delivered, back over to Punchestown for his first race of the new season."

"I'm sure my Dad will be happy to hear that, Mr. Cannon. He always appreciates repeat business."

"And so he should," Cannon replied, thinking of the support Joel Seeton and others had given him over the years. Seeton continued to do so by keeping White Noise in the stable, which he didn't need to, now that the horse had recovered from injury.

"Well, I'd better be on my way then," Kelly said, shaking hands first with Cannon, then with Telside. The two men stood back from the horse box as Kelly jumped in the cabin, started the engine, waved from behind his window and drove towards the open gate.

"Nice guy," Cannon said, pointing towards the back of the truck as it turned onto the road, then disappeared from view.

Agreeing, Telside said, "That's two down and one to go, Mike. Santa's Quest, that's Sutcliffe's horse, should be here tomorrow from Hawkers' place. With luck we can get all three into their routine quickly because we've only got a few weeks before we start the season proper. I'm sure Sutcliffe, as with all our new owners, will be keen to see what you have got planned for his horse and oh, by the way, I've got to give his agent a call asap to make arrangements with him so that they can come up here and have a look around. Unfortunately they can only come up on weekends though, due to Sutcliffe's show every weekday."

"Bloody hell," Cannon said, "you'd think they'd give us a bit longer wouldn't you."

"Well we did agree to a visit when you accepted their invitation to take the horse on. Plus the poor animal has been stuck inside his box ever since Warren died. I think it's only fair that they come see him exercise so that are happy with what we are all about."

"Fair enough, Rich," Cannon replied, pointing upwards. "And talking about being inside I think we'd better get inside ourselves. That rain that has held off until now looks like it is starting again."

Telside stuck his hand outwards just as a few droplets landed on his face. Suddenly increasing in frequency heavier drops began to land on his cap and the shoulders of his coat. Without speaking again both men went in opposite directions. Cannon to the house and his own office and Telside back to the stables, where he wanted to check on the new arrivals, making sure that they were properly settled for the rest of the day. They would be left to rest until Sutcliffe's horse arrived the next day, then after a veterinary examination all three would begin training again. It would likely be a slow process, each horse tested in stages, slowly put under pressure as their workload increased. While they knew how good White Noise was, it would be important that they brought him along slowly after his injury. A repeat would be devastating. Regarding Rory's Song and Santa's Quest, Cannon and Telside would need to find out more about each of them. Previous form compiled on paper from the previous season, didn't always translate to success during the next one. Some horses improved, others went backwards. The start of a new campaign was always exciting for everyone, but it wasn't without its dangers either.

Fionn Kelly relied on his GPS to get him back to Holyhead. This had only been his second trip on his own, having been previously limited to driving in Ireland. It wasn't too often that the business was given assignments like the one he had just finished. Most of the bigger stables used larger companies to move their livestock. Small jobs like single or two horse trips across the Irish sea were few and far between.

The journey would take about five hours if he included a short stop along the way. It was a couple of hours longer than going home via Liverpool but the trip on the ferry was so much shorter. In addition there were more sailings and the cost was considerably cheaper. With luck he would arrive in time for the early evening sailing just after six pm. He was looking forward to having a short nap on the ship, which was expected to get into Dublin somewhere in the region of nine thirty. That was more than enough time to get the empty horsebox back to the yard and be in his own bed by eleven.

Ninety minutes into his journey he pulled off the M6 just north of Wolverhampton and parked his vehicle away from the lunchtime crowd that had concentrated their cars near the entrance to the Moto Hilton Park services. He was hungry and needed to relieve himself.

As he climbed out of the cab, he didn't notice the white panel van that had stopped directly behind him. Two men, both much physically stronger than him, and dressed completely in black, balaclavas covering their heads jumped out of the sliding door, catching Kelly off-guard. One of the men grabbed him by the shoulders, the other quickly covered his mouth with a firm hand before stuffing it with a wet sponge. Kelly gagged, unable to call out. Within seconds he was bundled inside the van. Shouts rang out and a third man, the driver, pulled the van out from behind the horse box, his door still hanging open, and sped out of the car park and onto the motorway. The three men inside the vehicle knew that there were cameras all around the parking area, and on the various buildings that made up the complex. They were aware that vision of the abduction would in time be available to the police and that their van would be seen on motorway CCTV. However with time on their side and false number plates on their vehicle, their plan to dump the van in the forest near Cannock Chase just a half hour drive away, meant that they were confident of escape.

Keeping Kelly subdued during the drive to where their own vehicle had been hidden was the easy part. Torching their van with him inside it, and disposing of their clothes, boots and all traces of having been involved with Kelly's murder took a little more planning. The men however knew what they were doing and by the time they left the scene the white van was a blackened shell, torched by the flames that shot out from the front and side windows scorching the panels as the glass exploded. Inside, Kelly was dead before the flames touched his body. The fumes and smoke that entered the van after the men had poured petrol all around the wheels, along the sides and across the roof before igniting it, added to his already restricted airways. The tape placed across his mouth and used to tie his hands and feet together had seen to that. While taking care to remove as much evidence as they could regarding their presence at the killing site, including footprints and other possible clues that the police would be looking for, they had watched the van burn and slowly collapse in on itself. The low cloud above quickly gorged the black smoke that rose up from the burning hulk, making it almost impossible to be noticed from any distance. Once satisfied with their work, having changed into new clothes which they had left at the site in advance of their return, the three men walked the half mile to where they had hidden a non-descript white Honda and drove off. The men would split up near Ellesmere Port in Cheshire, ninety minutes' drive away.

CHAPTER 12

The morning had broken with another reddish sky. The temperature had dropped slightly from the previous day, the clouds breaking, then reconverging as if to tease them. The morning's work was over and Telside had shared the good news that both White Noise and Rory's Song had settled in nicely since their arrival. In addition, all three horses that had been taken ill through contaminated feed were now on the road to recovery. Cannon agreed with Telside that they should all remain in their boxes for a further forty-eight hours, until they were ready to exercise again.
"No point rushing it," Cannon said.
"Agreed, Mike. There is still plenty of time to get them ready for their first outing. I don't suspect it will change any of our plans."
They were sitting together in Cannons' office. It was a place where they met regularly on non-race days to talk about the morning's exercises, issues with any of the staff, equipment needs and a multitude of other matters that never seemed to end. With tea in hand, Cannon indicated the computer screen that he had been working on, just before Telside arrived.
"I've laid out various options and races for each of our horses over the next few months, starting in about six weeks," he said. "I've used the fixture list for the rest of the calendar year and want to start at Stratford-on-Avon, Ludlow and Huntingdon in the first few weeks. Those courses are not too far away and I don't want to spend too much time away from home if I can help it, especially now that Cassie is expecting."
Cannon had told Telside of the news as they had watched the first lot go through their paces. They had been sitting inside the SUV studying each horse as it worked. Time pieces and watches were unnecessary when it came to the various pieces of work that each horse and rider was being asked to complete. Fitness and speed would come in time, but good schooling of the horses and getting them to jump and be brave at the obstacles was more important to Cannon than anything else. Bad habits were difficult to change and safety of horse and rider were paramount as far as he was concerned.
With his usual positive response at the baby news Telside had shook his friends hand and patted him on the back, offering him hearty

congratulations. Cannon's decision to run some of his horses locally made sense, especially those of less ability. The more seasoned and better horses would need to wait a little while longer before making their seasonal debut.

"The local meetings may not be the best races but I've been working on a plan to give every horse a chance of going up in class by the end of the season," Cannon said. "I think if we want to get White Noise to Cheltenham next year and into the Champion Hurdle then we need to keep him focused on the two to two-and-a-half-mile trips. I don't want Seeton thinking of taking him 'chasing, the horse has great speed and if he stays sound throughout the winter I think we can qualify him."

Pointing to the screen again, Cannon moved his mouse to show Telside when and where every horse in his stable was to run. In some cases there would be two of his horses in the same race. The spreadsheet was extremely detailed including track name, dates, event type and horse's names. Shaded in a cell alongside each horse was the jockey that Cannon hoped to use at that specific meeting. Depending upon injury, availability and form, the jockey would be confirmed closer to the time, but one had to get in early and book a rider before he was assigned to another ride. A large part of Cannon's administrative duties each day was to contact a jockey's agent to secure who he wanted to ride for him. There were regulars that he used, but even they weren't always available, and he needed to have a back-up where possible. Telside noted that Cannon had not put Tom Crichton up to ride Rory's Song at any meeting as far as he could see.

"No, I haven't," Cannon replied. "I want to see what the horse does with an experienced jockey first before I let Tom ride him in a race."

"I'm sure he'll be disappointed if the horse proves himself after the boy does all the work on him."

"He probably will, but if that's the way it pans out, well so be it. I'm sure the boy will be happy to get a few rides this year. However, it will only be once I'm comfortable, then I'll be happy to give him a few starts. We don't want another Ray Brollo."

The two men continued discussing the spreadsheet, with Cannon making the occasional change based on Telside's input. Immersed in the task for twenty minutes they hardly noticed the change in the weather. The clouds that had been threatening had eventually decided to dispel the occasional shower. This was followed by a quick dump of heavy rain before there was a break allowing a slither of sun to shine through before the gap closed up again. It was during a second rain shower that there conversation was disrupted with the arrival of a large horse float, the bulk of it just managing the fit through the gate as it turned off the road from Woodstock and into the yard. The running lights of the truck shone through the window into Cannon's office before the vehicle turned ninety degrees and came to a stop.

Bright lights on the side of the truck, situated near the roof line, shone downwards lighting up the signage and a decaled logo. It read, 'Hawker Racing Stables'.

"This must be Sutcliffes' horse," Telside said, standing up to peer through the window. "I'll go and speak to the driver so that we can get him offloaded. I can't wait to see what he looks like."

"Okay," Cannon replied. "I'll be out in a minute, I'll just save these changes on the spreadsheet and I'll be with you shortly."

Left alone, Cannon tapped the keyboard as speedily as he could. He could hear Telside talking outside with the truck driver, their voices muted through the window. As he began to save his work he noticed the truck starting up again. He assumed that Telside had requested the driver to move the vehicle closer to the stable entrance so that once offloaded the horse could be given a walk before being taken into its new box. Looking through the window, he noticed the damp of the early afternoon, the grey sky still leaking occasionally. Picking up his coat that lay on a small chair to the side, he didn't notice his mobile phone that he had placed on the edge of his desk, drop onto the carpeted floor. The action of turning to the doorway while thrusting his arms down the sleeves of his coat and pulling the two sides together had caught the device, whipping it and making it spin off the desk landing next to one of the legs of his chair. As he reached the front door of the house he heard the phone start to ring. Caught in two minds, he was unsure whether to return to his office and answer it or let it ring out. Knowing that Michelle would normally call him on the landline at this particular time of day if there was any issue and that he had spoken with Cassie during the last forty-eight hours, he decided to let the caller leave a message.

He guessed that he wouldn't be outside for long and as Telside would arrange for the new arrival to be properly looked after, he expected that he would be able to listen to any messages left for him, shortly. Standing alongside Telside they watched as Sutcliffe's horse was led around in a tight circle. After the long drive, it was necessary to let the animal stretch its legs. The big gelding was an impressive beast. His coat gleamed despite the dull day. The few spots of rain that had landed on his back since he had been removed from the trailer, disappeared into the almost black skin. Cannon noticed the intelligent eye and the swagger. With a head that seemed perfectly chiseled at the end of a long gracious neck, this was very special horse flesh.

The driver of the truck walked over and introduced himself to Cannon.

"Bryce Kidd, I'm the former Head Lad at Warren Hawkers' stables," he said, pointing towards the man who was walking with the horse. "That's Phil Tobin. He's been Santa's Quest's groom ever since the horse came to us."

"Former Head Lad?" Cannon questioned, referring to Kidds' comment and noticing the irony behind the name. The man standing before him was in his late thirties at least, and certainly no child. Standing at less than five feet two, (one metre, fifty-eight centimetres) he could have been a jockey himself. He had ruffled and unkempt blond hair in a style that reminded Cannon of Boris Johnson, the former UK Prime Minister. His eyes were a sharp blue, his face oblong with a strong chin. Dressed in jeans, with a dark green jersey under a brown leather jacket and matching leather boots, he gave the impression of being immediately in charge of what was going on around him. It was a kind of leadership quality that Cannon admired. There was no arrogance involved, just efficiency.

"Yes. Former," Kidd said. "With the boss's death, our entire operation is being closed down. Horses are being dispersed by their owners to different trainers, and the staff down there are looking for other jobs. I've been given three months to find something else before I'm out of work."

"I'm sorry to hear that," Cannon responded. "Are there no vacancies anywhere?"

Pointing across to the groom, Kidd said, "Unfortunately not in the immediate area, no. Some places closed during Covid, leaving very few active racing stables near to us. Phil and I were lucky while the pandemic was on, we kept our jobs and we've had a few good years since then…..up until now that is. As I said earlier, Phil has been with him since the day the horse arrived at the stable and just as the horse was starting to build a good reputation as a potential future champion, he is going to lose his job and his association with the horse because of what happened to Warren."

Cannon conscious of the sensitivities of the situation nodded in sympathy. Racing was full of such stories. Many owners didn't see what went on behind the scenes of a racing yard. They only saw their horses on racecourses or on TV, not in the stables where they were being taken care of by youngsters who worried more about the animals welfare than the owner likely did. In addition some owners rarely understood how little grooms were paid. The bill that trainers sent to their clients rarely spelt that out. He wasn't sure if it applied to Sutcliffe, but to Cannon the man could just as easily be one of those owners.

Thinking back to Telside's original comments about the issue, he wondered whether Rich had been right, and that by taking on Sutcliffes' horse there was baggage associated with it, that he wasn't yet prepared for.

"I guess the last six weeks or so have been pretty tough then?" Cannon asked.

"You can say that again," Kidd replied, disconsolately. "It's been nothing short of horrendous. Firstly getting the news of the accident, then trying to keep the staff calm before giving them the complete picture of what Warren's wife decided to do with the business made my job a lot more difficult than it should have been. When Mrs. Hawker said she wanted to sell out, I was hoping that someone would take it on as a going concern, maybe lease the place initially…another trainer perhaps? But no…nothing."

"I'm sorry to hear that," Cannon replied, sympathetically. "Didn't Warren have an assistant? Someone with a license working for him who could manage the stables for her in the interim, while they looked for a buyer?"

"The closest to that person was me. I was his assistant, but in name only. We hadn't done anything formally, everything was done on a handshake. I've been slowly working towards going on my own, but I've still got a lot more work to do, not least of which is to build up some capital. This has all come a bit too soon unfortunately," he added, nodding to where Telside was now directing the groom to take the horse. Cannon turned around to take a quick look at the disappearing backside of the horse along with the backs of Telside and Phil Tobin. The rain began to fall again. "Come into the house," he said, pointing at the sky, "there is something I want to ask you."

CHAPTER 13

The arrival of Sutcliffe's horse and the subsequent conversations had caused him to change plans and lose track of time. Working with Telside after Kidd and Tobin had left to return to Taunton, he was still busy in the stables when Michelle arrived home. He hadn't noticed her car until he was on his way back to his office and as he strode to the house, he felt a shiver run through his body. The rain continued to fall, more heavily now than earlier in the day. By the time he crossed the front door's threshold his hair was soaked, his shoulders damp. Mud and other detritus caked his boots.
"Take them off," Michelle said, pointing at his feet.
"Can I take this coat off first?" he asked, closing the door behind him, cutting off the breeze and the damp that tried to muscle their way into the room. She smiled in response, turning away, leaving him standing there as if to say, "okay."
He began scraping away straw one foot at a time, balancing himself on the mat just inside the front entrance. Once he was done, he placed the boots to one side.
Finding her in the bedroom, he apologized for the fact that he hadn't been around to greet her when she got home. He had noticed several sodden bags of groceries still on the dining room table and he guessed that she had carried them in herself despite the heavy rain.
"I was caught up with the new arrival," he said, apologetically, "Rich and I had to make a few changes this afternoon from what we had originally planned. I had a chat to Warren Hawker's Head Had who brought the horse and he told me that there were a couple of quirks that I should be aware of."
"What kind of quirks?"
"The first one is that he likes to bite…..hard! The second is that he likes to rear up on his hind legs and threaten people if he doesn't get his way."
"That doesn't sound any different to some of the other horses you've had over the years," she replied.
"That's true, but in order to make sure that no one is left in any doubt as to the risk the horse may pose, Rich and I will keep an eye on him for the first couple of days and give him time to settle in. It

may be that the horse has gone a bit stir crazy given the amount of time he's been cooped up in his box and I don't want to have anybody get hurt."

"Will it work…your plan?"

"I hope so, but there are no guarantees and that's what concerns me. If the horse does get riled up then we may have a problem. It's why Rich and I were doing what we were this afternoon, a bit of a juggling act! We've rearranged things regarding which of the staff will look after which horse in the short term, to make sure nothing serious happens. With White Noise being back I was hoping to get everyone into a routine as quickly as possible, but it seems that nothing ever goes as planned. The contamination scare didn't help either. I didn't know until Hawker's Head Lad told me, that Sutcliffes' horse was going to be a potential problem. Even Rich wasn't aware."

Michelle looked at the concern on her husband's face. It was obvious that something else was bothering him. She wasn't sure if it was the horse or the owner, but it was apparent that the arrival of Chester Sutcliffe's animal had unsettled Cannon somehow. She wondered if having such a high-profile owner as part of his clientele was playing on his mind. Was there an unrealistic expectation of success which, if not achieved, would be used against him? Her intuition was that Cannon, for some unknown reason, now had second thoughts about training for Sutcliffe, and that concerned her. It wasn't like him. She decided to bite her lip, at least for now.

There were signs that someone had been inside the building. Subtle changes that had caught the eye. It was obvious that whoever had been there had been looking for something. The question was whether they had found it or not?

Standing outside again, DI Dave Walsh was furious at the breach, taking his anger out on the young Constable who been assigned night duty.

"What the feck were you doing?" he asked, sarcastically. "I suppose you saw nothing and were fecking sleeping most of the time? Weren't you? You fecking eejit!"

Trying not to go too far overboard, Walsh had tempered his language slightly, using a colloquialism rather than using 'fuck' outright. The young Constable wasn't entirely to blame. Whoever had managed to break into the house obviously knew what they were doing. Anyone with such enterprise had some balls, he thought, and that gave him an additional headache. That conclusion alone confirming to him that whoever was involved, was no opportunist.

"I'm sorry, Sir," Constable O'Callaghan stammered, "I honestly didn't see a thing. Nothin' at all."

"Well if you're asleep son, you generally don't." Walsh replied, turning away from the young policeman, and heading back towards the front door of Sam Quinn's house, which he had deliberately left open. Stopping two yards from the opening, he turned around to face O'Callaghan again who was now standing against his police car, staring at the grey sky, unsure what to do with himself. The bollocking he had received was still ringing in his ears.

"Hey!"

"Yes, Sir?"

"Get a call into the station, Constable. I want a crime scene team and forensics back on site within the hour! Do you hear me?"

"Yes, Sir," Callaghan replied, enthusiastically, anxious to get back into Walsh's good books.

"Good," the Detective responded, "and be quick about it," he added unnecessarily. He could tell that his message had gotten through to the youngster and that was all he wanted. He had decided to leave the matter there, the tongue lashing he gave deemed enough. No point in taking it further or suggesting any disciplinary action be taken against Callaghan. The paperwork alone and the time it took to get any form of proper hearing with 'People and Culture' was just insane. A waste of money too, he thought. The process would have taken him off the frontline for days and likely over a period of many months too.

It was Police Command who needed to be taken to task as far as he was concerned. The entire Wexford Division of the force was overstretched. The number of cases piling up on desks when measured against the quantity and skill level of the resources on hand was completely out-of-whack. Everyone knew of the problem, but no one appeared to want to own it. The result; the sending of a boy to do a man's job.

Walking into the building again, he faintly heard O'Callaghan talking on his car's radio. Taking slow and methodical steps throughout the house, Walsh scanned each room again, touching door handles as needed and light switches when required. His hands were encased in disposable plastic gloves which he used to ensure that any fingerprints left by the intruder would be collectable by the forensics team. He doubted there would be any, but what he didn't doubt was that there was something valuable in the house that someone wanted. It was one of the pillows that had originally given the game away He was standing at the doorway of Quinn's bedroom again. When he had been inside the house the previous day he had watched the forensics team as they worked. When they had completed what they had been doing, he had noticed how the pillows on the bed had been left. Earlier, when he had stood where he was now, he could see a few small impressions where someone had tried to place the pillows exactly as they had found them. Walsh surmised that the intruder had moved the bedding to look what was underneath them. With the sheets and duvet still intact it was the smallest of alterations that had led to him to realize that someone else had been in the room. Once he had drawn that conclusion he had scoured the rest of the house looking for any other differences. Again, he noticed small adjustments. A bottle of soft drink lying flat on the shelf in the fridge now had its front label facing downwards. He was sure that it had been facing upwards previously. The washing machine door was slightly further ajar than it had been. The tops of books on a shelf in the lounge seemed to be more in line than when he had seen them last. These were only slight and hardly noticeable changes but were enough to convince him that someone had been throughout the house at some point overnight. Being observant was what had made him a good detective, but until he had more to go on than a gut feeling, he was still floundering. He needed answers to his questions. If Quinn was murdered for something he had in his possession, then why hadn't he handed it over to his killer? It was obvious that if had he done and was murdered afterwards, then why would anyone want to break-in again if they already had what they wanted? Was it just to confuse the police? He doubted that was the case. Risking being caught for no reason made no sense. The people behind the killing knew exactly what they were doing. On that basis alone he gathered that whatever the intruder or intruders were looking for, they hadn't found it as yet and were likely to come back at some stage.

As he contemplated various scenarios in his head he heard Callaghan calling him from the front door. The young Constable was standing at the opening. It was clear that he was anxious about entering the building. He called out to Walsh once again.

"Sir! Sir!" he shouted, receiving a gruff, "What?" in response, as Walsh wandered down the passageway to where he was standing.

"Forensics are on their way, Sir," the Constable said.

"Good," Walsh replied. "and thank you."

Feeling slightly less intimidated Callaghan nodded, smiling slightly. The Detective appeared to be less threatening to him now, certainly less than he had been just thirty minutes earlier.

As Walsh was about to speak again, his mobile began to ring. Checking who the caller was before answering, he groaned, expecting to be quizzed immediately about where he was physically and what he was doing there.

"Hello, boss," he said, in Gaelic. "I was going to call you later. I'm at…"

He wasn't allowed to finish his sentence. Superintendent James Kelleher cut him off. "No need, Daithi," Kelleher stated. "I need to speak with you urgently."

"What about?"

"A bit of news I just received. I think you might find it interesting."

"Can't it wait, Sir? I'm on site at the moment, at Sam Quinns' place," he added, "waiting for forensics and the CS teams to arrive."

"I thought they did the job yesterday?"

"They did, Sir, but I need them again. As I just mentioned, I was going to call you later and fill you in."

"Well, it can wait. Get yourself back to the station, immediately. I think you'll find what I've got for you, is more than a little interesting."

With the order issued, Kelleher ended the call. Walsh looked at the phone in his hand, the screen now black, its silent face seemed to be laughing at him.

"What was that all about?" he said to himself, curious as to why his boss hadn't filled him in straight away as he normally would have done. What was so secret that could only be discussed in the office?

Standing in front of the house, the blue 'Police, do not cross' tape bending and swaying in the wind, Walsh watched as two police mini-buses began the short drive from Quinns' front gate to where he was standing.

Pointing a finger at Callaghan, he said. "Just make sure that no one comes down that driveway other than official vehicles on Garda business, do you understand me? And I want every single one that does recorded, their picture taken and the time noted of when they arrive and when they leave."

"Yes, Sir."

"Good," Walsh replied, "and you can start with this lot," he added, watching as the two vans pulled up to a stop a few yards away. Tossing a small notebook at Callaghan that he removed from an inside jacket pocket, he said, "Here's a spare one of mine. Use it exclusively while you are here. I'll get it back from you later."

As the two teams piled out of their vehicles, Caoilinn Murphy began taking charge of her own team, giving instructions about what she wanted the forensics team to focus on. The other team were a pair of crime scene investigators.

Walking over to Murphy, Walsh interrupted her, "Sorry to have brought you out again, Caoilinn, but can I have a quick word?"

"Sure," she replied, "I'm all ears."

Knowing that she was a woman with no time for small talk or anyone who tried to tell her how to do her job, he tried to be diplomatic as he spoke to her about his requirements and expectations.

"Oh and any joy with that piece of paper?" he asked, referring to the scrap that was found in Quinns' throat.

"Not as yet, but it's still being analyzed. I'm doubtful we'll find any DNA on it apart from the victims, but the writing may provide us with something useful."

"And the paper itself?"

"Just normal copy paper. Bought anywhere."

"So nothing unique about it?"

"No," she answered, simply. "We'll analyze the ink as well, but I'm not confident that it will reveal anything either."

Sarcastically, but with a smile on his face, he said, "Nothing like being positive then?"

"Piss off," she replied, with a straight face, before saying, "Are we done here, Daithi? We've got work to do you know…as you requested."

"Okay, okay," he said, hands held up in mock surrender.

She gave him a dirty look, then went back to talk with her team. Shrugging, Walsh turned his attention to the two CSI men. He walked over to their van. Both men, who he knew from previous occasions, were almost ready to enter the building. With their feet and heads covered in blue plastic and with gloved hands holding clipboards and miniature torches, they appeared almost comical. He spoke to the senior of the two.

"Good morning, Donal, how are you?"

Donal Murray, a thirty-year veteran of the force was a jovial man. Bald, with a face like a bulldog and with a body of similar proportions, he had a nature entirely opposite to his looks. Another serious rugby player in his day, which endeared him to Walsh, he had twice represented his country before injury forced him to end his career. Now in the twilight of his days in the Police his mind was still on the job despite having already announced the date of his retirement. He greeted Walsh like an old friend. "I'm fine Daithi," he said. "Lovely day."

Walsh looked up at the heavy white sheets above him. There was no sign of rain as yet, but he was convinced that things would change soon enough.

"I guess it is," he answered, without contradiction.

"So what do you need from Brian and me today?" Murray asked. His partner, Brian O'Clery, standing a few feet away acknowledged Walsh with a quick, "Hi"

"Just one thing."

"Which is?"

"I'm convinced that someone has been in the house overnight. I had Constable O'Callaghan watch the place all night but he didn't see a thing." Stopping for a second he recalled his earlier conversation with the young policeman. Deciding not to deride the young officer again in public, he kept quiet about their earlier conversation, adding, "That tells me that whoever it was, knows their business. It means that it's at least their second attempt as well. We think that nothing was stolen when Sam Quinn was murdered, and from what I can tell, this second attempt appears just as fruitless."

"Because?" questioned O'Clery.

"Because they left everything as they found it. Well, almost."

"And that proves what?" O'Clery again.

"I'm surmising, call it a gut feeling, but if they had found what they were looking for, my experience tells me that they would have ransacked the place. To confuse us as to their motive. By taking any number of things it would be easy to conclude that this was an opportunistic break and entry, a simple robbery, but I've said from the very beginning that there is something unusual about this case."

"So, what are we looking for?" Murray asked.

"I honestly don't know, but my guess is that whatever they came for, and the reason you are here, is still in that house. We need to find it before they come back a third time."

Murray smiled, a huge grin across his face, his plastic cap sliding to one side of his head. He loved a challenge, and this case certainly fitted the bill. "We'll do our best, Daithi, but to not know what we are looking for, makes it very difficult you know."

"I understand," Walsh replied, "but I have faith in you. Something is hidden inside that house and if we need to tear the place apart to find it, we will.

CHAPTER 14

Telside had made the phone call to Tony Burke and his arrival along with Chester Sutcliffe was highly anticipated. The two men were expected over the coming weekend, Sunday being the preferred day.
They had less than seventy-two hours to get KK, the nickname the staff had quickly given to Santa's Quest, into a routine. It was up to the horse to comply.
"Why KK?" Cannon asked, somewhat bemused when Telside had told him of the horse's nickname.
"Apparently it's short for Kris Kringle, the German Father Christmas," Telside had replied, "I think it works," he continued.
They were watching the second lot parading, walking around in a large circle before they were to head up to the heath. The sun had risen an hour earlier, and the cloud had broken up for a while, allowing the dew on the grass and the condensation that had settled on the gutters of the stable roof, including the downpipes, to quickly evaporate. A slight mist had carpeted the heath when the first lot had exercised earlier, and Cannon was thankful that there were no incidents, falls or injuries, as a consequence.
The three newcomers into the stable, including White Noise, were amongst the ten horses circling. Each had been given an appropriately skilled rider to take them through their paces.
Brooks had White Noise, nicknamed Winnie. Crichton was on Rory's Song, called simply Rory, and KK was ridden by Lester Crouch. The latter's experience would come in handy should Sutcliffe's horse act up as he was prone to do. As they watched the horses circle, carefully studying the actions of each, Telside commented how quiet and compliant Crouch's mount was being. There had been no attempts to bite nor rear, which Cannon put down to the way Crouch handled him.
Just as he was about to ask Brooks to "lead off" and take the lot up to the heath, KK suddenly reared up on his back legs, taking Crouch by surprise. Fortunately the experienced rider was able to hang on as the horse reared a second time, front legs thrashing as if to ward off anyone who tried to stop him.
The riders of the other mounts moved quickly, trying to keep out of

harm's way. Crouch wrestled with the reins, fighting to stay on the horse's back, his saddle slipping backwards slightly. After getting a couple of kicks in the belly from Crouch the horse put all four feet back onto the ground, snorted its discontent and stuck out his tongue as if to tell anyone who would listen that he was the new king in town. A few seconds later Cannon walked towards the still slightly agitated animal and praised Crouch for staying in the saddle. As he stood alongside, the riders knee at eye level, KK suddenly swung his neck viciously, bared his teeth and tried to take a chunk out of Cannons' hand while he was patting the horse's neck.

Fortunately his experience of working with thoroughbreds over the years saved him from a mauling. However he did receive a bite to his left hand, the horse sinking its teeth into the flesh leaving a deep gash on his palm and the back of the hand.

"Shit!" Cannon shouted in pain, immediately noticing the blood that began to ooze from the wound. He covered the gash with his right hand trying to stem the flow with applied pressure.

Telside reacted immediately to what KK had done, raising his arms and moving them in a windmill-like motion. His intent was to scare the horse into back-pedalling thereby giving Crouch time to control the horse again before turning it away from Cannon and himself and trotting it back towards the stable block. There would be no schooling for Kris Kringle today, he thought.

"Are you okay, Mike?" Telside asked, worriedly.

Looking at the wound, Cannon nodded. "It looks far worse than it is, I think, but I need to get it cleaned up and dressed. If necessary I maybe need to get a jab. Fortunately it doesn't look like it needs stitching."

Telside had a quick look at the bite. "I agree," he said, sympathetically. "Look, let me go and sort out the bloody horse while you go and get fixed up. I'll meet you on the heath when you can. In the meantime I'll get Simon to take the rest of this lot up there for me, and we can get them going through their paces. You and I can catch up when you are ready, but if you do need a doctor let me know and I'll make the arrangements."

"Thanks Rich," Cannon replied, blood now staining the cuffs of his shirt and the rib of his jersey, his right hand basically useless in stopping the flow. "I'm sure I'll be okay. I want to see how the others go, so I'll see you up there shortly," he added, still annoyed with himself at what had happened.

"Okay."

Cannon made his way into the house. Michelle had long gone. The start of the new school year just a few days away, scheduled to start the following Tuesday. The silence inside the house unnerved him slightly as he struggled to find what he was looking for; a first aid kit usually kept in a bathroom cupboard, under the sink. He was conscious of blood dripping on the carpets and tiles and it took him longer than expected to open the box once he had been able to extract it. Using the supplied scissors, sterile wipes, antiseptic cream and gauze pads and bandages he managed to dress the wound, taking nearly forty minutes. As he struggled through the process, cursing his luck and repeating a few "fucks" he heard his mobile phone ring a number of times. It was in his office on his desk where he had hurriedly left it before looking for the first aid kit. He was happy not to answer it, given he was busy, but was hopeful that each caller would leave a message. If they didn't do so, then he surmised that the call was unimportant, probably a scam call, he thought. If the caller did leave a message then he would listen to it as soon as he could and respond accordingly. As he finished putting bloodied gauze and cotton wool into a dustbin, his left hand now partially wrapped in a clean bandage, he suddenly remembered that someone else had tried to call him the previous day. The caller hadn't left a message which was why he had totally forgotten about it.

Picking up the device and readying to make his way up to the heath, he checked the missed calls, noting that there were four, one of which was from the previous day. All the numbers were the same. Numbers that he did not recognize at all other than they began with 353 which he knew to be Ireland. Initially he thought of Jim Cochrane but he already had his friend's number saved in his 'Contacts' list and he knew that a mobile number from Ireland would start with an 89. The number displayed was a landline number. Again he assumed it to be a series of scam calls, deciding not to respond and made his way out of the house.

He was sitting in the driver's seat of his SUV, a few hundred yards from the heath where Rich and the second lot were in full flight, his hand throbbing as he drove slowly up the dirt track. The morning light had softened somewhat as a large band of cloud crossed the countryside blocking out the sun and bringing with it the prospect of more rain. Cannon was always happy for more, he preferred wet and soggy ground for the majority of his horses to run on. Hard or firm ground in his opinion was not ideal for jumps racing and he was occasionally faced with the dilemma of having to run his horses on dry tracks or those affected by heavy frosts. If he believed that a horse he had declared to run in a race could be injured due to the state of the track, he would have no hesitation at scratching it. It was a philosophy he lived and trained by. He was hopeful that Chester Sutcliffe understood this, and he intended to make it known to the former politician when they met in the coming days. The matter was non-negotiable and given the way he was currently feeling about Sutcliffes' horse, he would be more than happy to let the bloody thing go somewhere else, even before he had had a chance to see it in work; his left hand could attest to that.

Parking the car then clambering out, he made his way to where Rich was standing.

"How are you doing now?" the older man asked, stamping his boots on the ground, trying to get some feeling into his toes.

"I'm okay," Cannon answered, showing Telside his bandaged hand, "how are things going here?"

"Looks like….," Telside began, just about to go into detail about the horses that were running past them in even time, some jumping over hurdles, others over 'chase fences, when Cannon's mobile phone began to ring. Cannon looked at the number shown on the screen, noticing that it was the same Irish number he had noticed earlier.

Ignoring the call he put the phone back into his pocket giving the caller another opportunity to leave a message. Forty-five seconds later the phone beeped with a 'voice mail message' notification.

"I'll have a listen when I'm back in the office," he indicated. "So tell me, how is Rory going?

"To be honest Mike, slowly!"

Cannon wasn't too put off by what he heard. He gingerly placed a pair of binoculars to his eyes and scanned the heath until he was able to see the horse cantering towards a 'chase fence. Rory was paired with another horse, Edge of Forever. Both cleared the fence easily, landing together, though Rory was slightly unbalanced losing a bit of ground as they both picked up the bit again and made for the next obstacle.

"If there is any consolation Mike, he may be slow but it looks like he can jump and can stay all day. I think he may do well in races over three miles and upwards."

"I suppose that's something," Cannon replied, slightly disappointed by what he had heard. "Let's see if we can get some speed into his legs. I'll design a program for him so that we can get him to the races before December. Perhaps a novice chase at Huntingdon?"

"Fine with me."

"And how is White Noise doing? I hope Simon is taking it easy with him," Cannon queried. As he scanned the heath the big grey horse came into view, skimming his way across the ground before easily clearing the practice hurdle. With ears pricked he galloped away from his practice partner confirming that he was enjoying his work. Cannon smiled. It was early days yet, but all the signs were looking good.

"As I told you, Rich, he's never looked better. I'm sure Joel will be happy to hear that the horse is back."

"Yep, he seems to be a different animal. His work is impressive even at this early stage. I think it will be useful to get a clock on him in a few days to see how he improves over time. If you decide not to take him to Punchestown then the meeting at Cheltenham in November would be a good place to start his campaign I think. It will give him a look at the place, especially if we want to get him into the Champion Hurdle next year."

"Maybe," Cannon replied, "we'll see. In the meantime you've given me an idea about Rory. There's a 'chase over three and a half miles on day two of the festival in March, maybe we can get him into that?"

"A big ask," Telside replied, "but given his staying ability, anything is possible. I just hope he can keep his mind on the job when he jumps. He still seems a bit clumsy, but nothing we can't fix."

Cannon agreed. What they had in front of them were a mixture of animals, some more athletic than others, but as far as he was concerned athleticism was only one component of what made a successful National Hunt horse. Bravery and a desire to win were just as important. Some horses could run fast but lacked the confidence to take on a fence. Others were brave, some unfortunately were stupid or just plain crazy.

In addition to getting them fit, it was a trainer's job to teach a horse to jump a fence or a hurdle properly. To help it to settle and relax when it cantered or galloped, and to have courage when necessary.

The two men watched as the second lot completed their work before Cannon again went through his regular routine, obtaining feedback from each rider and observing how each horse appeared to have handled the work. Any relevant issues or concerns, he again noted in his notebook. Once he was happy, he let Simon Brooks take over and lead the horses back to the stables.

As the neighs, whinnies and sneezes died in the dullness of early morning, cloud having packed together again to keep the sun at bay, rain not too far away, Cannon stood alongside Telside. Both remained silent breathing in the fresh air that seemed to taste so much better on the heath. Telside knew from Cannon's demeanour that something was on his mind. He waited for him to speak.

"I'm not sure about Sutcliffe's horse," he said, "despite what it did last season. He seems very coltish, a bit highly strung. What do you think Rich?"

Telside did not respond immediately. He stared out over the expanse of turf that lay before them, the town of Wootton just visible in the distance. A strengthening breeze kicked up pieces of grass disturbed by the horses, and he felt the chill of an early winter.

"I suggest we take our time," he answered eventually. "If Sutcliffe isn't happy with your plan then let him take the horse somewhere else. We've always had that option."

"That's true."

"And anyway, it's early days. We haven't even seen the horse in action yet.....other than when he tried to take a piece of you," Telside joked.

Looking at his bandaged hand, Cannon nodded. Yes, it was too early to make a judgement call on the horse and perhaps he was more concerned about the owner than anything else? Maybe his disquiet was compounded by the events of the morning, the bite on his hand throbbing again.

"I suppose you are right, Rich," Cannon conceded. "I'll withhold judgement until after the visit on Sunday. I assume you're coming?"

"Yes. Wouldn't miss it for the world. I might bring the missus along as well if she's well enough, she's a bit of a fan of his show it seems."

"I didn't know that."

"Me neither," Telside laughed. "I'm always in bed when he's on, so

I've never watched it. The only thing I do remember was reading about him a few years back when he left parliament, but that's all. His agent is the chap I spoke to."

"And he's coming as well, I believe."

"Yes. Apparently it was he who chose you."

"I suppose I should be flattered. Anyway, let's get on. I need to get back to the office and sort out some paperwork. If there are any problems with the cooldown or morning stables let me know. I'll see you shortly. We can have a look at KK with Lester once I've finished."

"Right-o," Telside replied, making his way to his car, as Cannon did the same. Within five minutes both were back at the yard. The cloud cover had grown thicker and the morning darker.

CHAPTER 15

He was about to listen to the voicemail message when his mobile rang again. It was the same number as before. Getting annoyed, he sat back in his chair letting the shrill of the phone continue for a few seconds. His initial reaction was to let the caller ring off. He had had his fair share of scam calls over the years and he knew that scammers used all sorts of techniques to fool people as to where the call was coming from. A call from the Philippines or the sub-continent could easily be made to suggest that it was coming from anywhere in the UK. Virtual Private Networks easily masked a callers identity. Taking a deep breath, he pressed the answer button, ready to unload on whoever was on the other end of the line.

"Yes, what do you want!" he said, sharply, not mentioning his name as he would usually do. He didn't want to give the caller any information to use as a hook with which to haul him in. However the moment he heard the words, "Mr. Cannon, it's….," he knew exactly who it was.

"DI Walsh," he said, "what a surprise. You're lucky I answered. I was just about to listen to a voicemail left yesterday. I assume that was from you?"

"Yes, I've called a few times."

"I noticed," Cannon apologized. "I've been a bit busy since I got back and I didn't recognize this number."

"It's obviously not my mobile, it's my office number."

Apologizing again, Cannon gave Walsh the space to divulge why he was calling.

"It's about CB & Sons Transport."

"What about them?"

Walsh took a second or two to answer. "Do you know Fionn Kelly?"

"No. Should I?"

"Perhaps not," Walsh replied, spuriously.

"I'm sorry," Cannon commented, having noticed the subtlety of Walsh's response, "you seem to be suggesting that I should."

"He was the driver who delivered the two horses from Ireland to you, a couple of days ago."

"Oh yes, now I remember. A young guy, mid-twenties or thereabouts. What about him?"

With his usual penchant for directness and without warning, Walsh replied. "He's dead."
"What?!" Cannon exclaimed. "How?"
"He was murdered."
"Bloody hell."
"Exactly."
Sensing something else was behind the news of Kelly's killing, Cannon said, "I'm so sorry to hear what happened, but can I ask what it has to do with me? I only spoke with him for about fifteen minutes. Once he dropped off the horses he left straight away."
"Did he say anything to you?"
"About what?"
"Where he was going next? His movements?"
"No, he just said that he was heading home. That he had a ferry to catch."
"Anything else?"
"Nothing that comes to mind. The only other thing he said was that he would let his company know that we would likely use them again as I was happy with their service. The two horses he delivered had been well looked after during the journey."
"And that was it?"
"Yes."
There was a short silence. Cannon waited for Walsh to speak again. He was still curious as to why the Detective had called so many times in an attempt to contact him.
"You see, Mr. Cannon, something is bothering me about this case."
"Which is?"
"It's this, and I'm sure you'll understand where I'm coming from given your police background and all."
"Go on."
"There have been two murders in what is less than a week. Both of which included victims that had a connection to yourself. Don't you think that's a little curious?"
"I'd hardly say connection, DI Walsh, but I can see the coincidental timing."
Cannon had never believed in coincidence. There was always a reason behind it as far as he was concerned, and the moment the words left his mouth he sensed that what Walsh was suggesting was about to engulf him.

"And that's my problem, Mr. Cannon. Two murders and both have your name associated with them."

"You think that I was involved?"

"As I said when we met the other day, I'm keeping my options open."

Disturbed at the insinuation, Cannon asked, "Where was the young man, killed anyway? I haven't really left my yard since he dropped off the horses. The only place I've been to, is the heath behind my place."

Ignoring Cannons' comment, Walsh said, "I don't really want to disclose the full detail, but I can tell you that he never left England."

"What happened?"

"Again I can't say too much, but the Staffordshire police should be in contact with you in due course. They have some information that may be relevant which they have shared with me."

Cannon was stunned, his mind racing. "I still don't get the link to me though," he said, trying to tease out a little more information that he knew Walsh would likely have. "How did the police in the Midlands connect Kelly's apparent murder to Sam Quinn?"

"They didn't. I did."

Knowing how the police operated, not always willing to share information beyond their own jurisdictions, Cannon was surprised at the comment. Since Brexit happened he guessed that cooperation across the Irish Sea with the Republic was even less than it had been in the past.

"I put two and two together and I've come up with four," Walsh said.

"Despite the close working relationship between the Police Service of Northern Ireland, the PSNI and the An Garda Siochána (AGS), it's other links and connections that help at times like this."

Cannon knew what Walsh meant. The informal network that he had cultivated during his own time in the police was often a better channel to use than the official one in obtaining information. It was much quicker and word of mouth through unofficial channels required no red tape or paperwork.

"So can I assume a Staffordshire Detective put out a call for information about Mr. Kelly through the PNC?"

"You know too much, Mr. Cannon."

"And that enquiry somehow ended up with you?"

"Indirectly. It helps to have friends up north."
"Who passed on the query, given Kelly was from the Dublin area?"
"And his only reason for being in England was to visit you."
"Hardly a visit, but I can see your logic," Cannon conceded.
"And that's the reason behind the call," Walsh admitted. "I need your help."
Cannon was confused slightly. "I thought I was a suspect just a minute ago?" he said.
"I didn't say that Mike," Walsh replied, "I said that I'm keeping my options open."
Cannon noted that this was the second time Walsh had changed how he addressed him during a conversation. He wondered if he could really trust the policeman, but he let the matter slide for now.
"And yet you need my help?" Cannon laughed.
"Yes."
Pausing to consider his reply, Cannon knew that by not having any detail about Kelly's death meant that he had little to add to what he had already told Walsh. However, he was curious to find out what had happened and why, the subject piquing his interest. "So, what is it you want me to help you with?"
"I don't know to be honest. I'm working on an assumption."
"Which is?"
"Either someone wants to get you, frame you…"
"Or?"
"That someone you know is involved in these killings."
"And that leads us where?"
"As I said, I don't know. But what I would like you to do is keep your eyes and ears open for me…..please." Walsh requested. "If you can do that, then that would be very useful."
The request was so vague that Cannon nearly said so, but he decided to bite his tongue. Stranger things had been requested of him in the past, but to keep a look out for………for what, was the most unusual. How would he know what to look for, when Walsh himself was unsure?
Reluctantly he agreed to help, silently hoping however that both cases would be solved without any significant involvement from himself. He expected the police in Stafford and Wexford to do their job. He would assist where he could, and he let Walsh know accordingly.
"That's all I can ask….for now," the Detective accepted.

Terminating the call, Cannon again sat back in his chair. He couldn't see any connection between himself, and the murders of Quinn and Kelly and he wasn't sure if Walsh was telling him everything he knew. He would keep an open mind on that one.

As he sat thinking about the request, he stared at his bandaged hand which he had ignored while he had been talking. The bite was throbbing again, he decided to take some pain tablets. As he stood to make his way out of his office towards the bathroom a thought suddenly hit him. He sat back down again, picked up his phone and tapped out a number, fulfilling his promise by taking the initiative and calling the Staffordshire police on Weston Road, some one hundred miles away.

CHAPTER 16

The white Mercedes turned into the yard, splashing through the puddles that had gathered over the preceding twenty-four hours. It was later than they had expected. Burke had indicated their arrival time with Cannon the previous evening, sending him a text message. It was nearly 11.30 and they were almost ninety minutes late. With the stables already settled after Telside and his staff had completed their rounds for the morning, mucking out, grooming and feeding the inhabitants, Cannon was more than a little annoyed at the arrogance shown by his visitors. He was busy talking on the phone with Cassie, having taken advantage of the no-show when the sound of the car arriving, roused Michelle and she peered through the lounge window. Cassie's joy at being a mother in the Spring was infectious and he was disappointed at having to end their call as the car doors opened.

"I assume that's them," she said. "Should I get the door?"

"Let them knock," Cannon replied, still slightly agitated. "I'll quickly call Rich and tell him that they've finally arrived. It'll take him a few minutes to get here anyway."

It took Burke and Sutcliffe a minute or two to extricate themselves from their car. As he stepped out of the vehicle, Sutcliffe pulled on a fawn Barathea mid-length coat. He stood silently for a few seconds and looked around at the yard, the stable buildings, Cannon's house and the garden along the one side of it, all of which were as neat as a pin. He was impressed with what he saw, mentioning his observations to Burke as they walked towards the front door. While the rain had stopped an hour or so earlier, a swift breeze had taken the edge off the forecasted temperature. It was clear to both men that summer was long dead and that autumn had rapidly followed in its wake, the grey leaden sky even suggesting an early winter.

Michelle answered the door after Burke had rapped his knuckles upon it, with a 'rat-a-tat' rhythm. She greeted both men before introducing herself and asking them inside. She noticed Sutcliffe entered first, his eyes assessing her, almost undressing her. She felt a sudden chill, noticing him scanning the contents of the entrance hall and then the lounge where she requested that they make themselves comfortable. It was obvious that Sutcliffe was a man who took in the detail of his surroundings, whether for immediate or later use she couldn't decide. The image that he portrayed on the TV was exactly how he appeared in public, somewhat aloof, certainly arrogant. Dangerous perhaps?

Burke was far more engaging and thanked her on behalf of both of them after she offered them something to drink.

"Tea, coffee, perhaps?"

"No, thank you, we don't have a lot of time," Burke replied. "We're here to get an idea from Mr. Cannon about his plans for Mr. Sutcliffe's horse after the transfer from the late Mr. Hawker. Unfortunately we need to get back to London as soon as we can so that Mr. Sutcliffe can prepare for his show tomorrow night. Do you ever watch it, Mrs. Cannon?"

Michelle noticed how formally Burke spoke to her, finding it quite unnerving.

"Occasionally," she replied to his question. "I'm a school-teacher, a Head of department actually, so I don't have a lot of time in the evenings. Also we go to bed early as Mike has to get up before dawn most days. On Friday nights I watch if I can, but it's not every time," she apologized.

Sutcliffe smiled, "Well I'm pleased to hear that you do watch whenever you are able to," he said. "It is appreciated."

Michelle quickly tried to assess if there was any sarcasm in the tone of his voice, but the comment appeared neutral, balanced. A typical politician she thought.

Wondering where Cannon was, she was about to suggest that she go and find him when he walked into the room. The three men shook hands, Cannon apologizing for not being immediately available when they had first arrived and letting them know that he was making arrangements for them to see the horse. "I was just calling Rich Telside, my Assistant," he explained. "He'll be here shortly. His wife was going to come along as well as she is a big fan of yours. Unfortunately she's a little under the weather, so Rich may be a few minutes late as he needs to make sure she's comfortable. She's in her seventies."

"How did he travel up?" Sutcliffe asked, ignoring Cannon's explanation. The man was so direct and without any attempt to be civil that it seemed to Michelle that he was acting as if he was still in Parliament, attacking the Prime Minister during question time. Cannon ignored the abruptness of the question, responding in a way that let Sutcliffe know that he wasn't a guest on his TV show, nor would he be intimidated by the man's background or history.

"He was a little bit flighty," he said, understating his concern about the horse's behaviour, before showing them his still bandaged hand. "I don't think we knew of his foibles until he was dropped off, but now that we do…"

Leaving the sentence unfinished, he stared at Sutcliffe for a second, wondering if the horse had taken on some of its owner's characteristics. He realized that he was making a quick assessment of the man, as first impressions did count as far as Cannon was concerned. He had done it many times over the years; at crimes scenes, in interview rooms, at race meetings. He knew from experience that an individual's true nature was something that many tried to hide. Politicians were good at hiding their motives, their true thoughts. Cannon had dealt with many characters of a similar ilk in the police force itself. So-called colleagues who were trying to find their way to the top. Schmoozing their way up while trying to keep others down. Eventually the combination of internal politics, a lack of resourcing and the continuous dealing with human detritus (inside and outside of the police) had ultimately taken its toll, resulting in him leaving the force for good. As he waited for a response from Sutcliffe, the silence between them palpable, uncomfortable, he realized that what he and Telside had feared was potentially true. Sutcliffe was going to be a challenging owner and just how long their relationship would last, only time would tell!

"I'm sorry to hear about the mishap," Sutcliffe said, finally. "I assume it was a once off?"

"Fortunately yes, but…"

"That's pleasing to hear," Sutcliffe replied, cutting Cannon off again. "Are we able to see him now?"

"And the rest of your facilities?" Burke added, keen to be seen as part of the team. His client was the owner, but it was he who managed all the business affairs including those related to Sutcliffe's horses.

"I'll give you the tour," Cannon answered, obligingly. "My 2-I-C Rich Telside should be getting the horse ready. If you'd just follow me, please?"

Michelle shook hands with both men again, "Just in case I don't see you before you leave," she said, as Cannon opened the door to the cold and damp waiting for them outside. With a flourish the trio of men left Michelle behind, but not before Sutcliffe gave her an unexpected peck on the check as she held the door open. Unsure whether to feel violated or not, she rubbed a handkerchief across her face as she contemplated what had just happened.

Reaching the stable block where KK had been resting in his stall, Cannon unbolted the big barn doors.

"I see you haven't padlocked the doors," Sutcliffe said, "is that not unusual, Mr. Cannon?"

"We do at night," Cannon replied, "but during the day there are any number of reasons to go in and out, so we make it easier for those that need to, by not locking the door."

"You know that Santa's Quest is the best horse I've ever had, Mr. Cannon, so I'm curious as to how you intend to keep him safe during his time here."

Despite getting annoyed and thinking that the tenure referred to by Sutcliffe could be a lot shorter than he imagined, particularly if the less than subtle insults continued, Cannon bit his tongue. As planned Telside had already been into the stable block and Cannon noticed that he had put a leading rope onto the horse's head collar and was walking with the animal towards them as they stood at the now open doors.

"The staff have named him KK, after Kris Kringle," Cannon advised, observing how placid the horse now appeared as it walked alongside Telside. "We'll probably call him that whenever we send updates about his progress."

Sutcliffe did not seem impressed, watching as Telside brought the horse outside, walking him around in a circle, allowing everyone to get a good look.

"He probably needs to put on a little bit of weight," Cannon said. "He's lost some muscle mass over the weeks while stuck in a box, but I believe we can get him almost race fit, and in a reasonable condition within about a month or so."

Burke pursed his lips and nodded as if he understood what was being said. Sutcliffe was less complementary. "How has his schooling gone so far?" he asked.

"It hasn't yet," Cannon replied. "He'll be doing some work for me from tomorrow."

"And why is that Mr. Cannon?" Sutcliffe asked, conspiratorially.

"Simple. He arrived a few days ago and he nearly took my hand off the very next day. Given his state of mind I've been keeping him quiet until tomorrow. It's obvious that we need to iron out a few behavioural faults he has, in order to get the best out of him."

Again Burke nodded, then he glanced towards Sutcliffe saying, "Makes sense to me, Mr. Cannon. I'm sure you know what you're doing."

Without taking his eyes off Sutcliffe's face, Cannon waited for a response to his statement.

"I assume you've had a look at his races?" Sutcliffe asked.

"Yes, I have."

"So you know that he has talent."

"From what I've seen, yes I do. I'm sure Warren Hawker would have told you that as well."

"Yes, he did, Mr. Cannon," Burke interrupted. "It's such a pity that we lost him just as he was beginning to get the best out of the horse."

"Very sad indeed."

"Which is why I chose you," Burke stated, "well at least one of the reasons."

"How do you mean?"

Burke looked at the ground for a second as if he was trying to find the best way of getting his point across. "It's quite simple actually. Firstly your record as a trainer of national hunt horses is very impressive. More so when one considers that you have such a small stable compared to some of the large outfits. That was one consideration."

"Anything else?"

"Yes, there is, and please excuse us for highlighting it."

"And what is that?" Cannon asked.

"The fact that you are a teetotaller."

Cannon cringed inwardly. He wasn't sure if he should respond or not to Burke's comment, fighting to contain himself as a sense of anger grew at what was being said. How deep into his background had Burke gone? What did they really know about him? He cautiously let him continue.

"When we, I, contracted with Warren I didn't know at the time that he had a drinking problem. It only came to light after he was killed and so we, I, wanted to ensure that whoever we gave Santa's Quest to, to train, was someone we could rely on to take the horse to the next level."

"I see," Cannon replied, rubbing his chin subconsciously, "and that's…?"

"And that's why we are here, Mr. Cannon. Simple really," Burke concluded, smiling.

Cannon pursed his lips together, his brow furrowed into a frown. Trying to contain his anger at what he had just heard, he was unsure if he should tell them to take the horse with them or not? He looked across to Telside who remained stony faced.

"So what are your plans for the horse then, Mr. Cannon. What can I expect?" Sutcliffe asked suddenly, breaking the short silence that had swirled around them. It was said in a way that appeared to be seeking a commitment against which to hold him liable.

Sensing a kind of trap, and parking the immediacy of Burke's previous comments, Cannon said, "If he's good enough, maybe we can get him into the National or even the Gold Cup, but let's not get ahead of ourselves, those races are pipe dreams for most owners and trainers."

"But not for you, I heard, Mr. Cannon. You've actually been there." Burke added. "It was because of your success, that I suggested we bring the horse here in the first place."

"It was hardly a success," Cannon responded. The memory of losing the great race at the very last fence due to actions of the owner, was still a sore point for Cannon whenever he was reminded of it. "And anyway time marches on, KK is a different challenge for us and until I can see for myself what he's really capable of, we'll start with low expectations and build up from there."

Appropriately scolded, Burke nodded a fake understanding, deciding not to comment any further.

Sutcliffe asked, "How many horses do you have in training here, Mr. Cannon?"

"Around twenty-four at any one time. There are others in the yard under my care as well, some are in various paddocks across the country having a good rest or recuperating from injury, and others are waiting for their owners to decide what to do with them. By way of example the owner may ultimately decide to move their horse elsewhere, sell them or even retire them. Also some of the horses here today may not run for a year or two and others may only have a single day at the races after which they are moved on to other trainers or are sold off because of where they finish in their races. The cycle is endless, which is why to get a horse to a big race means that they need to stay sound and the owners need to be committed and to be patient." He wasn't sure if the dig at Sutcliffe had gotten through, but if it did, the ex-politician did not show it.

"Do you run your horses subject to an owner's wish or do *you* decide where to run them?" Sutcliffe asked.

"I'm the one who decides where to place each horse, which race and when, but I usually do so after discussion with the owners."

"So how far do your horses travel?"

"Why do you ask?" Cannon responded, sensing there was something else behind the question.

"Because, if I can, I like to attend the race meeting when my horse is running. I always try to go whenever the Flat horses race and I'll try to do the same with Santa's Quest."

"If it's any consolation, I run them all over the country. As far north as Musselburgh, Ffos Las in Wales or even Chepstow, which I'm sure you would have been to given Warren Hawkers' stables are in Taunton."

"Do you ever go to Ireland?" Burke asked.

"Not often," Cannon replied. "But as it so happens I was there for a few days last week and I intend to take a couple of horses over there later this year to race. Why do you ask?" he repeated.

"It's for my sake," Sutcliffe said, ready to explain the reason behind the question. "In order for me to get to Ireland on a week day, see my horse race and then get back for my show in the evening would be very difficult. Even Musselburgh or Kelso in Scotland would be a challenge. So I was hoping that Santa's Quest would get to race at courses which suited my schedule."

Cannon smiled inwardly. This was what he had expected would happen. "Well as I told you earlier, we'll see how he goes and depending on what he shows me, I'll let you know my thinking and when I'd like to run him." He pointed towards the horse, which for some reason appeared to be on its best behaviour, his hooves clattering on the concrete as Telside continued to lead him around. "I'm sure you'll appreciate that I have a number of horses in the yard that have ability. So as heads up I'll be managing and training the horse as I would any other. No favourites, no special treatment, other than veterinary, and ideally no outside interference."

Telside was surprised at Cannons' candour and the approach he was taking with Sutcliffe, but he knew that his friend was right. It was necessary to establish the boundaries of their relationship up front. If a client didn't like the results of Cannon's work then they always had the right to remove their horses and take them elsewhere. Cannon was putting the principle on the table. He waited for their reply.

Sutcliffe looked up at the darkening sky, smiled, looked at his watch and then placing his hands into his coat pockets said, "We need to leave in fifteen minutes, so can you quickly show me what training and treatment facilities you have here Mr. Cannon? I'd like to see what I'm paying you for."

CHAPTER 17

It had taken longer than anticipated but at last he was back at the races. The Huntingdon course was bathed in a wintry sunlight which reflected off the lake situated in the middle of the track. Fortunately despite the grey skies that had persisted over recent weeks there had been no repeat of the flooding that had occurred in prior years. The rain that had fallen had made the track soft but not heavy.

It had been a busy few weeks since Sutcliffe's visit. With the season having started Cannon had taken his time with all the horses under his care. White Noise had improved significantly since his return has had a number of others, and the plan to take him to Punchestown was already in train. Rory's Song had only improved slightly but Cannon had brought him to the races to give the horse an opportunity to blow out some cobwebs. He was scheduled to run in the second race, a class five novice chase of nearly three miles. The distance was a little too short for the horse, but today wasn't about winning, it was to see if Cannons' intuition was right or wrong.

As he made his way from the car park to catch up with Simon Brooks, who had driven the horse box with Rory and Chocolatier on the two-hour trip from Woodstock, he contemplated what to do with Chester Sutcliffe's horse. Ever since he had taken it under his wing, he had been regularly bombarded with requests for updates. Most of them came via email but occasionally there were phone calls. The majority were from Tony Burke acting for Sutcliffe, but occasionally Sutcliffe would call himself. When he did, he would make Cannon aware of how well his flat horses were doing and would seek answers as to when Santa's Quest would start racing. The fact that Sutcliffe refused to use the stable nickname or even shorten the horse's name in conversation or in written form, indicated the arrogance of the man. On a number of occasions Cannon had almost gotten to the point of asking Sutcliffe to remove the horse but decided at the last minute to hold his tongue. The need for information by an owner was understandable, but sometimes it seemed that Sutcliffe and his proxy were taking things a little too far. The only reason Cannon kept his peace was because of his pride, an attribute within him that he didn't necessarily like, but in a prior life had paid dividends. It was his pride and his drive that had helped him solve cases. At the point of giving up, as many others would have, he had persisted. That attitude had given him the strength to walk away from the career he had loved and to start something new. His career as a trainer had been at the very bottom of the ladder and he had built up his business and his name through hard work and perseverance. Sutcliffe and Santa's Quest/KK were hard work but Cannon had a program for the horse and he was going to stick with it. If everything went well, he would take White Noise and KK over to Punchestown for the Winter Festival in a couple of weeks, which reminded him that he needed to make the necessary travel arrangements. He hoped to use CB & Sons again but he wasn't sure what the situation was currently. Since Walsh's last call he had not heard anything further, for which he was grateful. The death of Fionn Kelly had been buried in the middle of the news cycle a few days after the tragedy, a small article inside the Daily Sentinel was the only report written about the incident. As far as Cannon could tell, no one had been arrested and the case remained unsolved. The Staffordshire police had not even bothered to contact him either, despite his attempt to contact them. He assumed that whoever was leading the investigation did not see any value in talking to him. On that basis he felt that Walsh's request for help was now null and void and he couldn't see how his presence at any racecourse would provide clues as to who was behind Kelly's murder or indeed that of Sam Quinn.

He found Brooks in the allotted stables, along with one of his team, Andy Scanlon, a young rider who was just starting out in the industry. They were readying Rory's Song for his race. Chocolatier was in the stable next door, occupying stall number thirty-four. There were seventy-six runners in the racecard, using over three quarters of the course stabling facilities, ensuring plenty of movement of horses and handlers. A busy day was good for the sport and a boon for the course itself, especially being the first meeting for the season, and to have as many runners across the six races was a bonus. Big fields of runners made for a spectacle and it was that which enticed spectators to come through the turnstiles.

"How was the trip?" Cannon asked, watching as Brooks pulled on a pair of blinkers over the animal's head. The cups on either side of the head gear would ensure that the horse would only be able to see directly ahead of it rather than be able to use its extensive field of vision of almost 300 degrees plus. During schooling it was clear that the horse was consistently distracted, looking around at what was going on, not concentrating at the task at hand and therefore occasionally blundering at a fence. This would create a problem in a race, increasing the risk of a fall, putting both horse and rider at risk. Cannon had subsequently schooled the horse in blinkers and this had helped enormously. Bright red with the letters MCR, 'Mike Cannon Racing', stamped upon them, the blinkers matched the colours that the jockey, Xavier Mountjoy, would be wearing in the race. They were Cannon's own colours; White with a red diamond in the middle, both front and back, red sleeves and a white cap. They were rarely used as he only owned a couple of horses himself, Rory being the second. His other horse, Featherweight Tim, was on the long-term injury list and would not run at all this season. Even trainers of their own horses couldn't guarantee that they would ever race.

"It went okay, boss," Brooks answered, once he had finished the tricky task of connecting the Velcro straps of the blinkers under the chin of the horse. "We had a small problem near Northampton where there was a bit of traffic jam due to an accident, but overall it was uneventful."

"That's good to hear," Cannon replied. "And how does he seem to you, Simon?" he added.

Patting the horse on the shoulder, Brooks let Cannon know that Rory's Song was relaxed and ready to run.

"Not too relaxed I hope?"

"Well he stays all day, so I guess being chilled is his way of reserving energy."

"Umm," Cannon replied, wondering if his purchase and the comment about the horse being slow was coming home to bite him in the backside. "Well let's hope when Xavier gets on board, it'll wake him up a bit."

"I hope so too," Brooks said.

"What about Chocolatier, how is he doing?"

"He's still a bit edgy. He seems to have settled down for now, but if he attacks those flights like he used to, then I'm not sure what will happen."

"I'd hoped the schooling we've done with him would have calmed him down. Maybe he's just feeling a bit antsy because it's his first day at the track. All the hype and activity may be a bit upsetting for him. I think you should put the earmuffs on, that might help."

"Will do, boss. If you can just hold Rory here for a second I'll help Andy put them on."

Two minutes later Cannon was on his way to the Owners and Trainers bar in the Fairfax Saddles suite. The Goodlift Stand, which allowed panoramic views over the course, was already beginning to fill with spectators. The crowd was growing quite quickly in anticipation of the first race and the sun was just winning the battle with the passing clouds as they drifted away from the Cambridgeshire course on their way eastwards to East Anglia, Norfolk and the North Sea. The breeze held a definite chill, which would test the riders as they traversed the right-handed course. A head wind down the home straight could be quite challenging for tiring horses at the finish line. Despite the track being very flat with little undulations, because the going was declared as soft, the end of each race could be a slog. It would be interesting to see how things developed.

Cannon found who he was looking for. Bill McBride was a farmer from Newington, south of Oxford, a big supporter of point-to-point races and was the one who had brought Chocolatier to him during the middle of the previous season. It was McBride's first serious national hunt horse and he was as nervous about the forthcoming race as the horse itself had appeared to be.

"Drink?" he asked, holding up a pint pot that was already half empty, despite the fact that it was still just after midday.

"No thanks, Bill," Cannon replied, shaking his client's hand. "A bit early for me."

Rarely drinking anymore, which Burke had reminded him of, Cannon ordered some tea and a couple of sandwiches for both of them, then luckily found a spare table for them to sit at. They talked for a few minutes, Cannon doubting that McBride would need much encouragement to enjoy himself over the next few hours. He was a small man, mid-fifties, with thick grey hair under a tartan patterned cap. His bulbous nose complemented the veins on his cheeks as he swallowed the rest of his beer in one gulp. Stifling a burp, he looked at his empty glass then suddenly got up from his chair, offering Cannon another tea.

"No thanks," Cannon replied, watching as McBride made his way to the bar again. Under a dark blue jacket, a light blue shirt-tail hung out from beneath a green jumper, brown corduroy pants and black boots completed the man's wardrobe.

Smiling to himself, Cannon noticed the occasional individual cast an eye over McBride's choice of dress as he made his way back to the table.

"So how's my boy doing?"

"He's well," Cannon replied, "but he's still a work in progress, Bill. I'm just a bit concerned about his jumping ability."

"How so?"

Cannon explained his concern and expressed his hope that Chocolatier would get around the course without hurting himself. "If he jumps well, then he has a chance. There's not too much depth in the race, and he's certainly fit enough."

McBride was relieved, suggesting another drink was needed. Cannon again declined and advised him to slow down a little.

"I have a runner in the next," he continued, as the result of the first race was confirmed over the PA system. A battle of three horses over the final furlong had resulted in a tight finish which required a photo to split the first two. The remainder of the field of nine had come in at various distances behind each other. There had been no horses fall, and only one had been pulled up. However, from the commentary on the race, and the time recorded for it, it was obvious that conditions were tough out on track.

"I'll see you later," Cannon said, "in the parade ring, after the fourth race has finished."

With a smile and a wave of his hand, McBride agreed, leaving Cannon to make his way to the parade ring. Walking down the stairs to the ground floor, he passed numerous faces who were heading upwards to the first-floor lounge. Most were dressed for the weather, some however had decided to be fashionable. Young women dressed in floral prints and high heels shivered as they clambered upwards, several holding onto their partners or friends, giggling as they staggered. Behind him a stream of people were making their way towards the parade ring at the back of the stand. At such a small course it was like a sea of humanity crisscrossing each other as people moved from one place to another. Cannon was always curious about the way people behaved on racecourses. In most cases, and despite the amount of alcohol drunk, there were few incidents on course, the vast majority there to enjoy the racing, not to get into or cause trouble. As he made his way through the crowd, he didn't notice the tall, well-built man, who followed him. With a square jaw and deep dark eyes that were barely visible due to the flat cap that was pulled low down on his head, the man kept at least ten yards behind. Dressed in jeans and a black overcoat with a belt that was tied around the waist, he wandered towards the parade ring rails as Cannon made his way inside. Standing at the back of the crowd, the man watched as Cannon waited for Rory's Song and Xavier Mountjoy, to make their way into the ring. Watching every individual Cannon acknowledged or spoke to as the ring began to fill with owners, trainers and jockeys, the man used his mobile phone to film what was happening inside the ring. He apologized to those around him when he raised his phone above their heads, pretending to be a friend of one of the owners whose horse was running in the race. When he was satisfied he had what he needed, the man drifted away. He would be back to do the same for the fifth race.

David Walsh sat in his office in front of his computer, ruminating on what to do. He was frustrated. The lack of progress on the Sam Quinn murder had meant that he had been assigned other cases to investigate. "No progress means no resources," he had been told by Superintendent Kelleher. "Let the Brits do what they need to and if they find anything useful, well …." The implication was obvious. Maybe the murder of Fionn Kelly had nothing to do with Sam Quinn and they had seen a link that wasn't there. With no feedback from Cannon for weeks now, Walsh was even beginning to doubt his own instincts.

As he continued reading a report on a recent domestic violence killing, the perpetrator having breached a court order against his partner, he sighed for the third time. The problem was getting worse. Social media had exacerbated coercive control and sexual violence issues against women and the increase across the country in femicide was a national disgrace. He rubbed his eyes, the strain from reading the screen had made them itch. Ready again to continue reading, he moved the cursor on his screen just as the phone on his desk began ringing.

"DI Walsh," he answered, robotically, placing the receiver to his ear.

"Good afternoon, Daithi," Caoilinn Murphy said, her no nonsense voice reverberating forcefully down the line.

"Hello Caoilinn, what can I do *you* for?"

"Funny!" she replied. "You should be on TV."

The irony of his comment when he considered what he was reading made him realize how insensitive his response had been. He apologized for it.

"I'll forgive you," she continued, "though thousands wouldn't."

"I appreciate it," he replied, appropriately chastised. "So what's up?"

"I'm about to send you the final report of my findings from the Quinn killing, so I thought I'd give you a heads up."

"Anything useful?"

"To be honest, not much, and that's the reason for the call."

"Go on."

"Well, we did some analysis on that note that we found."

"And?"

"Nothing. The pen used seems to have been a simple rollerball. Blue ink, bought on-line or at a WH Smith, anywhere at all frankly."

"And the handwriting?"

"Someone left-handed, but that's it."

"Anything on the paper?"

"No, and that's what bothers me."

"Because?"

"Whoever was involved in this, knew exactly what they were doing. They were extremely careful not to leave any trace of anything at all. In fact when I read Murray and O'Clery's report…."

"The CSI team," Walsh interrupted. "Yes, I read it myself."

"And you'd know that they didn't find anything useful either. All they gave me to work with were those things that one would expect to find. Quinn's fingerprints on a glass, his DNA from a toothbrush, hair samples from a comb, a towel, nothing to suggest that there had been anyone else in that house."

"What about outside?"

"From what they passed on to me. I could only establish the presence of Quinn, and of that race horse trainer, the one who found the body."

"Cannon?"

"Yes, that's right."

"Doesn't that seem strange?"

"Yes, it does. But that's your problem to figure out why, not mine. My job is to analyze a scene and the contents, your job is to find out who was involved and get them convicted."

"Which is difficult if we have no clues."

"Precisely. That's what I'm saying," she said, her tone suggesting that she was talking to an idiot. "The murder of Quinn was conducted by professionals, not amateurs."

"What about the gun used?"

"A Glock 17. Used by armies and special forces across the world including the FBI, CIA."

"Fu…Bloody hell!" Walsh exclaimed, conscious of not wanting to swear, just in case she took umbrage at him, given her mood. He knew that in the UK handguns were extremely difficult to obtain legally, but in Ireland despite the law, there were hundreds of thousands of handguns legally owned. To try and track down every legal Glock owner would be a fucking nightmare, he thought.

"Finally," she continued, "we did some analysis on the bullets used. There were no identifying marks on them at all. They had been completely removed."

"Which again confirms a professional hit."

"Yes. And whatever abrasive was used to take off the markings was washed off with something like acetone or an acid wash of some type."

"Is that it?" he sighed.

"More or less," she replied. "I didn't want you to be disappointed with the report so I thought I'd let you know before you received it."

"Well, all I can say is thanks for nothing, Caoilinn," Walsh answered, diplomatically.

"It's always a pleasure, Daithi, but in this case…..Anyway, I'll email the report through to you in a few minutes."

Putting down the phone, Walsh rubbed his eyes again. The screen in front of him had gone into screen saver mode, for which he was thankful. The content was distressing enough but what he had just heard from Murphy disturbed him even more. He kept his eyes closed, thinking, dissecting the conversation, wondering what to do next.

Disturbed? Disturbed?

The word kept coming back to him. He knew that someone had definitely been inside Quinns' house but what they were looking for he had no idea. Murray and his team had spent three full days looking through every single part of the house. They had removed box after

box of individual items; notebooks, diaries, a laptop, mobile phone, bills and multiples of varying paperwork. The report that they ultimately produced provided little in the way of offering a reason as to why Quinn was murdered in the way that he was; Executed. An analysis of his emails and text messages confirmed that as a long-time widower and farmer he kept to himself most of the time. His communication was pretty basic, only using outlook for email, and having no social media presence other than a basic website that only consisted of two pages. It was there that he advertised the horses he had for sale. Even his text messages were limited to a couple of drinking buddies who he met with every Tuesday night at Whites Bar just a short drive from his house. Walsh had sent Callaghan and another Constable to interview the pair and obtain statements of what they knew of Quinn and to establish their whereabouts on the day of the murder. The information received had confirmed what Walsh had expected. No one had heard or seen anything or could even imagine any reason for the killing. Plus nobody they interviewed had any clue as to what the note found in Quinn's throat meant.
Disturbed?
Something else was disturbing him. He reached for the mouse on his desk, minimizing the report he had been reading and opening a folder labelled, 'S. Quinn - Foulksmills'. As he did so, the email from Murphy arrived, a pop-up notice appearing on the bottom right of his screen. Ignoring the message, he found what he was looking for. It was an email he had sent to the New Zealand Police in the capital, Wellington, some weeks prior. He had been trying to get in contact with Quinn's daughter having provided the police there with her details and an understanding that she lived in Dunedin. The response he had received had been unhelpful. He read it again.

Unfortunately we have been unable to locate Mrs. Julie Whitman (nee Quinn) in the Dunedin area. However, from a search of various records, including citizenship awards, voter rolls, property and income tax records plus employment information, we can confirm that Mrs. Whitman (nee Quinn) was granted a decree absolute some eleven years ago. We have also been able to establish that she left New Zealand almost nine years ago on a flight to the US leaving from Dunedin, via Christchurch arriving in Los Angeles. Since that time, she has not returned to New Zealand. We suggest that you contact the US Department of Immigration and Citizenship to further your enquiry.

Looking at the date of the email, he noticed that it was nearly five weeks ago. Since then there had been no progress in finding the woman. Even publicly releasing the detail of Quinn's death and requesting her to get in touch with the police had drawn a blank. With no other relatives alive, it had required the coroner to make the decision to allow a public health funeral to go ahead. The matter of Quinn's estate however, was still subject to probate as no will had been found, neither in the house or in electronic form on the laptop. Local solicitors had been contacted as had those in other counties, but again there was only dead ends.

The entire case was unusual. He had sensed it right from the very start, yet he couldn't work out why. Quinn's background did not show up anything odd. He had never been subject to any police inquiries since he moved into the area some twenty years prior. He had no known association with any specific group that they could find, leading Walsh to conclude that Quinn was a just a farmer, murdered for reasons as yet unknown. What still troubled him though was the note, and the execution style killing. What the hell did it mean?

"Bollocks!" he suddenly said to himself, slapping a hand on his desk, the sound of which carried to some of his team working outside his office. "Bollocks! Bollocks! Bollocks!"

Standing up to his full height, he ran a hand through what was left of his hair, his demeanour threatening as he paced his office.

The sight of his boss in full flight was intimidating, something he was beginning to get used to the more he worked with him but having stuck his head around the door of the office, PC Callaghan immediately regretted having done so. It seemed like Walsh was acting like he was on the rugby field again, ready to lead fourteen other men into battle.

"Are you alright, Sir? Can I get you anything?" Callaghan stammered, half expecting to have a box-file thrown at him.

Walsh glared at the young Constable, before taking a moment to compose himself, the red mist in his eyes slowly clearing. He realized that his frustration needed to be channelled into action and not inertia, and with such a small team, he needed them to be motivated not cowed.

"I'm sorry Callaghan," he answered. "I apologize for my outburst, and yes, yes, there is something I need?"

"Coffee?"

"No. No, thank you, but come in and sit down, take a seat. Let me tell you what I want you to do for me."

Cannon was pleased with the result and the feedback from Mountjoy as to the way Rory's Song finished off his race.

"He did well for his first race of the season," the jockey said, as he began unsaddling the horse in the enclosure. "He tired at the end which is understandable, but he did try his best."

"I guess fourth of eleven isn't too bad," Cannon said, watching the jockey unbuckle the leather straps and remove the saddlecloth from the horse, which was blowing quite hard, the chest expanding and contracting quickly as the lungs sought oxygen. Simon Brooks held the reins, standing at the head, keeping the horse still. It was his job, now that the race had been run, to take the horse for a short walk. After which he would wash him down with a hose before returning him to the stables where he would be groomed then be required to wait until after the fifth race. Once Chocolatier had run and had been through the same post-race process, they would both be loaded into the horse box for the long drive home.

Mountjoy replied to Cannons' comment, "One positive that you can take away Mike, is that he jumped superbly throughout the race. That's a testament to his schooling."

Cannon smiled as Mountjoy provided a summary of how the horse felt underneath him during the race, explaining how he went into each jump and indicating that there were no concerns that he needed to be aware of.

"Thanks," Cannon said, "Now all we need do is make up the fifteen lengths that separated him from the winner." He pointed in the direction of a group of owners that were standing together in the number one box, ready to smile as a photographer hurried them together with their horse for the obligatory photo.

"That will come in time, Mike," the jockey stated, shaking hands and thanking Cannon for the ride before turning and make his way to the weighing room in order to conclude the formalities of the race. Giving his runner a final pat on the neck, Cannon watched as Brooks led the horse away. He was happy with the couple of hundred pounds prize money they had won. "It's a start," he said to himself as began to leave the now almost empty enclosure. Most of the punters and spectators had moved on to either collect their winnings or to commiserate in the bars. Only the winning owners, still smiling and taking selfies, kept him company. He grinned at the joy winning owners always exhibited in victory, no matter what grade a horse raced in. A win was worth celebrating. About to make his way to the racecourse office to pick up the saddle cloth number for the fifth race and drop it off with Brooks, he noticed out of the corner of his eye, a tall man standing alone just under the eaves of the Paddock bar that overlooked the winners enclosure. He appeared to be watching the group of winning owners but Cannon sensed something else, the eyes were clearly focused elsewhere. As he tried to study the man's face, the stranger turned, grabbed a door handle and opened a door into the bar, disappearing into the crowd within. Unsure if he was being overly sensitive or judgemental of the individual, when he arrived at the racecourse office building Cannon took a few minutes to write up his immediate observations of Rory's race and the feedback from Mountjoy, then added a comment in relation to the man he had seen. After collecting the items he needed from the office, he made his way to the saddling boxes where Chocolatier was waiting.

An hour later he was back inside the Parade ring standing alongside Bill McBride. It was obvious that there had been a few more drinks consumed since they had last spoken. McBride's cheeks were flushed red, and the internal combustion of the alcohol he had consumed was keeping him warm. Unsteady on his feet he had greeted Cannon again as if they hadn't seen each other for weeks.

"How is my choccy going to go?" he slurred, tugging slightly on Cannon's coat, which was now completely buttoned up since the sky had turned from watery sunlight to a soft drizzle. An occasional shower had thinned out the crowds. Some had decided to leave, others had taken shelter in food courts, bars and restaurants. Only the brave few sat on the small stands surrounding the parade ring, either under umbrellas or with jackets and coats held above their heads. A cold breeze sent a chill through them as they watched the parade for the penultimate race.

"If he doesn't try to knock down the hurdles, then I think he'll run well," Cannon stated, answering McBride's question. "But it's a big field of runners so I hope he doesn't get lost out there. I know he doesn't like to get crowded in his races, so hopefully Xavier will be able to keep him on the outside."

"Does that mean I should back him?"

Cannon shook his head. "You know I never give advice about where to put your money Bill, but I notice from the betting that no one else does either."

Before he had made his way into the ring, Cannon had checked the betting for the race on the totalizator and with the bookmakers. The betting was five-to-one the field, meaning the lowest bet for a pound would provide a five-pound return for a win. Chocolatier was at fourteen-to-one with six horses ahead of him in the betting and seven others at even bigger odds.

"I'll take that as a yes," McBride said, as his horse continued being led around the ring.

It was a bad decision.

CHAPTER 18

The interview with his latest guest, the Minister for Health and Social Care, had turned ugly very quickly. Chester Sutcliffe had challenged the Minister on a number of issues and she had fired back with answers and counter arguments that he said were generalisations, full of cliches and diversions from the facts. Tempers flared and while it made great television it did little enhance the Minister's standing. At one point Charlie Scott spoke directly into Sutcliffe's earpiece from the control room, telling him to calm down a little, which annoyed Sutcliffe immensely. Only two minutes earlier Scott had been encouraging him "to go for the jugular."

Watching the show at home Burke had smiled at the way his client had been able to get under the skin of the 'Honourable' Julie Mason. She must have expected to be grilled, but her advisers had obviously misread the tea leaves with regards to the extent of Sutcliffe's questioning and the detail into which he would go. Her responses had been embarrassing and she clearly came off third best in a duel of two.

While he sipped his beer he had noticed from her body language that she was desperate for the show to end and would have walked out if she could. The optics would have looked extremely bad if she had done, and it was to her credit that she rode the wave right until the end. Unfortunately she had crashed off her board by then.

The post show production meeting would be interesting, he thought.

CHAPTER 19

They discussed the aftermath of the race meeting the following morning, standing inside the stable block while the staff worked around them. As they talked, water was being sprayed on concrete floors, fresh hay was being laid and food bags were being filled. The first lot of horses were being walked around, warmed-down after their gallops. A second lot of only four were already on the heath under the supervision of Simon Brooks. Cannon had given him instructions as to the exercise and schooling he wanted for each member of the quartet.

"How has Chocolatier pulled up today?" Cannon asked Telside, the horse having had a disastrous race at Huntingdon, trying to smash down all the hurdles, rather than jump them. Mountjoy had pulled the horse up halfway through the race for fear that the animal would hurt himself or indeed fall.

It had been the sensible thing to do but had caused some considerable alarm to Bill McBride who, in his inebriated state, had bet three hundred pounds on his horse to win.

"He seems to be okay," Telside replied. "The Vet said that he has a few cuts and grazes on the skin over the hind cannon bone, both near and off sides that will need treating. Also there is a bit of heat in the forelegs that will need some anti-inflammatories and cold packs but thank God for the leg wraps. The horse would have damaged himself irreparably if he had raced without them."

"I know, and unfortunately it was my fault."

Telside placed a hand on Cannons' shoulder. "No it wasn't, Mike," he said sympathetically. "It was just one of those things. The horse has been well schooled and he was fit enough, but for some reason he decided that he didn't want to race."

"Well that's as maybe, but that doesn't change the fact that we have a very unhappy owner."

"Because of the result or because of the money?" Telside asked, cynically.

"Probably both I suspect."

"Well, Bill can be a little up and down at times."

"I guess so, but it's understandable. I'll just have to give him the bad news that Chocolatier is not going to run again for a while. I suppose the Vet is recommending rest?"

"Yes, at least three weeks or until the inflammation goes down."

"Then we'll need to take our time with him after that. Maybe put him out to pasture for a month or so? Slowly work him back up to fitness and get him to settle better when he races. I thought he'd worked it out but I was obviously wrong. Perhaps we'll need to take young Crichton off when the horse is back and put someone else on who can school him a bit better?"

"That's probably wise, Mike."

"Thanks, though to be honest I'm not sure we'll still have him after the way McBride carried on when we were in the unsaddling enclosure."

"Did he say he was going to take the horse away?"

"No, but as I mentioned, he was very upset."

Telside nodded, considering Cannons' comment as he watched his young team continue conducting their morning routine. Buckets were being filled with water and piles of manure were bagged to be placed in large piles, at least eight bags high. Eventually they would be moved to a spot near the front gate of the yard and sold to gardeners and other passers-by for use as compost or fertilizer. "I guess we'll have to wait and see what happens then?" he said, finally, "It won't be the first time we've lost a horse to an owner's whim."

"That true, Rich, but I'm concerned how badly wrong I was. As you know we've been trying to get each horse ready for their first start of the season with the hope that they will improve as they get fitter and deeper into the winter. Obviously all the plans for Chocolatier are now out of the window. What if I've got it wrong with the others?"

"Do I hear self-doubt creeping in, Mike? That's not like you."

"I know, and that's what is concerning me," Cannon opined. "You and I have worked together for years now, Rich, and we've progressively gotten better horses to train, which is great. But, with better horses come higher expectations, and the question is whether we can live up to those."

"I'd hardly say that Chocolatier meets that threshold, Mike. He's an average horse, as are a few others in the stable. Neither the owners nor you can expect miracles from that quality of animal."

"You're right Rich, but there are some…"

"Like Sutcliffe, you mean? Is that what this is about?"
"Strangely, yes."
"In what way?"
Just as Cannon was about to continue, the second lot arrived back from the heath. Simon Brooks jumped off White Noise, keeping hold of the reins as he landed on the ground.
"How did it go?" Cannon called out, amidst the noise of horses hooves on the concrete and the chatter of the other riders who were readying themselves for the usual debrief.
"They all schooled well, boss. We did exactly as you asked and I can see improvement across the board. I think Santa's Quest is ready, as is White Noise."
"Do you agree, Lester?" Telside called out. "Is Santa's Quest ready to race?"
"Yes, Mr. Telside, I think he is. He's enjoying his work and he has a bit of class about him," Lester Crouch replied, confidently. "He's really come on in the past few weeks and he settles nicely in the run now. Plus, he's not tried to bite anyone for weeks and he hardly kicks out any more."
Cannon instinctively looked at his hand which had now healed completely, the memory of the bite still haunting him slightly. In order to address the problem Sutcliffe's horse had posed, he had introduced a regime of deprogramming and then rebuilding the animal's understanding that it was a follower of instructions and not the leader of the herd as it would normally want to be. It had taken a while but by all indications the methodology had worked. Cannon was pleased at the outcome.
"And the others?" he asked.
"Thunder Three has only been back for a couple of weeks after being kicked and Winter Garden still has some work to do after that feed problem. Maybe another few weeks before either will be ready to go," Brooks answered.
Cannon thanked him and the other riders after receiving their detailed feedback. He would write up the notes he made when back at his desk. Turning to Telside he said, "I've just had an idea, Rich. After second feed, come down to the office and you can let me know what you think."
"Sure, no problem Mike," Telside replied, "I'll see you shortly."

CHAPTER 20

"I need a break," Sutcliffe said. "All these editorials in the government-aligned press are ridiculous. It's as if they don't want anyone to question what the Government is doing, and I'm fed up with the comments made in response, especially from Chris."

They were debriefing after the interview with Julie Mason. Scott, Sutcliffe and the rest of the production team were seated in a meeting room where they routinely discussed the previous show and well as made the necessary arrangements for the next one. Background research on the guest or topic, media postings, promotions and the advertising approach were all part of the process.

Sutcliffe's comment had come out of the blue, particularly his less than subtle dig at Chris Blakman.

"What do you mean?" Carol Boyd asked, "the publicity we are getting is fantastic. It's great for the show," she continued, ignoring his comments about their CEO.

"That's as maybe," Sutcliffe replied, "but not for me."

"What do you mean, Chester?" Charlie Scott, questioned. "The show is going from strength to strength and you're the star of it. It's exactly what we all hoped would happen when we started this thing."

Sutcliffe sighed. He had heard this song many times before. People were riding on his coattails and their own careers were growing because of it.

"Look," he said, his voice calm but pointed, "I know you may not always see things the way I do, but there is another side to being successful."

"Which is?" Boyd asked.

"Stress, anxiety, the expectation to always be in control. Not to mention how my relationships with my former colleagues in Parliament suffer."

"But you're out of there now, Chester," Scott said. "What does it matter what they think."

"It matters because I need those people. To get the facts rather than the spin. You know how it works Charlie, I scratch a back here and a back there and in turn they scratch mine. How do you think I managed to nail down Mason last night?"

"So what do you want to do?" Scott asked, fearing that Sutcliffe was about to resign and terminate his contract.

"As I said, I need a break. Three weeks."

The Producer stared at the ceiling. It was as if he could see Chris Blakman in his office four floors above. For a second he imagined what response he would get from the CEO if Sutcliffe was off the air.

"Okay," he replied, "but before we say anything, either upstairs or via a broadcast, we need to talk about the why and from what date. The public will expect it at the very least. So let's you and I talk about it in private and I'll advise everyone here what we are doing after I've met with Chris."

"Agreed," Sutcliffe replied.

"Good, so if you and I can stay here," Scott said, "the rest of you can get on with some work." He pointed towards the door, swinging his arm gently to encourage the others to leave. "Go on, get a move on," he added, silencing the complaints of Carol Boyd in particular, who wanted to stay behind to hear about any decisions being made. Her protest was unsuccessful, and she followed the rest of the team into the waiting hallway, taking her time as she slunk away. Her face told the tale and what she was thinking about her banishment.

Once they were alone, Scott said, "What's this all about, Chester? It's not like you to spring this on us."

"Did your friends find the girl yet? The one in the audience? You said you were going to follow it up."

"No, not yet. Why?"

Taking a few seconds, Sutcliffe reached into the inside pocket of his jacket and pulled out a folded piece of paper. When opened it was approximately the size of an A5 sheet.

"This was pushed through my letterbox this morning. It was lying on the hall floor and was exactly as you see it. No envelope, just the folded paper. I don't even know how it got there. Whoever did it must have got past the concierge desk somehow."

"Would does it say?"

"I'll read it to you, but before I do, this must stay between us. No one else to know about it, right? Not Chris, not Tony, nobody."

Receiving a nod of agreement, confirmed with a mouthed "yes" Sutcliffe continued, his voice tinged with fear as he read the words that had caused him so much distress overnight.

"You may think you are clever, Sutcliffe, but you're nothing but scum! Taking pleasure in using that silver tongue of yours to criticize, attack and demean people is disgraceful, sick. Stooping so low as to use an individual's failures or weakness against them is just unforgiveable. Perhaps you should look at your own failings first? Some of those you feast on may forgive you in time, but I don't!"

Stopping to look into his Producer's face, he noticed how Scott seemed to be in total shock. Turning back to the paper he continued reading.

"The public seem to taken by what you do, your popularity growing each week, but do they really know who you are? No, I don't think they do. You are a bastard! It's odd how people have fallen for your act but on the other hand it's not unexpected, given the lies you tell. Well, it's time to end this charade. Do you remember Mark Chapman?"

"That's the guy who killed John Lennon in New York, wasn't it?" Scott interjected.
"Yes, that's right."
"Is there anything else?" Scott asked, curiously.
"Yes. It ends with a simple highlighted sentence."
"Go on."
"I'll be watching your every move, watching and waiting! Until…."
When Sutcliffe had finished reading, he put the note on the table. Scott stared at it as if the paper was cursed. "Sounds like a nut-job to me," he said eventually, trying to convince himself that the letter was a hoax. "Surely you can't take it seriously?"
"I think it's from the woman," Sutcliffe replied.
"Why do you say that?"
"It's just a feeling. After I saw her in the auditorium I just knew something would happen. Something like this."
"But what happened was years ago, why would she want to threaten you now?"
"I don't know. Maybe she wants money?"
"Perhaps we should take this to the police?" Scott suggested.
"No!" Sutcliffe exclaimed, "No, we need to sort this out ourselves."
"But how are we going to do that? We don't even know who it's from," Scott replied, pointing at the note.

"Which is why I need the break. I need the time off to think. Hopefully being off screen it will draw out whoever is behind this."
"And then what?"
"I don't know," Sutcliffe replied, "we'll have to cross that bridge when we get to it."

CHAPTER 21

"What did he say?" Cannon asked.

"He said he would let me know, but he thinks it should be okay," Telside replied.

Sitting in the warmth of Cannons' lounge, they were watching the racing from Wetherby on TV.

"Poor Buggers," Telside added, pointing out the rain that was lashing down at the course that lies between Leeds and York. It was the club's first meeting of the year and despite it being a mid-week event, it had been well supported until the heavens opened, halfway through the card of six races. He supped his tea, bony hands wrapped around the mug. Between each race Cannon and he had discussed what they intended to do with their horses over the next few months, planning different campaigns for each of them all the way through to the new year. This included taking White Noise and Santa's Quest/KK to Punchestown, the latter subject to Sutcliffe being in agreement.

"When will he get back to you?" Cannon quizzed, knowing that he needed an answer quickly so that arrangements could be made to transport the horses back across the Irish sea.

"He reckons it should be by tomorrow."

"Good," Cannon replied, indicating the TV, "This meeting reminds me that I need to get the nominations in with Weatherbys soon. The racing at Punchestown is in just over a week on the Saturday, so I've got until next Tuesday midday to get the entries in. If I can get it done by tomorrow, I'll give CB & Sons a call to see if they are happy to take the job."

"Talking about that, what happened to the poor boy that was killed. Has anything come of it?"

"To be honest Rich, I don't know. I haven't heard anything other than that first call from DI Walsh. Since then, nothing at all."

"So, I guess it's just been deemed to be a random attack?"

"Possibly, but I'm not sure. I think Walsh is not as convinced as perhaps the Staffordshire police are, and anyway that's their problem not ours."

"Very well," Telside replied. Looking at the TV screen again, he noticed that the start of the next race had been a straggly affair. The starter had let the field go when a number of runners were not facing forwards, some were still circling while others were jig jogging away from the starting tapes. Turning up the sound, they heard the commentator suggest that the bad weather and low visibility may have been the cause for the ragged beginning of the race but doubted that it would be called a false start.

"Not sure I would agree with that," Telside said, seeking Cannons' opinion.

"I agree with you Rich. Sometimes though these things all come down to the final result. If a couple of horses that were disadvantaged at the start end up winning or running in the first three, then its deemed to be just one of those things. And, as you know, sometimes it's the jockeys who get the blame, not the officials, when things like this happen."

Telside nodded. He had watched more races than he could care to remember over the years. Some had been mired in controversy and others forgotten even when the issues were the same. Whether it was jockeyship (good or bad), trainers doping their animals to win or lose or even simple betting plunges, there would always be something to keep the conspiratorialists busy about the integrity of racing. As they watched the race conclude with an outsider winning at 25 to 1, and the favourite finishing a long way back in sixth, Cannon said, "It will be interesting to read the Stewards report on this one. The two horses that were impacted the most at the start were the first and third favourites."

"I agree, Mike, though it won't change the result. I guess if you were on the favourite though you'd be a bit annoyed."

"Bloody right, Rich, I'm glad it's not our problem. We have enough of our own to worry about as it is, and the season has only just started. So, let's hope White Noise does us proud at Punchestown, it will be a great result if he can do something on his first outing."

"And if we can get Santa's Quest a start, then we may have a couple of stars in the stable."

"Yes, well that's up to Sutcliffe giving us permission as we said earlier, plus the horse running up to expectations. If he races like Chocolatier did then we could be in trouble. I don't think Sutcliffe suffers fools lightly and it's only due to his manager that we have the horse in the first place."

"I suppose so, but it does also mean that you have a reasonable standing in the game and that's why he choose you to take over from Hawker."

Cannon nodded. Prior to the visit from Sutcliffe and Burke, he had been a little unsure as to how they would view him and his operation, but after he had shown them around the facilities and discussed his philosophy about racing he believed that both men had warmed to him. Sutcliffe had been particularly aggressive initially, seeking answers to numerous questions. Burke on the other hand had stayed quiet for the majority of time, asking a few questions which seemed to be couched in a way that justified his decision to recommend Cannon to take over from Hawker.

A few minutes later after picking up the remote, Cannon turned off the TV because as they were talking a short ticker had appeared, scrolling along the bottom of the screen advising that the rest of the meeting had been abandoned after the running of the previous race. It seemed that the riders had decided that the course had become dangerous due to large pools of water beginning to flood the back straight, particularly on the landing side of two of the fences. There was also a problem at one end of the racetrack due to the deteriorating ground. A number of divots and holes had been uncovered which could result in a horse breaking a leg if it stood in one of them, potentially putting it and the life of its jockey along with those horse and riders following, in jeopardy.

"I guess it was a sensible decision," Telside said.

"After the stuff up of the start of that last race I think it will give the officials a bit of a way out, but yes I agree Rich, with the weather up there getting worse, it was definitely the right thing to do."

CHAPTER 22

"I've got an idea," Burke said, his excited voice from sixteen miles away causing his client to lower the volume on his mobile which had been lying on a small side table next to him. The man's exuberance sprang from the instrument like a Punch and Judy snake jumping from its box. "How about a few days away to help get your mind of things?" he added.

"What do you suggest?" Sutcliffe replied, as he sat in his armchair sipping a small brandy and watched the last of the sun's rays filter through the balconied windows of his sixth floor South Kensington apartment.

In the background a CD was playing on low volume, Leonard Cohen, very droll but it suited his mood. He had been thinking about the letter he had shared with Scott and all that it implied.

"Well, I had a call from Cannons' stables and they want to take your horse to Ireland to race on Saturday week. I think it might be good for you to take the opportunity to have a few days over there and watch the horse run. What do you think?"

"I was hoping for something a bit more exotic," Sutcliffe replied, non-committally. "Somewhere with a bit more sun."

"I suppose I could arrange that if you wanted, Chester, but you did say that you were impressed with what Cannon was doing, so I just thought that given they had called me to get your permission it would be nice to combine the races with a bit of a holiday. It's not too cold yet and irrespective, a few days away in a cosy cottage or hotel can only do you good, keep your mind off things."

Taking a sip from his brandy snifter, Sutcliffe considered the pros and cons of what was being suggested. Firstly, he had sought a short time away from the spotlight which had been given. Secondly, he needed to work out how to address the threat from the letter without alerting any one as to what it meant to him, especially Burke. Thirdly he wanted to see his horse race again. It had been a long time since the horse had run. Ever since Hawker had been killed, he had worried that Santa's Quest would languish and never develop or reach its full potential unless it was managed properly. His confidence in Cannon had been underwhelming to say the least until he and Burke had visited the Woodstock stables, however he later conceded to Burke that his agent had chosen well.

He quickly came to a conclusion. "Okay, let's do it." he said. "I'll go over next Wednesday and come back on Sunday."

"Excellent, I'll let Telside know that they can go ahead. In the meantime, between now and then, what are you going to do?"

"I've got something I need to look into," Sutcliffe replied, thinking about the letter that was inside the jacket pocket where he had hidden it again after sharing the contents with Scott. Between now and the trip across the water he would use the time to do his own investigation. Normally he would be busy chasing his staff to find out as much as they could about his guests that were to appear on his show. Now however it was up to him and him alone to discover who was the anonymous sender of the note. He needed to build a trap. Burke interrupted his thinking just as the Leonard Cohen CD came to an end. The sudden silence alerted Sutcliffe to Burke's question, which was whether he was happy for him to make the necessary arrangements regarding flights times, airport car pickups, hotels type and car hires?

"Yes, that will be great," he replied, only half hearing what had been said to him.

"Okay well I'll get started on it and hopefully I'll have everything sorted for you by tomorrow morning."

"That would be perfect," Sutcliffe said. "I assume you'll send me the itinerary once you've booked and confirmed everything."

"Yes, and I believe from Telside that they'll arrange an owners ticket for you to collect on site, on the day of the races."

"Do you know where they are racing?"

"Yes, at Punchestown. Have you ever been there?"

"No, have you?"

Burke scoffed. "You know that I rarely go to any race meeting as I don't have the time, plus I'm not an owner. I just do the magic of getting you the very best of what you need, because that's my job."

"And a damn fine job you do, Tony."

Taking the platitudes in his stride, Burke let Sutcliffe know that he would email him with all the travel details once he had them, but to expect the correspondence by no later than by mid-afternoon the following day.

Having finished the conversation, the two men ended the call simultaneously. Sutcliffe walked over to his CD player replacing Leonard Cohen and putting on a CD by Lou Reed, having not got into streaming music over the internet, preferring instead the tactile nature of the inserts from a CD jewel case. He also enjoyed the feel of vinyl whenever he decided to play something from his aging record collection. People could call him a dinosaur if they wanted to, but it was a choice that he was happy to defend. As has sat back again, letting the music of Reed surround him, he started to hatch a plan to find the woman behind the note that had surreptitiously dropped into his life, bringing back memories that he had hoped would never resurface.

CHAPTER 23

Having been given the green light to run, Cannon had completed the formalities, nominating the two horses in the scheduled races. As it was the first day of the Winter Festival of racing and he wanted to see where White Noise was in terms of getting back to his best, he had placed him in the first qualifying race in the 'full circle series'. This was a series of ten hurdle races for horses with ratings up to 130, which started and ended at Punchestown after four months of qualifying. Five of the ten races were to be held at Irish tracks and five others across England, Scotland and Wales. If things went according to plan and White Noise did well in his first run back and then improved over the season, Cannon felt that the horse may need to forego the grand finale and concentrate on the main game which was Cheltenham and the Champion Hurdle. Time would tell. Santa's Quest was nominated for the main chase on the same day and unfortunately had to miss out on the biggest one of the weekend due to that race, the Grade 1 Chase being held on the Sunday. When they had sought approval from Sutcliffe to race, Cannon had no intention of running in the Grade 1 anyway as he still had not been able to fully assess the horse's ability, despite its success to date. Also, with limitations on Sutcliffe's time Cannon had decided on the handicap steeplechase as it was to be held immediately after White Noise's race.

The next job had been to confirm with the transport company that they were willing to move White Noise and Santa's Quest across to Punchestown, particularly after what had happened to Fionn Kelly.

It had been a difficult conversation and Cannon had not been able to add much about what had happened, other than offering the lady who took the bookings his sympathies and best wishes, which she graciously accepted. It was a relief to him when she confirmed that CB & Sons would be happy to take the job of transporting his horses to Ireland and return them to his stables in Woodstock, despite what had happened to Kelly. She indicated to him that the management had no reason to believe that there was any connection between what had happened previously and Cannon's racing operation. After confirming the dates when he needed the horses to be collected and delivered to the Irish racecourse, along with the dates for the return trip, he thanked her again.

His final task in connection with the trip back across the Irish sea had been to contact Jim Cochrane and let him know that White Noise had been thriving and was to race in Ireland for his first race back after injury.

"That's great news," Cochrane said, "I'm looking forward to seeing him run."

"Do you think you'll be able to attend in person? To be on track?"

"I wouldn't miss it for the world. After all, a star patient of mine is on the comeback trail, and I'd be very disappointed if I couldn't see him in his first run post treatment."

Cannon smiled. He was pleased to hear Cochrane's enthusiasm. Because their last time together had been so rushed and under such difficult circumstances both men hoped that this time, events would go much easier, much smoother. Cannon did not raise the issue of Fionn Kelly's death but did mention that CB & Sons would be responsible for transporting the horses from his stables to the racecourse and back again. Surprisingly Cochrane did know about Kelly's murder. "It was on the news over here the day after it happened," he said. "Such a tragedy. The poor boy."

"I agree," Cannon replied, unsure what else to say.

"Do the police have any clues as to who was behind it?" Cochrane asked.

"I'm not sure. Someone was supposed to contact me from the local police where the body was found, but I've never heard anything from them, so I honestly don't know."

"Well let's hope they find that people behind it. It's a bloody disgrace, that's what it is."

With nothing else to add, Cannon wished Cochrane a good afternoon after confirming where they would meet next. The plan was to catch up again on the Friday evening before the Punchestown meeting.

"I'll be staying at the Westgrove Hotel in Clane," Cannon had said. "Maybe we can catch up for a drink the night before? Say seven o'clock?"

"Sounds good to me," Cochrane had replied, "sounds good to me."

CHAPTER 24

Liam Kennedy made the phone call that he wished he hadn't needed to.

"We've looked everywhere," he said, "it's not there."

"Are you sure?" he was asked.

"Yes, absolutely. My man has been in several times and found nothing."

"Do you think the police may have discovered it?"

"I doubt it if we couldn't. I suspect it wasn't kept in the house at all. Maybe he destroyed it?"

"No, he wouldn't have done that. It was his insurance policy."

"Well," Kennedy said, "if it was, it certainly didn't help him in the end did it?"

"No, I guess not, though perhaps your man was a little exuberant."

"I don't think he had much of a choice to be honest. If he hadn't done what he did, then the whole thing could have come undone?"

"I'm sure you are right, but remember I'm paying you to find it, so keep looking."

"We will, though I still think there is a link between Quinn and Cannon."

"In what way?"

"That's something I am still trying to work out."

"Don't you think the police may have come to the same conclusion?"

"It's possible, though I'm not sure. Either way, as long as they are unable to link you, nor I, with what happened, then we're okay."

There was a short grunt down the line, a sort of uncomfortable acquiescence to Kennedy's statement, followed by a long silence.

When the phone line finally went dead, Kennedy knew that the conversation was over. The objective however was still the same. Until there was no more money on offer, he and his team would continue to do the job the best way they could. He needed to call Campbell and get everyone together so that they could decide on their next move.

CHAPTER 25

"Have you been able to find out anything else?" Sutcliffe asked.

He was standing at the window of his apartment, his hand holding his mobile flat against his ear, staring down at the traffic. The red tail-lights of the vehicles moving down the street looked like dragon's eyes, while the occasional puff of exhaust fumes as a car lurched away from where it had stopped, ready to move again, seemed to indicate that the dragon had awakened.

"No, I haven't," Scott replied, "it seems like she's playing a game."

"Why? For what purpose?"

"Maybe for maximum leverage. Perhaps she wants to scare us to get the most out of the situation?"

Sutcliffe wasn't convinced. It had been a long time ago and he couldn't see why she was being so secretive if she was looking for some form of recompence. "Why now?" he asked rhetorically, "why after all these years?"

"Who knows, perhaps she's run out of money and she has seen how well your career is going so she wants to take advantage of it?"

"That's possible I suppose, but if that's the case why the threat? Why would she want to kill me? If she wanted money why not just say that?"

Scott hadn't wanted to use the phrase but given the circumstances he felt that he had no choice. It was the only explanation. "Revenge?" he asked.

"But we both know that it was an accident."

"I agree which is why I suggested we go to the police," Scott retorted. "If her intent is not to blackmail you and me, but she is seeking payback for what happened then let's get the cops to find her before this thing gets any more serious than it already is."

Sutcliffe contemplated what his friend was saying. He knew that Scott was right, but the whole mess didn't sit well with him. Having come off the air for a break, the last thing he wanted was more drama to follow him back onto it. No, they needed to find her before she decided to break cover and bring the whole sorry episode out into the public domain. He was surprised that she hadn't posted anything on social media already but surmised that by keeping her cards close to her chest, she was holding out for something more.

"How long do you think we have?" he asked.

"I have no idea," Scott answered, "that would depend on your movements. If she can't get to you, then it will buy us more time to find her."

"But she knows where I live."

"That's true. Which is why you need to stay put until we do."

"But I can't stay here forever. I'm off to Ireland next week for a few days to see my horse run and also to have that break and recharge the batteries."

"Are you going alone? If so, that's not very clever. You'll definitely need someone to keep an eye out for you, to watch your back."

"Tony is coming with me. It was his idea to move the horse to another stable after Warren Hawker was killed and the trainer wants to run the horse in Ireland for his first start with them. It seemed like a good idea to go and watch, so we gave them the go ahead."

"Perhaps," Scott answered, reluctantly. "I'll see if I can find out anything else about her. In the interim, until you are ready to leave on your trip, I suggest you don't step a foot outside of your place."

"But that's ridiculous," Sutcliffe protested.

"Look Chester, you are no longer in the government. You don't have protection anymore like you used to, so that leaves you exposed. Remember her message, the reference to Chapman and the fact that she would be watching your every move."

"Of course I remember! I read that bloody thing so many times before I even showed it to you."

"Which means that you know that you need to be careful."

"Both of us do."

"I suppose so, but it's you she's after," Scott repeated, "you're the one with the high-profile position and it looks like she wants to bring you down with this….this issue."

"I get it, Scott, but it's not just me, I think she wants to get both of us. As I said earlier something has triggered this, but I'm buggered if I know what."

"A bad choice of words," Scott stated, referring to Sutcliffe's trigger comment, reminding him again how John Lennon met his end at the hands of Mark Chapman outside his Manhattan apartment in 1980.

Sutcliffe turned away from the window just as a strong breeze suddenly whipped up sending dust and light stone, that pigeons and other birds had dropped onto the balcony, to whack against the glass. In the heat of the moment, the sound made him flinch, imagining that the rat-a-tat were shots being fired at him.

"Fuck," he shouted, as he dived behind a couch with the phone still pressed to his ear. His initial reaction to the pinging of stones against glass was to use the furniture as a shield against the gunman that he thought had begun peppering bullets at him through the closed window.

Scott heard the sudden commotion and Sutcliffe's expletive, shouting back down the line to hear if his friend was still alive.

"Yes, I'm fine," Sutcliffe answered, mildly out of breath. "I just overreacted a little."

"Shit, you scared me for a second," Scott said, "I can tell that this has clearly gotten to you hasn't it?"

"What did you expect?" Sutcliffe replied, angrily, as he slowly moved around the couch and sat down, his hands shaking slightly, his phone visibly tapping the side of his head despite his attempt to keep himself calm.

"I don't know," Scott replied. "but we need to get this thing resolved before you are due back on the air."

"That's not very long,"

"I know but we don't want something like this to hang over your career like the sword of Damocles."

Being aware of the inference and the story of Dionysius, a tyrannical Sicilian King who trusted no one other than his daughters to shave him and thought that he was under threat of constant assassination, Sutcliffe suggested that he wasn't that paranoid. However, he did agree with Scott that the sooner there was an answer as to why their shared history had suddenly come to light and what it meant to them both, the happier he would be.

"Me too," Scott replied, letting Sutcliffe know that he would leverage all his contacts to try and find the woman. "And remember, stay inside, let the concierge know that you are not expecting visitors and tell them that no one should be allowed up to your floor without your express permission."

After giving Scott's suggestion a few seconds consideration, Sutcliffe agreed, making the call to the front desk via the building's intercom system as soon as they had finished their conversation. As an extra precaution, he also used the building's app on his mobile phone to confirm the same arrangements. Feeling a little more secure, he called Tony Burke to make sure that every detail of their trip to Ireland had been formalized. Receiving the necessary assurances, he poured himself a brandy, closed all the curtains in his lounge and sat down on a single armchair staring at, but not seeing, the TV news. His mind was racing. Something was not quite right, but he had no idea what was bothering him.

CHAPTER 26

The feedback from the US did not fill him with any confidence at all. DI Walsh read the short note that O'Callaghan had presented to him. Allowing the young Constable to sit on the only other chair in the office, on the opposite side of the desk, Walsh flicked the page with the forefinger of his right hand as if to brush away its content. He had read the note for the third time but the message stayed the same with each reading, the words mocking him.

We regret to inform you that we have been unable to trace Mrs. Julie Whitman based on the information you have provided to date. Our search was limited due to the fact that our computer system was upgraded eight years ago and records prior to that time were archived. Given that the dates referred to in your request for information were prior to that period, it would require additional resources and an extended amount of time to research your request. As you have indicated that no crime appears to have been committed by Mrs. Whitman in the US nor indeed in the Republic of Ireland we feel it would be an unnecessary use of our limited resource to continue with your inquiry. Should you decide that it is absolutely essential for us to review our decision based on any additional information pertinent to your case then please provide us with such detail that we can review appropriately.

"It seems like she just dropped off the planet," Walsh said to himself, almost forgetting that O'Callaghan was sitting quietly, watching, waiting for an instruction.

"Perhaps she's dead, Sir?" the young Constable offered, placidly. "Or she doesn't want to be found."

"Anything's possible I suppose," Walsh sighed, reluctantly but quickly coming to a similar conclusion. He had been involved in so many investigations over the years, many of which had reached dead ends. Perhaps this was another?

He placed the note on top of the file which contained the information they had gathered so far in connection with Sam Quinn's murder. There were numerous documents inside, all of which he had reviewed several times. Statements from the likes of Cannon and others, forensic reports, background checks, financial details, even tax assessments, none of which indicated why a relatively small-time farmer and horse trader would be murdered the way that he was.

He picked up the note again staring at it as if it would speak to him. It didn't. Knowing that he had other cases to tackle, he made a decision for his small team to stand down. He would have to shelve the Quinn murder investigation until some additional evidence was forthcoming. After dismissing O'Callaghan from his office, he sent an email to Kelleher regarding his decision and justifying why he had made it. Couching his words carefully, he let his boss know that the investigation was on hold rather than stopped completely. He wanted to make sure that the case was not seen as cold, but that it wasn't very warm either.

He waited for the likely backlash.

CHAPTER 27

CB & Sons Transport had fulfilled their promise.

Despite the tragedy of Fionn Kelly's murder and subsequent funeral, the business had continued operations as if nothing had happened. A two-day shutdown to appropriately grieve for their loss was deemed the only course of action that they could take. Business was business. Insurance claims, equipment replacement, staff support services and a police investigation were problems to be solved or endured, but Management could only do what it could, deciding to leave anything outside of its direct control to others.

The horses had arrived at the course stables on schedule a few days prior to their races. They were in excellent condition despite the ferry across to Ireland having been a relatively bumpy ride. This was primarily due to a small low-pressure system crossing the southern-most part of the country before turning north and dumping plenty of rain across Wales and the North-West of England.

After looking over each animal to ensure that they were ready to race the next day, Cannon smiled. It was obvious that they had enjoyed their work earlier that morning. White Noise and Santa's Quest had galloped alongside each other in the middle of the course, each showing that they had not lost their desire for racing, both indicating by their responses to their riders' urgings that they were keen to get back into the action.

It was now Seven am and Cannon had been up since five. He had already sent a text to Michelle rather than call and wake her, to let her know that he had arrived safely after his previous afternoon's flight had been delayed again (not unusually) and that he would call her later in the day. His two grooms/exercise riders had arrived separately, Lester Crouch had been brought over to look after Santa's Quest, his usual groom and rider, while Jamie Strickland, a long-term member of Cannons' staff, and ex jockey, had been given the responsibility of looking after White Noise. Normally this would have been Simon Brooks, Crouch's best friend, but Cannon and Telside had deemed it necessary for Brooks to stay back in Stonesfield to help Telside maintain the regimen and the routine required by the other horses in the stables. It was a philosophy that almost every racehorse trainer in the world abided by. Horses loved routine, especially when in training. The regularity of exercise, feeding, schooling, treatment and down time were essential to get the best out of a racehorse and Cannon could see that the two animals in front of him had profited from that process. With coats now washed and brushed, they both looked extremely healthy, but he knew that both were not totally fit as yet. He didn't need them to be one hundred percent on day one, because he wanted them to improve during the season. Trying to judge when either had reached full fitness was difficult however, especially with chasers and hurdlers. Time on the track and racing against opposition was the only way of knowing at what stage they were at. Cannon was hopeful that his current assessment was correct and that both would run good races the following day. The contrast between White Noise, a grey, and that of Santa's Quest, a large bay, as they stood a few metres apart in their respective stalls, was obvious. The former was built for speed, the latter had power and endurance, a genuine chaser. With luck White Noise would make Joel Seeton a happy man by the time the race meeting was over. Cannon was hopeful that Chester Sutcliffe would feel the same, at least he wanted that to be the case, but that was out of his hands now. He had done everything he could as a trainer, it was now up to the horse to fulfill his owner's expectations.

He had enjoyed the past couple of days, staying on his own. The accommodation that Burke had arranged for him at the Barberstown Castle Hotel some twelve miles from the racecourse had been a perfect choice. The charm of the fourteenth century castle once owned by Eric Clapton had left its mark on Sutcliffe slowly easing away the stress that he had been struggling with ever since the letter had arrived.

The conversation with Scott and the subsequent need for caution had eventually subsided, particularly once he was out of his apartment and he had arrived in Ireland. For two days he had lost himself in magazines, sleep and anonymity. Never leaving the hotel he had eaten alone at the same table for breakfast, lunch and dinner, only being recognized by a couple when he entered the lift to go to his room the previous evening. It had been a little unsettling initially, but he sensed that his concern was in response to being alone for a few days. Being isolated for a period did have advantages but it was not something he believed he would ever fully get used to.

As he and Burke sat in the Barton Room finishing their coffee after dinner, he thanked his agent for making the arrangements.

"I'm glad you liked it?" Burke responded. "I thought the surroundings would help you unwind, and the level of discretion here is amazing isn't it?"

Sutcliffe agreed, letting Burke know that even if he was recognized, the staff and management had not let on, having kept as discreet a distance as possible, treating him just like any other guest.

"Which is why I chose the place," Burke answered. "I've been here before, and I've always enjoyed it."

"You did well, Tony, a great choice," Sutcliffe said, taking a sip of his coffee, before asking, "by the way have you spoken with Cannon at all during the day?"

"No, should I have?"

Sutcliffe shrugged his shoulders. "I was just wondering how the horse is doing," he said. "I'm looking forward to tomorrow as it's been a long time since I've been able to attend a race meeting in person and it would be excellent if this trip ended with a win."

"I agree, but given there are so many local trainers with chances in the race, I'd suggest a good showing would be enough, wouldn't it? I know I suggested Cannon take on Santa's Quest, but it's a big ask to get the horse to win his first race with a new trainer."

"Warren Hawker did it," Sutcliffe replied.

"Yes, but that was at his local track at Taunton. It's a far cry from Somerset to here," Burke advised. "Anyway, let's see what happens, we may be surprised. Cannon is a good trainer, and he knows his stuff."

"I'm not doubting that," Sutcliffe replied. "His philosophy and attention to detail was evident when we went to see his place, but that is different to getting a positive result on the track. Remember this is my best horse, flat or jumps, and while Cannon has a good reputation, so do I, and that is something that is very difficult to maintain ongoing."

"You're point Chester?" Burke queried, unsure what his client was getting at, but noticing the subtle change of tone in Sutcliffe's voice and the lengthy sigh which accompanied it..

Taking a last sip of his coffee and placing the now empty cup on the matching saucer on the table, Sutcliffe dabbed his mouth with a napkin, taking much longer than Burke would have expected to answer his question. Uncertain whether to reveal what had been on his mind a few days ago, and which had been forgotten until this very moment, he put his hands together as if in prayer, placing his elbows on the table and leant forward.

Whispering, he said, "I think someone is trying to blackmail me."

"What?" Burke replied, incredulously. "Who? Why?"

"It's a long story, happened years ago."

"What did?"

"An accident."

"An accident?" Burke repeated. "What kind of accident? Where?"

"In Croatia, on the Dalmatian coast fifty kilometres south of Split. A place called Brela."

"What happened?"

"A girl drowned, fell off a cliff. We…."

"We? Whose we?"

Staring into space for a few seconds, his thoughts jumbled, Sutcliffe castigated himself for raising the subject. Having been in control of his emotions for the past few days, the notion of going back on TV, going public again in less than forty-eight hours, and trying to act normal when there was a threat over his head seemed ludicrous. He was faced with a dilemma, and it was eating him up inside. His style, his on-air reputation had been built on getting to the truth behind issues that others wanted covered up. It was this characteristic, this dogged determination that had brought him many admirers in political circles, ultimately leading him to the position he held before suddenly resigning from his party. His leaving without explanation rankled with many of his former colleagues and left many of them to speculate as to why. So far he had been able to keep his reasons safe.

Apart from Scott, no one else knew what had happened to the girl or her sister, and he had hoped to keep it that way. Over time he had wrongly rationalized that what had happened was just a stupid teenage prank, something that could have happened to anyone. He had effectively blanked the incident from his memory until it had suddenly and inexplicably caught up with him. With no news from Scott, he wasn't sure what to do, which was why he had opened up to Burke. Realising what he had done, he knew that he had no choice but to swear Burke to secrecy before revealing any more detail.

"I know I've never mentioned this before," he said, "but as my agent, I think it would be better that you hear this from me. After all, if this comes out it may be the end of my career or even my life."

CHAPTER 28

The morning had broken with a mottled red sky and a fresh breeze that the locals took in their stride. By midday the Punchestown course was alive with more than eight thousand punters who were there to enjoy the first day of the Winter festival, irrespective of the weather.

While rain threatened, and clouds gathered in the South-West, the late autumn sun continued its struggle to provide a little bit of warmth to those brave enough to be without coats.

Cannon was glad that he had prepared. A beige scarf around his neck augmented his black knee length woollen coat and his beige chino trousers. Standing next to the running rail as the horses for the first race jogged along the track to the start, he stared at the turf. The breeze overnight had dried the track slightly, but it still seemed loose enough, and if any rain arrived during the afternoon the potential of downgrading the track from good to soft or even heavy was likely. Knowing the capabilities of his two runners he didn't mind if White Noise ran on heavier ground, but Santa's Quest preferred it slightly firmer. It was unfortunate that their respective races meant that White Noise would race before Sutcliffe's horse.

As he turned away from the rail in order to make his way to the stables a hand landed on his shoulder, surprising him to the extent that he let out a "fuck me!" He instantly apologized to a group of young women who were standing a few yards away, plastic wine glasses in their hands, oblivious to his outcry.

"Sorry, Mike," Jim Cochrane said, apologetically, "I didn't mean to surprise you like that, but I've been looking all over for you."

The two men shook hands as Cochrane continued with his explanation as to why he had been unable to have the drink they had arranged to have the previous evening.

"I had one of my patients go down with colic, spasmodic in fact. It happened about an hour before I planned to leave so I had no choice. It was either meet you or potentially lose the horse."

"I understand," Cannon said. He had been disappointed to receive a text message the previous evening, a few minutes before their agreed catch-up at seven, explaining that Cochrane would need to take a rain-check, but he also knew that when one is involved with racehorses anything could happen at any time. It was an occupational hazard even when one tried to keep to a routine. "How is she doing?" he asked, as they made their way through the crowd that had begun to consolidate on and near the stands, getting themselves ready to watch the first race.

"I think she'll pull through, but it was touch and go. Fortunately, it doesn't look like she'll need surgery. My Vet spent most of the night with her, but he only arrived around nine. By that time, I'd done all I could to keep her comfortable."

"Sounds like you did a good job."

"I just did what I had too," Cochrane answered, self-effacingly. With his reputation for managing horses back to health he was always concerned when the potential to lose one arose. Not being someone to seek credit for his successes but conscious of his failures, he took Cannons' comment in his stride.

"Anyway," he asked, "how is White Noise today?"

"Come and see for yourself," Cannon replied. "We may as well go and take a look now rather than just before his race. It will give you a bit more time to say hello."

Cochrane laughed, following in Cannon's footsteps just as the on-course commentator announced that the first race had started. A roar went up from the crowd as the nine horse field of novice chasers began the day.

"Maybe we should quickly find a spot to watch?" Cannon said, turning his head to check if Cochrane had heard him above the noise of the crowd.

Cochrane nodded, confirming that he was happy to do so. "Under the Hunt stand?" he shouted, as the runners raced past the winning post for the first time. A loud cheer rose up from the crowd only to be followed by a groan as one the runners fell at the very next fence.

As they moved through the throng, just about to enter through the glass doors of the stand, Cannon looked up to the numerous groups of people leaning on the rail which overlooked the forecourt where he and the majority of spectators were standing.

Out of the corner of his eye, he saw a face that he thought he recognized. A man seemed to be staring at him, watching, following his progress until he and Cochrane disappeared inside the building. It had only been only a fleeting glance, but Cannon was sure he had seen the face before. As he pushed and prodded his way towards a

TV set that was attached to a large metal stanchion, part of the building's superstructure, the crowd around them grew more boisterous as the remaining horses in the race entered the final bend, ready for a last push to the finish line. Joining with hundreds of punters, Cannon and Cochrane watched as three runners reached the final fence together. With all three clearing the obstacle, the race to the line became one of resilience and heart. As the whips cracked, gaps appeared between the combatants and with a loud cheer from the crowd the favourite eventually pulled away from the others to win by two lengths. As the chatter died down around them, Cochrane suggested that after he had seen White Noise, that he and Cannon have the drink that they had planned to have the night before.

"You've still got ninety minutes before your race," Cochrane indicated.

"True, but I still need to catch up with my other owner. His horse is in the race after White Noise."

"That being Chester Sutcliffe?"

"Yes, how did you know that?"

"Simple," Cochran smiled. "I looked in the racecard and saw your runner and who the owner was."

"So, you know who he is?"

"Yes, I remember him being a big-wig in the government at one stage and then out of the blue, he quit politics without any explanation. I read about it at the time."

"Do you ever watch his show on TV?"

"No, I don't have time for that," Cochrane answered. "I have enough to keep me busy with than watch bullshit on TV."

"I'm not a fan either," Cannon said, as they began making their way to the stables, "though on occasion my wife does watch."

"How is he then? As an owner?"

"I've had very little to do with him to be honest. He came to the stables once and today will be the first run of his horse since I took it on."

"Why did he choose you?"

"I don't think he did. His agent recommended me. His previous trainer was killed in an accident."

"Does the horse have a chance?" Cochrane asked, changing the subject.

Cannon took his time in answering. He was always uncomfortable to

tip any of his runners no matter how confident he felt about them.
"If he runs as expected then he will be competitive."
"That's very diplomatic, Mike. I'll take that as a maybe."
"Your just as good with people as you are with horses," Cannon laughed.
"Better with the former," Cochrane replied, "much better."
They were almost at the stables; their passes had allowed them to walk through the necessary checks at various gates without any problems.
"Talking of people," Cannon remarked, "I have to meet up with Sutcliffe and his agent between the second and third race. Would it be okay if you stay with White Noise and my team after our drink? Ideally right the way through until I can get back to the stables and get him ready for his race in the fourth?"
"Sure. Any reason?"
"No," Cannon lied, thinking back to the face in the crowd. "It's just that with having to entertain Sutcliffe I won't have much time to get down there and make sure I'm happy with everything. If you're there I'll have one less thing to worry about. With two races back-to-back it just means that I'll be running around a little."
"Okay."
Arriving at the stalls where White Noise and Santa's Quest were waiting for their races, Cochrane smiled. His grin contrasting with the gloom that had suddenly enveloped the immediate vicinity. Low clouds had blown in, eradicating what was left of the sunlight. Tiny spots of rain appeared on the ground. The weather seemed to be turning, but so far it was indecisive.
"Hello big fella!" Cochrane shouted, reaching over the stable door and giving White Noise a pat on the neck and rubbing the horse's face. "How are you doing? It's been a while."
Jamie Strickland standing inside the stall with the horse held the animal's bridle as Cannon introduced him to Cochrane.
"So, what do you think?" Cannon asked, pointing at the now repaired leg that Cochrane had worked on.
"He's looking really well, really well," Cochrane answered, continuing with a note of caution. "Let's hope his leg holds up. It would be a bloody shame if it doesn't. He's a lovely horse."
"I'm sure he'll be fine," Strickland said. "He's done everything asked of him at home and he's a gutsy type."

Death Claims its Prize

"He has to be if we want to get him to Cheltenham," Cannon added, "and I'm sure you're right Jamie, but you never know until they start to race again and today's the day that journey begins."

"I might have a quiet twenty on him, each way," Cochrane uttered suddenly. "From what I can see of him, I'm quietly confident."

Cannon rolled his eyes. Having been non-committal earlier he didn't want to get into whether White Noise was expected to win or not. He just wanted the horse to race well and return safely. The same applied to Santa's Quest who was standing quietly in the next stall and if the horse was getting excited about being back on a racecourse, he wasn't showing it. The horse seemed calm and relaxed, all the problems of the past, the kicking out, the biting, had been resolved through sheer hard work by every member of Cannons' team.

"As I mentioned earlier, Jim, I'm not a betting man but we have big hopes for White Noise. As you're aware we are trying to get him into the Champion Hurdle next March. He does need to win today or at least get close. If he doesn't then we may need to rethink our plans. Not sure if that helps you decide whether to back him or not?"

"Listen, Mike, I did my research before I got here. I would have told you last night if I hadn't had to cancel. All I wanted was to see the horse. I know from working with him on his rehab that he has a heart as big as a lion. As I look at him now, all I can say is that he's ready."

"He has a few locals to contend with don't you think?"

"Yes, but I have confidence in you."

"Hopefully not misplaced."

"Misplaced enough to go fifty each way," Cochrane replied with a huge grin, before slapping the horse on the neck again. Turning back to Cannon, he asked, "So what about that drink then?"

Leaving the two horses in the care of Crouch and Strickland, Cannon and Cochrane made their way towards the Owners and Trainers bar. When they arrived they struggled to make their way through the throng of people who were watching the on-course TV's. The field was getting ready for the second race, and it took some hefty pushing and shoving before they were able to order their drinks. Cochrane was surprised to see Cannon choosing tea over anything stronger, as he had ordered himself a Jamesons.

Standing at a waist high table with a young couple who appeared to be on a first date, they watched the second race being run and won.

The couple had screamed at the vision until a horse they were following was pulled up. Cannon noticed their owners badges, surprised that such young people would be in a position to own a racehorse given the state of the economy and the ongoing cost of living debate. As he considered the numerous owners he had served over the years, trying to remember their backgrounds, he suddenly recalled the face of the man he believed had been watching him. He wasn't sure if he had imagined it or not, but he knew from experience not to ignore the feeling. He was sure that had seen the same man, a look-alike or at least their doppelganger somewhere before, and it unnerved him. While he mulled the issue over in his mind he failed to notice Cochrane touching him on the arm, trying to get his attention.

"Oh, sorry, Jim," he said, trying to appear calm, but still thinking about why he was feeling uncomfortable. "I was miles away just then."

"That's okay. I just thought I'd make my way back to the horses while you go and find your owners as agreed. I'll see you back down there later. After the next?"

With another handshake the two men went their separate ways. The bar had now completely emptied. Owners, members and trainers had gone off to see their runners and get the jockey debrief. Those whose horses had finished racing went off to celebrate if they had been successful, and if not would commiserate by going home. The ebb and flow of the crowd followed a similar path. A gathering at the parade ring, a collective movement to the running rails or the stands, then post-race a crush in the food halls, restaurants and bars. Cannon knew where to find Sutcliffe; in The Watch House, with its stunning view over the finishing straight and the rolling green hills that gave way to the Wicklow mountains beyond.

The issue had not been raised again and Sutcliffe was feeling more relaxed now that he had another confidant. While he had been reluctant to open up initially, the fact that his agent had a vested interest in him made it easier to do. Whether Burke would ever question the morality of the issue or walk away from him in response was never considered. Sutcliffe knew Burke better than that. Both agreed that what had happened could not be undone and as such the matter needed to stay buried, each committing to make sure that it did.

Burke offered to use his contacts who could potentially and discretely find out more about the woman behind the threat, promising to use all his resources to discover who she was and what she really wanted.

"Wanting you dead is one thing," he had said, after Sutcliffe had relayed the back story, "but actually going through with it, is another."

"Maybe," Sutcliffe had concurred, "but if I end up in prison then I may just as well be dead."

Burke had nodded an understanding. The two men had then closed the subject when Burke suggested that Sutcliffe, "leave the problem with me."

He had been happy to do so but was unsure if the words of comfort from Burke would help resolve matters as easily as they sounded.

Sutcliffe had heard those very same words before.

"It's nice to see you again, Mr. Cannon," Sutcliffe said, rising from his chair, "I hope you have some good news for me?"

Cannon smiled and took the chair opposite Burke who had remained seated. Around them a sophisticated noise and quiet chatter filled the restaurant as waiters moved silently between multiple tables, delivering drinks and various food courses to those well off enough to be able to enjoy the best of what the course had to offer. Cannon guessed that as with all such venues, by the time the last race began most tables would be empty and the once calm atmosphere would have been transformed into a boisterous party. He knew from experience that money was never a factor that controlled decorum and looking around him he could sense that the festival was soon to kick into gear.

"Well, I can say that the horse is well, if that's what you mean?" Cannon answered, pointing at the glass window of the restaurant and indicating the track. "If the rain comes however then it may not work in his favour as there are a couple of runners in his race that are mud larks. If it's too wet then that's not good for him as he seems to prefer some give in the ground but not too much, so let's see."

Picking up a bottle of sparkling wine, Sutcliffe offered to fill an empty flute that stood in front of Cannon. "No thanks," Cannon replied, "but I appreciate the gesture."

Sutcliffe smiled then topped up his own glass before doing the same for Burke.

"Do you know that this is the first time I will have actually seen this horse run, in the flesh I mean?" Sutcliffe announced. "When he was with Warren I was only able to watch his races on TV."

Cannon thought the comment ironic given Sutcliffe's fame was as a consequence of his TV show. Gesturing again to the track, he said, "Well you couldn't have chosen a better place to come. It's a lovely venue, the people at the festival are here to enjoy themselves and the racing as you may have seen from the first couple is excellent."

"I'll drink to that," Burke said, taking a swig from his glass.

"Have you been here before, Mr. Burke?"

"Tony, please," Burke replied, "and yes, I have been to Ireland before, several times in fact, but never to the races."

"Have you ever been to a meeting in England?"

"No. Until Chester became my client I had no interest in racing at all."

"And now?"

"To be honest, not really," Burke admitted. "But as my client here does, I'll do whatever he wants me to do to help him enjoy it."

Cannon nodded, noticing the brief glance that each man made towards the other. He concluded that with them being so close, matters of a personal nature that they would only share with each other would naturally develop over time. Whatever they were, were none of his business, as those between he and Rich were likewise nobody else's.

"And for that, I am extremely grateful to you," Cannon continued, though not completely sure if he was. Depending on how Santa's Quest performed in the next hour or so, he may well see a different side to Sutcliffe from that which he had seen so far.

"Your welcome," Burke replied, toasting Cannon by tilting his glass towards him then taking another sip of his drink.

Cannon noted that Sutcliffe had gone quiet for a few minutes. It was obvious that there was something on his mind.

"Are you still going back to London tomorrow, Mr. Sutcliffe?" Cannon asked.

"Yes, I'm back on TV screens on Monday night, and I have a

Death Claims its Prize

production meeting on Monday morning."

"I suppose all good things come to an end?"

He wasn't sure if he had hit a nerve somehow, but Cannon observed the slightest flinch in Sutcliffe's body in response to the comment. The reaction was both unexpected and intriguing.

"You are right Mr. Cannon, and unfortunately my holiday, my break, is over."

"Did you enjoy your time being off the air?"

"Yes, I did. The past few weeks have been really enjoyable. I've had chance to relax, read, catch up on sleep and drive around the country on my own, totally inconspicuously, before finally ending up here. What a way to finish don't you think?"

Before Cannon answered, he wasn't sure, based on his previous visit, that driving around the countryside was considered relaxing, but he decided that perhaps he had been unlucky and that not everyone on the roads drove as manically as he had experienced. "I couldn't think of a better finale," he suggested, "though I need to temper that until after your horse runs." He pointed to the window again. Beneath their position, beyond the glass, punters and spectators had started to gather as the runners for the third race came onto the track. In the distance, beyond the hills, the sun had disappeared and the sky had turned black. The earlier warmth of the day was slowly fading, however the buzz from the crowd and the party atmosphere still seemed all pervasive as cheers and whoops continued to rent the air.

Indicating the crowd and the mass of heads facing towards the track, Burke said, "It looks like it doesn't matter to them if their choice doesn't win, they're here to have a good time."

"That's right, Mr. Burke," Cannon answered. "That's exactly what racing is all about. The prize at the end of any race is not the trophy or the money, it's the enjoyment of being involved with the sport. Which is exactly what you see outside."

Cannon noted that Sutcliffe responded with a slight grimace. It was if he had taken his comments and viewed them cynically, interpreting them as if Cannon was trying to lower Sutcliffe's expectations about the forthcoming race. While that was not the intention, racing was a great leveller and no matter how much one wished for a positive result, horses were not robots. Sometimes expectations were dashed, other times results surprised even the most optimistic of trainer and owner.

Death Claims its Prize

Recalling what he had said to Telside about Sutcliffe being a potentially difficult owner, what Cannon observed in response to his comment suggested that the gloom on the horizon could be a portent for what could happen after the fifth race. Santa's Quest's race.

A waiter quietly appeared at the table from behind Cannon's right shoulder, his lilting voice questioning if they wished to order food, as the kitchen was taking last orders. When Sutcliffe reached for one of two menus that stood between a small posy of cyclamens and a set of salt and pepper pots in the middle of the table, Cannon used the opportunity to excuse himself. Despite the protestations of Burke asking him to join them, he leveraged the need to get White Noise ready for his race and agreed to meet them again in the parade ring before the fifth.

"Should we put some money on your horse in the fourth?" Sutcliffe asked, as Cannon rose from his seat.

"I'll leave that to you, Mr. Sutcliffe."

"And how about mine, in the fifth?"

Once again Cannon was prudent in his reply. "There are a number of great local trainers here whose horses have raced on this track before and the locals don't like to lose," he continued, looking at the waiter who appeared to be taking in everything being said. "My view is that your horse is an extremely good one. If his attitude is right then I think he'll do well." Pointing outside towards the betting ring where the bookmaker's boards seemed to float in the sea of humanity made up of onlookers, the true professional punters and the curious of mind, he added, "I see Santa's Quest is at eleven-to-one at this stage. That's good odds as far as I'm concerned...."

He let the comment hang in the air for a few seconds then smiled and turned away. Making his way out of the restaurant he heard the announcement that the third race had begun.

He had lost Cannon for a while, being unable to follow him into the areas restricted to trainers or those which required a specific ticket or booking, such as the restaurants. This had been expected, so Liam Kennedy was not too concerned. He would find his prey again during the course of the next two races, when Cannon would be more accessible, more visible.

So far it appeared as if everything was going as planned. Campbell had confirmed with him that he had found a perfect spot and would remain where he was until the job was done. Thereafter, they would meet back at a small bed and breakfast that they had already checked into the previous day. It was a few miles north west of Carlow in the Killeshin Hills, about fifty-five kilometres away from the racecourse. It had been chosen as they suspected that once the Garda got involved they would assume that those they were looking for would have made their escape across the border or via Dublin. Kennedy had always been known as a good scenario planner and a mission like this one required attention to detail in order to be successful. While he had been challenged with the idea, along with the cost, he had left his boss under no illusion as to what they needed to do.

"Either we do this properly, or not at all," he had said.

The expected argument in response to his plan was over before it had really started, the push-back never came and so he had sweetened the deal slightly by offering to "search the house again, if we get time."

Standing against a railing at the back of the main stand, Kennedy dragged on his vaping machine sending billows of mint scented smoke into the air. Above him, a low dark veil had gathered and he watched as the clouds from his e-cigarette appeared to mix with the ever-increasing swirling mass of nimbostratus that brought with it an increasing threat of rain. As he waited, keeping a keen eye out for his quarry, a straggle of punters rolled around the side of the building. One individual appeared to be worse for wear, clearly having overdone their celebrations. The five-person group were on their way out of the course in advance of the coming rain, or more likely due to making poor choices which resulted in them improving the lot of the bookmakers as well as the tote. Moving slightly deeper into the shadow caused by the stand's structure that towered above him, he could hear the voice of the on-course commentator reach a high pitch crescendo as the third race reached its climax. The roar of the crowd appeared to make the building shake as the winner crossed the line five lengths ahead of its nearest rival. As the commentator expanded on the result, calling out the name, number and jockey of the first three finishers, Kennedy noticed Cannon suddenly appear from beyond the other end of the stand. He was heading in the direction of the stable block, his back quickly disappearing between the food vans and numerous mobile TV production vehicles. A mass of cables littered the ground and snaked along the floor before vanishing into buildings and up into satellite dishes which sat on the roofs of the vans. Satisfied that he hadn't been seen, Kennedy took a final puff of his vape then slowly made his way to the parade ring. He was in no hurry. As he sauntered along he pulled his coat a little tighter and his hat slightly lower in an attempt to hide his face. Texting Campbell as he walked, he asked a question of whether or not the possibility of heavy rain would impact their plans.

He received a reply almost instantly; "No."

CHAPTER 29

The parade ring was abuzz with activity. Seventeen runners for the main hurdle race of the day. Joel Seeton had been in touch, wishing Cannon all the best and letting him know that he would be watching the race on TV. It was a lovely gesture as far as Cannon was concerned, especially considering that White Noise was Seetons' horse.

As Cannon watched Jamie Strickland lead White Noise around the ring, he could hear the announcements being made regarding the coming race. With so many runners, six of which were those of Billy Milligan, the local trainer who had already been successful in two of the three races so far, it was no surprise that White Noise was quoted at around sixteen-to-one. Cannon was of the view that the price was way too generous but it was what it was. He assumed that the vast majority of bookmakers were more scared of Milligan winning the race with the favourite, than giving White Noise any real consideration. If Cochrane did put twenty pounds on him at that price, then should the horse win, there would be one very happy horseman in their midst. Not only would there be a financial gain, but the professional pride of getting the horse back racing after his injury would be immense.

"What's your verdict?" a voice suddenly questioned, taking Cannon by surprise.

Standing next to him, wearing Joel Seeton's racing colours of blue and grey halves, yellow sleeves and a red cap, was Niall Sullivan, a local jockey who Cannon had been able to convince to take the ride.

"Under the circumstances I couldn't be happier."

"That's good," Sullivan answered, his strong accent and shrill falsetto voice made him difficult to understand in the noisy environment. With spectators standing four deep around the perimeter of the ring, owners and trainers congregating together deep in discussion and the oncourse announcements continuing, Cannon was obliged to bend down in order to talk with the jockey.

"As far as instructions and tactics for the race I can only give you two," he said.

Sullivan gave a half smile. Both men knew that instructions were nothing more than mere words when it came to a race. With so many runners it would be almost impossible to implement them anyway. There were multiple, almost infinite number of scenarios that could play out, so Cannon wanted to keep things simple.

"What do you suggest?" Sullivan answered, adjusting his cap slightly.

"Simple really. I think a couple of Milligan's runners will lead and they'll try to run the legs off the field in order for his other runners to take over later. So, just stay on the outside if you can and follow the favourite until you are ready to go for home."

"And the second thing?"

"Don't fall or fall off," he joked.

Sullivan grinned in return. Falling off a horse was an occupational hazard no matter how hard one tried to stay on it.

"I'll give it my best," Sullivan replied, just as the bell rang indicating that the jockeys should mount their rides and make their way out onto the course.

They waited until Strickland led the horse around to where they were standing, then Cannon gave Sullivan a leg up into the saddle. "Good luck, come back safe," he said, as White Noise jig jogged away, while the jockey adjusted the stirrups to his required riding length.

Cannon looked up at the sky, the clouds had darkened. He wondered if the rain would arrive during the race or a little bit later, just in time to spoil Sutcliffe's party. Turning around to join the rest of the owners and trainers now readying to leave the parade ring and make their way to the stand, bars and other viewing spots, he scanned the crowd for the face that he knew he had seen previously. He had tried to recall where he had seen the individual before, but he wasn't one hundred percent sure. What he was convinced off however was that he was being followed. For what reason and by whom he still had no idea.

CHAPTER 30

The field circled around waiting to be called into line. Seventeen horses faced twelve hurdles over the two-mile, two-furlong journey. The wind had strengthened but the rain had stayed away for now. The silks of the jockeys ruffled and crinkled as they sat expectantly, nervously waiting for the off. Some held the reins tightly to prevent their mounts turning away from the line that they had been called into. Others had a loose grip in order to keep their horses relaxed.

Ahead of them a man with a white flag appeared in the centre of the track, a request for the field to advance towards the starting tape.

Amidst the jostling to get a good spot Niall Sullivan took a conservative position, not wanting to get caught in the scrum when the tapes were eventually raised.

Cannon stared through his binoculars across to the hurdle course which lay on the inside of the chase track. From his spot on the stand in the owner and trainer's area, which was directly in line with the winning post, he scanned the field as they gathered together in readiness to race.

Beside him was Jim Cochrane, nervously picking at a small piece of skin on his lip.

White Noise was positioned exactly where Cannon wanted him to be as the race began. The big grey, one of three in the race, was easy to spot and was in ninth place as the field clattered into the first hurdle.

A gasp went up from the crowd as a runner came down at the obstacle. The large TV screen near the finish line showed the horse's jockey hitting the ground then being lost from view as the rest of the field continued on their way, some stepping on the figure lying on the ground. The field continued to race on leaving behind a prostrate human and a mount struggling to get back to its feet. Within seconds however the fallen horse's instinct kicked in, and sans-rider, and without apparent discomfort, it was back on its feet and began to chase the pack ahead.

White Noise remained in the same position for the next half mile, jumping well and showing no signs of being affected by injury. Cannon followed the horse's progress as the field started to string out, like a ribbon, along the undulating track. By the ninth flight the favourite had taken the lead. Four of the field had been pulled up and

Death Claims its Prize

there had been two fallers. Of the remaining eleven runners, seven continued with their chase to catch the run-away favourite, the others seemed to be somewhere between pulling-up or finishing the race in their own time.

At the tenth, favourite backers began to scream as the horse began to tire. A poor jump caused it to lose its momentum and the six-length lead was soon eroded to two lengths as three runners came out of the pack to challenge for the win.

At the penultimate flight, the favourite slammed against it, barely able to lift its legs and it was quickly passed by the three chasers, one of which was White Noise.

Letting his binoculars drop, their weight being carried by the strap around his neck, Cannon watched as White Noise took on the last two remaining Mulligan horses. The group of three surged together towards the final jump. Cochrane began to shout, his twenty-pound bet less important to him than seeing his handiwork being rewarded. Just before the final hurdle, White Noise sat a length behind the other two runners and was gaining ground.

"Be careful," Cannon said to himself under his breath, as he watched Sullivan gather the horse together underneath him, readying for the final two-hundred-and-fifty-yard sprint to the line. Once over the obstacle it would come down to the horse's heart and the desire to win.

The two runners ahead of Sullivan reached the fence just milliseconds before he and White Noise did. Unfortunately by taking one another on for the lead, they had begun to affect each other's concentration and by doing so one of the horses, Seven-Up, hit the hurdle hard, coming down with a crash on the green turf. The falling jockey curled up into a ball, and began rolling clear, fearful that the rest of the field would be over the jump within a few seconds. If he was still lying on the ground he could easily be stood on or at worse kicked. The second horse, Silver Dancer, vying for the win, also jumped the fence poorly almost unseating the jockey. Somehow, due to nothing more than supreme horsemanship, his rider managed to remain in the saddle, but their momentum was lost. White Noise cleared the hurdle then cruised past Silver Dancer as if he was standing still. A roar rose from the crowd, joined by Cochrane and Cannon, when Sullivan took the lead. White Noise's jumping had been superb and it seemed from a distance that there was no sign of his previous injury.

On the run in to the winning post, a mere two hundred yards, White Noise began to wobble slightly. The amount of time being away from the track was beginning to tell. With the horse's fitness still not at its peak, the first run back was beginning to have an effect. Silver Dancer, who had now recovered from its blunder, began to close the gap between them, rapidly.

With the crowd urging, screaming, and the whips cracking, both jockeys pushed their mounts to the limits. As White Noise reached for the finish line, Silver Dancer made a bold lunge towards it, but was unable to reel him in, crossing the line half a length adrift.

Cannon was ecstatic as was Cochrane.

"Well done, Mike," Cochrane said, "what a great race and a great training performance by you and your team."

"It's not just me, Jim, you know that. It's a multi-faceted effort across all disciplines, including everyone at your place."

"Nonetheless a great result for you."

"Yes, I'm happy," Cannon said, "though it was a bit too tight for my liking, I was hoping to win by a bigger distance to be honest."

"I can understand that," Cochrane answered, "but a win is a win, so go and bring him into the enclosure. You can get a debrief from Sullivan about the race and what he thinks of the horse itself.

Cannon agreed, "Why don't you come with me? We couldn't have done it without you."

Cochrane smiled. "It's what I do, Mike, it's my job. No, you go ahead, I'll see you back at the stables," he suggested. "I'm happy to help young Crouch get your other runner ready for the next."

"Thanks," Cannon replied. "It'll be a bit of a rush as I have to meet Sutcliffe and Burke in the parade ring before the race, so anything you can help me with would be appreciated."

"I'll give him a call after the next," Cannon mentioned to Cochrane, as he watched Jamie Strickland walk White Noise away to be washed and scrubbed clean. He was referring to Joel Seeton after receiving feedback from White Noises' jockey. It had been extremely positive. Sullivan had told him that the horse had "travelled within himself and had done just enough to win."

It was what Cannon had hoped to hear as the inference was that improvement was likely in subsequent outings. After the prize giving Cannon had managed to give the horse a quick examination and there appeared to be no signs of distress or injury and recovery from the race seemed normal. He would have a clearer picture of how much the race had taken out of the horse in the morning once the lactic acid built up in the animal's body had dissipated and the muscles had cooled

Having rushed back to the stables where he checked the saddle, nose roll and other equipment that had been put on Sutcliffe's horse, he thanked Cochrane for helping Lester Crouch get everything ready. Cochrane had been able to "run his hands" over Santa's Quest and had commented on how well the horse looked.

"He's well put together," Cochrane said, as Crouch finished putting the final touches on the horse's coat. "He has a huge behind, so there is lots of power there."

"Agreed," Cannon replied. "He's certainly an impressive chaser. We'll know today though if he has the heart for it."

"Hasn't he won most of his races to date?"

"Yes, but today's a little different from where he has raced before. The undulating course and stronger local opposition over this trip may make it a bit more difficult for him."

"I suppose so, and I'm sure Billy Milligan won't like to be beaten again today."

Cannon laughed. He had been congratulated by the Irish trainer for White Noise's win a short time earlier, but Cannon could see that Milligan was not happy. "I'm sure you are right, Jim," he said, "but we all know that racing is a great leveller and you can't win all the time."

"I don't know about that. Billy likes to win every time."

"And if he doesn't?"

"Well I suppose things can get a little feisty."

"Meaning?"

Cochrane remained silent for a second. It was as if he had a secret to share but was afraid of the consequences if he did. "Shall we say that he's been known to use tactics in a race that are not particularly fair."

"Such as?"

"As he did in the last race, where he had six runners."

"But nothing happened."

"I'd suggest that's because he expected either Silver Dancer or Seven-Up to win the race after they got to the front."
"And?"
"There was no need for them to impede White Noise."
"Impede? Surely if they tried that then the stewards would intervene?"
Cochrane raised his eyes heavenwards. The look on his face said it all. "You know as well as I do that there are vested interests in racing. Sometimes fairness is defeated by pragmatism."
Cannon nodded. His expression pained. He moved to one side and whispered to Crouch to take the horse to the parade ring. "I'll see you there in a couple of minutes."
"No problem," the groom replied.
"And if Sutcliffe is in the ring already, tell him I'll be there as soon as I can."
The big bay had been on his best behaviour until now, but as the horse was led away, Cannon could sense that he was starting to put his game face on. It was as if the horse knew what was to come and had begun dancing on his toes as if ready for action.
Turning to face Cochrane, Cannon said, "Milligan has three of the seven runners in the next, do you think he'll try anything?"
"I don't know. Whatever they do it's very difficult to prove, but I just wanted you to be aware of the possibility."
Cannon squinted his eyes as if he was thinking of something. "Let's go," he said, finally. "My owners await."
Cochrane nodded, "Lead the way," he replied, conscious that Cannon was mulling over what they had discussed.

The rain had arrived and the deep blue umbrella battled the elements unsuccessfully. By the time Cannon had walked into the parade ring, his coat had darkened as the fabric struggled to repel the downpour.
Standing next to Sutcliffe, Tony Burke held the shaft of the brolly trying to keep his client as dry as possible. Unfortunately the breeze had strengthened and the wind whipped at their trouser legs creating damp patches around their ankles and shins.
Ten yards away a group of six had mustered, gathered around Willie Milligan like ants around a sugar bowl. With three runners, two of

which were owned by the same person, quiet optimism exuded from the group as they collectively laughed at something Milligan was pointing at. The rain and wind seemed to be having little effect on their enthusiasm despite it being obvious to all that the change in weather conditions could have a significant impact on the forthcoming race. Slippery ground could easily affect a horse, and all fences when approached at speed, especially those with open ditches, were more difficult to jump when the ground was particularly wet or sticky. Cannon had always trained his horses to respect the weather but never to be frightened of it. 'Soft' ground was his preferred going, but if the rain changed it to 'heavy' then he would not mind at all. Santa's Quest was a horse that loved slogging through mud and Cannon reassured Sutcliffe accordingly.

"He looks very well," Sutcliffe said, pointing a damp arm towards Lester Crouch and Santa's Quest who paraded in front of them, the horse still dancing on his toes.

"He is," Cannon replied, taking a quick look at a couple of the other runners who were now squelching through puddles that had accumulated around the perimeter. All of the grooms leading the horses around were drenched as none of them had any protection from the rain other than improvised ponchos or very thin raincoats.

With so much rain falling even the crowds had stayed away from the ring except for a few hardy souls who had brought with them the necessary wet weather gear. Cannon scanned the empty seats and the rails checking whether anyone was paying him particular attention but the sparse crowd meant that those who wanted to hide would have been unable to do so. Still not sure if he was being a little paranoid, he started to relax, giving Sutcliffe and Burke his complete attention.

"This jockey, Sullivan, he seems pretty good," Sutcliffe stated.

"Yes, he's not bad," Cannon answered, down playing any expectations. He realised that Sutcliffe was anticipating a win, irrespective of the competition, and as Cannon had chosen who was to ride the horse, it would be him in the firing line if things went pear shaped.

"Didn't he just ride the winner in the last race?" Burke asked, seemingly oblivious of what was going on around him. "And that was your horse, Mr. Cannon?"

"My horse to train, but I don't own it."

"Oh, sorry. I must have read the details incorrectly in the race card. I just saw your name and...."

"That's okay. I do own a horse that I bought here in Ireland, but he's back in Woodstock at the moment."

Burke smiled an apology again just as the jockeys for the race jogged into the ring. Despite the short distance from the jockey's room to the parade ring by the time each of them had found their trainer, owner or a representative of their runner they were also completely soaked.

"All part of the job," Sullivan said to Sutcliffe, when asked about the rain. He seemed impervious to it, while the TV host seemed decidedly uncomfortable as the skies continued to discharge its contents. Aware of others starting to leave the parade ring, Cannon suggested that he meet Sutcliffe and Burke in the owner's bar, "in the next ten minutes."

The offer was immediately accepted and as soon as they were alone Cannon questioned Sullivan whether there had been any "issues" during the previous race.

"Like what?" Sullivan queried.

"Any attempt to impede you, or box you in between horses?"

"No, nothing that I could see, and anyway getting boxed in happens all the time."

"But not always deliberately," Cannon countered.

"True, but to try and prove that is almost impossible. Notwithstanding how it looks on TV. Anyway, why do you ask?"

"No specific reason," Cannon replied, coyly.

"Ummm," Sullivan growled, as if he wasn't convinced at Cannons' response.

"Anyway, about Santa's Quest..."

"Yes?"

Taking a minute, Cannon let Sullivan know of the horse's temperament and the apparent change in behaviour since he had been transferred to Cannon's yard. "He'll stay all day, and he has an excellent turn of foot if you need it. His jumping is immaculate at present so I suggest you ride him how you see fit."

With such a broad description of the horse, and his capabilities, Sullivan climbed into the saddle once the mount bell had been rung. As he did so with Cannon's help, he asked, "What did Sutcliffe say about me earlier?"

"Nothing really."
"Nothing?"
"Yes."
"Are you sure?"
"Yes. He just told me that the horse had better win. That was it."
"No pressure then, Mike?" Sullivan replied.

The seven-horse field had completed a mile as they turned right-handed and away from the now significantly diminished crowd. The rain had continued unabated leaving the bookmakers all alone on their stands as the remaining spectators retreated into the betting hall under the stands or into the still functioning bars.

Cannon, Sutcliffe and Burke were seated at their table having said goodbye to Cochrane who was already on his way home. Cannon stared through the glass windows of the restaurant but the rain splattering against them and the now low cloud that had settled over the nearby hills and which streamed across the course made it impossible to see what was happening. The TV sets inside the room were muted and the on-course commentary was difficult to hear unless one was outside. Turning to the TV, they could see that all seven runners were still in the race, despite two of them being tailed off from the others. At the mile and half mark the leaders met the seventh fence, Sutcliffe's colours of white with a St. George cross on the front and back, red sleeves and red cap were barely visible through the gloom but could be seen landing neck and neck in joint second position, two lengths adrift of one of Milligan's runners, the second favourite.

"He's travelling well," Cannon advised, following the rhythmic action of his charge as they reached the next fence, which seemed to arrive extremely quickly. The front three horses successfully cleared what was an open ditch, but the fourth horse knuckled on landing, dislodging its rider. A groan escaped from a group sitting at a table some twenty feet away. Cannon assumed they were the connections of the horse. Fortunately it had been able to right itself without injury and continued to race with those horses that had earlier been behind it. Up ahead the three leaders were heading towards the next right-hand bend which would start the long turn into the straight before the final two fences and the finish line. At the eighth fence all three cleared it easily, their jockeys leaning into the necks of their mounts as one by one they landed safely, their footing still sure. With only a length between all three, a close finish was expected and Cannon noted Sutcliffe begin to tense with excitement. At the next, Santa's Quest was in second place, a half-length ahead of the third runner and a two lengths behind the leader. Still jumping well, Santa's Quest soared over the birch finding himself in front as the leader landed awkwardly losing some momentum and being relegated to third. Those who had remained on course were enjoying the battle giving full throat in support of what was a mighty tussle. Within seconds, as Santa's Quest set off for the last fence which was on the bend, Sullivan found himself being headed again by the horse that had been a half-length behind him at the penultimate fence. The second favourite, who had been leading earlier, was slowly drifting back and was now two lengths behind. Sullivan urged his mount on, quickly coming alongside his opponent. The two jockeys rode as if their lives depended upon it, reaching the final fence together. Santa's Quest was on the outside, his rival closest to the running rail. Cannon peered through the glass but the rain trickled down the window obscuring his view. He turned to watch the TV screen again just in time to see Santa's Quest and his rival steady themselves before clearing the top of the fence with ease. However, as they landed on the other side of the fence, both horses crumpled. Legs disappeared from under their bodies and their jockeys hit the ground hard. Sullivan was speared into the turf, his rival crashed through the running rail sending splinters of plastic flying in multiple directions. For a brief second there was a deathly silence in the restaurant, even the commentator on course was dumbstruck.

Sutcliffe stood from his chair continuing to stare at the TV which now showed the horse that had been in third position, now in the lead. As the TV tracked the race through to the end, Cannon put his head against the glass, shielding his eyes from the lights of the restaurant hoping to see Santa's Quest running freely on the course somewhere. Unfortunately he could only see the other horse that had fallen with him at the last fence.

"I've got to go," he said, letting Sutcliffe know that he would find out what had happened to Santa's Quest as soon as he could.

"We'll wait," Sutcliffe said.

"Okay meet me in the owner's bar. I'll get there as soon as I can."

"What are you going to do, Mr. Cannon?" Burke asked.

"I need to find out how Sullivan is and what's happened to the horse."

Cannon pointed at the TV where the winner was being led from the track. "They probably won't show what's going on but take a look over there." He pointed at the window, where blue and red flashes of light pierced the increasing darkness that seemed to be eating up the hills beyond. "That's the course ambulance. Those jockeys could be in a very bad way. Let's hope not too serious, but with both horses falling at the same time and at that speed, God knows what damage has been done."

"Where is Santa's Quest?" Sutcliffe asked, "I see from the screen they have managed to get hold of the other horse."

"I don't know," Cannon said. "I'll let you know once I have more information." Without another word he made his way out of the restaurant, finding himself jogging towards the steward's room just as an on-course announcement was made for him to "please make his way" there.

"Fuck," he said to himself, his mind reviewing what he had been able to see of the fall and correlating it with the Steward's request for him to present himself immediately.

As he made his way through the remaining crowd, who were concentrated under the stand or under whatever shelter they could find, a further announcement was made, letting those who were still waiting for the final race know that the remainder of the meeting had been abandoned.

Glimpsing at various TV sets that hung against walls, the picture showed the course, ambulances, and a blue screen being held up by several attendants who were fighting against the wind and the rain that continued to fall relentlessly. Cannon noticed how the fabric was buffeted inwardly then outwardly like a child's balloon as it inflated then deflated before re-inflating again. He felt his stomach drop.

As he pushed through the door of the administration building to make his way to the steward's office, a voice called out his name. It was the Chief Steward, George McIlroy.

"Mr. Cannon, could you come with me please?" he asked, holding an arm outwardly and requesting Cannon enter through a door marked 'Stewards Only.'

Death Claims its Prize

Before he was even completely inside the room, Cannon turned to McIlroy who was starting to close the door behind them.

"Is Sullivan okay? How is my horse?" he asked, the urgency in his voice indicating his concern about what had happened on the racecourse

McIlroy took a deep breath. He was a man in his mid-seventies. Grey haired, with a pencil thin moustache and a thin face. His cheeks told of his history of drinking too much whiskey and the loose skin on his neck, his battle with weight. Dressed in a blue jacket with a club tie, white shirt and grey slacks, he exuded the demeanour of a gentleman.

"I'll let you go in a few minutes, then you can go and see what's going on out there, but I need to have a quick chat with you first. As you no doubt have heard, we have abandoned the last race."

"Yes, I did hear that. I'm assuming because of the weather? It's clearly treacherous out there."

"Yes, yes it is, but that's not the reason."

"It's not?" Cannon queried. "It is because of the fall. Is Sullivan okay? My horse?" he repeated.

"I think both jockeys have injuries but it's too early for anyone to say to what extent. A very quick assessment from the paramedics in the ambulance that was following the field is that there are a few broken bones and lacerations. Mr. Sullivan appears to have been severely concussed."

"Shit," Cannon replied, rubbing a hand over his face.

"My main concern however is with your horse, Santa's Quest. Owned by Chester Sutcliffe I see."

"What of it?"

"The oncourse Vet has had a quick look at the horse."

"And?" Cannon interrupted, fearing the worst.

"I'm afraid to tell you, Mr. Cannon, that the reason your horse fell at that fence wasn't due to the weather or being brought down by the other horse alongside.....it was because he was shot!"

CHAPTER 31

The decision not to release any information to the public or the press about the shooting had been agreed by all parties. The police had made the recommendation so as not to alarm the general public and the racecourse management and Stewards had agreed, as did Cannon. Detective Inspector Patrick O'Shea had been given the task of investigating the 'incident' and had arrived at the course within forty-five minutes of the crime having been reported. He had been enjoying a drink after a long shift, in Kavanaghs, his local, when the call came in. The six minute drive from the Naas Garda station along with Garda/Constable Conor Lynch, allowed him enough time to read the limited detail the 999 operator had been able to compile.

As he stood in the pouring rain, his dark blue raincoat turning an even darker colour and his shoes squelching in the mud of the racetrack, O'Shea turned a full 360 degrees trying to get a sense of where a gunman could have hidden in order to be able to fire the shot that killed the racehorse.

With the exception of the public spaces inside the course and the parking area, ninety percent of the track was easily visible from the perimeter fences. Some spots were tree lined, others were open to the fields beyond. Pointing towards the south he suggested that the gunman had likely hidden in a small copse of trees just on the apex of the course.

"It's just a guess, mind you," he said. "We'll need to do some further investigation before we can draw any final conclusions."

Standing next to him, Cannon looked down at the body of Santa's Quest. The poor animal lay where it had fallen, blood still oozed down the chest where the bullet had penetrated. The six-inch wound stared at him like an angry mouth, the raw flesh, ragged and ugly, lay exposed to the elements. Cannon knew that when the bullet had hit the horse and the poor animal crashed to the ground, its heart would have kept on pumping until there was no life left. He was angry and frustrated and was trying to contain himself, his mind racing with questions. When he had left the Stewards' office he had been taken by car to the scene and upon arrival had called Burke and suggested to him that he and Sutcliffe leave for their hotel. He told him that he would fill them in on what was going on, once he had more information.

"Of course," Burke said, reminding Cannon that Sutcliffe and he were due to fly back to London early the following morning.

"I'll be in touch later," Cannon had replied, "hopefully within the next couple of hours."

That was ninety minutes ago.

"Can the horse be taken away now?" Cannon asked, continuing to stare at the twisted limbs, the wide-eyed face and the open mouth of his former charge that was lit up by the headlights of the horse ambulance and the three other vehicles that were on scene. The rain flashed through the beams of light, each drop illuminated as it fell to the ground before disappearing into the turf.

"I suppose so," O'Shea said, "I don't think there is anything else we can do here. Once the bullet or bullets have been removed then we'll have something to work with. In the meantime perhaps we can go somewhere dry and you and I can have a chat?"

Taking a long last look at Santa's Quest, Cannon ran a hand across his face, trying to convince himself that it was the rain affecting his eyes.

"Lead on Inspector, lead on," he said.

"Do you think he's got the message, yet?" Kennedy asked.

"I'm not sure."

"Well what else can we do?"

"You need to get back to that house, it must be there. There's no other place."

"Why don't you ask him directly?" Kennedy questioned.

The silence at the end of the line was deafening. Kennedy waited, hearing little except the sound of a TV in the background. A news report. "Because even if he has it, I'm not supposed to know."

"Okay," Kennedy conceded. "You're the boss, but just remember how much you owe me."

"Payment isn't an issue. Payback is," came the simple reply.

The click at the end of the line confirmed that the conversation was over.

CHAPTER 32

He was alone in the Steward's room. While he was waiting for O'Shea, Cannon called Telside giving him some brief details about what had happened and asked him to keep the matter to himself.

"Don't mention it to anyone, not even Michelle," he said.

"I won't."

"Thanks Rich, I appreciate that."

"How are Lester and Jamie doing? It must have been a hell of a shock."

"I haven't told them about the shooting. Lester is upset obviously. He thinks Santa's Quest fell and broke his neck, which is bad enough. Jamie is also struggling but I told them both to concentrate on White Noise, getting him ready to be picked up tomorrow so that he can go home."

"And how about Sutcliffe?" Telside asked.

"I haven't spoken with him as yet. I will do once I've finished with the Stewards and the police. I'm not sure when that will be though."

"And how about Sullivan and the other jockey? I was watching the race, but it was difficult to see with all that rain as to what happened to them."

"I understand from the ambulance men who were working on them when I got over there, that both were pretty shaken up. Bones can mend but the biggest concern was the concussion that Sullivan received. He was walking okay but was complaining about headaches, a sore neck and his shoulder."

"Gee, Mike. If you don't mind the pun, it looks like both jockeys dodged a bullet there."

Cannon grimaced. "You are absolutely right, Rich," he replied, just as the door to the room opened and O'Shea, George McIlroy and two other men entered. The policeman had been able to dry himself off slightly, but his shoes seemed to squeak and squelch. The other men were bone dry. Cannon was introduced to the newcomers. Both were race day Stewards who served on the committee which McIlroy chaired.

After everyone had taken a seat, McIlroy turned the meeting over to O'Shea.

"As you all know, the incident of a couple of hours ago now is being treated very seriously. The entire course is being regarded as a crime scene and I will need your cooperation to try and understand what went on here and why."

He looked at each of the four men in turn before continuing with his commentary. "I'm obviously not sure yet if this attack is on the club, any specific horse or rider or indeed on the sport itself, but one thing I am sure about is that we have a dangerous person or persons out there that need to be apprehended as soon as possible."

"So what happens next?" McIlroy asked. "I don't think the shooting will remain a secret for too long. With those on scene, ambulance folk, the Vet and his staff, along with the drivers from the knackers yard and others, the news is bound to leak out sooner rather than later."

"You're probably right, Sir, but that doesn't mean we need to jump at the very first shadow. I need some additional information first."

"Such as?"

"Did anyone see anything unusual during the day? Why this particular race?"

"Or horse," Cannon added.

"Yes, or horse," O'Shea repeated, looking to Cannon for any additional comment he wanted to make. The room fell silent, everyone waiting for Cannon to speak.ABeginning a jumble of thoughts together he said, "During the course of the meeting, I noticed someone appeared to be following me. I wasn't sure if I was just being overly sensitive or paranoid but based on my personal history I had an uncomfortable feeling all day."

"About?" McIlroy asked, quizzically.

"I wasn't sure until now."

"Go on," O'Shea encouraged.

"Mr. McIlroy and the rest of the members here will know that the horse that was shot, was, is, owned by Chester Sutcliffe, the ex-MP and Minister who is now a TV personality. I think this killing, this murder of his racehorse is more to do with his current high profile than it is to do with racing."

"What makes you think that, Mr. Cannon?" the Inspector asked.

"It's just a feeling."

"A feeling?" one of the other Stewards asked, sarcastically.

Cannon stared at him, a short man with red hair and a beard, dressed in tweed. A flat cap which had taken the brunt of the weather was lying on the table in front of him. No more than five foot six, he looked like a gnome.

"Yes, a feeling," Cannon answered, "or maybe I should have said, intuition."

The gnome squirmed slightly, as Cannon was asked to explain.

"Before I began training horses over ten years ago now, I was a Detective Chief Inspector in the Oxfordshire, Midlands and surrounding areas of England for more years than I care to remember. During that time I got to work on so many cases that intuition about a case often preceded any factual evidence I could gather." He pointed at O'Shea. "I'm sure the Inspector would agree with me that by keeping an open mind, and one's eyes open, sometimes the smallest clue can help solve the biggest or more complex of crimes."

"So what are you saying, Mr. Cannon?" the gnome asked.

"That in my opinion the answer to what happened today has something to do with Chester Sutcliffe himself."

"Is that all you have, Mr. Cannon, just this wild speculation?"

O'Shea put up a hand to silence the gnome from asking any further questions.

"The person you thought was following you. Had you seen the individual before?"

"No."

"So why do you think this person was indeed watching you?"

Taking his time to answer, Cannon looked at McIlroy, then the gnome and finally the other Steward who had remained mute throughout the entire conversation.

"As I said before, intuition."

The gnome exploded with a laugh before withering under O'Shea's gaze. The Detective quickly realised that he had little more to go on than when he had first requested the meeting, so he decided to let everyone go, but not before offering the floor to everyone and going around the room.

"Is there anything else, Mr. Cannon? Anything at all you want to add?"

"Not at this stage," Cannon lied. It was the second time he had done so during the meeting, "but if I do think of anything then I will definitely let you know."

O'Shea nodded. It had been a long day and a shooting at a racecourse was the last thing he needed.

CHAPTER 33

They were seated away from the others in the hotel bar. Cannon had finished his tea, the empty cup sat on the silver tray along with a half-filled tea pot and a small milk jug. A quiet sophisticated noise enhanced by the soft lighting and background music made it easy for them to chat without being overheard. The occasional chink of glasses or the soft pop of a cork amidst the gentle whispering of dating couples masked the concern that showed on Sutcliffe's face.

"As I told you before, I have no idea why my horse would be singled out."

Cannon grimaced slightly, the low lighting hiding his face as he studied Sutcliffe's body language. Even an ex-politician couldn't hide everything he was thinking. Sitting alongside his client, Burke asked Cannon what he thought was going on.

"I'm not sure," he answered, honestly.

"So what happens now?" Sutcliffe questioned.

"That's up to the police. They have my statement, they have the TV footage and they may want to talk with you at some stage, but for now I suspect they will try and conduct their investigation as covertly as possible to minimize any public concern or panic."

"Do they have any ideas?"

"I don't know," Cannon replied, "but if they do, they are not saying."

"Would an animal rights group do this?" Burke queried.

"It's possible I suppose, but doubtful. Ireland is big on horse racing and to shoot a horse like that wouldn't go down well with the general public, no matter what the cause is."

"Fuck it," Sutcliffe said, sighing loudly, before taking a large swallow of merlot and then heavily plonking down his empty glass onto the table. A young couple turned to stare at him at the sound. He was clearly upset and exasperated about what had occurred. Turning to Burke he touched him on the arm, saying, "Perhaps we should go to the police anyway? Tell them what we know?"

Cannon noticed the brief shake of Burke's head in response to Sutcliffe's comment. "What do you mean?" he asked. "Is there something else going on that I should know about?"

It took a few seconds before Burke responded. "I was hoping to keep this quiet in order to protect Chester from any possible fall out,

but for your information, Mr. Cannon, and yours only, Mr. Sutcliffe has been subjected to a number of threats recently."
"Threats? By who?"
"I don't know," Sutcliffe replied.
Even in the low light Cannon noticed from the way his eyes moved to the left rather than looking straight at him, that Sutcliffe seemed uncomfortable with his reply. Many advocates believed that this type of eye movement was evidence of a lie being told. Cannon had even been trained that way; to look for such signs, when he was learning the ropes as a Detective. However, Cannon had never totally believed in such simple theories. Over the years he had used his experience and a dose of gut feeling when looking for inconsistencies in statements, words, body language and actions, in order to draw conclusions. He sensed that Sutcliffe knew more than he was letting on.
"I think….," he began, when his mobile phone started ringing. Looking at the screen, he asked to be excused and after walking away into the hotel lobby, answered the call.
"Why am I not surprised?" he said, even before hearing the voice of DI David Walsh say, "Hello."
"I just heard, Mr. Cannon, so I thought I'd give you a call."
"Just heard?"
"Yes, about what happened at Punchestown."
"Word gets around quickly," Cannon added, sarcastically.
Walsh let the comment go. He understood where Cannon was coming from and was aware that his contacting him now after being silent and uncommunicative for several weeks would be irksome, perhaps even considered opportunistic.
"I know this is not the right time, and I'm sure you have plenty on your plate at the moment, but I wanted to touch base and see if you would be available tomorrow sometime, assuming you are still in the country?"
"To do what, Inspector?"
"David, please…and, well, I'm hoping I can have another chat with you ."
"About what?"
"The Quinn case."
Cannon was taken aback by the comment. With no contact from Walsh or anyone else from the Irish Garda, he had assumed that the

investigation into Quinns' murder was either resolved or ongoing. Either way he hadn't expected to be asked for help…again. He wasn't even sure if he could. "Look Inspector, err, David, I'm booked on a flight tomorrow afternoon at two, so I can spare a couple of hours up until midday, does that work for you?"

"Tell me where you are staying. I'll come and pick you up at nine," Walsh said, in a way that seemed overly officious.

"Okay," Cannon agreed, somewhat reluctantly, before providing the details of his hotel.

"Excellent," Walsh replied, thankfully. "I'll tell you where we are going when I see you," he added, then immediately ended the call.

Smiling to himself at being conned by Walsh, he made his way back inside the hotel bar only to find the table where he had been sitting, empty. He hadn't noticed Sutcliffe and Burke leave but as he had been engrossed in his conversation, it was likely that they left while his back was turned to the bar's entrance.

Making his way back to his room, he pondered whether to let DI O'Shea know about the threats that Sutcliffe had begun to tell him about. Entering the lift, he decided against it as he had no details nor indeed had any idea whether what Burke had alluded too was relevant to what had occurred at the racetrack or not. He assumed that should the Irish police interview Sutcliffe, then any threat towards him would form part of the narrative around the shooting of the horse. Getting back to his room Cannon called Michelle who was already aware that Santa's Quest had been killed.

"I'm so sorry to hear about it, Mike," she said, her voice tender and filled with compassion.

"Yes, it was just an unfortunate accident. A freak fall."

"How did Mr. Sutcliffe take it?"

"He's obviously saddened and disturbed, but he seems philosophical about it,"

"Well then, I suppose that's something to be grateful for."

"Yes, I agree," he replied, before asking her how she was coping with everything at home, then letting her know that DI Walsh had been in touch with him again.

"What did he want?" she asked.

"My help with something."

"Do you know what about?"

"No, he wouldn't say, but I told him that I'm on a plane at twelve tomorrow."

"Okay, well whatever he wants, be careful. Remember it's not your job anymore, so try not to get too involved," she pleaded, knowing that she was likely talking to the deaf.

"I will try," he said, honestly. "I really will."

CHAPTER 34

There was no sign of Sutcliffe or Burke when Cannon went down to breakfast. Being alone allowed him to make a couple of phone calls while he ate. When he checked out of the hotel he was advised that Burke and his client had left in a hurry, the concierge informing him that he had arranged for them to be taken by taxi to the airport just before six am.

As he waited in the lobby for Walsh to arrive, Cannon made a quick call to Telside, explaining to him in a little more detail the circumstances surrounding the death of Santa's Quest and Sutcliffes' reaction.

"Bloody hell!" Telside exclaimed, sadly, "who would want to do that to the poor horse?"

"That's the sixty-four-thousand-dollar question, Rich."

"And?"

"Apparently, Sutcliffe doesn't know."

"Do you believe him?"

"Let's put it this way, Rich. He knows something, but he's not letting on what that something is."

Cannon could sense Telside frowning.

"And before you ask, Rich, I have no idea what it is that he's hiding."

"Or even why?"

"Exactly. It doesn't make sense to me. Whatever issues there are that need addressing, I would have thought that the best thing for him to do, would be to go to the police."

"And yet he hasn't," Telside said.

"Exactly. Which make me wonder why."

"So what are you going to do?"

"Nothing. It's not really my problem. The police can handle it, if and when Sutcliffe asks them to get involved."

"But aren't they involved already?" Telside queried.

"Only as far as they can be I suppose, which is the shooting at the course yesterday. If there is something else going on or relevant, then it's up to Sutcliffe to report it."

Pleased to hear that Cannon was staying away from trouble, Telside changed the subject. "How is White Noise doing this morning?"

"I spoke with the Jamie earlier. He told me that White Noise ate up everything and seems to have got through his race extremely well. Jamie's also taken Lester under his wing and is keeping him busy so that he doesn't dwell on what happened yesterday. They are getting White Noise ready to be picked up later this morning by CB & Sons. The horse is booked on the late afternoon ferry. He should arrive home sometime tomorrow morning, and I'll be home long before then."

"And what's going to happen with Santa's Quest's body?"

"I'm not sure, though I expect the bullet or bullets that killed him will be removed for ballistic testing, after which the police investigation will follow whatever line they think necessary."

"And you? What are your plans?"

"There's no change. I'm on the plane at two this afternoon as planned. I should be home around four thirty."

"Do you need to meet with the Stewards again?"

"No, it's out of their hands now I believe. They agreed that it's a matter for the police, and I told them everything I know yesterday."

"Except what Sutcliffe told you last night."

"Yes, but hopefully he can tell them that himself."

"Fair enough," Telside said. "So what are you going to do now. You've got a couple of hours to kill I suspect. Perhaps you can go into Dublin and buy a few baby clothes," he added, laughing.

"It's a bit early for that, Rich, but it's a good reminder. I should give Cassie a call and see how she is going with her morning sickness."

After finishing the call, he was about to dial his daughter's number when DI Walsh walked into the hotel foyer.

Greeting him like a long-lost brother, Walsh's handshake suggested that he was extremely happy to see Cannon again, even offering to carry his luggage to the car.

"It's okay," Cannon remarked, as he pulled his small suitcase the short distance to where Walsh had left his vehicle in front of the hotel.

Once they were inside the car and out of the wind which seemed to swirl about like a demented demon, sending crisp packets and other rubbish skittering across roads and into drains that were still partially blocked from the previous days deluge, Cannon asked the obvious question.

"We're going to visit some friends of yours," Walsh replied, as he merged the police car into the traffic.

"Friends?" Cannon queried, trying to clarify in his own mind who Walsh was referring to.

"Well, maybe I should correct myself....associates then."

Cannon was a little annoyed at the cryptic response. He tried to work out if Walsh was taking the piss or if he was being serious. For someone who he knew little of, other than through their earlier meetings and brief phone conversations, he concluded that the Detective was serious.

"Not sure I have either, to be honest," Cannon said in reply, as their vehicle entered the N4 motorway heading North-East towards Dublin City. Cars instantly flew past them in the right-hand lanes doing well over the speed limit, reminding Cannon of his earlier visits. He wondered whether any of those passing Walsh's car would have done so if it had not been unmarked? "Anyway," he added, "you know I only have a couple of hours available before I need to be at the airport."

"Don't worry, where we are going is only about twenty minutes from there."

"So are you going to tell me, then?"

Walsh continued to watch the road ahead, coming up behind a large truck before indicating his intention of moving into the middle lane. As he did so, a motorbike screamed passed, sending up spray from its back wheel and across their windscreen. "Bastard!" Walsh reacted, turning on his windscreen wipers just in time to see the motorbike jink in and out of the traffic ahead before disappearing into the fast lane.

"What do you know about CB & Sons Transport?" Walsh asked, regaining his composure and briefly turning his head to look at his passenger.

"Not much. I found them by accident when I needed a couple of horses to be transported over here. They were a cheaper option than anyone else. Why?"

"I've had a look into them since Fionn Kelly was murdered and I'm convinced that somehow what happened to him is linked to you."

"Me?"

"Yes."

"Why do you think that? I don't know anyone involved with the business."

"And it's that which got me thinking. Two murders where the only common denominator is yourself and then, yesterday, a horse being shot on a racecourse which again is directly linked to you."

"I agree that there is something going on, but you don't think I'm involved do you?"

"As I said when we first met, I'm keeping an open mind."

Cannon laughed, sarcastically "Are you thinking of arresting me?"

"Should I?"

"That would be your call."

"Do I have any reason to arrest you?"

Cannon sighed, then peered out of his side window at the passing fields for a few seconds, before turning to look back at Walsh who continued staring straight ahead.

"I'd suggest that if you thought so, you would have done it already."

"Which is why I asked you to come along with me this morning. I made an enquiry before I called you last night, after I heard about the shooting."

"And?" Cannon asked.

"The one that was shot, and the other one…"

"White Noise?"

"Yes."

"They were both transported by CB & Sons."

"Yes, as I told you, I found them very reliable. In fact White Noise is being picked up by them this afternoon. He's on an overnight ferry."

"Which is why you and I are paying them a visit."

"I already gathered that," Cannon replied, beginning to wonder if Walsh really believed that he had anything to do with the two murders.

She was waiting in her car for him to arrive home. Parked down the street a few doors away from the entrance to his building, she had been there since before dawn, readying herself to act the moment she saw him. The sun had risen at a quarter to eight, almost two hours ago, but had not been seen due to the steel grey skies that had begun covering the city two days earlier. It was still gloomy as he exited the taxi carrying his bottle green suitcase. By the time he was unlocking the door she was almost upon him. He turned just in time to see her raise her arm.

"DI Daithi Walsh," he said, showing the young girl at the small reception desk his police identification. "Is the boss in?"
She was in her late teens and clearly flustered and intimidated by Walsh's unexpected arrival. Cannon smiled at her trying to offer some comfort against her distress, but it seemed to make her even more uncomfortable.
"I'll get him for you," she offered, picking up a phone and asking them to take a seat while she did so.
"I'm happy to stand," Walsh replied, looking around at the single three-seater grey fabric couch that was pushed up against a wall. There was nothing else in the three-metre square room other than the desk, a large PC screen that the girl had been using and her chair. The couch had seen slightly better days but still appeared to be useable, so Cannon left Walsh to his own devices, making himself comfortable. He looked at the walls which were all empty of decoration other than a number of photographs of different trucks with the CB & Sons logos on them, that were plastered on the wall directly behind the desk.
A single door to the left of where the girl was sitting had a 'staff only' sticker plastered on it and was abruptly opened by a man in his early sixties. Cannon noticed that he stood ramrod straight. He was around five feet ten inches tall (one metre, seventy-six), very good looking with deep blue eyes and a strong nose. His chin, like his head was covered in grey hair, the beard neatly trimmed. Dressed in casual clothes, black jeans and a beige jersey, he looked as if he had just come from his tailor.
"Mr. Boyle? Conor Boyle?" Walsh asked, introducing himself again, then doing the same with Cannon, who was now standing. "Is it okay if we have a chat?"
"What about?" Boyle queried, seeming genuinely confused.
Walsh looked around at the room then at the receptionist. "Is there anywhere we can talk....privately?"
Boyle rubbed a hand against his temple. "We're only a small business, but yes, I'm sure I can find a room somewhere, even if it's my office."
Turning to the receptionist he checked whether a spare room was

available to them, only to decide that he would have to use his office. He asked the two visitors to follow him through the 'staff only' door. As they trooped behind him, Boyle suddenly realised where he had heard the name.

"Ah….Mr. Cannon," he remarked, extending an apology, "I'm sorry I didn't twig just now, I didn't realize it was you. I hope I didn't appear rude?"

Responding by letting Boyle know that there was nothing to concern himself with, Cannon noticed Walsh's face. He could imagine the cogs within the Detective's brain whirring, trying to connect the dots between Boyle's attempt at familiarity and Cannon's comment of not knowing anyone in the business.

Once they were seated in the office, which was incredibly neat and tidy, almost stark like the reception area, Boyle asked Walsh how he could be of assistance.

"I'll get right to the point, Mr. Boyle," the policeman began, "I'm investigating a murder that took place down in Foulksmills a short while ago, you may have heard about it?"

"No, I'm sorry, I haven't."

"Are you sure?"

"Yes, I'm positive." Boyle replied.

Cannon was curious. He watched the way both men reacted to the other, still trying to understand why he had been asked to join Walsh in the meeting in the first place. From what he had gathered from their earlier chat in the car, Walsh had nothing but spurious speculation about Cannons' involvement with Boyle's business. He wondered what strings Walsh was trying to draw together.

"Your man, Fionn Kelly," Walsh stated.

"My partner's late son, what about him?"

"Did the police in England ever come back to you with any requests for information about him? Any thoughts on why he was killed?"

Boyle shook his head. "Other than letting Darragh and I know what had happened, no they didn't. Darragh has been on to them a number of times but as far as I can tell they have treated it as a random attack. A hijacking is what they called it."

"And you have no idea why Fionn was targeted?"

"No."

Walsh sighed. He gestured towards Cannon then turned back to face Boyle again. "Mr. Cannon here was unfortunately dragged into the murder down in Foulksmills that I just told you about. It was he who found the body."

"I'm sorry to hear that," Boyle replied.

"And it was he," Walsh continued, "who Fionn made his last delivery to, before his death."

"I still don't …."

"Don't you think it curious that these events occurred so soon after Mr. Cannon started using your services?" Walsh interrupted.

"Look," Boyle said, raising his voice slightly, "I don't know what you are getting at, but I had nothing to do with any of this. Why would I?"

Walsh suddenly changed tack, Cannon noted it immediately. He had done it himself many times before, straight out of the police handbook.

"Yesterday," Walsh said, lowering his voice conspiratorially, "one of Mr. Cannon's horses died on Punchestown racecourse. One of the two that your business had transported over from England and were due to return this afternoon."

"Yes, I heard. I'm sorry about that," he said sympathetically, in Cannon's direction. "But these things happen in racing, don't they?"

"Yes, they do," Cannon answered, speaking for the first time.

"But what you don't know, Mr. Boyle," Walsh added, "was that the horse in question, died because it was shot."

"What?"

"You heard me, Mr. Boyle. The horse was shot dead."

"By who?"

"You tell me," Walsh replied.

"How would I know? Look, I still don't know what you are getting at, Inspector."

Cannon studied Boyle's face, his eyes, his shoulders, his entire demeanour. He appeared genuinely concerned about what was being relayed to him.

Walsh continued. "Don't you think it unusual that three deaths have occurred, all of which seem to tie your business to that of Mr. Cannon here?"

"I guess so," Boyle replied, "though all I can suggest is that it's purely coincidental. As I said earlier, I know nothing about a murder in Foulksmills and if you hadn't mentioned the horse shooting I wouldn't have known about that either. It wasn't mentioned in the papers anywhere was it?"

Walsh did not respond to the question. He turned to Cannon asking him whether he had any questions of his own.

"Just one," he said. "Fionn Kelly's father, Darragh. You mentioned that no one from the police in England had been in touch with him."

"As far as I know."

"What's his view of what happened?"

"It's the same as mine. Unbelievable. He's still struggling to get over it, if he ever will."

"Can we speak with him?"

"I'm sure that can arranged."

"Is he available now?"

"Unfortunately not," Boyle replied.

"Why is that?" Cannon asked.

"He was so devastated after Fionn's murder that I told him to take time off."

"So is he at home?" Walsh questioned.

"No, he's in the US. I told him that he should get away for a while. He did have family there at one time but not anymore. Now he's just travelling to keep his mind off things. He's been there for a couple of weeks already, due back in another four."

Cannon nodded, "Thank you," he said, "and thanks for taking care of my horses." He gestured to Walsh to have the final say.

"Please don't mention anything about the shooting yesterday," Walsh stated. "I've told you in good faith and in confidence, Mr. Boyle, hoping that it would jog something in your memory about Mr. Cannon or his horses. Also I want to ask that you keep your eyes peeled for anything unusual you may see around the place. Finally, please treat what I've told you seriously…for your own safety and for that of your business."

"Of course, Inspector."

"And if anything does come to mind, please can you give me a call on this number?" Walsh passed a simple white card across the desk with a Garda logo printed on it. It contained his mobile number and his email details.

Leaving the card where it was on the desk, Boyle stood from his chair then walked the two men back to the reception area. They shook hands before Boyle returned to his office and Cannon and Walsh to the unmarked police car.

"What do you think?" Walsh asked, once they had both put on their seat belts.

"I think it's time for me to go to the airport," Cannon said, a hand rubbing across his chin. As Walsh put the car into gear, Cannon couldn't help but agree with the Detective that there were too many coincidences associated with CB & Sons, something he never liked.

Back in his office Boyle closed the door before locking it.

He picked up his mobile and dialled a number. The ringing in his ear seemed interminable and he was about to hang up when a voice answered with a raspy greeting.

"We need to talk," Boyle said.

CHAPTER 35

She sat opposite him, motionless. It was as if she was afraid, but in reality he was the one who trembled.

"What do you want?" he asked, looking at the woman he had last seen nearly two decades ago. She was still slim, her light brown hair, with a blond fleck, was cut in a tapered-pixie style which fell just onto her shoulders. She was just as attractive to him now as she was when they had first met. Her green eyes, small nose and soft mouth were accentuated by a flawless skin. Despite him feeling uncomfortable at seeing her he took in her blue slacks, white polo neck jumper and the black peacoat. It was obvious that she had done well for herself. He noticed that she spoke with a strange accent. A mixture of several. He waited for her to answer.

"What do you think?" she replied.

"Money? An apology?"

She stared at him for a second then stood up. He followed her with his gaze as she walked across the room to a small bookshelf. She pulled out a book at random, skimming through the pages before returning it back in the same spot. "William Ebenstein?," she said as she picked up another book, "Churchill: Walking with Destiny, my my, pretty heavy reading."

"It's what I do…did," Sutcliffe replied, correcting himself. He remained seated in the only armchair in his lounge.

"And it's what you did that I'm here to talk to you about."

He squirmed in his chair. He knew that it was a bad idea to let her in, but he had decided to do so in order to find out what she wanted. So far she had not given him any clue. He was conflicted with her demeanour. She didn't appear afraid of him, but he was of her. The anonymous printed letters he had received previously were threats to his life, his career, so he had every reason to be concerned about her motives. He was hoping, indeed he was gambling on the fact that she would be wanting money in order to keep quiet about what happened rather than simply wanting to take revenge.

His eyes followed her as she continued walking around the room. She pointed at various paintings on one particular wall and the photographs of Sutcliffe with numerous politicians, actors and business leaders that adorned another, "Some of these are quite recent," she said. "I recognize a number of them."

"Yes, they are," he replied, non-committally, still wondering where this encounter was going.

Sitting down again on the couch, she leant forward as if she was about to make a proposition to him. Her demands.

"Can I ask you why you didn't respond to my letters, my emails?"

"Respond?" he replied, exasperatedly. "Why would I do that?"

"Why?"

"Yes, why! And anyway, how can anyone reply to an anonymous letter, especially a threatening one. You're lucky I didn't bring in the police."

"That's a low blow," she said, "after what happened."

Showing a little bit of humility, he frowned then nodded, saying softly, "You're right, I'm sorry."

"So, I'll ask you again, why did you not respond?"

"With what? When someone tells me in a letter that they are going to kill me, and insinuates that I'm a liar and a fraud, you don't think that I would offer an invitation to a time and place to do it, do you?"

She looked at him strangely, wondering if he had suddenly gone mad. He seemed puzzled, just as he was when she caught him on the doorstep with a suitcase in his hand, a few minutes before ten am. It was also obvious to her that he was genuinely frightened when she had approached him. So, in order not to cause a scene, he had let her follow him into the building where she had noticed the airline tag on the bag that he was carrying. She guessed that he had been up very early and was still a little sleep deprived, which may have accounted for his confusion.

"Kill you?" she queried. "Why would I do that?"

"Because of what happened?"

"What happened was an accident."

Sutcliffe stared at her. He wasn't sure what was going on, and he found himself tensing. Was she toying with him? He needed to be wary. "But she died, your sister died."

"Yes, she did, but it wasn't your fault."

"But she drowned, while I was there. I remember it as if it was yesterday. It still haunts me."

Death Claims its Prize

Sutcliffe suddenly found himself reliving what had happened nearly twenty years prior. He and Charlie Scott had been on a six-week holiday, journeying across Italy and into Croatia, spending time along the Adriatic coast. They hired a boat in Brela and had planned to sail it down to a small town called Drvenik, the next day; some forty-five kilometres South. While they were getting the boat ready with supplies, two young girls, twins, backpacking along the coast, came into the harbour and they began talking. It wasn't long before the girls asked to join them on their adventure. Sutcliffe and Scott liked what they saw and were happy to have female company. By early evening, bottled water had turned to bottled beer, complimented by grilled sardines and squid, bell peppers, rice and wine.
Before midnight they had paired off and by the time the sun rose, Sutcliffe and Scott had slept with both girls.
The trip down the coast was a disaster. While the weather was warm, with a deep blue, azure sky, and the sea was calm, the lack of wind and experience of both men meant that they struggled to sail to their destination. After a couple of hours of collective hangover laughter followed by frustration, they decided to anchor the boat in a small cove below the town of Promajna. Their intent was to stay for a few hours then take the boat back to Brela. The girls had agreed, suggesting that they spend the afternoon on the beach, which was easy to get to from where they were anchored. The water was clear and less than five feet deep at most.
Cheese, bread, wine, olives and few tomatoes were carried to a shady spot and the rest of the afternoon passed by slowly, until Sutcliffe and one of the girls decided to find a 'quiet spot.'
Climbing up a bank they soon found themselves on the opposite side of a bluff which acted as one end of the cove. The drop to the sea from the bluff was almost vertical, at least thirty metres. The view was spectacular and Sutcliffe had suggested that the two of them use the opportunity and the remoteness to have sex again. The girl had agreed but suggested that he had to catch her first as she didn't want to be seen as "easy." Sutcliffe thought her comment contradictory given what had happened only hours earlier, but as they were both in a playful mood, he agreed. He had barely started chasing her when she stood too close to the edge of the cliff with her hands stretched out in front of her as if to ward him off. She tumbled backwards, grasping at the salty air as she plummeted head over heels towards

the sea, her screams lost in the breeze that swirled over the sea. Sutcliffe immediately peeked over the edge of the cliff but he couldn't see the girl anywhere. For a few seconds he froze, silently looking skywards, before letting out a fearful howl of his own that carried down the bluff to Scott and the other twin. Running back to the beach to tell the others what had happened, the two men almost collided as Scott raced up the pathway Sutcliffe and the girl had taken earlier. Sutcliffe out of breath tried to explain what had occurred, demanding that they had to get around to the other side of the bluff and look for the girl. They were standing twenty metres above the beach when the other sister stumbled towards them demanding to know what was going on. Sutcliffe explained what had happened and the girl, panicking, screaming, continued on up the path to see where her sister had fallen from. Scott looked around and made a suggestion.

"Let's go," he said.

"Where? What do you mean?"

"Back to Brela. Let's get out of here."

Sutcliffe had looked at his friend, trying to understand what he was suggesting. Trying to comprehend. "What about the girl? We need to find her? We can't leave her, she might be injured."

Scott had shaken Sutcliffe by the shoulders, demanding that he listen to what was being said to him.

It took less than two minutes before both men were in the water, wading the short distance to the boat. They carried everything with them that they had used or touched, leaving nothing other than a single towel that the remaining sister had been lying on. With nothing of theirs left behind, no one would ever know that they had been there. By the time the remaining sister found her way back to the beach, the boat had gone.

The flashback had occupied his mind for less than ten seconds. He stared at her again. He recalled her name……..Julie.

"What do you want?" he asked again, hoping to bring the nightmare to an end, but still unsure of her motives.

"I want to know why you haven't acted."

"Acted? On what? What are you talking about?"

"The letters, did you not read them?"

"Letters? The only letters I got from you were threats. You called me a liar, said that you intended to kill me….all because of what happened to your sister."

"Look," she answered, "what happened to my sister was a long time ago, and if I had wanted to get back at you I would have done it already. But….," she said, pausing to ensure that her words came out correctly, "But, the only thing that I could hold you accountable for, was…was…. for leaving me, us, on the beach that day."

Sutcliffe sat still, unmoving, trying to reconcile what she was telling him versus his own memory of that fateful day, nearly twenty years prior, and the threats that he had recently received. He waited for her to continue. A sad sigh escaped her lips as she spoke again.

"Rachel, my sister, survived the fall. I found her floating face up about twenty feet from the base of the cliff. I had swum around the bluff and because the sea that day was like glass, there were no waves to push her back against the rocks, so I was able to drag her back to the beach."

"What?" Sutcliffe answered, his eyes moist with tears as he pictured the scene. He quickly wiped them away with the back of his hand.

"Between breaths she told me what had happened. That the fall was due to her own stupidity."

"So what happened to her?"

Julie Quinn lowered her eyes, her voice dropped almost to a whisper. "She died….in my arms…on that beach."

"I'm sorry," he replied, his contrition real. "We should have stayed. We panicked. I panicked."

"The post-mortem report said that she died from post-immersion syndrome."

"What does that mean?"

"It's when a person who has inhaled water experiences airway spasms and difficulty breathing."

"Could she have been saved? If we had stayed would it have made any difference," he asked, wondering if things would have been different, almost wishing that he could turn back time.

"No. I did try CPR but because she was also an asthma sufferer and had the beginning of COPD, chronic obstructive pulmonary disease, her lungs just gave in. I only found that out later."

"I'm so sorry," he repeated.

She continued with her explanation as if she hadn't heard him. "We were both exposed to numerous chemicals growing up on our farm in Ireland, it was how her lungs were impacted so badly."

"And you?"

"I was lucky," she smiled, "Rachel always spent more time with my dad than I did, especially when he was working the land. Even as a kid she was always playing in the different barns where he kept the supplies. Chemicals of all types, Herbicides, Pesticides, Fungicides, Weedkillers. And then, when he was using them, she would often be with him. On the tractor, in the stables….almost like a barnacle on a ship's hull."

Sutcliffe smiled at her analogy, suddenly feeling a sense of relief. It was as if history had been rewritten. The guilt he had felt for years had been partially pardoned, though he knew that by running away he was still complicit in some way to Rachel Quinn's death. He knew that it was something he could never undo.

"Can I ask you something?" he said, gently.

"Yes."

"You said earlier that you sent me numerous letters by email."

"Yes, I did. It's why I'm here. It's why I tried to see you at the studio."

"What were the letters about, if they weren't threats?"

"Politics."

"I'm sorry?" he replied, surprised and wary at her comment.

"Politics," she repeated.

"I don't understand."

"It's a long story and it may sound strange, so despite what I said earlier that you weren't responsible for my sister's death, I wrote to you because you were the only person I knew who I thought could help. Also, and to be perfectly honest, I wanted some payback from you for what happened to my sister."

"How?"

She sighed again, before standing for the second time and walking to his apartment window, looking down at the street below. "I wrote to you to save my dad. I wanted you to reveal to the public, the government, that there are people in this world who don't believe in the Good Friday Agreement and who still want to fight the war."

Sutcliffe ruminated on what she had said. The Good Friday Agreement was what brought the 'troubles' in Ireland to an end. A political agreement but not a universally accepted one.

"I'm sure there are," Sutcliffe said eventually, in response to her comment. "It was always understood that not everyone would be happy. It would be naïve to think otherwise."

"I know, but some are more unhappy than others."

"Go on," he encouraged.

Turning to face him, she said. "I wrote multiple times to you because as an ex-politician who now has a platform to speak out on various issues, I was hoping that you would help expose those who are still fighting the war."

"And as I told you, I never received any of your letters, your emails."

"So you say."

"It's true."

"So what happened to them?"

"I have no idea," he answered, repeating that the only letters he had received recently were of threats to his life.

"Perhaps that's due to some other reason?" she questioned.

"Maybe," he answered, not wanting to consider why, but aware that he had upset any number of people during his time in the government or on his TV show. He looked at his watch, he needed to get a move on, to get himself ready, before he had to leave for the TV studio.

"So what is it you want from me?" he asked.

"I want you to help me find who killed my father."

"Isn't that a subject for the police?"

"They are already looking into it."

"Well if you are aware of that, then why haven't you told them what else you know?"

"Because I don't want anyone to know that I'm back."

"From where? I noticed your accent earlier. It sounds Australian."

"New Zealand mixed with the US."

"You've been around," he stated, blandly.

"Yes, I have."

He looked at his watch again, then in an attempt to bring things to a head took a deep breath and asked, "Okay, okay, so if you don't want to go to the police, how do you expect me to help you?"

Her response took the wind right out of his sails. All the bravado he had been expressing instantly disappeared like a balloon rapidly deflating.

"Did you know Warren Hawker?"

"Yes, why? What about him?" Sutcliffe replied, stunned to hear her mention the late trainer of Santa's Quest.

"I met him when he visited the racehorse trainer I was working for, in California."

"You met him?"

"Yes, I spoke with him for a few minutes. He said he was there to visit a few stud farms and to meet some local trainers while he was on holiday. He told me that he was representing an owner in the UK who was interested in buying a few horses."

"That sounds reasonable to me. Did you know he trained a horse of mine?"

"No, I didn't, but when I saw on a local news report that he had been killed in a car accident in Nevada, I knew that I had to come home. I'd written you several letters by then but I hadn't had any response. Unfortunately by the time I made it back after serving notice at my job, my dad had already been murdered."

"Hold on, hold on," Sutcliffe replied, as he tried to understand the connection between Warren Hawker and the woman in front of him. With his arm outstretched pointing in her direction, it was if he was trying to grasp hold of a rope that was constantly out of reach. His thoughts seemed like smoke disappearing into the air.

"What does Warren Hawker have to do with your dad?" he asked.

"Everything," she replied.

"You'd better sit down and explain," he said, deciding that hearing what she had to say was more important, after what had happened at Punchestown the previous day, than leaving her and going off to his pre-production meeting.

After she had sat down again, she took another deep breath, then continued to elaborate. "I don't think Mr. Hawker was visiting the States for the reason that he claimed he was. I think he was trying to find out something."

"Do you have any ideas as to what?"

"Confirmation!"

"Of what?" he pressed, starting to get annoyed with her cryptic answers.

"A theory. Exactly what I'd written to you about."
"But what is this theory and how would he know about it?"
"I'm not sure, but I have a view."
"Which is what?" Sutcliffe replied, indignantly, as if his intelligence was being tested. "It's all starting to sound a bit fanciful to me."
"Perhaps but let me ask you a question then. If you didn't get my letters then who did?"
"How would I know. And does it really matter?"
"Of course it does, especially if somebody acted on them."
"What did they say, these letters of yours?"
"Exactly what I said before. That some people were still fighting the war and that my father knew who they were."
"And what exactly did you want me to do with that information?
"Highlight it on your show. Let the government know that there are still those who pose a threat to the Good Friday Agreement and to expose them."
"But one could only do that if there was evidence to back up your claims. Do you have any?"
"No."
"So there is nothing to talk about is there. This entire conversation has been a waste of time," he said angrily.
Staring at him, she said, "All I can tell you is that my father had kept a record. It was a list with details on it that a lot of people would kill for. He said once that it was his security. It kept him alive."
"What was on this list?"
"I don't know, but what he did say was that if something ever happened to him, something suspicious, then the list should be made public."
"And you think your father was killed for the list?"
"Yes."
"So where is it?"
"I think he hid it somewhere in his house."

CHAPTER 36

The mood in the yard was sombre. Cannon had arrived back just as the rest of the team were heading home after completing their work for the day. A few of the staff asked him about what had happened to Santa's Quest, before congratulating him on White Noises' win. The death of Sutcliffe's horse was still being stated officially as a result of a fall. O'Shea had requested that it remain that way until further inquiries had been made.
"How are you feeling, Mike?" Telside asked, noticing that Cannon appeared tired. The drive back from the airport had been a frustrating one due a number of accidents on the M40 just South East of Oxford. It had added an extra hour to the trip and Cannon had parked his car thirty minutes after the sun had set. They were standing at the barn door where White Noise and Santa's Quest would normally be housed. Tomorrow, only one of them would be. The lights above the barn and those from the house cast shadows across the yard. The temperature had dropped significantly and despite it being dry, the chill in the air caused Cannon to shiver.
"I don't know," he replied. "I'm still trying to get my head around what happened."
"Do you have any ideas?"
"About the shooting?"
"Yes. I mean why would anyone single out Sutcliffes' horse?"
"I'm not sure, yet, but I have an idea."
"Do you want to tell me? I mean do we need do anything different around the yard at this stage? I wouldn't want to put any of the staff or the horses in danger, you know."
"At this stage, no, it's business as usual. I think that what's going on has nothing to do with us directly. I think I, we, have just got caught in the middle of something."
Telside heaved a sigh of relief. "Thank God for that," he said.
"Indeed, Rich, though we still need to be wary."
"Why?"
"I think someone has been following me. I noticed a man watching me closely a couple of times at Punchestown and I'm sure I saw the same guy at Huntingdon."
"Following you? Why? Are you sure you're not imagining it."

"I thought that initially, but as you know coincidence and I don't go well together. What happened yesterday confirmed my suspicions."
"So what now then?"
Cannon smiled, his face was partially covered in shadow. "We just need to be aware, be careful but carry on as normal. Once White Noise gets back we'll see how he's travelled and if he's recovered well, then we continue with our plans for him….along with all our other horses."
"That's good to hear, Mike," Telside said, knowing that his friend had deliberately decided not to answer his question completely. Cannon had a habit of chasing up issues that affected him, his family, his staff, his livelihood, and this was another example. Telside was certain that once they had conducted a quick inspection of the horses now locked up for the night in their individual stalls, and before he had even completed the short drive to his house, Cannon would be sitting in his office trying to piece together what was going on. Deciding not to reveal what he was really thinking, Telside agreed with his boss that the yard should continue as Cannon had suggested; "as normal".

They had finished dinner, the empty plates, serving dishes and mugs lay scattered on the table. Michelle had insisted that he eat with her before he went to his office.
"I can see that something is troubling you," she said, "and you've been much quieter than usual. Is there anything I can do?"
He touched her hand. "No, I'm fine. Just a little tired."
"Umm," she answered, unconvinced. "I can see that, so why don't we go to bed early then?"
"Do you have an early start?"
"Just the usual, but I was thinking of you."
"I always have an early start," he replied, smiling at his own joke.
She wasn't particularly amused and she let him know. "The loss of that horse yesterday….you seem to have taken it to heart. Much more than you have in the past. Is there a reason?"
"Not really."
"Is it because it was Sutcliffe's?"
"No," he answered, not wanting to tell her about the shooting. He

knew that it would worry her.

"Well if it's any consolation, I don't really like the man," she said. "It seems that there is always trouble with everything he touches. Maybe after what happened with his horse, you'll be shot of him?"

Cannon noted the irony of her words. Maybe Michelle was right, he thought. Perhaps he needed to let things go, to not get involved any further and allow the police to do their job

"His show on TV is popular because he's controversial and I read somewhere that his political career was just as hectic," she was saying as he focused back on her. "It wouldn't surprise me if he had skeletons in any number of cupboards, which was probably why he left politics."

Cannon was surprised at the vigour of her comments. It wasn't like her.

"You seem a bit angry," he said, referring to the fact that she had raised her voice.

"I am to be honest. I've watched your face ever since you arrived home. You seem distracted and distant. It's not like you."

"I'll be okay," he said, "I just need to sort something out."

She stared at him for a second, then standing up from the table she began to gather the plates together. "I know you well enough by now Mike, to notice when there is something on your mind. If you don't want to tell me, then that's fine. All I can ask though is for you to please be careful. You have a grandchild on the way, so just think about that ….," she said gently, as she turned and walked away into the kitchen.

Cannon was about to turn off his computer when his mobile started to vibrate. Michelle had already gone to bed an hour earlier. He wasn't sure if she was still awake and reading or not but was conscious of the fact that if she was waiting for him, she would be extremely upset if he answered it. Fortunately, he had put the phone on silent and on flight mode when his plane left Dublin airport and had forgotten to turn it back on to ring despite turning flight mode off, hence the silent vibration.

He stared at the number and he knew instantly who was calling but was unsure whether to answer it or not. He hadn't realised that it was way past ten o'clock but he knew from his past life that late night phone calls were often made by policeman. This was one of them.

"Hello, Inspector," he said, as quietly as he could.

"Good evening, Mr. Cannon," DI David Walsh replied, "I'm sorry to be calling you so late, but I just wanted to let you know that there has been a development in the Quinn case."

"That's good to hear, Inspector, err, David."

"Do you want to know what it is?"

Cannon thought the comment unusual. "Is it relevant to me?" he asked.

"I'm not sure yet, but I thought I'd let you know anyway."

"Right now?" Cannon asked, looking at his watch again.

"I'll be quick."

"Okay," Cannon replied, reluctantly, "go ahead."

Walsh told him how he had been contacted by Patrick O'Shea. "It seems that Chester Sutcliffe has had a visitor. Believe it or not it was Sam Quinn's daughter, the one I have been trying to get hold of since his murder."

"Bloody hell!" Cannon exclaimed, louder than he should have. "What did she want?"

"She believes her father was murdered for something that he has hidden in the house."

"Does she know what?"

"A list or a document of some sort."

"Which would seem to confirm what you have thought all along. That someone was looking for something when Quinn was killed."

"And subsequently…"

"I didn't know that," Cannon replied.

"I didn't tell anyone, but someone entered the house again after we removed Quinns' body."

"So what now?"

"I need your help again."

"To do what, Inspector?" Cannon asked.

He could almost hear Walsh smiling down the line when the policeman said, "To be my eyes and ears."

"Sorry?"

"We've set up a call with Sutcliffe and Quinns' daughter for tomorrow at midday. Both DI O'Shea and I will be on it, and I'd like you to join. Unfortunately, the two of us can't take a flight to London at the drop of a hat to meet with them and engaging the British police to investigate a crime in Ireland, even when there are UK citizens involved, such as Sutcliffe, is never easy. It's the same with Finn's murder. That killing is outside of my jurisdiction so I have to leave that investigation to the British police."

"Don't I know it," Cannon replied, thinking back to his past. "So what type of call are you setting up?"

"A Zoom call."

"I've never used one of them," he replied.

"Don't worry I'll send you a link by email."

"Umm…okay, but what do you want me to do?"

"Just watch and listen."

"And then?"

"If there is anything that you think needs checking or following up on then we can talk about it afterwards."

"I'm not sure how…."

"Mike. You were the one who found Quinn's body. The first on the scene. Who knows what could be said that may jog your memory."

Cannon was about to decline, to change his mind. What Walsh was asking of him didn't seem to make any sense.

"And there's something else," Walsh continued.

"What?"

"The bullet that was used to kill your horse."

"What about it?"

"It came from a L96 rifle."

"Bloody hell," Cannon replied, suddenly realizing the implication. A piece of the puzzle had just fallen into place.

"Exactly," Walsh replied, "exactly."

CHAPTER 37

White Noise arrived back at the yard just before ten. Telside and his staff had been busy finishing their tasks of cleaning, feeding, watering and grooming after the mornings exercise and schooling. The Vet had been called in earlier to check over a couple of horses that had picked up niggles and cuts from their work. One horse, Safe Haven, an eight-year mare, had worked poorly and she was seen to be off her feed. It was soon established that the mare had suffered an exercise induced pulmonary haemorrhage (an EIPH), and a small bleed was found in one of her nostrils. Cannon was informed by Telside, and a decision was made that the horse should be taken out of training for a while so that the horse could be 'scoped'. This would ensure that the cause of the bleed could be found, and a treatment plan to address the problem be put in place. The health of his horses always came first as far as Cannon was concerned.

He had just finished talking to the owner of Safe Haven when he noticed a van through his office window trailing a single horse box with the CB & Sons Transport logo on the side, drive past, and then stop deep inside the yard.

After making his way outside, he found Telside next to the van just as the trailer was being opened in preparation for White Noise to be unloaded. Standing alongside Telside was Jamie Strickland who had travelled with the horse.

"How was the boat?" Cannon asked, as he joined the pair.

"It was nice, Mr. Cannon," Strickland replied, "though I did feel for Lester. He was very quiet for most of the trip."

"I can understand that. I think all of us are going to miss Santa's Quest, particularly as we were just getting used to him."

"What happens now then?"

Cannon shared a glance with Telside. With the cause of death still officially under wraps, it was important that the staff continued with their day-to-day activities and not be sidetracked. The demise of Sutcliffes' horse did not need to effect the running of the yard. Yes, there would be a certain level of sadness, but hopefully it would be countered by the success of White Noise and the other horses in the stables. Life needed to go on even while the police investigation was continuing.

Answering the question as forthrightly as he could, Cannon said, "We celebrate White Noise's success, and we plan for more. It's what we do and it's why we are here."

Cannon watched Strickland smile slightly as he looked down at his feet. It was if the young groom couldn't look into Cannon's eyes. He clearly understood the sentiment that his boss was relaying but hadn't fully understood that death was actually part of the game.

Telside put his hand on Strickland's shoulder. "White Noise looks tremendous," he said, as the van driver finally lowered the ramp, unhooked the safety straps from the horse's head and led White Noise back onto terra firma. "You did an excellent job," he continued, "take him down to his box and give him a long drink and a good rub down."

"Will do," Strickland replied, with a grateful smile.

They watched the young groom lead the horse away, both men casting their eye over the animal as its hooves echoed on the concrete floor.

"Looks like he's recovered well," Telside said.

"And no obvious distress from the boat ride either," Cannon added.

While they talked, the driver of the van began to close up the trailer by fixing the ramp to the back of the horse box, securing it with six bolts and then finishing the job with two heavy padlocks.

"Are you heading straight back?" Cannon asked.

"Yes, sir," the man answered. He was heavy set, well over six foot four (one metre ninety-three), with legs like tree trunks and a beard that made him look piratical. Not someone to be messed with. His appearance seemed incongruous when one considered that his job was one of caring for racehorses and transporting them safely. He spoke with a gentle lilt, his inflexion clearly Irish. "I've been told to get back as soon as I can," he said, "after what happened previously."

"Are you on your own, Mr….?" Cannon asked.

"Yes, I am, and its Eamon, Eamon Boyle," he held out a hand.

Cannon and Telside took turns to shake the man's hand, thanking him for delivering White Noise back home safely.

"It's no problem at all," Boyle replied. "We do this every day, taking horses all over the country and all over the world. Hong Kong, the US and sometimes even Australia."

"I thought you were a small business," Cannon asked.

"Well, we are technically, but we have lots of agents and partners we contract with to get the job done. We're still small in the overall scheme of things, which is the way we like it."

"And your dad is happy to keep it that way?"

"Yes, as is his partner."

"That's Fionn Kelly's dad?" Cannon asked.

"Yes."

"How is he doing?"

"I believe he's okay. He's been in the US for nearly six months now doing some work there, trying to establish new relationships. I'm not across all the details but I know from my da' that he took Fionn's murder very hard."

"I can understand that," Cannon replied. "We were very sorry to hear what happened. Let's hope the police find out who did it and why."

"To be honest I couldn't care about the why," Boyle replied, bitterly, "I just hope that whoever they are, are caught soon and the bloody book is thrown at them!"

"Me too," Cannon agreed, as Telside nodded his own confirmation in support of Boyles' comment.

Ten minutes later, the van and trailer had left the yard. Telside went off to check on how the staff were getting on with settling down their horses for the afternoon. With no declarations for the day, there would be no more movement of horses to or from racecourses after the arrival of their Punchestown hero. Accordingly, things would quieten down within the next half hour. By the time Cannon got back to his office, he had a number of questions in his head that he added to those he had already written down soon after he had returned from the morning's work on the heath.

He still had another hour to kill before the call at twelve; he needed to think.

He found the button, eventually. After joining the call by following the link sent to him by Walsh, he had maximized the screen and had responded to the question asked of him, but the others were unable to hear his reply. Having been told where the mute icon was, he answered those on the screen, with a "Yes" he could hear them.

The obligatory, "Can you hear me now?" from his end followed.

Confirmation was ultimately received, much to everyone's relief.

After resolving all the technology issues, Walsh advised them that he had invited Cannon to attend the call, for reasons that would be made clear later. He then introduced him to Quinn's daughter.

"I'm sorry for your loss," Cannon said, as he watched the screen which was made up of four square windows. One each for the two Detectives, another for Julie Quinn and Sutcliffe who were seated together, and his own.

"It was you who found my father?" she asked.

"Yes. I had an appointment that day to see him, to look at a couple of horses that he was selling. Unfortunately, he was dead by the time I arrived."

She nodded a thank you to him, and he noticed her eyes fill with tears.

Watching the others, he saw what appeared to be O'Shea typing something and within seconds Walsh took charge again, addressing Julie Quinn directly.

"Ms. Quinn, before Mr. Cannon joined us, I told you of my attempt to contact you in recent weeks regarding your father's death. I also mentioned to you that Mr. Cannon was engaged by Mr. Sutcliffe to train a horse of his, after the sudden death of a Mr. Warren Hawker, the horse's former trainer."

"That's right," she answered, "though nobody in the US ever tried to contact me. I suspect with all their issues surrounding migration they didn't even think to check that I had already left the country."

"You may also be aware from Mr. Sutcliffe that the very same horse I am referring to was killed while participating in a race in Punchestown, just two days ago," Walsh continued.

"No, I wasn't aware," she answered, looking at Sutcliffe.

"This is why Detective O'Shea is here. He is investigating the matter as the death of the horse is suspicious. Mr. Sutcliffe quite rightly contacted my colleague after your conversation yesterday, particularly given the information you shared with him. I understand that you believe you know why your father was killed."

"Yes, I do."

"Can you share those reasons with us?"

Taking a deep breath, Julie Quinn went through her rationale. What she shared was nothing new other than a reference to "his security in relation to the troubles."

"What do you mean by that?" Cannon asked, seizing on a piece of information that he hadn't heard previously.

She stared down at her hands, inspecting them. It looked like she was trying to find some comfort within her entwined fingers. She slowly raised her head and looked back into the screen, her face reddening as if she was embarrassed.

"I told Mr. Sutcliffe here a number of things yesterday," she began, "but what I didn't tell him was that my father was a former IRA member."

"Former?" Cannon questioned, doubting that such a thing was ever possible.

"Yes. He told me once that he had been a controller of IRA finances in the South of the country. He said he managed numerous channels where large donations and other sources of money for the Movement came from, but that he was never involved in any operational activity. Effectively he was the money man with a record of where money came from and where it went."

"And this was his protection?" O'Shea queried.

"Yes, he told me that even before the Good Friday Agreement was concluded, he had walked away from the Movement and had turned his back on those who wanted to keep fighting the war. He said that he wasn't afraid of exposing everyone involved if they didn't let him be. He had had enough of the killing; the war was over, and he wanted to get back to farming. In fact, he said that he only did the job because the IRA coerced him into it and that they had threatened to kill my mother and me if he didn't. Fortunately…." She stopped suddenly, choking up, her voice cracking and tears formed before rolling down her cheeks. They all waited, remaining silent, until she had composed herself again. After apologizing and drying her eyes she appeared ready to continue.

"Go on," Sutcliffe said, encouragingly, conscious of the emotion he could hear in her voice. She offered him a sad smile in response.

"Fortunately," she repeated, "I was unaware of the threat to my late mother and me at the time. He kept it a secret from us, and I only found out about it recently after we had reconnected."

"Why was that?" Walsh asked.

"I moved away. I emigrated to New Zealand due to….due to," She looked across at Sutcliffe then faced the screen again, "due to an internal family matter. My father and I had a fall out."

"And you lost touch?"

"Yes. He didn't even know that I had moved to the US."

"So why did you reconnect with him?" Walsh asked.

"Because of what I'd found out when I was working in the States."

"Which was?"

"That some people over there are still supporting the cause and have been for years. I wanted to confront him about it. To find out if he was still involved."

"And was he?" Walsh asked.

"No, but that's when he told me about what he was forced to do and why."

"What happened after that?"

"Nothing, at least initially. I thought about things for a while but eventually I realised that I couldn't sit idly by given what I had found out, so I decided to do something myself."

"And did you?"

"Yes," she replied. "I wrote to someone who I thought would be able to help me."

"And did they?" Cannon asked, hoping to clarify something that had been niggling at him. He had been watching the screen closely observing how the eyes of Sutcliffe and Julie Quinn narrowed on occasion. It was as if they were both holding something back.

"No," she said, in response to his question.

"So, what did you do?" Walsh again.

"I wrote other letters, sending them by email, and then a few months ago my dad began receiving strange phone calls and threats to his life. He believed there were in connection with the records he had kept."

"How do you know this?" Cannon interrupted.

"Because he told me. I called him a couple of weeks before he was killed to tell him that I was coming home."

"Why did you decide to come back?"

"Because I wanted to find out why my letters had not been responded to and not acted upon."

"Who was this person you wrote to?" Cannon asked.

She turned to stare at Sutcliffe, who waited for her to reveal to them what had happened to her sister as the reason for her writing to him. She didn't mention her twin at all, she remained silent on the matter, though her response confirmed Cannon's suspicions as to who the recipient of her emails was.

"It was Chester Sutcliffe."

Bingo! Cannon thought.

There was a brief silence between the five of them. Walsh typed something on a keyboard which Cannon noticed O'Shea respond too.

"What did you say in these letters?" Walsh questioned.

"I told him about the list that my father had."

"Why Mr. Sutcliffe of all people. Why not someone else?"

"Because, he was the only person I knew who I believed was remotely accessible to me. He has a platform," she lied.

She glanced at Sutcliffe again, fully aware that he was feeling uncomfortable. "I wanted him to use his experience in politics and his status on TV to expose those who haven't yet accepted that the war is over."

"Don't you think that by doing that it would have put your father at greater risk?" O'Shea said.

Both Detectives knew from their own experiences that crossing former members of the IRA was not a clever thing to do. They had seen the results of individuals taking such a stand over the years and when the victims were found by the police, they were generally not a very pretty sight.

"I'm not sure," she answered, somewhat naïvely, "but when I spoke with my dad about coming home, something didn't seem right."

"Why?" Cannon asked.

"Because the threats he received only started *after* I wrote to Mr. Sutcliffe, and that didn't make sense to me, so I wanted to confront Mr. Sutcliffe about it."

"So, Mr. Sutcliffe," Walsh asked, "why did you not respond to Ms. Quinn's letters?"

It was a reasonable question.

"Simple really," Sutcliffe replied, "I never received them. I explained all this to Julie, yesterday."

"Oh, come now Mr. Sutcliffe, do you expect us to believe that?" O'Shea questioned.

"Look Inspector, I can assure you that had I known that Julie had written to me, I would have answered." Again, Cannon saw the subtle glances between the two. He wasn't sure if anyone else had noticed but it became clear to him that by being on the call as an observer, Walsh had been right to ask him to attend. He would discuss what he saw with the two Detectives later, deciding to ask Sutcliffe the obvious question instead.

"So, if you didn't receive any correspondence, Mr. Sutcliffe, then who did?"

"I have no idea, Mr. Cannon, and what business of yours is it anyway?"

Cannon felt angry at the repost. He wanted to let Sutcliffe know by how much but decided that he had to tread carefully and so dialled down his reply slightly. "It's my business Mr. Sutcliffe, because a racehorse, yours, was killed while under my care. Under my Trainer's license I have an obligation to the public, to the industry and to my team, including the jockey I hired to ride the horse, to ensure a safe and secure environment. Those obligations also require me to let the relevant officials know if there is something going on that impacts the integrity of the sport. That's why it's my business!"

Sutcliffe glared at the screen. The scowl on the ex-politician's face suggested that if there hadn't been sixty odd miles between them, Sutcliffe would have physically attacked Cannon. It was enough to confirm to Cannon that Sutcliffe didn't like being put under pressure and was clearly hiding something. He could give out criticism and malign people, but it was obvious that he wasn't able to take it himself. Walsh filled in the silence that had been created by Cannon's answer, asking Quinn if she had anything else to add.

"No, not really," she said, aware that they were no closer to finding out who was behind the killing of her father. Walsh then opened the floor to the others, asking if there was anything they would like to add to the conversation?

O'Shea asked if she had the address to which her letters, the emails she had written, were sent.

"Yes," she replied, "it was Mr. Sutcliffe's official email address."

"So you never sent anything to his home address?"

"No, I didn't know it until I came back from the US. I managed to get it from one of the production assistants at the TV station when I attended one of his live shows. I pretended that I had a gift that I needed to deliver to him. She gave it quite willingly which surprised me."

"Do you know her name?" Walsh asked.

"No, I'm sorry I don't."

"Bloody stupid woman!" Sutcliffe exclaimed, suggesting that he had an idea which one of the crew at the TV station would be the likely culprit.

"What about you, Mr. Sutcliffe? Anything?"

"Just one thing."

"Go ahead."

"Yesterday, Julie…Ms. Quinn, told me that she had met Warren Hawker while she was working at a stud farm in California and that she believed he had something to do with all this."

"In what way, Ms. Quinn?"

"I don't know, it was just the things he did, the way he acted, the questions he was asking. They didn't seem to make sense for a racehorse trainer. Especially when he said that he was looking at horses to buy for a client, particularly yearlings."

"Why was that?"

"Because it was the wrong time of the year," Cannon jumped in, abruptly.

"Sorry, I'm not with you," Walsh replied, wondering what Cannon was alluding to. He asked him to explain.

"In the US the breeding season is roughly March through to early June. Most stud or breeding barns would have sold off their crop of yearlings by the time Hawker visited them in May/June. The primary focus of those farms at that time of year would have been getting the mares in foal."

"So?"

"If Hawker was looking to buy something, the horses that would have been born and still at foot would be weanlings, horses no more than a few months old," he said.

"Which means?" O'Shea asked, intrigued at what Cannon was implying.

"It means that Hawker would have known that, and it's probably why his behaviour seemed odd."

"So you think he was doing something else?"

"Yes," Cannon answered, as definitively as he could.

"What was it?"

"I believe that he was trying to confirm that the list of donors and other information Ms. Quinn told us about actually exists, and that he was trying to find out whose names appear on it."

CHAPTER 38

It was two days after the conversation with Julie Quinn and Chester Sutcliffe, Cannon was busy in his office. He had been pleased at the work most of his horses had done that morning and was readying himself to leave for the races at Ludlow. His intention was to go on to Mansfield after the race meeting, where he planned to stay overnight. Cassie and Edward were to drive down from Bolsover and they would have dinner together. He would return to Woodstock the following morning. Michelle had agreed to stay at home as she had certain responsibilities at the school which made it impossible for her to take a couple of days off.
"You go," she had said, when the opportunity to race at Ludlow had availed itself.
"But what about you?"
"I'll be okay and I've got enough to keep me busy anyway. It's parent/teacher night next week and I need to prepare. The half term break is only two weeks away."
He wasn't overly happy that she couldn't come with him as he had been away from home a number of times in recent weeks, and he thought that it would be nice to spend a couple of days together, even if he would be busy with the horses he was racing at the Shropshire course. Ludlow is fourteen miles from the Welsh border and according to the late Poet Laureate John Betjeman, was "probably the loveliest town in England". Cannon enjoyed racing there as it was a lovely course, the atmosphere relaxed and the people were always friendly. He also liked the fact that he could use the race meeting as a nursery of sorts, particularly when he had horses with potential that needed to learn how to win. The competition there often included horses from some of the best trainers in the country, and by running his own horses against them he believed that he was able to use the experience as a way to assess their future. He wanted to see if they could one day race at Sandown, Aintree, Kempton Park or Cheltenham. The two horses he had accepted for Ludlow included Rory's Song and Winter Garden. Cannon had seen the improvement in Rory since his first run and was hoping that this time the horse would do better than his fourth place at Huntingdon. Winter Garden however was having her first race after the incident with the

contaminated feed. Cannon wasn't completely happy with running the horse so soon after the scare, but the Vet had given the mare a clean bill of health and Telside was convinced that 'The Garden' was ready.

As he crammed the last of the items he needed for the day into his backpack which he had placed on top of his desk; binoculars, trainer and access passes, his notebooks and a printed copy of the racecard at Ludlow, he searched for his phone. For a second he couldn't remember where he had left it, then he realised that it must have fallen onto the floor while he was packing the bag. Looking around his desk he eventually found it lying underneath his lightweight suitcase which contained a change of clothes, underwear, toiletries and shoes.

As he picked it up he glanced through his office window and into the yard. Outside the weather was mild, the sky almost cerulean in colour, partially hidden by mid-level cloud. A glimpse of the sun could be seen when it occasionally broke through the passing canopy that continued to drift eastwards across the county. The track at Ludlow was expected to be heavy after the recent rains but Cannon was hoping for soft going rather than heavy. If the sun and wind did their job then maybe he would get his wish. Ready to leave he turned off his computer, picked up his phone and put it into his jacket pocket. Then he slung his backpack over a shoulder and was about to pick up his suitcase when the mobile began to ring.

"Shit!" he said out loud, fumbling within his pocket to grab the phone and see who was calling. If it had rung ten minutes later he would have been in his car and the phone would be on speaker via his Bluetooth connection.

He recognized the name. Taking the backpack off and placing it onto the floor, he dropped into his chair.

"Hello Inspector," he said, with a sigh, "you caught me just as I was about to leave."

"You off somewhere then?" DI Walsh replied, cynically.

"To the races. You might remember that it's my reason for being."

The sarcasm wasn't lost on Walsh, but he ignored it. "I just wanted to give you an update," he said.

"Regarding?"

"Julie Quinn. Her story checks out."

"So you followed up my suggestion?"

"Yes. She is who she said she is, and you were right, there was something between her and Sutcliffe."
"What was it?"
Walsh told him about the death of Julie Quinn's twin sister and how it affected the Quinn family, breaking them apart resulting in the surviving sister moving to New Zealand.
"So that's why she wrote to Sutcliffe and then came back from the US sometime after she met Warren Hawker," Cannon said.
"Exactly."
"Anything else?"
"No, though we are still trying to find out about the letters, the emails, where they went."
"And who acted on them?" Cannon questioned.
"Yes."
"Any ideas?"
"It could be anyone. If Sutcliffe didn't get them, then who did?"
"I wouldn't know either. Maybe you need your boffins to check Sutcliffe's email account or something?" Cannon answered. He was beginning to form a view as to what had happened in his own mind but felt that it was too early for him to say as it was pure speculation on his part. What he had concluded however, related to Sutcliffe's former trainer. "About Warren Hawker," he continued.
"What about him?" Walsh replied.
"I believe he was murdered."
"What? Are you sure?" Walsh stammered.
"Yes, I'm certain of it."
"What makes you think that?"
"Because of the anomaly in the police report…and something else."
"I'm not with you."
"When we went to see Connor Boyle he told us that Darragh Kelly was in the US. He said that he had been there for two weeks to get over the trauma of his son's death."
"That's right."
"But here's the thing. When Boyles' son, Eamon, delivered White Noise back to our stable, he told Rich and I that Kelly had been in the US for six months already, and while he wasn't across what Kelly was doing there, he believed that he was establishing relationships. I suspect he was, or is, trying to warn those long standing IRA donors and sympathizers out there about the possibility of being exposed

and was trying to make alternative arrangements with them."
"That's fair enough Mike, but what does it prove?"
"It suggests to me that there is something that Conor Boyle is not telling us and I think it's to do with Warren Hawkers' death."
"What do you mean?"
"Well as I mentioned earlier, I said there was an anomaly with the report surrounding Hawkers' death."
"Yes, so what was it?"
"Hawker had supposedly died in a single car accident by running off the road late at night and had been drinking."
"Agreed."
"Well, I don't believe it."
"Why?"
"Because Hawker didn't drink at all."
"How do you know? Walsh asked, sceptically.
"When Sutcliffe's horse was delivered to me, I had a chat with Hawkers' Head lad, Bryce Kidd. I wanted to sound him out about a job. He had three months to find a new one after Warren's death and I thought he might want to consider taking over from Rich at some point."
"So?"
"He told me that Warren was an alcoholic, a reformed one. He had stopped drinking nearly fifteen years ago after doctors had told him that if he didn't then he would be dead within two years."
"Do you think he relapsed?"
"No, Kidd was adamant that Hawker would never have touched a drink while he was in the US or anywhere else for that matter. He'd even banned his staff from celebrating with beers or wine when his yard had a win."
"So where did the alcohol come from that's in the police report?"
"I don't know. I guess the police out there saw the so called accident as an open and shut case. One of DUI. Also I'm assuming that there wasn't an autopsy done on Hawkers' body given that he was a foreigner, supposedly on holiday. Kidd never mentioned a post mortem having been done here either, before the funeral."
"So if he was murdered, by who and why?"
"As we both dislike coincidences I think Conor Boyle or someone associated with him, like Darragh Kelly, was involved. As far as the why, I think they were trying to stop Hawker from uncovering some

information that he was looking for."

"What type of information?" Walsh asked, sensing that Cannon had taken the focus away from the investigation into Quinn's death, which in itself was still far from being solved.

"I believe he had been sent to the US to follow up on Julie Quinn's emails and intended and find anyone who could be on her dad's list."

"So whoever got the emails, had a personal reason to send him out there?"

"Yes, and it resulted in his murder."

Walsh was quiet for moment, trying to process what Cannon had been saying. While he was thinking, Cannon continued with his theory. "I think another conversation with Conor Boyle is in order. Maybe you can take him in for questioning? Get the truth behind Darragh Kelly and where he is. Even get the cops in the US to track him down."

Walsh considered what Cannon was proposing. It was worth a try.

"Mike, there is one thing that I still don't understand though, re your logic."

"What's that?"

"Fionn Kelly's murder. We still don't know who was involved with that do we?"

"No."

"Nor why."

"I think the why is in retaliation for Hawkers' murder. Almost payback in some way. It's as if whoever was involved was trying to send a message that they know of the records, the list of donors, and they know that someone is trying to stop them finding it."

"Which would tie in with Quinns' death."

"Yes, whoever murdered Quinn, likely killed Fionn Boyle and also shot Santa's Quest. While we don't know who just yet, we have some clues already. Hopefully when you interview Boyle again, we'll get a little closer to the truth?"

CHAPTER 39

The Ludlow meeting was sparsely supported. The crowd was small compared to Huntingdon and Punchestown but that was expected given it was a week day. The racing however looked competitive, and Cannon hoped that his two runners would show him what they could do. His personal interest in Rory's Song was obvious and he looked forward to his 'chaser improving on his position last time out. Winter Garden was another proposition completely. The mare had been declared to run in a novices handicap chase and because it was her first race of the season Cannon just wanted her to get around safely, no matter where she finished in the field of nine runners.

The weather had turned a little greyer by the time he had arrived on course and parked in the O & T car park. He had immediately made his way to the stables to check on his horses but remained vigilant with regards to anyone who may be keeping an eye on him.

Both animals had travelled up well. Each seemed lively enough and both were bright eyed. The owner of Winter Garden had been unable to attend the race but was happy with Cannon's view of where the horse was at. This meant that apart from the two grooms who had driven the van and horse boxes to the course, he had no specific catch-ups or a need to entertain anyone on site. He spent a significant part of the meeting having conversations with other trainers and owners in the various hospitality facilities as it was always useful to see if there were any of the latter who were looking to move their horses from their current trainer, and at such a relaxed meeting nobody seemed to be too put out by the practice.

Rory's Song ran in a handicap chase over a distance of just less than three miles, finishing strongly to run a close second. It was a much-improved run than previously and Cannon was pleased to see how the horse had cleared the fences without any issues, though he knew that Ludlow's chase fences were considered easier than those of other courses. The finish had been exciting and it showed that Rory's increased fitness meant that he could run out the distance. Losing by a half head was nothing to be sneezed at particularly when the winner was the odds-on favourite, trained by one of the Premier trainers in the country.

Winter Gardens' race was a different affair. A slightly shorter trip than that of Rory's Song, but it was over the same fences. Unfortunately she lost her rider at the very first fence, a jump that used to be called 'Trippy or Trappy Trevor'. Years prior the fence was considered dangerous but had been moved in the early 2000's and made much easier. This didn't always stop a horse from falling and while Winter Garden didn't actually fall, she seemed to wobble slightly on landing and it was her jockey that fell off. Cannon was extremely disappointed at what happened but he took it in his stride.

While his grooms were in the process of packing up, readying for the trip home, Cannon made his way to his car. There was only the last race to come and he had no interest in it at all. He wanted to get on his way to the hotel in Mansfield. On arrival at the vehicle he found a note under his windscreen. It had been scrawled on the inside cover of the days racecard, the page having been torn off and folded in half. He looked around at the now almost empty car park trying to see if anyone was paying him any attention. There was nobody in his immediate vicinity, nor could he see anyone watching him from the near empty paddocks or stand.

'Stay away, it's not your fight,' was all that was written.

He quickly climbed into his car, put the note to one side, and made a call to Telside filling him in as to how each of the two horses had performed.

"Pity about Winter Garden," Telside said, "but at least she didn't fall. Maybe she was just a bit race rusty seeing as it was her first run for a while?"

"I think you're probably right, Rich," Cannon replied. "Anyway there is always next time," he added, philosophically.

"Of course. And Rory, are you happy with him?"

"Yes, he ran very well, finishing like a train and just missing out. If I can place him in a similar race soon then I think he'll win."

As he drove out of the course Cannon ended the call, and after a quick check of his GPS made a quick phone call to Michelle. She was still at school just finalizing a couple of reports for the upcoming Parent/Teacher meeting.

"How did it go, today?" she asked.

"Mixed, but positive."

"That's good to hear. How are you feeling? Are you tired?"

"I'm okay, looking forward to seeing Cassie."

"Give her my love," she replied.
"Will do."
They finished their conversation with Cannon saying nothing about the note he had found on the windscreen. He had placed it on the passenger seat where it sat like a coughing patient in a doctor's waiting room. It left him with an uncomfortable feeling.

The two hour plus drive to Mansfield was proving largely uneventful and it was already dark by the time he had passed the halfway mark. He hoped to arrive before Seven as Cassie and Edward were expected around half past.

Just south of Burton-on-Trent his phone began to ring again. He recognized the number; DI Walsh. "After our chat this morning I thought that was it for the day," he said, answering. "If we keep meeting like this, someone may start talking,"

He wasn't sure if Walsh got the joke.

"Can you come to Ireland tomorrow?" Walsh replied, without reacting to Cannons' attempt at humour.

"What?"

"I need you over here as soon as possible."

"Why? What's the rush?"

"I interviewed Boyle this morning and I've arrested him."

"What's the charge?"

"Suspicion of murder and accessory to murder."

"Have you any additional proof of his involvement in anything since we spoke?"

"No, it's still circumstantial, but I have managed to get hold of the police in Nevada and they are searching for Darragh Kelly."

"What did Boyle say?"

"He's playing a bit dumb, but when I challenged him he admitted that Kelly was in the US when his son was killed."

"Did he say why?"

"No, but I've made the arrest to see if I can break him. He obviously had a relationship with Sam Quinn, but as you know when you and I met him in his office he told us that he was unaware of who Quinn was. I want to raise the issue of the records that Quinn's daughter told us about and who may be trying to find them. I want to see how he responds which is why I need you here."

"Tomorrow?"

"Yes, if possible. After I've finished with Boyle I want us to go out to

Quinn's place. That list must be there somewhere, we need to find it before someone else does."
"But I thought you have searched the place already?"
"We have, but we need to look again."
"How long can you keep Boyle in custody for?" Cannon asked.
"I have a couple of days."
"Well, you may need that time. I doubt I can get there tomorrow. How about the day after?" Cannon said, wondering what Michelle would say, if and when he told her.
"The day after is better than none," Walsh replied, "I'll take it as a given."
"Okay," Cannon replied, reluctantly, "Okay."

Cassie was looking radiant. The pregnancy seemed to have done for her what many other mothers-to-be experienced. She was dressed in a black suit with a sky-blue blouse underneath. Her high heeled boots made her seem so much taller than when he had last seen her in the flesh. There was no obvious baby bump around her middle and because she was only in her seventh week she told him that she was not experiencing any morning sickness at all…..yet.
"So it sounds like you are one of the lucky ones," Cannon said, as they sat at their table. The Devonshire restaurant on Rectory Road, about six miles from where he was staying at the Midlands Hotel, had been recommended and from what they had seen from the menu and of the décor so far, they were in for an enjoyable evening.
Edward smiled at his father-in-laws' comment. He had always been the quiet one in the relationship with Cassie and was happy to let father and daughter bond again after nearly eight months from when they had last been together. Dressed casually in a beige jacket, white polo shirt under a light beige jersey and jeans, he looked every bit a proud first-time father even though the birth was still nearly thirty odd weeks away.
"Yes, I am very lucky," Cassie replied, in response to her father's comment. "I'm lucky in so many ways," she added, reaching for Edward's hand which she squeezed tightly.
"So, how are things going at the stable?" Edward asked, changing the subject.

"Not too badly," Cannon replied. "I bought a new horse in Ireland a short time back and I ran him today down in Ludlow."

"How did he go?" Cassie asked, excitedly.

"A close second, so I'm quite happy with him. It was only his second run for me."

"That's great," she replied.

"Yes," he responded, deciding not to mention what happened to Winter Garden.

"And how is Michelle?"

"She's well, just very busy. She would have liked to come up to see you but school got in the way. She sends her love."

"Well, give her our best," Cassie said in reply. "I'll give her a call myself on the weekend as well."

They were interrupted by a young waitress asking them if they wanted any drinks. Cassie ordered sparkling water, Cannon tea and Edward a cider.

"Last of the big drinkers," Cannon said, as they turned their attention to the menus that they had put back onto the table after initially giving them a quick once over.

After they had decided on their meals and the orders had been taken, they had a long conversation about their individual circumstances. Cassie's job at her law firm and how much maternity leave she could potentially take when the time came.

Edwards' position at the hospital in Chesterfield and how he was soon to be going to a conference in Germany to hear about the latest research in the haematological field.

"Sounds great," Cannon said, not really understanding much about blood cancers. Leukemia and Hodgkins lymphoma he had heard of, but there were so many others that Edward mentioned that went straight over his head.

"And you, Dad?" Cassie asked, "Anything exciting happening other than the start of the season."

He hesitated slightly, not sure whether to mention his involvement with the Irish police or not. He decided to keep his powder dry, not wanting her to worry about him. She had a baby to carry.

"No, nothing unusual," he said. It was obvious from her frown that she didn't believe him. 'Like father, like daughter', he thought.

When they had finished their meal it was close to nine thirty. Cannon paid the bill and once outside the restaurant shook Edwards' hand again, congratulating him for a third time. Then, he kissed and hugged his daughter before finally saying goodbye to them both and watched their taillights disappear into the cold dark night, slowly climbing back into his own car, a smile spread across his face.

On his way back down to Mansfield, he called Michelle again. She was sitting in the lounge already dressed in her house coat and drinking hot-chocolate.

"I've been asked to go over the Ireland tomorrow, but I told DI Walsh that it was impossible and anyway it was unfair to you."

"To do what?' she asked. It was obvious that she was uncomfortable with the idea. She knew from experience that he was involving himself in an issue that was likely dangerous. He hadn't really told her too much but she suspected that it had something to do with Sutcliffe's horse.

"The Irish police want me to help them find something for them?"

"Can they not find it themselves?"

"They've tried several times, but without success."

"So how do they think you are going find it if they can't?"

"They've arrested someone in connection with the death of Warren Hawker, based on a few ideas I had, and a couple of observations I'd made. They think that by me being there, it's possible that they can get more information out of their suspect than they have so far."

"About this thing that you are trying to find?"

"Yes. You see it's my view that Hawker was killed by someone associated with the company that has been transporting our horses to Ireland and back, and the police over there think I can help them with their inquiries," he lied, trying not to frighten her.

"Does that mean we could be in danger? You, me, Rich, the staff?"

"No, I don't think so. What's been going on has nothing to do with us," he said, expeditiously ignoring the fact that he had been followed at Ludlow earlier in the day, in addition to Punchestown.

"That's good to hear," she replied, sounding relieved, before changing the subject. "So when do you expect to be home tomorrow?"

"About ten I guess."

"Obviously I'll be at school by then. I'll leave you to book your own flights to Ireland for Friday, the day after tomorrow, if that's okay?"

"Sure."

"And Mike?"

"Yes."

"When you go on Friday, please be careful."

"Of course I will, and anyway I'll see you tomorrow night," he said. "Maybe we can go to bed early….what do you think?"

She knew what he was referring to, saying, "That all depends on what time I get my work done, and what time your flight is the next morning."

Cannon could sense that sex was the last thing on her mind and he decided not to push the subject. There would be other opportunities…if he played his cards right.

Shortly after finishing their phone call, he pulled up into the hotel car park and was in his room and in bed fast asleep within thirty minutes of locking the car door.

He had a fitful night. The ghosts of the past had come back to haunt him. It was as if they were able to enter his mind and shape his dreams at will. He dreamt of finding Sam Quinn's body and using his fingers to extract the note that was found down the dead man's throat. Then, suddenly, he was watching Fionn Kelly burn to death, finally waking as a scream of pain escaped his throat, his body soaked in a cold, clammy, sweat. He lay still, darkness surrounded him. He was breathing hard, tears streaming down his face. He realized that the two incidents in his dreams were related, and in his fevered mind he knew that he had enough to link the two killings to the shooting of Santa's Quest. Lying back in the bed he tried to clear his head, falling asleep sometime later, unsure how long he had lain awake for. Inevitably, he fell back into more troubled nightmares.

CHAPTER 40

He was on the road earlier than expected. His inability to sleep soundly meant that he was too early for breakfast so he checked out of the hotel just after six, driving south in the hope of getting home around eight o'clock. He decided not to bother calling Telside as he knew that his assistant would be busy with the two lots up on the heath, determining that it would be easier to find out how things had gone once he arrived home. As he drove along the still quiet road, he realised that he would have to ask Telside to look after the stable for another couple of days, which would mean some part of the weekend. He doubted that Rich would be concerned, but Cannon knew that with his friend getting older, there were limits! It was why he had sounded out Bryce Kidd. While nothing had been finalized between them, Kidd had indicated that he could be open to the idea at some point.

Chester Sutcliffe had a lot on his mind. The death of his horse in Ireland, the interviews with the police and the threats to his life occupied most of it. He barely heard what was being discussed at the morning's pre-production meeting. It was the third one since his return from Ireland and only the second since he and Julie Quinn had opened up to the police about their previous connection. While he had been assured that there would be no further investigation into what had happened all those years ago, the fact that the issue had been raised and was somehow linked to the death of at least one person, as well as his own racehorse, concerned him greatly. He looked around the room wondering if any of those sitting at the table, discussing the plans for the evening's show, had somehow got hold of Julie Quinns' emails or whether it was somebody else from his days in government? He had no idea what to think but seemed to find himself on constant alert. He realised that he was subconsciously checking to see how people reacted to him, watching their body language and listening to how they phrased their comments. It was as if he was back in Parliament and he felt that he could trust no one.

"You seem distracted, Chester," Charlie Scott said, trying not to come across too harshly. The fact that the story of Rachel Quinn's drowning had finally surfaced was obviously weighing on his friend and Scott was aware that Sutcliffe was concerned about how people would react to the news should it ever become public knowledge. After he had corroborated Sutcliffe's story and his own role in it, the police had indicated that the matter was closed as far as they were concerned and would remain so, unless any additional evidence was forthcoming.

The police also confirmed that public had no right to know what occurred years ago, but Sutcliffe knew that the prospect of a leak was always there. Scott waited for a reply to his question, but there was none.

"Are you okay?" Jill Sinclair asked, noting with concern how Sutcliffe glared back at her.

It was she who had given Julie Quinn his home address and he was suspicious of her motives.

"I'm okay," he replied to both of them in succession. "I was just thinking about tonight's guest," he lied. "I haven't had much to do with those who run the NHS Trust for Mental Health, but we all know that since the Covid pandemic there has been an explosion of issues related to the subject, especially in schools."

"That's why we have got Joe Hillman on to talk about it," Carol Boyd said, "It will be great publicity for us and for them….."

"If we can get him to be honest about the state of the service they are providing!" Sutcliffe interrupted, a little more aggressively than was reasonable.

Boyd stared back at him, not knowing how to respond. Arguments and sensible discussion were a cornerstone of their meetings but it was apparent to her that the situation today was not normal. The atmosphere in the room was tense.

Scott coughed animatedly as if to bring everyone back to the subject at hand. "Do you have anything to share with us Carol? About Mr. Hillman's background and any recent commentary that we can hold him too?"

Silently, her eyes focused elsewhere, trying not to look at Sutcliffe's face, she handed over a thin folder to everyone sitting around the table.

"I've compiled some information," she said, "that Chester can use as a starting position. I suggest that we hold back on a number of points until they are absolutely necessary. Depending on Hillman's answers to the initial question, Chester can decide to pursue that line of enquiry should he see fit or use these others that are more back-up questions but are more in depth."

"The whole idea of the show is to get to the truth," Scott said, feeling his comment was somewhat ironic, given what he and Sutcliffe had gone through over the past few days with the police; their own 'Coming to Jesus' confession. "So let's see if we can do that, while still entertaining the audience."

There was general consensus and agreement in the room with Scott's comment, after all he was the Producer of the show, and the meeting slowly wound down once each of them had had their say. While everyone else left the room, Sutcliffe and Scott stayed behind.

"Do the police know yet who sent you those threats?"

"No," Sutcliffe replied, "other than it wasn't Quinn."

"So who could it be?"

"I think it's somebody in this room. Either that or someone upstairs," he said, referring to Chris Blakman.

"But why would they want to kill off the goose that lays the golden eggs?" Scott asked.

"I don't know. Maybe you need to ask them, you're the bloody Producer."

"Perhaps I will, but I suggest we let the police do their bit first. If they can uncover who is behind all this, then hopefully we can all move on."

"I'm not sure about that," Sutcliffe replied. "I thought I'd got over the death of Rachel Quinn but what's happened over the past forty eight hours has brought it all back."

"That's understandable," Scott replied, "and I can see how it's affected you. Maybe during the show tonight you can try something? Ask Hillman about how trauma from years ago can affect a person when that event resurfaces at a future time."

Sutcliffe looked up from the table where he been focusing on the brief notes that he had been scribbling earlier in the meeting.

"That may not be such a bad idea," he answered, staring straight into Scott's face. "I assume we'll *both* benefit from it?"

A brief silence between them lasted longer than it should have. Scott was aware of Sutcliffes' inference. Leaving Julie Quinn alone on that beach, trying to find her sister had been Scott's idea. It made him uncomfortable.

CHAPTER 41

"If it's only for a day or so, I'll be fine," Telside said. "We've got a runner tomorrow at Stratford, their last jumps meeting for the year, and then we have two down at Hereford the day after. I'm sure the lads will chip in while I'm there and help keep the fort together while I'm off galivanting."
"Hardly galivanting Rich, but it's been a while since you've been to a track so maybe the change will do you good?"
The two men were standing in the kitchen. Soon after Cannon arrived back at the yard, Telside had made a bee line to the house to fill him in on the morning's exercises and how the schooling had gone.
"Things are looking up," he had said, after Cannon had put his luggage down in the bedroom and Telside had begun making the tea.
"I'm not sure Winter Gardens' owner would be in agreement, Rich, after what happened yesterday."
"Probably not, but at least the horse ate up everything this morning as did Rory, so there was no damage done."
"Except maybe to the jockey's ego?"
"That's true, but these things do happen."
Cannon smiled at Telside's positivity. Even when things went wrong he could always rely on his old friend to put things into perspective.
"And another thing," Telside said, handing over a mug of tea, "those we have running at Hereford, Chocolatier and Simply Guessed, are both training really well."
"And what about our old friend, Candlestick Quick, is he ready for his first outing at Stratford?"
"That could be a different story, Mike. He's working okay but I think he'll need another run or so before he reaches his peak. The distance in tomorrow's hurdle race may be a little bit short for him."
"And White Noise, seeing as you are talking hurdles, how has he done this morning?"
"Burnt the house down," Telside smiled, before taking a sip from his own mug. "If he continues the way he's going, watch out Cheltenham!"
"Easy Rich, there are few more hurdles to jump before then."
Telside laughed at the joke, and Cannon smiled. He was extremely

lucky to have such an understanding friend. It would be a very difficult day when their journey together came to an end. Unfortunately every day that went by brought them ever closer.

"Do you think this thing is nearly over?" Telside asked, taking another mouthful of tea.

"You mean the investigation into what happened to Santa's Quest?"

"And the rest."

Not having mentioned the note he found on his windscreen at Ludlow, he tried to play down the answer to Telside's question.

"I hope so. The police have asked me to go over to Ireland to have a chat with the management of CB and Sons. There seems to be some query as to *why* Fionn Kelly was killed and they think that there is some discrepancy between what they've been told versus what we know about it."

Cannon was being deliberately mendacious. He was hoping that by doing so, the focus of Telside and the rest of his staff was on the horses and that they need not be distracted from that by recent events. Everything that had happened so far had been away from the yard and he wanted it to stay that way. It had only become personal after he had found the body of Sam Quinn and if it meant keeping everyone else in his life safely out of it, he would do so. The death of Santa's Quest had unfortunately complicated things.

Putting down his now empty mug into the sink, he turned to face Telside who was busy draining his own drink.

"I've got to go and book my flights now, Rich. Is there anything else I should know about?"

"No, I don't think so, at least nothing serious."

"Go on," Cannon encouraged.

Telside took a deep breath. "I think we need to give young Tom a go," he said. "He's really applying himself and I think it's worth giving him a try in a race."

Cannon looked into Telside's face. He could see that his friend was serious and having always backed his judgement, replied, "OK, let's choose a suitable race for him and get him going. If you think he's ready, then I'm in."

"He's definitely worked hard enough to justify a start, Mike. He's applying himself really well and he's got great balance."

"So what you're saying is that he just needs an opportunity to develop his race smarts?"

"That, and to learn how to win."

"Well that's a harder thing to do, but I think you are right, Rich…it's about time. Will you give him the good news or do you want me to?"

"I'm happy to do it. In fact I'll tell him later during evening stables. I'm sure he'll be over the moon."

"That's fine with me, Rich. Hopefully I'll get a chance to talk to him as well before he goes home tonight."

"I'm sure he'll appreciate it, Mike. But just quickly, changing the subject, what time do you intend to leave in the morning?"

"I just need to check. If there is nothing that goes direct to Dublin until around lunchtime, then I may need to go this evening and stay an extra night."

"I don't think Michelle will be happy with that," Telside declared.

"No, I'm sure she won't. I think I'm already in the bad books because of being away so often recently. Michelle missing out on catching up with Cassie last night didn't help either."

"No doubt," Telside replied, imagining how much Cassie would have enjoyed talking with Michelle about what was growing inside her and how they intended to spoil the baby once it was born. "I think you may need to make it up to her at some point, Mike…maybe a weekend away before Christmas?"

"Maybe, Rich, maybe. Unfortunately with the season now in full swing, it's about finding the right time."

Putting a hand on Cannons' shoulder, Telside said gently, "There is always time, Mike. Remember how much you lost when Sally died? Don't let life get in the way, if you do, you may regret it later."

Cannon wasn't sure if Telside was talking about himself given his advancing years and his health scares in recent times, but he got the point, acknowledging it with a brief nod. "I'll think about it," he said.

She had only been home a few minutes, when he told her that he would need to leave within the next hour.

"The only flight that is going to get me there to meet with DI Walsh first thing tomorrow is at eight thirty tonight, out of Luton," he said. "And it's going to take at least an hour and a quarter to drive there, assuming that there are no accidents."

Michelle put her hands on her hips. She was obviously annoyed but knew that it was something he had to do.

"Will this bring everything to a head?" she asked.

He was reluctant to be definitive, but understood that there had to be an answer, a conclusion, at some point. What he knew was that someone close to Sutcliffe had reignited a war of sorts. Perhaps it was done with intent, maliciously, or perhaps inadvertently. Either way a resolution was needed before anyone else was killed or injured. The last thing Cannon wanted was for anything to happen to his family. The threat to himself, still sitting on his passenger seat of his car was a reminder of that.

"I hope so," he said, in answer to her question.

"But you're not sure?"

"Not completely, no."

"So how does going to Ireland help?" she asked, not unreasonably.

"The police agreed to question one of the main suspects about a theory I had, and they want me to hear what he has to say."

"Which would prove what?"

"That the war we all thought was over is still ongoing and someone wants to reveal who is involved with it, while others want to maintain the secrecy."

"And do you know who the individual is, who is behind all this?"

"No. Though I think I know where to find the answer."

"And that is?"

"Where it all started."

CHAPTER 42

Walsh was waiting for him when he came down to the reception.
"I thought it would be good to join you, if you are still okay with it?" he asked.
Cannon had arrived at his hotel just after ten fifteen pm. Michelle had told him to be careful repeatedly, before he left for the airport.
While he was in the taxi, shortly after arriving in Dublin, he had messaged Walsh to let him know that he would be available for an early start. Walsh had responded immediately, suggesting that the two of them meet up for breakfast.
They entered the dining room finding a quiet spot away from most of the other early risers who were currently surrounding the buffet.
"What did you find out from Boyle?" Cannon asked, as soon as they were seated.
"Initially, not a lot. He maintained his position about not knowing Quinn but it was obvious that the killing of Sutcliffe's horse had rattled him. It was as if he had seen it as a warning."
"From who?"
"He said he didn't know, but when I mentioned the issue of the list that we now believe Quinn was killed for, he was a bit more forthcoming."
"How?" Cannon asked, as a waiter arrived at their table offering them each coffee. Once the drinks had been poured and the waiter had moved on, Walsh answered Cannons' question.
"I told him that I had requested the police in the US to issue an APB to find Darragh Kelly and that I knew that he was lying about why his partner was in the States."
"I assume he tried to deny it?"
"Yes, until I mentioned what his son, Eamon, had told you."
"What did he say?"
"He tried to deflect. He said that someone was trying to stitch him up and close down his business, which was the reason why Fionn Kelly was killed."
"I suppose you had a good chuckle at that?" Cannon said, "You don't go around murdering people just because of competition."
"Exactly. It was when I turned it around and told him that I believed that Warren Hawker was murdered by Darragh Kelly, not because of

competition but because of what was at stake, that he opened up."

"In what way?"

"He admitted that he had been contacted by people in the US about someone asking questions over there in relation to donations to the IRA."

"That would have been Hawker."

"Yes, but because Kelly was already over there, apparently looking for new sponsors to add to existing ones, one of those involved was getting very nervous. They heard about Hawker poking around and wanted to know what was being done about it."

"So they had Hawker killed."

"He didn't confess to it, but I'm sure we can get that out of him?"

"How?"

"By finding that list!"

"Which must be at Quinn's place somewhere," Cannon replied. "It has to be."

As they left to make the two-hour trip to Foulksmills along the M11, the car that followed them out of the hotel car park remained a couple of car lengths away for a significant part of the journey. Occasionally it would pass them and exit at the next off ramp before rejoining the road shortly thereafter. A second vehicle took over the tailing of whenever the first left the highway.

Due to Cannon's previous experience on Irish roads he watched with concern from his passenger seat as Walsh weaved in and out of the traffic, noting at other times how numerous cars rushed by them, overtaking their unmarked police car at speeds in excess of the limit. Wary of the driving habits, Cannon made a mental note whenever he saw the same blue Hyundai Tucson and white Toyota pass them and then fall back, only to pass them again later on. He tried to see the faces of those in the front two seats whenever he could. When one of the cars was on their left, he had a glimpse of the drivers profile and when it was overtaking, he looked towards the passenger side. He wasn't sure if he was right, but something about one of the faces that he stared into on occasion seemed to resonate with him. As the traffic thinned out he became more convinced.

He let Walsh know, and the policeman made a call.

When they arrived at Quinns' farm, the place was as silent as the grave. The cool of the morning lingered and the thick grey clouds overhead sent a chill down the spine. After stepping out of the car, Cannon looked around, taking in the vista that he had last seen the day he found Quinns' body. Scanning the hills that were bathed in low cloud, he wondered if they were being watched. From what he knew so far, it was likely, and those that were out there had the means to take him and Walsh at any time they wanted.

"Where do you want to start?" he asked, noting that there was no indication of any police presence anymore. No blue tape, no forensic tents or any other signs of a crime having been committed. While time had passed, as was evident by some of the weeds now growing in the small back garden or through the gravel of the driveway, the silence seemed to suggest that death had come and claimed its prize and had since moved on. He felt a sudden sadness, particularly for Julie Quinn. It was as if her life had been beset by tragedy and in her attempt to reconnect with her father after so many years, misfortune had followed.

"Maybe inside?" Walsh suggested.

"Haven't you already been through the place?"

"Yes, several times, but perhaps you may be able to see something we couldn't."

"I doubt it, but I do have an idea."

"What's that?" Walsh asked, just as his mobile began to ring.

Cannon walked off ahead while Walsh took the call. By the time the Detective caught up with him, letting Cannon know that his earlier call had been acted upon, they were standing at the row of four stables, still empty of any equine occupant.

"Did you look in here?"

"I'm pretty sure we did, why?" Walsh queried.

"Just a gut feeling. But, if I wanted to hide something that was really important I would try and put it in one of three places. In plain sight, hidden in the usual type of places like a safe, or in somewhere that only I would be able to find it."

"Well there's not much in here," Walsh said, as he opened up the door of the first of the four empty stables. As he did so, a stench of manure hit him and he coughed, waving a hand across his face to obviate the smell that invaded his nostrils. "Shit," he said, as he gagged again.

Cannon smiled, remarking, "Obviously!"

Walsh did not see the funny side, standing aside to let Cannon enter the small dark and dank stable. There was a small globe suspended from the ceiling, but when he tried the switch nothing happened. "We cut off the power," Walsh said. "while we kept the place under surveillance."

Cannon nodded.

"I thought that anyone trying to search the property at night would use a light of sorts," Walsh explained, "and given the remoteness of the place and how dark it is out here, I had hoped that we would be able to pick it up from our observation point on the hill over there." He pointed towards a small mound a few hundred yards away.

"Assuming they needed one," Cannon replied.

"What do you mean?"

"As I told you earlier, those involved in Quinn's death are not your average thieves or burglars, these people are on a mission."

While Walsh stood at the door to the stable, Cannon turned on the light of his mobile phone and scanned the walls and floors. Dirty straw and manure in separate piles were strewn across the ground where they had fallen prior to the horse that had occupied the stable having been removed. As he continued to move the light across the walls, Walsh indicated that he would go to the other three stables and open the doors, to "get some fresh air inside them."

Alone, hearing Walsh's footsteps gradually recede as the policeman walked away, Cannon made an assessment of what was in the stable. An empty feed net attached to one wall, a half full water bucket placed in the corner about five feet off the ground, and a tie ring close to the feed net attached to a post that was part of the walls structure. A dirty green rug was flung over a nail that was embedded in the opposite wall. Cannon lifted it up to see if there was anything behind but all he found was a couple of dead flies that had attached themselves to the underside. Turning around he thought he heard a movement. He was right. A large rat ran from under the straw and out of the stable and into the cold grey day. The rustling sound made by the rodent put him on edge and he began to make his way to the next stable. As he walked out of the gloom, the days light was still bright enough to blind him for a second. He noticed Walsh walking towards him. "I've opened all the doors," Walsh said, "and Jesus, they all need it. They stink to high heaven."

"I'm not surprised," Cannon said, "and so would you if you didn't take time to shower or have a bath."

"I noticed that there is a hose pipe attached to the outside of the third stable, further up there," Walsh said, pointing to a red hose that lay twisted, some part of it wrapped around its frame and the rest sitting on the cement walkway that fronted each stable. "I assume that would be used to wash the floors and provide water for the horses?"

"Yes, for a small place like this, it's probably adequate."

"Ok, so what now?"

"We keep looking," Cannon said, taking a glance around the area again. He was starting to feel nervous.

The other three stables were laid out exactly as the first, except Cannon noted, the third one. There was no water bucket, just a water trough attached to a wall, much closer to the ground than where the buckets in the first two stables were hanging. After he had inspected the fourth stable he went back into the third.

"Did you notice anything?" Walsh asked.

"I'm not sure," Cannon answered, "but I may need your help."

Leaving the safety of the fresh air which he had been enjoying by standing at the open doors, Walsh walked into the stable following Cannon's lead, carefully watching where his feet landed.

Cannon passed him his phone. "Shine it here," he said, pointing at the base of the water trough as he moved his hands around the edge, feeling for something.

"What are you looking for?" Walsh queried.

"A catch of some sort."

"Why?"

"The base of this trough seems deeper than it should be and it's the only one in the four stables....why? The other three have buckets in them."

Walsh knelt down, he could see what Cannon meant. The metal of the trough seemed to be in two parts, the lower piece partially hidden by the depth of straw that was pushed up against it. Putrid water, blackened with grime, dust and dead flies lay in the half pipe shaped gully.

"Over here," Cannon said, indicating where he wanted Walsh to shine the light.

Moving his hand very slowly along the underside of the water-trough he eventually found what he was looking for. A small catch, so well hidden that it was almost to find if you didn't know where to look. It was right at the back where the trough met the wall. Cannon pressed it but nothing happened. Reaching for it again, he pulled it slightly towards him. As he did so, the edge of the trough that was facing away from the stable door came away. A small tray, roughly a foot (thirty centimetres) long and four inches (ten centimetres) high became visible in the harsh white light of Cannons' phone. Inside the tray was a book of sorts, more a leather-bound journal. They could see that it was old but it had obviously been used recently. The heavy clear plastic envelope that it was sealed in, was both a protector from water damage, as well as from dust, light and anything else that may have wanted to eat or destroy the pages.

Cannon removed it from its hiding place and both men stood, the light from the phone shining directly on their find.

"I think this is what everyone has been looking for," Cannon said, wiping his hand over the surface. "The reason behind Quinn's death."

"And thank you for finding it," a voice said.

Turning around, a familiar face and another with a familiar voice stood in silhouette at the door to the stable. Behind them two more men waited. It was what Cannon had been expecting. He hoped that Walsh's earlier phone call meant that his concern was being taken seriously.

CHAPTER 43

Tony Burke stood aside as Cannon and Walsh exited the stable door.
"I'll take that," Burke ordered, as Cannon brushed past him carrying the still sealed plastic envelope.
Handing it over to Chester Sutcliffe's agent felt like a kick in the stomach, but he had no choice. The three men accompanying Burke had guns pointing at Walsh and Cannon, and it was futile to do anything but follow their instructions.
"Glock 17s," Cannon said, pointing briefly towards the gunmen, "British army issue."
"Very good, Mr. Cannon," Burke answered, "I'm sure Mr. Kennedy, Healy or Flannery would be happy to show you how well they work, should you decide to try and make a run for it. After all they are well trained in their use."
"No doubt," Cannon replied, recognizing Kennedy as the man who had been watching him at Punchestown and probably at Ludlow too. "And I suppose they'd be happy to do any work for payment, as long as it's lucrative enough," he added.
"Shut your mouth," Kennedy interrupted, angrily. "You know nothing about us. You have no idea what we went through over here trying to keep the peace while being repeatedly attacked, shot at, murdered and ignored by those in power…and all that, for what? So that we could surrender!"
"I thought it was the IRA that was still fighting?" Cannon replied, glibly. "Maybe that's not the case?"
Kennedy glared at Cannon, pointing his gun threateningly at his chest. Burke put out a hand, asking Kennedy to take a step back.
"Just to add to the fun we are having," he smiled, sardonically, "I have a Mr. Campbell pointing a rifle at you from the ridge over there." He nodded towards another small hill that raised its head just behind the stable and ran a hundred or so metres down to where the eye could no longer see due to the uneven terrain.
"I suppose that's the same one used to bring down Sutcliffe's horse, my horse, at Punchestown?" Cannon speculated.
"Probably," Burke answered, nonchalantly.
"So what do you want?" Walsh asked angrily, deciding that standing

with his hands above his head was not for him.

"I think I have what I need," Burke answered. "Now all I need is…"

"To tell us why," Cannon interjected. "Why all this….?" he asked, indicating the three men that stood quietly in front of them, obviously waiting for instructions on what to do next. It was obvious that their training as professional soldiers influenced their approach to their work, even if they had a different paymaster now.

"Why?" Burke said, his voice malevolent, filled with hatred. "It's quite simple Mr. Cannon. Very simple."

"Revenge?"

"No, not revenge…justice!"

"For who?" Cannon asked, briefly looking around to see if could spot where the sniper with the rifle that shot Santa's Quest, could be hiding. The foliage below the ridge line was dense and the trees difficult to see into, so it was impossible to know where a shot could come from.

They waited for Burke to speak. Cannon asking his question in an attempt to play for time.

"Nearly thirty years ago, I lost a father and a brother, killed by an IRA bomb. Nobody was ever arrested or found to be responsible. Those involved got away with it….at least until now."

"What do you mean, until now?"

Burke tapped the envelope. "Inside this journal, are the names of those involved in numerous operations undertaken by the IRA. Not only that, but their backers, and their targets."

"How do you know that?" Walsh asked. "If we hadn't found it, you wouldn't have a clue what's written inside."

"That's true, but many of Julie Quinns' emails were very detailed. Full of speculation yes, but enough for me to send Warren Hawker to do some checking for me."

"Which set off an entire chain of events." Cannon stated.

"Not initially no. It was Darragh Kelly who started the whole thing."

"Because he was still collecting donations for the cause?"

"Yes, there are many personalities and business people in the US with long memories. Old Irish families who still believe that the north and the south should be one."

"So what?"

"Well, they are happy to give money to continue the fight, as long as their donations don't come back to them."

"Which means they…"

"Yes, Mr. Cannon, they use proxies. In many cases, racehorse trainers. People who have access to money that can be shipped across the world, under the guise of stud fees, prepayments for foals to be born, sales of champion racehorse sperm, an entire multitude of different things. Warren was able to verify most of this, but eventually someone found out what he was doing for me and had him killed."

"And you think that was Darragh Kelly."

"Which was why my friends here returned the favour."

"By killing Fionn Kelly, his son?" Cannon replied.

"Well, we did need to send a message somehow."

"How do you know all this?" Walsh asked, slowly lowering his arms before being made to put them back behind his head again, as he was pistol whipped across his skull by Tom Healy.

Falling back against the side of the stable, Walsh felt his warm red blood slide down the side of his face. He wiped a hand over the gash leaving his palm and fingers coloured red and sticky, as Burke continued with his diatribe.

"As I said, Ms. Quinn's emails were numerous and became more insistent over time, urging Chester Sutcliffe to act. The more she wrote, the more she exposed, eventually revealing the reason for this very journal. I just needed to find it."

"Why?"

"Because in here," he tapped the envelope, "are the names of those who supported terrorism across the UK, especially Northern Ireland and England. Names of those who sent money and those who used it for specific operations, those directly or indirectly involved. As I said, all I want to know is who killed my father and brother. I don't give a shit about the rest."

"Except you do," Cannon replied. "You want to know where the money came from don't you? You want to expose them too."

"All I want is justice, and the evidence is in here."

"So you think," Cannon suggested, trying to buy some more time and hoping that by doing so he could think of a way out of the situation.

"What do you mean?"

"I'm guessing that the journal you're holding has the names of US donors, the go-betweens, the racehorse trainers on both sides of the Atlantic, and the final recipients of the money."

"Yes."

"But what if you're wrong. What if Quinn was the recipient?"

"What?"

"Well, maybe he was protecting himself. Maybe he kept the money but wrote up the journal, the list, as pretence…to cover his stealing."

"I doubt that, Mr. Cannon," Burke replied. "The Movement had, and still has, pretty simple ways of dealing with those that try to undermine the cause. No, I think everything I need is in here."

Listening to the distant sound of the odd car driving away from their location, Burke seemed happy to bring the whole episode to a head. He had what he needed, it was time to bring the discussion to an end. Cannon noticed Burke make a simple gesture with a shrug of his shoulders and Flannery began to push him and Walsh back into the stable. Having almost run out of ideas to delay the inevitable, Cannon made one final play.

"How did you get hold of her emails? Those sent by Julie Quinn."

"Easy," Burke said with a smile. "That's what an agent does. I vet the correspondence of my clients."

"Even those of a personal nature?"

"Yes. I'm there to protect their reputation. To stop some crazy making representations that are false or likely to be damaging."

"But surely someone like Sutcliffe would know that you were the one accessing his email?"

"He would, yes. Provided he paid attention."

"And he didn't?"

"No. He was a politician, a Minister of the Crown prior to giving it all away. He had people to handle things for him before he was ever required to read or do anything….unless it was absolutely necessary."

"And so you did the same when you became his agent?"

"Yes, it was easy. Adding a simple dot in his TV station email address was enough to create a secondary mail box that looked like the correct address. No one ever picked it up."

"And all those emails went to you?"

"Yes, and those that I thought he should get, I just sent on to him. He never noticed that they were forwarded from the false address to the original one, as I just deleted that part of the message. He never saw any of Julie Quinns' letters."

"Which allowed you to do what you did."

"Until she showed up at the studio."

"So it was you who sent Sutcliffe the threatening letters, dropping them through his letter box at his apartment! You wanted him to think that she had come to expose him, for what happened to her sister!"

Burke decided not to answer, but his silence told Cannon all he needed to know. Turning to Kennedy, he said, "Let's get on with it. Once it's all over I'll be happy to settle our account."

"What about the list, the book?" Kennedy questioned.

"If I'm right the details of those that were part of the operation on the day my father died, and those who acted as go-betweens or third parties will be in here," Burke answered, tapping the envelope again. "That being the case, I'll have another job for you if those people are still alive."

Kennedy turned to Flannery and Healy. "As long as we get paid, it's fine with us, isn't that right boys?"

Cannon noted the term that Kennedy had used…"boys!" The army brass had a lot to answer for the way that young squaddies were treated during and after the troubles. It was no surprise that some decided to keep fighting an enemy that they believed their government had capitulated to. By contrast there were groups on the other side of the conflict that were likewise still wanting to fight. The murder of Fionn Kelly being a tit-for-tat response for the killing of Warren Hawker. The journal that Sam Quinn had kept and was now in Burke's hands was supposed to close the chapter, to stop the killing. Unfortunately it had resulted in the exact opposite.

"Give me your phones then get inside!" Kennedy shouted, pointing his gun at Walsh and flashing the barrel in the direction of the stable door.

Cannon took his time before handing over his mobile, fumbling with it as he tried to find the emergency call button. Flannery noticed what he was doing and punched Cannon in the stomach, doubling him over, causing him to retch. While still prone, a knee was slammed into his face and he felt an explosion of pain as he fell backwards against the stable wall, hitting his head hard on the wood.

"Little shit!" Flannery screamed, before bending down and pulling Cannon up by his jacket. Another blow to the head with a 'Liverpool kiss' rendered his victim dazed and he was thrown back into the dark hole that was the stinking stable. Landing on the dirty, foul-smelling straw, Cannon was just able to see through the blood that smeared his vision when the door to the stable was slammed shut. Walsh tried to help him up, reaching out in the darkness, blind until his eyes started to accustom themselves to the tiny slither of grey light that somehow found its way through the wooden slats of the stable door.

"Are you okay?" Walsh asked, still unsure where Cannon was. He could sense him on the ground somewhere but couldn't see where he had fallen. The rustle of straw became his direction finder, only to trip over him as their legs collided.

"Fuck!" Cannon exclaimed, as the big man's body landed on top of him.

As they struggled to stand up, they heard the sound of the stable door being secured. A bar was being locked into place to prevent it from being opened from the inside.

"What the hell?" Walsh shouted, rushing to the door, banging his fists as hard as he could on the old, splintered wood. A bullet zinged past his head, missing it by millimetres, deflected by the steel flanges that the wood of the door was attached to. He fell to the ground, landing in manure and straw, screaming invective and Irish profanities but remaining low in case another shot was fired.

Fighting the pain in his head and the ache in his shoulder where Walsh had landed on him, Cannon tried to listen to what was happening outside. The door to the stable had obviously been secured and it was unlikely that he and Walsh would be left to be found alive, which meant that something else was being planned. An execution of sorts.

The answer came quickly.

A smell.

The smell of fuel, of petrol. It was being splashed along the walls of the stable block. Fumes began to seep into the enclosed darkness and they began to gag.

"Use the lining of your jacket or rip your shirt," Cannon shouted, somehow remembering the training that he had been given during his days in the police. Covering his mouth and nose to minimize inhaling the invisible gaseous vapour would help keep them alive, if only for a few minutes. Despite his attempt to prolong the inevitable, he couldn't see a way out. He realised that death by asphyxiation was likely before the flames that were soon to engulf the stables, ravaged their bodies. Suddenly there was a roar as the fuel ignited. The walls of the stable seemed to convulse, contracting first then expanding as

Death Claims its Prize

the flames outside took hold.

"Quick," Cannon shouted, using the dim light from the flickering tongues that slinked their way through the door and the across the roof line, to direct Walsh to the water trough. "Use this," he said, as he began splashing the tepid liquid all over himself, across his bloodied head, his face, his jacket and the rest of his clothes. "It's not much," he shouted, through the noise, the smoke and the heat of the now raging fire that surrounded them, "but it may help keep us from frying…at least for a few more minutes."

Walsh knew that Cannon was trying to put on a brave face, even in the darkness, and he admired him for it. If they were going to die, then at least they would die fighting to stay alive. Following Cannons' lead Walsh used the last of the water the best he could. Smoke was now circling above them. The grey mist slowly creeping ever lower as it made its way downwards. It was getting difficult to breathe and both men began choking, coughing violently.

"We need to get as low as possible," Walsh croaked, ignoring the faeces and urine that the last occupant in the stable had left there. As they fell to the ground, they heard shots being fired outside. A gun battle began raging. Bullets from high powered rifles pierced the walls of the stables. The sound of screams and curses filtered through the noise of the flames that quickly ate away at the stable structure. The heat began to sear and singe at their clothes. Smoke and steam from the water they had covered themselves with rose upwards like winter nymphs that appeared suddenly before disappearing just as quickly.

Both men expected to die. They resigned themselves to their fate.

As the roof above them started to crack open and pieces of wood and tile and other debris from years past began to fall, they heard a loud bang and a heavy crash. A vehicle, its wheels spinning, engine running, screaming at high revolutions could be heard screeching and crunching its way towards their position. "Get back!" Cannon shouted, as a Garda Hyundai smashed through the walls of the stable. In the driver's seat, Constable O'Callaghan. Quickly reversing, he left a hole where bricks and wood had been glowing red from the heat. The gap was large enough for Cannon and Walsh to climb through together. As they tumbled out into the light, the roof of the stable collapsed. Both men were able to make ten metres before they fell to the ground, choking, gagging for the cold air that their lungs so desperately needed. It tasted both sweet and damp as rain had started to fall. Too little to put out a raging fire, but enough to cool blistering skin.

Cannon struggled to his feet, looking around at the carnage that surrounded him.

Spread out over a distance of twenty metres or so were six bodies. Two Garda policemen and four others. Tony Burke was lying face down, the left side of his head was missing. A police snipers bullet had taken him out. He had been the first to die. His cohorts had been able to use their skills as soldiers in an attempt to try and shoot their way out of trouble. Unfortunately due to the weight of numbers and superior fire power of the Armed Support unit that DI O'Shea had arranged as backup, and requested earlier by Walsh, they had eventually succumbed but not before killing two young Garda officers.

Walsh slowly picked himself up. He was exhausted and still struggling to breathe, taking in huge gulps of air as he tried to get his lungs working properly. As he continued surveying the scene, he turned to see part of the stable block collapse inwardly on itself. Sparks and flame flew up into the air and the crash of brick and wood disturbed the now eerily quiet of the killing field. A hiss joined the chorus as heavier rain began to fall onto the charred ruins, sending scalding steam skywards.

"Are you okay, Sir?" a voice said.

Walsh tried to focus on the question. Was he okay? He wasn't sure, he didn't know how to answer.

"Sir are you okay?" the question asked for a second time.

Slowly realizing where the question was coming from, he watched as O'Callaghan walked towards him holding out a mobile phone.

"It's DI O'Shea, Sir...it's for you."

Walsh took hold of the phone, noting that it was not his own. O'Callaghan smiled, indicating that it belonged to him.

"We got the other one," O'Shea said, simply, "the one who shot the horse, the sniper."

"How is he?" Walsh asked.

"Wounded, but he'll live."

Walsh nodded forlornly then handed the phone back to O'Callaghan without bothering to end the call. He noticed Cannon walking up to him.

"I think you saved my life," Walsh said, holding Cannon by the shoulder. "That water ….."

"No," Cannon interrupted, "it was your Constable here and his quick thinking. If he hadn't rammed that stable with the car, we'd still be in there." He pointed to the vehicle located around thirty metres away, its entire passenger side had been ripped away from the rest of the cabin. The force of the impact and the rapid reversal had torn the aluminium and plastic apart, tearing it like paper. Walsh nodded as Cannon made to walk towards the body of Burke. He had noticed the plastic envelope partially opened, lying on the ground, about a metre from where Burke had died. One end was flapping in the breeze and the cool rain that was steadily increasing was slowly invading the pages inside. As he bent down to pick it up, he contemplated some of the reasons why it had been kept, knowing from his own experiences that the past was never far away. It played a significant part in his life, no matter how much he tried to ignore it or push it aside. His own story, his own history had made him what he was today. The realization of that fact was always with him and the voices from those days, no matter how distant, and no matter how hard he tried to forget them, would never leave him. He sensed that what had happened to Burke so many years prior, had consumed him to the point that his ghosts had become real and the need to expunge them obsessive. So much so that he was willing to kill, to avenge a killing. Holding the envelope with the journal inside, he wondered which other ghosts would find their way out of the pages…only time would tell, but would they ever be silenced?

EPILOGUE

Darragh Kelly was charged with the murder of Warren Hawker in the US and was sentenced to life imprisonment.

Conor Boyle was found guilty of the murder of Cillian Lynch, his co-conspirator in the Warrington bombing in 1993, as well as the unlawful killing of at least two people that day. The victims were a father and son.

Ronan Buckley who had helped with the killing of Cillian Lynch had died in 2005 from bowel cancer, his role in the IRA was detailed in the list of activities, donors, payments and operations contained in the journal maintained by Sam Quinn.

The names of racehorse trainers and others in the US who acted as go-betweens and third parties to funnel funds to the IRA during the war and subsequent to the Good Friday agreement was acted upon discretely by the Irish and UK governments. Arrests were made where the evidence allowed. Some were high profile figures in the horse racing industry, breeders, owners, racing managers, while others were businessmen and women who had family connections to Ireland.

In Ireland itself, Sam Quinn's list helped the police arrest numerous individuals who had continued to act in roles within splinter groups that had branched out and away from the IRA itself. Aidan Murphy who sold Rory's Song to Cannon was one of them.

Finn Campbell was charged and found guilty of the murder of Sam Quinn. His record of ever being part of the British Army was expunged.

Due to the deaths of Tom Healy, Liam Kennedy, Jack Flannery along and Tony Burke, no one was found directly responsible for the murder of Fionn Kelly.

Chester Sutcliffe continues with his TV show. His audience and his popularity increases.

Julie Quinn has returned back to the US.

White Noise made his way up the Cheltenham straight. He was four lengths clear. The rest of the field were floundering as the grey cleared the penultimate hurdle. As the ground rose and the final part of the hill beckoned, the horse responded to his jockey's strong riding, charging towards the last fence and the winning post.

Cannon smiled as Michelle grabbed his arm. The cold of late January was lost on them both as she screamed encouragement. The festival trials day, the last day at the course before the four-day festival in March, was going to be a success. The other trainers and owners watched as White Noise cruised further ahead. Joel Seeton began slapping Cannon on the back in anticipation of his horse's victory.

"It's in the bag," Seeton shouted, trying to make himself heard above the noise of the crowd that screeched and roared as the race reached its climax.

Cannon did not respond. He had seen this movie before. White Noise had done everything asked of him since Punchestown, winning three hurdle races in a row and rapidly rising through the grades. Today's test was the biggest to date and it looked like he was going take the next step easily.

With the chasing pack having almost given up, the jockey in the greys saddle looked back through his legs. The race was won, all that was needed was to clear the last. Not wanting to leave anything to chance, he gathered the reins tightly, found his mark and the two of them, horse and jockey, cleared the final hurdle as one. Cannon shouted, raising a fist into the air as his charge crossed the line ten lengths ahead of the second horse. He turned and kissed Michelle on the cheek, before finding his hand being shaken vociferously by Seeton and a multitude of other trainers, owners and peers.

Turning to face the track, he knew that the main goal, the Champions Hurdle, was still eight weeks away. It was still a dream of his to win it, and it was highly improbable given the quality of horses that White Noise would have to compete with, but at least he now had a runner that was worthy of the event……..

TO BE CONTINUED

ABOUT THE AUTHOR

Other books in the Mike Cannon series:

- *Death on the Course*
- *After the Fire*
- *Death always Follows*
- *Death by Stealth*
- *Death never Forgets*
- *Death seeks you out*

Books in the DI Brierly series

- *Killing Mr. D (under pseudonym – Saul Friedmann)*
- *Damaged (under own name but writing as Saul Friedmann)*

A former Accountant with a lifelong love of horseracing. He has lived on three continents and has been passionate about the sport wherever he resided. Having grown up in England he was educated in South Africa where he played soccer professionally. Moving to Australia, he expanded his love for racing by becoming a syndicate member in several racehorses.

In addition, he began a hobby that quickly became extremely successful, that of making award-winning red wine with a close friend.

In mid-2014 he moved with his employer to England for just over four years, during which time he became a member of the British Racing Club (BRC).

He has now moved back to Australia, where he continues to write, and also presents a regular music show on local community radio.

He shares his life with his beautiful wife Rebecca.

He has two sons, one who lives in the UK and one who lives in Australia. This is his seventh novel in the Mike Cannon series.

Printed in Great Britain
by Amazon